T0361760

Fathoms

Books by Lisa T. Bergren

The Oceans of Time Series
Estuary
Rip Tide
Fathoms

The River of Time Series
Waterfall
Cascade
Torrent
Bourne & Tributary
Deluge

River of Time California
Three Wishes
Four Winds

The Remnants Trilogy
Season of Wonder
Season of Fire
Season of Glory

The Gifted Series
Begotten
Betrayed
Blessed

View more of Lisa's books
at lisatawnbergren.com

Fathoms

OCEANS OF TIME | BOOK 3

LISA T. BERGREN

Published by Enclave Publishing, an imprint of Oasis Family Media, LLC

Carol Stream, Illinois, USA.
www.enclavepublishing.com

ISBN: 979-8-88605-194-0 (printed hardcover)
ISBN: 979-8-88605-195-7 (printed softcover)
ISBN: 979-8-88605-197-1 (ebook)

Cover design by Kirk DouPonce, www.DogEaredDesign.com
Typesetting by Collin Smith, www.CollinSmithCreative.com

Printed in the United States of America.

For Mom, for everything.
You were the best, and I can't wait
to see you again on the other side.

1

LUCIANA

ays later, I still could not see.

Each morning, I awoke with hope. I'd blink, ready—so ready—to see anything at all. To note any sort of progress, only to face crushing disappointment. It was so weird to spend the night dreaming—with twenty-twenty vision—only to wake to darkness.

Oh, God, I silently moaned. *Is this it? Will you not heal me here? Now? Do you not hear me?*

A gentle knock on the door told me Chiara Greco had arrived. She'd apparently taken me on as her own personal patient, given that Adri was tending so many wounded Forelli knights. Those able to travel had returned from Castello Romano over the last few days; the more gravely wounded recuperated there. Thinking of that castello and the battle where I had been so badly injured— where Aurelio Paratore had given his life—made me nauseated.

I concentrated on Chiara's warm, reassuring voice instead. *"Buongiorno,"* she said, wishing me a good morning.

"Buongiorno," I returned, sitting up. I ran a self-conscious hand over my hair, knowing it was likely a mess.

Chiara lightly touched my hand. "You look lovely, as ever."

I paused. "My eyes . . . do they appear . . . odd?" I hated the insecurity of my question. But I had to know. They didn't have mirrors in medieval Italy—only sheets of burnished metal that gave a pretty good reflection. To not even be able to look in one of those left me feeling oddly vulnerable. I could feel the heat of her gaze. *Better to ask serious, stoic Chiara than my brother, who'd probably just make a joke out of it.*

Her gentle hands touched either cheek, keeping me still. "They have improved."

"Improved?"

"At first, one pupil was much larger than the other, indicative of your trauma."

"Now they are more alike?"

"Indeed."

"Does that mean they are healing?" I asked hopefully.

"Close and open them. Do you see light this morning? Shadow?"

I did as she asked. Was that light? "M-mayhap."

"I am going to cover your head with this blanket for a moment. Keep your eyes open."

Fabric enveloped me. "Is it darker?"

Was it a few shades darker than a moment ago? "Mayhap," I said again.

She pulled the blanket away. "And now?"

I sighed heavily. Was I only imagining things? "Mayhap." This time, the word came out a bit strangled, a knot forming in my throat.

She sat down on the bed beside me and wrapped an arm around my shoulders. "Do not lose hope, my friend."

"Too late," I said, feeling a tear slide down my cheek. Because hope slipped from my heart like water through a sieve.

She held me while I cried, placing a handkerchief in my hand. It was the first time I'd cried since I'd been injured, and my weeping soon turned to outright sobs. "I-I so wish . . . I'd only . . ."

I couldn't even form a complete thought to tell her all I was feeling. I was lost. Utterly lost. My mind as dark as my vision.

She said nothing. Simply handed me another handkerchief when I'd soaked the first. Gradually, my sorrow was spent, and I heaved one of those shaky sighs that signaled the end. "Have you seen this before, Chiara? People who lose their sight?"

"Many times," she said. "On the field of battle, such trauma is common."

"And out of all of those cases, how many regained their vision?"

She paused. Because she was afraid to tell me or because she was thinking? I missed the visual cues of communication, among a hundred other things about being able to see.

"I have treated twenty or more injuries like yours. And three-quarters of them regained partial or total vision."

"How long did it take for that to happen?"

"For some, days. For others, weeks. But in all . . ."

"In all . . ."

"In all of those who regained their vision, they noted some improvement the first week."

Which I had not.

"Come," she said, as I felt her weight leave the bed. "Let us get you dressed and your hair brushed. 'Twill do you good to take a turn about the courtyard. And my brother will soon return from patrol. 'Twould do *him* good to see you up and about."

I hesitated at the mention of him, wringing my hands and biting my lip. Giulio Greco. Drop-dead-gorgeous, blue-eyed, black-haired Giulio. A man who had captured my heart. A man I might walk beside—but never get to *see* again.

"Cease," Chiara said gently, as if reading my mind. "Cast your dark thoughts to the shadows. You need all the light you can gather. Every *inner* light you can muster, yes?" She pulled me to my feet and across the room to hold the back of a chair, knowing I tended to feel rather dizzy in my dark world. I could hear her open a trunk and then, with firm snaps, shake out the wrinkles of a skirt and bodice.

She helped me out of my nightgown and dropped a soft underdress over my shoulders as if tending to a toddler. I accepted the indignity—just one of many such experiences in my day—suddenly anxious to leave my room. To be outside again. To feel the heat of the sun on my face, even if I could not see the light. *You need all the light you can gather,* she'd said. And she was right.

"Into the chair with you," she directed, then set to brushing out my hair and forming a quick braid. She wrapped the braid into a knot, pinned a net over it, and lifted my chin. "Pretty as ever," she said. "Sighted or no."

I forced a smile, knowing she was doing her best to encourage me.

"Your brother fashioned this." She placed the slender end of a long stick in my hand. "'Tis a light willow branch he whittled into shape for you, suitable to test your path before you step."

I stood and tapped about, feeling a tiny surge of hope. It was a step toward independence. Instead of reaching out with my hands, waiting until I ran into something, this would give me warning. Didn't blind people count out steps to their normal daily destinations? Maybe I could find my way to the garderobe rather than use the chamber pot. That would be one indignity I could strike from the list.

Chiara took my arm and led me to the door, then down the hall. Even before we reached the courtyard door, I could feel and hear the rumble of commotion. In my room, the two layers of stone wall muffled all but the loudest of sounds, but even from there I'd known that Castello Forelli was full of knights. Siena had come to the Forellis' aid, and the garrison town of Monteriggioni had sent men too. Castello Paratore, now held by the hateful Andrea Ercole, was likely occupied by similar numbers of our enemies, with Firenze rushing to secure her.

"My brother has patrols running from dawn to dusk, and a fair number by moonlight," Chiara said, holding me back to allow horses to pass before us, then sliding left to avoid some other obstacle. "His thought is that a bored knight is a knight about to find some trouble."

"Wise man," I said. "What have they encountered out there? Have there been continual skirmishes?"

"Surprisingly, no," she said. "Neither Siena nor Firenze wants this to escalate into war. But each is like a pot on slow boil. Giulio figures 'tis only a matter of time. The creek has become a temporary border, with men on either side hurling insults and daring their enemies to cross it, no matter how much their captains attempt to dissuade them."

I pictured them all out there, trash-talking, trying to lure their enemy to make the first move. I was surprised it hadn't happened yet. Maybe the battle at Castello Romano had left *everyone* a little traumatized—*both* sides had lost good men that day. Many men.

I swallowed hard, remembering Aurelio Paratore and how he'd helped us, time and time again. How his intervention in the end—with Captain Valeri—had likely saved those I loved most, but cost him his own life. If only he had lived . . . we would not be in this mess.

As we got closer to the Great Hall, the number of people increased. I could smell the men—horseflesh and sweat and leather. Was it true that blind people gained a greater sense of hearing and smell? I'd have to ask Adri.

I could sense us drawing attention. Bodies turned toward us. Conversations quieted. Any woman among this many men was bound to be a pull. But I heard my name whispered, as well as words about my blindness and the hulking knight who had knocked me unconscious. I pretended not to hear, anxious to feel the cool chasm of the Great Hall enfold me. I wanted to pause and lift my face toward the sun, but not when I had an audience of a hundred or more.

"Make way!" I heard Giulio call.

Chiara brought me to a stop. I tried to swallow but found my mouth terribly dry. Why had I not asked for a cloth and a bit of coal powder to brush my teeth? *Oh, for a real toothbrush and some good ol' Colgate.* My free hand gripped the soft cloth of what

I knew to be my green gown, one that Giulio had said made my eyes all the prettier. *My eyes.*

"My lady!" he said, reaching us at last. He took my hand in both of his. "You have arisen!"

"Indeed." I smiled in spite of myself. He was so surprised! "Did you think I would forever be abed?"

"Nay." He squeezed my hand. "I knew 'twould not be long."

There was such joy in his tone that I knew Chiara had been right—he needed me to be up and about as much as I did myself. But after the men started whispering bawdy jokes about me being "abed," Giulio took my other arm and led me inside.

"Chiara," he said to his sister in the entryway, outside the armory. "Might we have a moment alone?"

"Of course."

He led me inside the Great Hall, and I took in the cool temperature of the big room and relative quiet—noticeable after the courtyard chaos—even as servants set the tables for the noon meal, still two or three hours away. My stomach rumbled and Giulio laughed.

"You sound as hungry as I. Come." He led me to a table, and I found the bench. "A bit of bread and cheese?" he asked someone.

"At once," she said. Did I imagine it, or did she stare at me for a moment before turning toward her task?

I lifted my skirts a little to move my legs across the bench and under the table. Giulio gently pulled a portion of my skirt from beneath my knee to cover my legs again. The brief brush of his calloused fingers along my calf sent a shiver running up my leg and side, all the way to my neck. He had not touched me in any intimate way since the accident, as if he feared he might do damage. I knew *that* brush of his fingertips was nothing but an attempt to help protect my modesty. And yet I still *felt* everything I'd always felt for this man.

Instead of buoying my spirits, the thought sank them. I might be totally in love with Giulio—but he ought not be saddled with me.

"What is it, my love?"

"Hmm?"

"Your face just fell. Is it not good, to be up and about?" He tenderly took my hand, interlacing our fingers beneath the table.

"'Tis good," I said, his touch bolstering me a bit. "For the most part."

"And the other part?"

"It-it only reminds me of how much I am missing," I admitted. "To not be able to negotiate crossing the courtyard alone is rather pathetic."

"Pathetic? I do not know this word."

"Embarrassing. Infantile."

He squeezed my hand. "Luciana. *I* have trouble crossing that courtyard, rife with knights. You must be more kind to yourself. Celebrate the small steps."

Gather any light you can, Chiara had urged me. *Celebrate the small steps.* These two were clearly siblings. Steady and wise. Like their sister, Ilaria. And their whole adopted Forelli clan.

The maid returned with the bread and cheese, and by the sound as she placed it on the wooden table, a jug of watered wine. Giulio poured for me and moved my hand to the cup. "'Tis just there. And your plate before you, as usual."

I was thankful for food that did not require a knife. But even that thought depressed me a little. I set down my bread.

"Luciana?" he murmured, turning toward me. He placed one leg on the outside of the bench, his other pressing against my knee. He tipped my face toward him, as if he could see something—anything—in my eyes. "What troubles you?"

"You do not need a woman who cannot find her own food and drink when it is *right before her.*" I sighed and shook my head. "My sight is no better than it was days ago, Giulio," I whispered. "It might never improve."

"I *do* need you." He traced my cheek. "Blind or sighted, I need you by my side. I love you, Luciana. And I wake each day thanking God that you lived through that battle."

I continued to shake my head. "But you fell in love with me as I was. Not as I am now."

He took my hand again, and by his firm grip, I knew I'd made him angry. "Who you are now, deep within, is who you have always been, my love. You are still healing. Give yourself time. You shall remember yourself."

Remember myself? What was there to remember? "I cannot fight. I cannot bathe or dress myself! I cannot sew or do anything useful at all, for that matter."

"We have servants who shall aid you."

"I know! I know that. But you, Giulio, *you*! You do not need a blind bride." The tears rose again, in spite of how I tried to keep them back. "You deserve a woman who is hale, riding beside you on patrol. Like Tiliani. Or Gabi and Lia. Is that not why you fell in love with me?" I wiped my face. "And what sort of mother shall I be? I cannot even watch over a toddler, let alone keep them safe!"

"Luciana," he whispered, pulling me against his chest. "Are we betrothed? Have I forgotten? Mayhap *my* head was hit too hard in battle. And you have conceived? When we have yet to consummate our union? Shall I fetch the priest with news of this miracle?"

I laughed through my tears and tried to push him away, but he held on to me. "You know what I mean," I said. "We must think of the future. We must."

"I understand your heart, dear one, but the present is enough to consider for now. Try and not fear the morrow." He kissed the top of my head, and I relished the moment of comfort. Of feeling my cheek against the curve of his neck, the scent of him—all sage and pine and road dust and leather after patrol. "On *this* day, I know I need *you*, Luciana Betarrini. Once wed, I shall tell you that every day of our long lives together. And we shall find our way to manage our massive brood of children," he added in a whisper. "Because I am so eager to bed you, I shall have trouble leaving it once you are mine. 'Tis been hard enough not to kiss you of late."

I laughed again, wiping away my tears. "Kissing shall not impede my healing. Gentle kissing," I amended, remembering a few of our steamier moments.

"Then by nightfall, prepare yourself for that. At the moment, we have a few too many witnesses about."

"But you do not mind them seeing you comfort me?" I straightened.

"Nay. They pretend not to see us anyway." He paused and caressed my hand. "Hear this, my love. I value you for you—far more than anything you can *do*. You could do nothing but sit in the solar, a servant reading to you all day, and I would be content to return home to you."

I stifled a sigh, knowing he only meant to encourage me. He'd be content—maybe. But would I? Could I find contentment in a permanently dark world?

Or would I risk forever losing everything—and everyone I loved—in trying to reach the tomb that could heal me?

TILIANI

I looked over to my cousin, Fortino, receiving a report from a scout. We would return to the castello when Benedetto relieved him. My father had forty-eight men in rotation, half of them standing guard at the creek and half patrolling back and forth along the border in groups of six. If a Fiorentini dared to cross, we would know about it. And this tenuous truce could not last forever.

The late August morning had started out warm, and while I

took pride in donning our blue tunics with the embroidered wolf insignia, come afternoon, I wished we did not have to wear them. The added layer over my leather chest plate set me to sweating as the sun cleared the trees and beat down upon us. I pulled a handkerchief from my pocket and wiped my forehead for the fourth time as Valentino untied his water skin and took a deep drink. Silently, he offered it to me. I took a quick sip, daring not refuse him—given that he had made precious few overtures toward me in the week we had been home.

I knew he was grieving Aurelio, more brother than friend to him. I was too. They had saved us at Castello Romano. Surely, if they had not intervened, we would have been killed. Every one of us, from my family members to every knight on the field. But when I mentioned that to him the next day, he had only one brief response. *"I wish I had died in his place."*

His words had stung. Made me angry. I felt forgotten. He wished he was dead? What about me and what we shared? Was that not something to bring him hope? Life?

Since then, he had retreated to his quarters. Slept. Risen each morn. Eaten a minimal amount. Patrolled at my side. Kept watch and made notes of enemy movements, as if he had always been a Forelli knight and not one of the Paratores. But he did so without heart and with but half a mind—as if more ghost than man.

He stood beside me now, staring across the creek at the Fiorentini, who jeered and taunted him in turn as the "Wolf-lover," "betrayer," and "traitor."

"We shall capture you, Valeri!" one massive knight threatened, but two hundred paces away. "And your death shall not be an easy one! You and your precious She-Wolf shall watch each other die as we drain the blood from your veins!"

He stared back, seemingly unmoved. I thought he had not even heard the man until he muttered, "And so I have made you more of a target than ever."

I took his hand, boldly staring back at the Fiorentini, the action itself a taunt in return. "Nothing could make me more of a target than being a Forelli She-Wolf. I have spent my whole life with that target upon my back."

I waited for him to respond, but he said nothing.

"My cousin shall soon arrive. Then we can return to the castello for a rest," I said. "'Twill do you good to be away from the border." *Away from the Fiorentini. Away from men who fought beside you but a week ago.*

He left me without another word, never holding my hand as I had his. Only bearing it as if my touch burdened him further. Had I made a mistake? Made him feel as if I was using him somehow to get back at the Fiorentini?

Ilaria came to my side, watching him stride toward his horse and prepare his mount. "He shall find his way, in time."

"Do you truly believe that?" I muttered. "I confess I am beginning to doubt." I wished we had time to forage in the wood for herbs and medicinals rather than Fiorentini. Time amongst the trees would bring him back to me faster than anything. Remind him of what was good—promising—in life rather than this daily reminder of death and disaster.

"'Twould have been difficult for him to ever leave Aurelio's side," she said, crossing her arms and staring over at the Fiorentini, who now turned their taunting toward us, shouting and pantomiming such foul things that we both itched to go after them ourselves. But we pretended to be unperturbed, "rising above," as my Zia Gabi and mama had taught us.

"It would have been better for him to choose," I said. "Rather than have the choice made for him."

"Aurelio . . . I was there, Til," she said in a hushed voice. "I saw him put your hands together. He blessed you. Together. *Blessed* you. He knew you would need each other as friends, if not anything more."

"Again, making Valentino's decision for him," I said, so clearly reliving it that fresh tears arose. "No man appreciates that."

"He made his decision when he accompanied Aurelio in coming to our aid," she sniffed.

"But what else could he do?" I returned.

My mind went back to that fateful day. The chaos. So many dead and dying. So few of us left, and so many Fiorentini continuing to arrive. Nay, in the moment, none of us really had a choice. Survival demanded movement. Immediate action.

One of the biggest of our adversaries stepped forward to shout a new, foul threat. Others beside him laughed. The Forelli men around us tensed.

"M'lady, grant me permission to shoot him," Otello said, coming to my other side. "I need not cross the border to do so."

"Oh no," I said, still staring the knight down, arms crossed. "Once this tentative peace breaks, he shall be all mine."

"Or mine," Ilaria said.

"But you may have any one of the others," I offered, sliding him a small smile. "All seem to be of the same ilk."

In contrast, Zio Marcello and Papa had forbidden any one of us to utter even a word in return. Those of us here, keeping watch at the creek, were to do nothing but stand. I smiled. Our lack of response clearly irritated them, which had escalated their threats over the last hour. They wanted us to attack, to begin the war that we all knew was coming. For it was always best to be able to blame the other side for what could not be ignored—trespass.

Trespass, I thought grimly. Even now, these Fiorentini stood on land that had been in Forelli hands for almost two decades. Well past a border that Aurelio Paratore had honored. Now we were back to the border that Aurelio's diabolical uncle Cosimo had claimed was ancestral. And the tomb that the Betarrinis might need to enter to heal Luciana's sight was a half mile into enemy territory. The only other one? Terribly near Firenze herself.

And we ourselves would be trespassers if we aided the Betarrinis in reaching either one of them, sparking the fire that threatened to engulf us all.

2

TILIANI

Fortino had just arrived with fresh troops to relieve us when we spotted the white flags, moving down the hill across the creek. "Make way! Make way!" the guards shouted. Fiorentini drew back like curtains on a window to let them through.

Six nobles in finery emerged from the crowd, led by twelve Fiorentini knights in full city regalia, with twelve more behind. Andrea Ercole rode among them, followed by Lords Vanni and Piccolomini. Beside him stood the young Lord Beneventi—the son of the man Valentino had killed—the man who'd tried to ensure my parents and I died, when we had reached the end of our sentence in the cages.

My jaw clenched.

"Allow me to handle this, cousin," Fortino said firmly, and I reluctantly stepped back. As the future lord of Castello Forelli, 'twas certainly his place. But I dearly wanted to be close if there was a chance to get to Ercole.

All of this was his fault. Ercole had set up the now-dead Beneventi. Made him believe Lord Romano had stolen from him. The blood of every dead man on Romano's land cried out for retribution. Luciana left blind . . . so many others injured, struggling to recover. Valentino shattered in his grief. 'Twas Ercole who had convinced Lord Vanni to his side, as well as Lord

Piccolomini. All by basing his case on lies, undoubtedly. My body trembled with rage.

"One more step back," Ilaria said in my ear, sensing my thin hold. Her fingers wrapped around my elbow, and I woodenly did as she bid. With a glance, I saw that Valentino had returned to my other side, gripping the reins of his mount so hard his fingers were white.

The Fiorentini nobles stopped at the creek, their front guards dividing to form a line, three on either side. "We wish to speak to Lord Forelli and any others of the Nine," Lord Vanni called. He and Lord Piccolomini pulled up in front with Ercole behind them.

Fortino and his younger brother, Benedetto, met them on their own war horses, hands consciously idle on the pommels. But I knew—as the Fiorentini did—that both could draw their swords in seconds. "You and your guards may cross the creek. No others."

Lord Piccolomini sniffed. "Allow us twenty-four additional guards."

"I assume you come here to speak of potential peace, given your white flag."

"*Potential* peace," he allowed.

"Then we shall treat you as respectful hosts until you return to your side of the creek. There shall be no need for more than twelve guards, two per noble. You have my word as the Forelli heir."

Lord Piccolomini glanced over his shoulder at Ercole and Beneventi. "I must have your word that *every* one of us shall be returned to this creek, unharmed. *When* we wish to return."

Fortino paused. "On my life," he pledged. He glanced around at our men, then me, Ilaria, and then hardest at Val, making sure he was understood—no one was to harm them. He turned his gaze back to the Fiorentini, and in his stance, I glimpsed the future lord in him. "Lord Piccolomini, trust me when I say that given our rage, a *hundred* men would not keep you safe if I did not keep my word. But we Forellis always keep our word."

"Very well," sniffed the older man, lifting a hand and directing his group astride their horses forward. The knights reassembled before them, and two by two, they came across the creek, the nobles at the back. After a week of thinking about the creek as the final line, I struggled not to view each *clop* of a horse's hoof as a minor transgression.

"Easy," Ilaria said in my ear, her grip on my arm tightening as Ercole and Piccolomini came closer and closer, following my cousin and his men, who pivoted to lead them down the central road. Valentino swung into his saddle and turned his mount, forming a barrier between us. They rode past, eyes forward, never looking his way. As a slight? Or because they knew Valentino was like a wounded, caged tiger?

"Come, let us get to the castello before them," Ilaria said after they passed. "We can take the western path and get there in time to warn your elders before they arrive."

Val nodded and I agreed, eager to know what this was all about and glad that I was no longer on duty at the front. When they were past, I stepped to Benedetto's side—who had assumed command from Fortino—waiting until he finished talking to one of his men.

"Captain Mancini led the last patrol west a half hour ago," I said. "He should return momentarily. As will the patrol from the east. We aim to beat the Fiorentini to the castello and warn our parents of their arrival."

"Take caution, cousin," Benedetto said, his brown eyes moving to study Val over my shoulder. "Your man is spoiling for a reason to tear into any of them."

As we all are.

"Fortino gave his word. Do not allow Valeri to veer from your task." His gaze now followed the last of the Fiorentini heading in the direction of Castello Forelli. "And send me word of what transpires, will you?"

"Of course." I turned to go.

He caught my arm and waited until I met his eyes. "Do not

make me regret this. If it is peace they seek, we do not wish to interrupt the process. Leave the rest to our fathers."

"Of course," I managed to say, pulling my arm from his grip in irritation. I did not appreciate his fatherly tone. He was but a year my elder, and I had nearly as much field and battle experience as he.

"He remembers what you endured in Firenze," Ilaria said, rejoining me as we hurried toward our mounts. "As well as on Romano's land."

"I do not need a nursemaid," I groused. "In either of you."

"Nay," she said lightly. "Only people to watch your back."

I mounted up, knowing they both sought only to protect me, and in turn, the family. Siena herself. *Grant me peace, Lord. Your vision and direction.*

Grace and mercy?

I do not yet know if I can pray for those.

Not when it came to Andrea Ercole.

LUCIANA

I'd avoided returning to the Great Hall—and all the people throughout the castello—for two days, but found I could not stay still. I had to move. Talk. Try and live some sort of life while I waited for healing.

Ten days after my injury, I still had not experienced any significant improvement. For days now, I thought I might catch the barest semblance of light and dark, but I questioned if it was just me imagining what I so desperately wanted.

Taking hold of the willow stick that Nico had crafted for me, I tapped forward, finding the edge of the wall and then the door of my room. In time, I reached the turret and the courtyard exit, where I knew a guard awaited. "Open it, please."

"M-m'lady," he stammered, "allow me to find you an escort."

"Nay. I am only going to the chapel. Surely I can make it fifty paces without trouble."

"The castello's courtyard is quite congested this afternoon. Would you not—"

"Nay. I shall do this myself. Now open the door, please."

"As you wish," he said reluctantly.

But I could feel his protective eyes upon my back and didn't hear him shut the door behind me. I knew it was protocol, especially with so many others inside our gates. With some guilt, I recognized that I'd probably put him in a predicament—maybe he'd promised to watch over me as well as guard the door.

And yet I could not feel sorry about it. It felt good—so good—to reclaim some semblance of my own power. To make a decision for myself, by myself. To have a guard obey my wishes.

He's used to She-Wolves in charge, I thought. And for the thousandth time, I thanked God they had paved a way. Had it not been the way of Castello Forelli, I doubted I would have lasted more than a week. I was too . . . foreign. Too . . . *other* for medieval times. But Gabriella and Evangelia and their mother had paved a road for women that was nearly as strong as the Romans' own. At least in this household.

I tapped my way forward with my stick and, in time, sensed someone approaching from behind. I tensed but concentrated on my path—and on hopefully not getting trampled by a horse.

"Hey, how are ya?" my brother said, taking my arm. He sounded a little out of breath. "Out for a leisurely stroll, eh?"

"Something like that," I muttered, not entirely glad for Nico's arrival. Had the guard waved him over? Pointed me out to him? Had I attracted the attention of others in the process? I didn't want them looking. Didn't want them all feeling sorry for me.

"Where are you headin'?" Nico asked.

"The chapel," I said, pretending confidence.

"Yeah, well you're about thirty degrees off and heading into some pretty serious horse traffic." He turned me a bit, and we set off again. I said nothing but felt the burn of a blush at my cheek. "Fortunately," Nico said, "I saw the padre just go in. It will be quiet—and safe—for you in here."

He opened the door of the chapel, and I paused. "Thanks, Nico. I don't need you to wait. I'll find the inner wall as I exit and can make my way back to the turret. That way I won't get off course again."

He didn't respond, apparently surprised. Because I didn't want him to listen in to my conversation? Or because I wanted to make it back solo?

"Nico, if I don't start doing things on my own, I'm gonna go crazy," I warned, lifting a hand.

"Gotcha," he said soothingly. "I'll be over by the stables. My mare came up lame, and a squire is getting me acquainted with a new one while she rests up. Shout if you need me."

"Th-thank you," I said, relieved he'd elected not to argue. I stepped through the doorway, but noted Nico didn't shut it behind me until Father Giovanni greeted me.

"Ahh, Lady Luciana! 'Tis good to see you up and about." He came to me and took my free hand in both of his. "What may I do for you?"

"I-I had hoped we could talk a bit. Is now a good time?"

"All my time is the Lord's. Please, please. Allow me to lead you to a seat here in the corner. Should someone come to pray, it will afford us a bit of privacy. How is your head today?"

I could feel my eyebrows lift in surprise, assuming at first he could sense what a head case I was. But then I knew he was referring to the migraine I'd endured constantly since I was injured. "You know, it might be a bit better this morning." I'd been so focused on getting out of my room, I hadn't stopped to think about it. Was that a good sign?

"Good, good." He squeezed my arm. "The bench is just here. If you will turn to your left, you can sit."

I thanked him and then bit my lip as an awkward silence rose between us. Where to start?

"Simply ask the first question you have in mind, child," he said reassuringly.

I huffed a laugh. "Very well. Why would God bring me here—all the way *here*—only to leave me blind?"

He paused. "Why would you assume he is leaving you blind?"

I frowned. "Why would I assume he is not? Lady Adri thought I would be seeing shadows by now, at least."

"Ahhh, yes. Well, let us say you are right. Mayhap you are blind for life. There are worse things, no?"

I stopped breathing. It was the first time anyone had not argued with me. Insisted that it would be different, in time.

"You could have died ten days ago, yes? Or been left in a coma? Or paralyzed?"

"Well, yes."

"This is not to say that losing one's sight is not terrible. 'Tis a significant loss," he said, putting a warm hand atop my own. "And if you are not healed, you must grieve it and grieve it fully. But your question was why God would bring you here—and leave you blind. He brought you here, yes. But he did not leave *you*, Luciana. He is with you even now. Here in this chapel. In your quarters. In the Great Hall. Wherever you go."

I sighed and shook my head. "That is well and good. But when I said *leave* I meant why would he not heal me? How much good can I do for him, for the Forellis, if I am helpless?"

He considered me. "I have learned a great deal about you, Luciana, since you joined our fold. And nothing I have learned would make me say you are helpless. You have great inner strength. Courage." He leaned closer. "And I wager that even fighting blind, you might be able to best the strongest man inside the castello gates."

That made me smile, in spite of myself. "I only might take a few more blows myself, before I do—in that I cannot see them coming."

"You shall compensate for that in time, if necessary. The blind I have known over the years develop an uncanny way of placing sounds. Knowing where people are—or even a mouse in the corner. That shall aid you."

I bit my lip. Maybe he was right. But there was so much more . . .

"Your next question, please," he encouraged.

"The blind you have known over the years . . . what did they do? To earn a wage? To make themselves useful?"

"Well, let me see." I could almost picture the small man tapping his lip, thinking. "A fair number are beggars, but I doubt that is in your future. One works in a bakery, kneading bread dough. Another washes floors. One is a fine lady and runs several businesses through instructions via her managers."

I had been a history major back home, gunning for a TA position at the university next year. What could I do here, in this time? What was I ever going to do, if we stayed? I'd been so wrapped up in Giulio I really hadn't stopped to think about that side of my life. Nico had his whole financial career figured out, finding a way to enter banking even *here*. But what could I do, teach? Some of the history I specialized in—the Renaissance— hadn't even taken place yet.

"I-I need a way to contribute. Back home," I said, knowing he knew our whole story, "I was studying to become a teacher. A *tutor*," I corrected myself. "But to do that, a person needs to read or write."

"There might be a way, in time," he said. "You might be able to still serve as a tutor, m'lady. Even now, some of our finest scholars pass along their knowledge as fine orators."

Orators. I took that in, slowly nodding. *That might work.*

"But I have seen how Captain Greco looks upon you. You are his intended, no?"

"Mayhap," I allowed.

"I think it is a foregone conclusion," he said, slightly chiding.

"If we can find our way," I said. "Given this new obstacle."

His hand returned to mine. "You are still as worthy a woman now, Luciana, as you were a sennight ago."

I paused. "Am I? As we have discussed, I do not know what I can do to contribute."

"Do you love Giulio for what *he* can do for you?"

I paused. "Nay. Of course not. I love him for who he is."

"What if he was the blind one?"

That startled me. It wouldn't matter. I'd help him find a way. But my love for him would remain.

"Those who find love—true love—begin with a foundation that cannot be shaken. Have you ever seen a house or tower built from the ground up, m'lady?"

I shook my head.

"The most important part is the foundation. If the builders do not build it correctly—if they fail to dig out sand and properly fortify the soil, it sinks. There are houses and towers everywhere that slowly lean in time—others that have fallen—because care was not taken for the foundation. What you and Giulio share is a foundation built on true love. Not for what you can *do* for each other, but because you purely love each other for *who you both are.* 'Tis much like God's love for us. He does not care if I am a potter or priest, beggar or baker. I am to accept that my foundation of faith is built on Christ's overwhelming, unfailing love alone. And a love like that cannot be earned, m'lady. Only accepted."

I heaved a sigh, thinking through his words. "You have given me a great deal to consider. Thank you, Padre."

"Of course," he returned. "Come to see me any time you wish to discuss it further, m'lady. My door is always open."

3

Luciana

As I left the chapel, I heard that Lord Romano and twelve of his men were coming through the gates. Bringing more of our wounded home?

The men called out in glad greeting, but a knight on the wall cried, "Captain Pezzati, Lady Tiliani rides in at a gallop! She is accompanied by Sir Valeri and Lady Ilaria!"

"Leave the gates open for them!" the captain returned as what I assumed were Lord Romano and his wagons drew deeper into the courtyard.

I tensed by the wall, waiting to hear more. Why such haste? The courtyard, so loud and raucous with men, became eerily quiet and still. Only the chickens and horses moved as the trio rode in and pulled up.

"What is it?" Marcello called, at last emerging.

"Fiorentini emissaries approach, bearing a white flag," Tiliani called, breathless. "They come to speak with you and Papa, Uncle. And Ercole and Beneventi are among them. Fortino swore that they would be given safe passage. Every one of them."

If it were possible, the courtyard grew quieter still. The gathering rage was palpable.

"They dare to come here," grunted a man near me.

"Through our own gates," returned his companion.

Marcello raised his voice so everyone present could hear.

"Hear this! These men, arriving shortly, do so as our guests. Until they are once more across the creek, every one of you shall treat them as you would any of the Forellis. If you do not, you shall answer to me."

With that, action returned. Calls rang out for water and stretchers to transfer the wounded from the Romanos' wagons to our own quarters. I tapped my way along the wall, and a man fell into step beside me. "May I lend a hand, m'lady? I hear tell your eyesight has not yet returned."

"Nay, it has not," I said lightly, trying to place his voice. "But thank you. I am quite able to find my way."

More men arrived, and I heard Giulio's name called. I hoped he might glimpse me—managing on my own—and wished these men would leave me alone.

Tiliani's voice rose above the clamor from the direction of the gate. "Where is my father? I must speak with him at once!"

I paused. She sounded alarmed.

"I think Lady Adri would insist," said the man near me, taking my distraction with Til for lack of confidence in my path. He took hold of my elbow.

I hesitated. I did not want to make a scene—the Forellis had more than they could handle at the moment—but I wanted it clear I was as independent as ever. "Unhand me, sir. Now. Blind or not, you know what I can do to you."

His companion laughed.

"I only meant to come to your aid," groused the first, releasing me.

"And yet if the lady says she need it not, you are to take her at her word," Giulio said, suddenly behind my shoulder.

"Yes, of course, *Captain*," said the first, as if subtly mocking his title. The two turned and departed, muttering between them and laughing. Not every fighting man—even at Castello Forelli—was the finest. With this many men called to serve, we definitely had some edgier dudes on the premises.

I began to tap my way forward again, as if unfazed by Giulio's presence. Had he seen me on my own? Or only when the men made a move on me?

"What do you suppose the Fiorentini seek?" I asked Giulio. "Why come here? Now?"

"I suppose they wish to avoid further battle, as much as we do. Mayhap they have a compromise in mind."

"Abandoning Castello Paratore and retreating behind the old boundary line?" I asked with false hope.

"If only it were that simple."

"If only." My stick hit the corner of the turret. "I best change into something more formal. Right? Or will m'lords not wish me to be present?"

"We all best be ready," he said shortly. He seemed to turn toward me, and I could feel his perusal. "I can see that you are putting that stick to good use. Who fashioned it for you?"

"Nico. He knows I am not accustomed to sitting about."

"That much I know well about you," he said tenderly, tucking a lock of my hair behind my ear. He knocked on the turret door. A small window opened with a squeak. "Lady Betarrini has returned," Giulio said. When the guard opened the door, he continued, "Lock the door behind us. I shall escort the lady to her quarters."

"Yes, Captain," the man said obediently, the door clanging shut.

"Margarete!" cried Giulio, startling me. "Come and see to your lady!"

"Yes, m'lord! I shall be there in but a moment!" called the girl from down the hall.

Giulio seemed to notice my reaction. "Forgive me." He took my arm. "I did not mean to frighten you."

I shook my head and tried to give him a smile. "You do not understand how many visual cues we use. I would have anticipated your shout had I seen you."

We reached my room, and he opened the door for me. Leaving

it open, he followed me in. When I set my stick against my chair, he came around and took my hands in his. "I missed you this morning, beloved." He brought them up and tenderly kissed my knuckles, one after the other.

"I missed you too," I admitted. How I'd longed to be astride a horse, on patrol! "And yet I had a very helpful conversation with Father Giovanni."

"You did?" he asked, hope flooding his tone.

"I did."

"Of what did you speak?"

"Ahh, I am not yet ready to share."

"Fair enough. I am glad you sought him out. He is a fine man."

"He is indeed."

"May I return to escort you to the Great Hall, once you are changed?"

I thought about that. Part of me had wanted to arrive solo. But I knew neither Giulio nor my brother would be okay with that. Nor was it probably wise. "Yes, please."

"I'll be right outside," he whispered, leaning closer to softly kiss my temple, sending shivers down my neck and arms as he reluctantly pulled away. Did I imagine it, or was he eyeing my lips? I turned toward him, inviting him to kiss me—truly kiss me—but the maid arrived then.

"Oh!" Margarete said. "Forgive me."

"Nay!" he said. "Stay. I am leaving now, reluctant though I may be. I shall await my lady in the hall."

"She shall be ready shortly," the girl promised.

He closed the door gently behind him, and Margarete guided my hands to the back of the chair. "Let us get you changed. I think you ought to wear the olive gown. Captain Greco favors you in green."

I smiled in agreement, finding hope in wanting to look especially fine for Giulio on this day. Finding hope in wanting him to kiss me—thoroughly kiss me again, blind or not. Finding hope in the fact that for the first time in days, my head did not ache. But also for the Fiorentini—that they might witness that they could blind me, but not keep me down.

"Yes, Margarete," I said. "That gown would be lovely."

TILIANI

I made my way through the mass of men in the courtyard, my entire body on alert, from heel to scalp. Many were as silent and tense as I was. Wondering where this would lead, if anywhere at all. Might we avoid another battle? War?

I hoped so. As I sought out my father, I itched for my bow, my quiver. Gall rose in my throat as I thought of those lost on the fields before Castello Romano. Aurelio, for one. Among so many others. Now here arrived Andrea Ercole and Lord Beneventi, thinking we could simply move past the horrible memories, not yet a fortnight old. Forget the dead and dying. The injustice!

Ercole had not once shown himself a purveyor of peace. He always had ulterior motives. What were they this time? The more I considered potential answers, the more I concluded we *must* not enter this meeting with mere hope and goodwill. We must be prepared for the unexpected. A threat, at the very least. *What does he want?*

I had to speak with Papa before they arrived. My uncle, too, if I could. To make a plan. Or at the very least, prepare to receive our enemy as one unified body.

I glanced at my hand, saw that it trembled, and quickly fisted it, hoping no one noticed. That battle had taken a part of me, I admitted to myself. I had engaged in skirmishes, attacks, before. But none had *taken* from me as the battle on Castello Romano's field had.

There, I had lost friends.

Brothers. Family. Aurelio. And nearly, my cousin Luciana.

And that left me spoiling for revenge.

Finally, I heard my father's voice over the din of men milling about. "Tiliani! Over here!"

I turned and spied him beside the entry to the Great Hall, beckoning to me. "Papa, may I have a word?" I asked, as soon as I reached him.

With a wave of dismissal to the two knights on either side of him, he immediately ushered me into the armory and closed the door. "What is it?"

"Ercole comes bearing a white flag, but he shall pursue more than peace."

"Undoubtedly," Papa said with a nod. "'Tis too soon for him to offer it. He would aim to bring us lower, first. Strive to hold something over our heads." He paced, tapping his chin. "I have long wondered why he returned *you* to us after the battle."

"Because we agreed to his terms—"

Papa shook his head. "He could have demanded more. Perhaps he is here to do so now." He shot me a warning look. "Mayhap he comes to collect a traitorous Fiorentini."

I faltered. "Val-Valentino?"

Papa covered my shoulder with a warm hand. I longed for him to give me some hint of a jest, break out into one of his customary cheeky smiles, but he was utterly sober. "You must prepare yourself, Til. Ercole may be here for him."

I gaped at him. "Why?"

"Some Fiorentini soldiers at Castello Paratore were previously loyal to Aurelio and therefore to their captain, Valeri. Perhaps Ercole wishes to remove any temptation of shifting loyalties by making an example of him."

I tried to swallow but found no moisture in my mouth. "We-we cannot allow it," I gasped, my heart twisting at the idea of them taking Val from us—from me—even though we were at odds.

Aurelio's loss had crippled us both. In time, as we healed, we would find our way back to each other.

But did Ercole have the right to demand we hand Val over to him? Was there some Fiorentini law regarding traitors that would give him license?

I steeled myself. It mattered not. For we stood on Sienese land.

Even with the door closed, we could hear the gate guards, announcing the arrival of the Fiorentini. Papa turned to go, but I grabbed his arm. "You shall speak to Zio Marcello?" I asked, hating the desperation in my tone but unable to curb it. "Ask him to help protect Valentino?"

He cradled my face. "I know you love him, Til. And we owe him a great deal. Do you trust me to do my best?"

"Always."

But even as I uttered the word, I felt the sinking futility of it. Because time and again, we had done our best to fight Lord Ercole. And somehow, he always ended up on top.

I followed him into the courtyard, coming alongside Domenico. He clenched his hands at his sides when Ercole rode through the gates, head held high.

I bumped Nico with my shoulder. "No one wants that man dead more than I."

"Of that I am uncertain. That's the man that *stabbed my sister*."

"One of his many crimes," I said. I nudged him again, half fearing he might leap at Ercole as he rode toward us. "Look at me, Domenico."

He reluctantly turned his dark brown eyes toward me for a moment.

"Breathe. No one shall touch any of the Fiorentini while they are inside our walls. To do so would end this very fragile peace. And possibly Fortino's life. Understood?"

"What if I find a way to hurt him but no one sees?" he hissed.

"Do not. My cousin gave his word."

I turned to stare at the contingent of men, now dismounting

by the stables. The young Beneventi offered an arm of greeting, but my father and uncle did not step forward to greet him in kind, leaving their own arms crossed.

Lord Beneventi looked about—every man, woman, and child staring at them as if we all wished to throw them into a fire—and then back to my elders. "Lord Forelli, might we retire someplace private to speak? Take some refreshment?"

"You are not a guest in this house," my father retorted. "As for privacy, there is no need. Say what you must, and then be on your way."

Beneventi brought up his chin as Ercole stepped up beside him. "Come now, Lord Forelli," he said. "We have as much rationale as you to be furious. Our family lost a fair fortune to Romano." He paused to glance back at Ercole, Piccolomini, and the rest. "And we lost as many men as you did. Including my father at the hands of Sir Valeri." He glanced around, as if looking for Valentino. Ercole did too. My heart raced.

My uncle poked a finger in Ercole's direction. "I shall say it once more. Your father was duped by that man, and it seems you were, too. You believed Lord Romano stole your father's chest of gold? I can guarantee that Andrea Ercole now has it distributed among his mercenaries, the chest itself buried in the forest. And now you are here to defend him and his false border?"

"I am here to defend Firenze and her land. But come, let us set aside our differences and—"

"Our differences?" my uncle sputtered. "More than four score of our men were killed defending an innocent man and his castello. Nearly as many were injured. And yes, you . . . you lost similar scores, including the only Paratore I have ever counted as a friend," he said, stepping forward to look down his nose at the man. "Your father *murdered* Aurelio Paratore. Never have I seen such a vicious, cowardly move. Pretending to acquiesce, and then stabbing him?"

"It had to be done. Paratore betrayed Firenze, as well as our family."

"He was defending innocence!"

"He rode to your aid," Ercole sneered. He said it as if we were vermin, and Beneventi nodded and crossed his arms.

I stifled a sigh. It seemed the son was as gullible as his father.

"He rode to the aid of all who were dedicated to protecting the innocent and defending truth," Lord Romano said as he pressed closer. Papa grabbed and held one of his arms. The poor man looked like he had personally borne the weight of every knight who had died on his soil.

Beneventi and Romano stood there, nostrils flaring, precariously close to coming to blows.

"Mayhap we should tell you why we have come," said Lord Piccolomini, trying to intervene.

"Please," Lord Romano sneered, still not letting his eyes drop from Beneventi. Zio Marcello put a hand on his shoulder, but Romano brushed it away. Still, he seemed to remember himself and managed to take a half step back.

"Get on with it," Papa said, gesturing to Lord Piccolomini.

The man fished a scroll from a pocket beneath his tunic, untied it, and handed it to Zio Marcello.

My uncle unfurled the scroll, scanned it, and then frowned at Beneventi. A vein at his temple bulged with rage as he handed it to Lord Romano. Seeing his expression of warning, the man whipped it from his hands and, with jaw clenched, began to read.

"You jest," he said, shaking his head, glancing up at Beneventi.

"We do not," Beneventi returned.

Lord Romano's face, already red, became an even deeper shade as he read it through again. Zio Marcello leaned toward Papa to whisper in his ear. Lord Romano threw the scroll to the ground between them and took Lord Beneventi's tunic in his hands. "My daughter *is but eleven years old.*"

His *daughter*? What was this?

Knights on either side pried apart the men, and Papa stepped between them, a hand on either man's chest. "Hold!" he cried. "I said *hold*!"

Beneventi straightened his tunic with a huff and glared at Romano. "Lord Ercole is, of course, willing to wait until she comes of age," he said, gesturing toward Andrea.

I struggled to understand. This was—a *marriage* contract? Between the young Lady Romano and *Ercole*? *Nay . . . Please, God. Nay!*

My skin crawled at the thought of it. *The filth had made a bid for a bride only eleven years old?*

"In turn," Beneventi said, ignoring the sputtering Romano, "we shall forgive your debt to me and begin to establish more friendly ties between our two republics." He lifted his hands. "We are reluctant neighbors, no? But the fact remains—our properties shall always form the boundary line. Why must we constantly battle? Lord Forelli was on the right track when he sought a marriage alliance with Lord Paratore. Let us resolve this in kind."

Zio Marcello scoffed. "You know as well as I that it shall not be that simple."

"'Twill be simple if both sides honor the agreement," Vanni said, taking charge of the negotiations. "You are clearly fond of the Romano clan, Lord Forelli. We shall find young Celeste a tutor and governess to accompany her to Castello Paratore, or Lord Romano may choose them himself. Over the coming seasons, she shall gradually feel at home and become fond of Lord Ercole before 'tis time for their nuptials."

Now my skin was truly crawling. This was not the first of such unions. Royals certainly made such agreements all the time, and some nobles followed suit. But most children were allowed to remain in their own homes until they came of age, not fostered in their intended's. And if they *were* fostered, it was generally among a robust family with plenty of women to protect and love the child—not a military compound like Ercole's home was likely to be. The thought of that precious little girl trapped in Ercole's lair . . .

The courtyard was rife with shouts of outrage and furious whisperings. Romano turned to argue quietly with my father.

"Of course, there is another option," Ercole said placatingly, quieting us all. He stretched out a hand toward me. "The Lady Tiliani could take my hand."

If my stomach roiled before, it was nothing compared to this. Ercole met my eyes. "You were betrothed to a Paratore once before. Why not accept me in his stead?"

Somehow I knew this was what he'd wanted all along. He had never planned to come after Val. And little Celeste was a pawn. *I* was the true prize.

The entire courtyard went silent, and I fought for breath. Either I sacrificed myself or I sacrificed Celeste.

"You cannot refuse us," Lord Vanni said. "For if you do, we shall attack again, and this time, not leave until we are in control of both Castello Romano and Castello Forelli. Siena shall lose this corner of her republic, along with many of her people. Mayhap both of your families. Lord Beneventi shall assume control of your castello, Lord Romano, and Lord Ercole shall assume control of Castello Forelli."

Men all around us erupted, jeering, shouting, threatening.

"We either establish peace," Vanni shouted, regaining the floor, "which shall benefit us all—via improved trade—or we shall exact payment the more difficult way."

"We shall not shackle either of our daughters' hands to that jackal's!" sputtered Romano, his face lined with incredulity.

"There is more for you to consider." Ercole slid another scroll from inside his own tunic. He handed it to Romano.

The man snatched it from him and furiously unrolled it. Could he even focus on the words to read them? But he apparently managed, because we all watched as his red-faced visage drained into a terrible gray pallor. He handed it to my father with a trembling hand. Ercole could barely contain his glee.

Papa read it, handed it to Zio Marcello, and glared at the Fiorentini. He turned to speak in a scout's ear, and the man set off at once. Zio Marcello slowly looked from the scroll to the Fiorentini.

"Your scout shall only verify that what we say is true," Ercole said smugly. "Even now, there are a thousand men ready to cross Arezzo's border. A thousand more on Perugia's. Should we not return to our side of the creek within an hour, they shall decimate this castle, and Lord Romano's—along with everyone in it."

I separated my feet, determined not to let my wobbling knees give way. My mother and aunt had raised a She-Wolf, not a fainting lady. And yet . . .

Two thousand men, plus the thousand Fiorentini already amassed on the other side of the border?

Siena had sent five hundred to hold off Firenze and could easily muster a thousand more of their own—but it would take two days for them to arrive. Monteriggioni had sent a couple hundred men who were already in and around our castello. Villeins would likely rise to our aid from our lands. But we were surrounded . . . and we would all be massacred between those forces, outnumbered three to one. How, *how* had they secured their agreement?

I stared at Ercole, shocked that he had managed to surprise us yet again. It *had* to be his doing.

"Shall we come to fetch Lady Tiliani in three days' time, or would you like to escort her to Castello Paratore?" Ercole asked, looking at his fingernails as if considering cleaning them. Then he threw up his hands with a flash of a grin. "I shall gladly throw a feast for my new family, as well as my new neighbors."

I saw no way out. It was either my life or the lives of my people.

Ercole cast out his arms with a welcoming smile. "Come now. Let this be the beginning of a new era of camaraderie and peace!"

"It cannot be so!" cried out a grave voice. Valentino? I turned to search for him in the crowd. "The Lady Tiliani is already betrothed to me."

My mouth went dry as Val pushed his way to the front. *My love, what are you doing?*

Papa studied him and then glanced at me. I widened my eyes briefly, inclining my head. He turned back to Ercole. "He speaks the truth. They are to wed this very night."

Ercole's brows lowered and lips clamped, not buying the lie. I was thankful that the entire courtyard held their breath rather than erupting into excited whispers of gossip.

"Then it shall be Lady Celeste," Lord Beneventi said, not recognizing Ercole's dismay. He, it seemed, had fallen for Ercole's lie: that he merely wished to wed for peace. But it was clear to me—and to the rest of the Forelli clan—that Ercole had come through our gates for one purpose, and one purpose only.

To claim me as his own. To finally, at all costs, subdue me. And in turn, bring low the entire Forelli clan.

He advanced a step. "You said you are to wed this night," he said to Val, still pinning me with his hazel eyes. Was the truth all over my face? "But you are not *yet* wed."

"'Tis too late," put in Padre Giovanni. "I have already blessed this intended union. What has been put before God cannot be set aside."

I tried not to gape at our priest. What he said was likely not an outright lie—I knew the man prayed for each and every one of us and our concerns, and had prayed over my longing to be together with Val.

Ercole scoffed in his direction. "All respect due to *God*," he said, "no wedding is acknowledged as binding until a bride has been bedded."

I gritted my teeth and saw my cousin take Valentino's arm to keep him from beating the smirk off our enemy's face.

"As you say," Papa allowed with a curt nod, his face coloring with rage, "but we Forellis consider it done. My daughter shall wed Sir Valeri, and no other."

Beneventi grabbed hold of Ercole's forearm. He wrenched it away in irritation and then Piccolomini faced him to confer in hushed tones. Ercole had one hand on his hip, the other gesticulating madly. Piccolomini raised a placating palm in response, his determined expression never changing. They whispered back and forth furiously for a moment. Ercole turned partly away, as if smarting from the decision, and Piccolomini curtly nodded toward us. "We shall resume our original bid for the young Lady Romano's hand."

Papa turned to Lord Romano with a commiserating look. It was their turn to share quick, furiously intent words. Despite the outrage, none of them could disagree—to do so would be to condemn our people to death. They were in a terrible position.

"I-I need to consult with my wife," Romano said at last, clearly trying to buy time. "We-we shall have to find her a governess and tutor."

While Ercole's fellow lords saw this as acquiescence, the thunder behind Ercole's eyes proved he was not yet bested. He would take out his anger on little Celeste. And safely wed to Valentino—if it were truly to come to pass—I knew I could not abandon the child to his fury. After all, it could have been me. In many ways, it should have been me.

I was speaking before I really considered it fully. All I could think of was defending that innocent girl, caught up in a web she had had no part in weaving. "I shall be her governess."

All eyes turned toward me. Papa's narrowed. *"Tiliani."*

Ilaria took my arm. "What are you *doing*?" she whispered.

But every passing second made me more assured. Would it not be good for me to be inside those walls? Could I not find a way to aid my people when they came to free us both? A way to bring Ercole down from the inside out? As a married woman, I would not only be qualified, but I would have greater protection.

Married. A married woman. My mind could not make sense of the words. And I dared not let my heart consider what this actually meant, let alone how Valentino actually felt. It would have to wait.

"Excellent," Lord Vanni said, rubbing his palms together. "*Two* beloved daughters of Siena shall be even better than one in establishing peace. That only leaves finding a suitable tutor. I know a young man in Firenze who—"

"*I* shall be her tutor." Luciana, in her dark-green gown, stepped closer.

With a start, Giulio moved to intervene, but I put a hand to his chest. "Wait," I whispered. "Let her have her say."

Ercole let out a scoffing sound. "A stray dog would make for a better tutor than a blind woman."

"I have lost my sight, not my brain," she returned, taking another step forward, hands resting on her stick. "I am a nobleman's daughter. Educated at university in Britannia, in history, as well as letters. Between us, Tiliani and I shall see to your daughter, Lord Romano. You may trust *us*."

I shifted nervously. Normally I would leap at the opportunity to have our newest She-Wolf at my side. But *would* she be of aid to me in Castello Paratore? Or would her lack of sight make her as vulnerable as little Celeste?

The determined set of her chin eased my concern. Would it not be better to have her beside me than some silly tutor I did not know? Even blind, she would still be able to fight.

Ercole was rubbing his chin, his keen eyes flicking from me to Luciana. He moved toward me, but Papa put a warning hand to his chest. He ceased his approach but not his stare. "You undoubtedly have some scheme brewing in that pretty head of yours," he sneered.

He was not wrong. We would find a way to free Celeste from the devil's lair. We had to. "My only desire is to serve my people, my *lord*," I said, with no semblance of respect to his ill-begotten title. I moved closer to him and gave my father a quick look, silently telling him I had to stand on my own here. Papa reluctantly dropped his hand and retreated as Ercole and I turned to face each other. "I would rather be drawn and quartered than abandon that innocent girl to your despicable whims," I said.

He smiled thinly and leaned toward me. "And drawn and quartered shall you be if you do anything but see to my little future bride's welfare. Is that understood? Should you attempt any measure of subterfuge within my walls, or should you try and turn her against me, I shall make Celeste *watch* as you are dismembered. And then I shall hang the pretty Lady Luciana from my wall." He paused and smiled, catlike. "Mayhap in a cage like you endured in Firenze, so that all your kinsmen may watch her slowly die."

I refused to even blink. It would be two or three years before little Celeste came into her womanhood. Surely we could find a way to free her and reclaim Castello Paratore long before then.

"You scheme, even now," he hissed, eyes narrowing. "But I do not fear your plans. I have always managed to keep several steps ahead of the Forellis. And having all three of you in my keep shall buy us years of peace and prosperity."

"Then it is done?" asked Lord Piccolomini, glancing at the sinking sun. "We must soon return to the creek in order to send messengers to our allies, telling them to stand down."

Papa and Zio Marcello looked to Lord Romano.

The man ran his hands down his wan face and looked to me and then over to Luciana and back. "You shall keep watch over my precious daughter, Lady Forelli?" he asked, his voice tremulous.

"Day and night," I pledged.

He turned to face Ercole. "I agree to this, as long as the Ladies Forelli and Betarrini are by Celeste's side. All have heard your threats this day. But should *anything* happen to them, either by your hand or God's, this agreement is null and void."

Outraged, Ercole shook his head, but Lord Piccolomini stilled him with a clearing of his throat and firm look.

I stifled a smile. As much as Ercole might have masterfully organized this trap, his fellow lords clearly held power of their own. They had agreed to this, undoubtedly after a handsome financial gain, but he was not free to do entirely as he pleased.

Mayhap sensing the same, Lord Romano pressed on. "And lastly, when she comes of age, Celeste shall have the ability to choose if she takes your hand. Should you treat her as the treasure she is," he said through narrowed, challenging eyes, "she shall *surely* choose you over time. But if she does not wish to take you as husband, she shall be returned to Castello Romano unharmed. Those are *my* terms. Agreed?"

Lord Piccolomini cleared his throat again as the silence stretched between them.

"Agreed," Ercole said stiffly, putting a hand to his chest and bowing slightly before he moved to lead the others out. "However," he said with a wink, "I think you shall find that I can be quite charming when I set my mind to it. Mayhap even more so with the young and innocent."

My uncle and father had to bodily hold Lord Romano back as the Fiorentini turned to mount up and swiftly depart through our gates.

4

LUCIANA

"What have you done?" my brother asked in hushed astonishment and rage. "Luci, you can't go in there!"

"I can and will," I said.

He pulled me along, sidestepping various people and obstacles as he rushed me to a place we could speak more freely. "You are hurting me, Nico," I griped, trying to shake off his hand.

But he did not release me. Instead, he grabbed my other elbow and shook me. "Not as much as Ercole might hurt you! What were you thinking? He *stabbed* you. He-he . . ." His voice became thick, as if fighting tears. "He almost killed you, Luci. And now you . . ."

He released me, and I could picture his hands going to his mouth, staring at me in horror and dismay.

"I could not let Tiliani go alone!" I said. And the timing of this opportunity was not lost to me after my conversation with Father Giovanni. God's doing, perhaps? Here, now, I could be of some *use*! Aid Tiliani and Celeste!

"Yes, *yes*! You could've!" He took my arm again, but this time, his touch was filled more with warning than anger. "Giulio is coming our way," he said with some relief. "Maybe he can make you see what an idiot you're being," he whispered. "He looks like he wants to throttle you more than I do."

But I turned toward the sound of Giulio's footsteps as he approached, emboldened. "Do you not see? Either of you? I can be of aid to Til, even in my blindness. Together, we shall find some means to bring Ercole down, while you all figure out how to waylay these forces from Perugia and Arezzo. Help drum up support for Siena."

"Drum up?" Giulio repeated in confusion.

"Rally. Pull people together," Nico explained irritably. "And in the meantime, Luci will be in the lion's den."

"I prefer to call it the She-Wolves' lair," Tiliani said, joining us. "You heard Romano. If anything happens to us, this agreement is null and void. Ercole shall not harm us." She said nothing of Valentino's claim of betrothal. How could they have kept it a secret? Or had it been what it seemed—a desperate ruse to protect her?

"It might be hours, even days until we find out if you are in trouble," Giulio said, voice strained. I could picture him, rubbing the back of his neck, consternation lining his face as he looked to me.

"We can demand that we send a morning and evening missive, testifying to our well-being," I said.

"We can also demand that we take Celeste for walks along the allure where you can clearly see us, as well as into the woods," Tiliani said. "As her governess, I shall insist upon it for her good health. She is not to be treated as a prisoner, and neither shall we. If they truly desire peace, then they shall have to act accordingly."

"We weakened the wall before Aurelio took charge," I put in. "And it appears that Ercole has not yet discovered it. If worse comes to worst, you could bring it down."

"And risk your lives too?" Nico asked.

"At least it is something in our favor," I said with a shrug.

"This is crazy, Luci," Nico said in English. "All of it."

"Don't you see?" I returned in English. "This puts me within reach of the tomb—the tomb that can heal me, should I choose to try."

"Only if *I* can get there too."

"As we said, we shall not be treated as prisoners," I went on, this time in Tuscan. "I must see my twin brother at times, yes? And an eleven-year-old girl will be entering Castello Paratore's gates in three days' time, the fate of all of Siena on her little shoulders. Is it not good that Tiliani and I can be there, to help her bear the load?"

"'Tis brave," Giulio allowed. He moved closer, his hand moving to my hip. "And though I loathe the idea, I am proud of you both. Fiercely proud. Your sister is right, Domenico. We shall find a way to utilize their placement, inside the walls. And bring Ercole down from within."

"Valentino approaches," Tiliani said, as if in warning. "And we have . . . much to discuss."

TILIANI

"You pledged yourself as *governess*," Valentino said, grabbing my upper arms in aching misery. "Willingly agreed to enter Castello Paratore's gates. To sleep within reach of that—that *jackal*."

"*Valeri*," Giulio warned.

"'Tis well, friend," I said, barely glancing his way. "Please. Give us a moment."

Reluctantly, Giulio moved away.

I did not fight Val. Only waited. Tears brimmed in his eyes. And . . . God help me, I relished it. 'Twas the second sign of life I had seen in him in days—the first, his claim on my hand. "We had no choice."

"You had a *choice*!" he growled. "My bid for your hand was your way to stay safe and sound, here at Castello Forelli!"

While I did not care for his anger, I took comfort in the fact that he was finally more man than ghost. But then a shudder of regret ran through me, knowing what drove him. I knew he had lost Aurelio, more brother than friend. That was what had brought him back to me now.

Fear of losing me too.

I waited for him to relax his grip on me and, when he did, reached up to rest my hand on his chest. "Please, my love. Truth be told, had you been in my place, you would have made the same decision. To protect the innocent. Yes?" I felt him shuddering, as if fighting tears. Had he yet wept for Aurelio? Mayhap not since that terrible day. "Do you remember telling me how the Paratores took you in? Were you not a child, like Celeste Romano?"

He briefly met my gaze, his only affirmation.

I took his hand between both of mine. "Think about how glad you were for Lady Paratore's attention. Your dear Cook's. How you needed help and hope, even as a child of the streets. How much more vulnerable and innocent might Lady Romano be? And with *Ercole* as her intended?"

He lowered his forehead to meet mine, and we stood there, sharing breath, as he absorbed that thought.

"I could not let her go in there alone," I whispered. "Luciana and I will find a way to get all three of us out—when the time is right. Once my father and uncle reestablish relations with those who threaten us and secure Siena's greater support, we shall return to you."

He lifted his head to look at the others, then back to me. "Might we go somewhere?" he whispered.

"Of course." I took his hand even as my parents hastened toward us, having seen the Fiorentini out through our gates. I raised a hand to them, silently asking them to wait—knowing they were likely coming to speak of our nuptials.

No one could make any sense of this—make it right—but us.

We pressed into the turret and climbed up the stairs to the top of the wall. Once there, he leaned against the parapet and took a few deep breaths, as if gathering himself, and then offered his arm. I took it—letting him lead our course and our discussion—as we walked the allure.

"So you shall go to Castello Paratore, in three days' time," he said faintly, as if recounting a dream.

"In three days' time," I said. "More than enough time to come up with a plan to meet."

He glanced at me in surprise. "You believe Ercole shall allow you to freely enter and exit?"

"Castello Paratore shall be in need of medicinal herbs as much as Castello Forelli," I said with false assurance. "We might meet in the glade, at least once a week."

He turned to me, hope easing the lines in his face. "By happenstance?"

"Nay," I smiled. "By agreement. I am to be a governess, not a prisoner. They demanded Lady Romano's hand in an effort to establish peace. Keeping Luciana and me locked behind the gates shall not improve relations. Especially if I am a married woman. I shall make Ercole see that."

He laughed softly and wiped his face of tears. Then he took my hand and brought it to his lips. "M'lady, I believe you could talk your banker-cousin out of his last florin."

We shared the first smile we had in some time. Here he was, suddenly returned to me in ways I had despaired might be lost. At last! *At last* . . . Hope flooded through me.

I tipped my lips up to him, inviting him closer. I ignored a pair of guards passing us. He nodded at them and then looked back at me with some surprise, finding me still waiting.

"You try me, Tiliani," he said, gazing down at me then along either side of the wall from us. He ran a hand through the dark waves of his hair, then reluctantly looked back to me, so intense.

"Try you?" I said innocently, tipping up a bit on my toes, bringing our lips closer.

In response, he gave in. 'Twas like an ice dam in the stream giving way to spring's relentless momentum when our lips finally met. He pressed me back against the wall as our kiss deepened, and I pulled him closer, meeting his need with my own. When he leaned back at last, we stared at each other, slightly out of breath.

"I had wondered if you would ever kiss me again," I whispered.

He gave me a sad smile. "Oh, I always intended to do so. I have only been a bit . . . lost of late."

"I understand, beloved. I mourn him too. We shall mourn him for some time."

He shook his head in disgust. "'Twas such a waste. The Fiorentini wish for peace now? Why could they have not sought it a fortnight ago? Before killing so many? Before killing Aurelio?"

"Aurelio was always suspect, with his genuine fondness for us. Beneventi, Vanni, Piccolomini . . . they must have some financial gains to be made by granting Ercole lordship of the castello and her lands. Once we are inside, Luciana and I shall undoubtedly discover more."

He cradled my face between his two calloused palms and looked at me with those soulful eyes I loved so well. "God help me, Tiliani," he muttered. "God help me. I do not wish you to feel forced to accept my bid, regardless of what is about to come to pass. We could protect you by pretending to wed. Or wed but not consummate our marriage, so that you would be free to annul it in the future."

I reached up and pressed my fingers to his lips. "Nay. *Nay,* Valentino. I want you as my husband if you truly wish to take me to wife. I *want* you. But we must speak to my parents at once."

I dropped my hand, and for the first time in weeks, I saw a beatific smile light across his face. And then he bent to kiss me again in a way that made me forget everything else . . . whether past or future. For in his arms, finally in his arms, all I could think of was the present.

We met my elders in the solarium. My father looked us up and down and arched a brow as his lips twitched. But my mother, as usual, was very serious.

A jug of wine and four cups had been set out, alongside a tray with cheese, smoked sausage, and bread. Upon Mama's invitation, we took seats across from them. Papa's elbows were perched on either arm of his chair, his fingers steepled before him. After pouring wine for each of us, a maid bowed her head and then slipped out the door, closing it behind her.

Papa clapped his hands together lightly, once, then clasped them. He focused on Valentino. "There is no time—nor reason—to mince words. You had not yet come to me asking permission to court our daughter, let alone wed her."

Valentino blinked slowly and turned to look at me. "Truthfully, I never imagined that I might attempt to claim the heart of one such as your daughter, m'lord." He bit his lip and let out a sigh. "And I find that I have little to offer her, or you," he said, meeting my parents' gaze. "I am a knight with but two horses and armor to my name. I am neither welcomed in my own republic nor yours, truly. Which puts me—and mayhap my lady—in a precarious position."

"Our people shall accept you in time, Valentino," Mama said. "You and Aurelio and your men saved us at Castello Romano."

"And we occupied Castello Paratore, holding it for Firenze."

"In an attempt to ally with us. That is far different than how Ercole holds it now," Papa said.

"Our people accepted Lord Rodolfo Greco once," Mama said, "when he left Firenze behind and joined us. Why should they not accept you?"

I saw now what Mama and Papa were doing. They were discussing betrothal as though it was not a force of hand from Ercole's threats. They were letting Val choose me—choose us— with his own will and honor. They were not presenting courtship or betrothal out of pressure or obligation. How I loved them for it!

Valentino looked to me, then back to my father. "Your daughter is worthy of a prince's hand. Someone like Aurelio. That is who you sought in Firenze, yes? A nobleman with lands, not a penniless knight."

Papa heaved a sigh and leaned forward, hands splayed. "As you might have discovered, my daughter has a mind of her own. Her heart is hers to share with whom she pleases. And I believe she has chosen you, Valeri."

Valentino dragged his eyes to meet mine, as if again verifying that this was true.

I smiled sadly. How many times, in how many ways, would it take for me to convince him? Was he so wounded that he might never accept his worth in my eyes? "You have held my heart for some time, Valentino," I said. "Do I not hold yours?"

"M'lady," he said gruffly, "I believe you have held mine since the moment I first saw you. I fought to stay out of the way. But I confess that every minute Aurelio was with you, I wanted it to be me in his stead."

"As I wanted it to be you, in turn," I said. "In the end, I believe Aurelio knew it was inevitable. 'Twas why he put your hand on mine. A final blessing."

Tears rose in his eyes. He reached for me, and I went to him. "Could this truly come to pass?" he asked, his heart in his eyes. "Might you truly do me the honor of being my intended bride?"

I smiled, tears rising in my own. "'Twould be my joy, Valentino."

"Very good," Papa said, grinning. He rose and so did my mother. "We are so pleased for both of you."

"So pleased," Mama said, hugging me tightly, then turning to accept a kiss on both cheeks from Valentino.

5

TILIANI

Upon Papa and Mama's departure, Valentino took me in his arms and simply held me for several long minutes. "Am I dreaming?"

"If you are, I am dreaming too." I looked up at him. "And I very much hope 'tis *not* a dream."

A slow smile spread across his lips. For the first time, I saw joy—true joy—in his sad, world-weary eyes. He laid a hand on his chest. "You have done me such an honor, m'lady. To think you might allow me to court you, to even dream that you might take me as your husband—"

"'Tis a mutual honor, Valentino," I said, caressing his face. "Do you know how long my parents have sought a suitable companion for me? There are not many men who can stomach a woman such as I."

"Which is fortunate for me," he said, touching his forehead to mine. "Because I deem you perfect."

I laughed under my breath. "I can assure you I am far from that."

"Perfectly imperfect then," he amended. "For me." He lifted his chin. "Now, what say you in regard to forgoing courtship and exchanging our vows this very night? Would you like even a day to consider?"

I pulled away from him and went to the solarium window,

peeking through the opening to the bustling courtyard below. I rubbed my arms against the chill of evening. He enfolded me in an embrace from behind, and I leaned my head back against his shoulder. How grand it felt to be held by him! Memories of our kisses made me smile. What would it be like to not have to stop? To give him my body—all of me—once free to do so?

"Part of me wishes to wed within the hour," I said. "And part of me will miss the months of courtship. The waiting and the wanting of you," I went on, turning in his arms, "is rather a sweet experience."

"Or an excruciating form of torture," he said. He put a knuckle under my chin and looked into my eyes.

I swallowed hard, my mouth suddenly dry. I sank to the nearest chair and took a long, slow sip of wine. Valentino did the same beside me, leaning forward, his forearms on his knees.

This was the illusion of a decision. I knew what had to be done—I *must* marry Valentino to keep from Ercole forcing me to marry *him*. But I willed away that knowledge and allowed myself to approach this moment as though it were a decision without ties. A decision I was thinking through with both heart and head.

Valentino did not stop staring sidelong at me, patient and steadfast.

"I do not wish for you to ever look back at this day and feel you were pressed to do this," I finally said. "Solely to protect me from Ercole."

"Do you jest?" Both brows rose in an arc. "'Tis the same as if I was pressed to take hold of a king's treasure trove. Who would turn away from such a bounty, so freely offered?"

I thought about the months ahead. "'Twill likely be that we shall spend weeks or even months apart, until we find a way to bring Ercole down and free Lady Celeste from this hateful betrothal." If we could get Luciana and Domenico to a tomb, she would find healing. But I knew there was no promise they could return. The thought of Giulio without Luci, Ilaria without Nico, made me wince. Especially when I thought again about experiencing this new separation from Valentino.

"We are only promised the day before us, not the morrow," I said. I rose and reached for his hand. "We have seen how lives change between sunup and sundown. And if something were to happen to you, Valentino Valeri, I would forever regret not making the most of every moment I had with you."

His eyes searched mine, and he gently pulled me into his lap. "So you are saying—"

"I shall be your bride. This very night."

Mouth slightly agape, he seemed momentarily speechless. "Now I am truly dreaming," he managed.

"Then mayhap," I said, leaning in, "I must kiss you awake."

LUCIANA

We were in the Great Hall, making our way to the front dais for supper, when Ilaria stopped us. "Giulio, Tiliani has asked us to attend her."

We hesitated. Domenico was right in front of us, and I could feel the brush of his sleeve as he turned to face us. Did that mean we should go too?

"Come along, Betarrinis," she said, giving my arm a squeeze. "She sent for me and my brother, but she shall not mind your presence too."

"If she does, we can wait outside," I said.

We made our way up the turret to her floor. All the Forellis shared this wing, but Tiliani had chosen an upper room, insisting it had the best air flow via the tiny arrow-slit windows. I had forgotten how perilous it was to make my way up—or down—the circular, stone steps, given my blindness. Ilaria turned and took my hand behind her back and Giulio moved below to take my waist in his hands.

"We have you," he said. "Follow Ilaria's lead. She shall warn you if you face a taller or shorter step than most."

But we moved at an aggravating pace. Nico finally let out a sound of exasperation and told them to make way. "I'm giving you a piggyback ride," he said to me in English.

"No, Nico," I protested.

"Give me your arms," he said over his shoulder, in English. "At this rate, we won't find out what's going on until next year."

"Whatever," I said, knowing arguing with him would be fruitless.

After ten steps he was huffing. "Sheesh. You better lay off the gnocchi, baby sis."

"Shut up," I said. "This was your idea."

"If I didn't do it, Giulio was about to carry you up himself. I could see it in his face."

"That would have been far more romantic. And less embarrassing than being carried like a sack of potatoes. Skirts don't really allow for efficient piggyback positioning."

"Noted," he said, panting. "But we're here." Despite his teasing, he was decidedly gentle as he set me to my feet, holding on to my arm until I was steady.

Giulio put a hand to my lower back, and once I had a firm hold on his arm, we moved on.

I wondered how I might manage the stairs in Castello Paratore. Especially with a child in tow. I'd have to figure it out. My stick would aid me too.

"Ahh, there you are!" Tiliani greeted us, when we at last reached her door. "And Luciana and Domenico! Good, good. You shall want to hear this too."

We entered her room, and Giulio closed the door behind us. Tiliani grabbed my hand—and presumably Ilaria's too—and dragged us toward her bed. "I have happy news, friends."

I perched a hip on the side of the bed, relieved to be still and not negotiating stairs.

"I think we can guess," Ilaria said, a smile in her voice.

"I have agreed to marry Valentino. With my parents' blessing, we shall wed this very night."

"Congratulations," I said tentatively. So Val *hadn't* been bluffing with Ercole.

Giulio cleared his throat. "May you two forever be under God's hand."

"Forever," Ilaria said.

"Forever," Nico repeated, catching on to what I was belatedly thinking.

Was saying "congratulations" not a thing in this era? Probably not. I could picture their confusion over my choice of words, but thankfully, they had moved on.

"Is this truly your choice, Tiliani?" I asked. "Or your father's?" Perhaps the question was rude, but after our encounter with the Fiorentini, it had to be asked.

To my relief, Tiliani laughed. "My parents left it to me and Valentino to decide. But it is desired by all parties. The only way to safely care for Celeste without being a target to Ercole is if I am already wed. And if my desire in courtship was to eventually wed Valentino, why not do so now? I do not believe anything shall change after weeks or months or even years of courtship. Nor does he."

"'Tis wise. And clever," Giulio said. "By rights, he shall have reason to see you. At least periodically. We could use this to our advantage."

Did I imagine that he looked in my direction as he said it? I felt the heat of a blush.

"And yet are you certain, Tiliani?" Ilaria asked. "Is Valentino truly the one with whom you wish to spend the rest of your life?"

"I am certain," she said. "Truthfully, I would prefer a few days to settle into the idea of it. But we do not have those days, and I do not believe anything would change."

"I agree," Giulio said as he laid a gentle hand at my lower back.

I stiffened, hoping he was not getting any ideas. His hand slipped away. I might have to accept that I may never see again, but I did not have to rush into a wedding, too.

"What shall you wear?" I asked, thinking that I remembered that most medieval women wore blue.

"It matters little to me," she said happily. "What matters is that this very night, I shall join hands with Valentino forever."

"I am so happy for you," I said, hearing the genuine joy and anticipation in her voice now. "And for him. That man needs some reasons to smile again."

"Indeed," Giulio said. "You honor him so,"—it sounded like he kissed her on both cheeks—"and shall make him smile for years to come."

Tiliani and Ilaria moved off the bed. The lid of a trunk creaked, and then I heard the ruffle of material. The search for a suitable gown, I presumed.

Giulio's voice came low and private toward me and Nico. "May I have a word with you both?"

Again, I stiffened, worried this was going in the wrong direction.

"Y-yes," Nico said, sounding taken aback. "Of course."

"Mayhap we could do so outside?"

I rose and tentatively took Giulio's arm, wishing Nico had been within reach. We moved into the hallway, and my brother closed the door. We turned toward one another in a small circle, so that we could speak without being overheard.

"Their plan to wed this night is a good one," Giulio said. By the agitation in his voice, I could picture him rubbing the back of his neck, or his mouth. "Why should Luciana and I not do the same?" he said in a rush.

I froze. Did Nico do the same?

"That was foolishly stated," he hurriedly amended. "Domenico, your sister already holds my heart. I want nothing more than to make her my own. Forever. Would you do me the honor of granting my wish for her hand—"

"No!" I frowned and shook my head. "No. *Nay.* That is not how we do such things. You ask *me*, not *him*," I hissed, recognizing I was disproportionately angry, but could not stop my rising fury. "I do not want to marry because my friends are marrying. I do not want to marry because it is a 'good idea.'"

"'Twould afford you a measure of protection, just as it will for Tiliani."

"Yes, but she is *ready* to marry Valentino," I whispered furiously. "I am not . . ."

I left the rest unsaid, unsure of all that I was totally feeling, thinking. *Ready to marry you? Not now? Not when I am still blind? Not when I feel so much is out of my control? Not when I might have to go home to contemporary times . . .*

"I-I see," he said, and the hurt and ache in his tone stole half my breath.

Nico stayed uncharacteristically silent.

"Giulio, I am not saying I will never be ready. I simply cannot wed you yet. Not when we have to try and reach the tomb. Not before my eyesight has been restored."

He paused, seemingly attempting to gather himself. "I told you, beloved," he said, stepping forward and taking my hand in his. "I do not care if you are blind. I want your heart alone."

"But I care," I whispered, tears rising in my eyes now. Why could he not understand? He was being so sweet, but how come he didn't get this? "*I* care, Giulio. *I* want my vision back. *I* want to see again. I want to gaze into your beautiful eyes. See every sunset *with* you. Please. Please help us reach the tomb. Mayhap even this very night we could—"

"What of the risk that Ercole might force *you* to wed him once he has you in his castello?" he interrupted.

"You heard him. In his eyes, I am vermin because of my malady." My throat caught on that last word. "And if we cannot steal our way across the border, mayhap residing on the other side shall afford us the opportunity to reach the tomb."

"If they catch you entering the tomb, either now or later, they shall hang you for witchcraft."

"Mayhap that is a risk I must take."

"You are willing to risk your *life* for your sight?" he asked, as if stunned. "What of me? What of us?"

"That is unfair." I gripped his hand as he tried to pull away. "Think, Giulio. Truly think about it. What if it were you who was blind? How would you feel marrying me then?"

"'Tis different for a man."

"For me, 'tis no different. No different at all."

He let out a long, slow sigh, and I allowed him to pull away then. Was he running his hands through his hair? Over his face in exasperation?

Tiliani's door flew open then, and the girls emerged, laughing. Taking in our tense scene brought them to a halt. "What is this?" Tiliani asked. "Nay. You cannot quibble. Not when I'm about to wed!" She swept past us. "I shall tolerate nothing but joy in this castello this day! Do you hear me? There is strife enough in the coming days. We shall borrow none of it. Now come along, friends! Come with me!"

"Yes, m'lady," Giulio muttered. His footsteps followed them.

Leaving only Nico to offer me his arm.

The mood in the Great Hall was a mix of somber and celebratory that evening. Celebratory for Tiliani's and Valentino's approaching vows, but somber over the cause of them. For Lord

Romano, I knew it was the imminent threat to his young daughter. I did not envy him going home in the morning to break the news to his wife. As much as I'd studied it in college—actually *witnessing* children pledged as tokens of peace was a whole different thing. And to Ercole of all people! Tiliani and I had to find a way to help her escape. Because there was no way we would leave her behind.

I held tightly to Giulio's arm as he led me in. We'd exchanged nothing except stiff pleasantries when he'd collected me for dinner. I could hear wine splashing into goblets, trenchers set out on tables. People quietly greeting one another. Could they sense our tension?

"Hello, Luci," whispered a woman from my right. She gave my hand a gentle squeeze.

"Adri," I said, finding comfort in the older woman's presence. With the arrival of more wounded from Castello Romano, she had likely been tending to patients all afternoon.

"Come and sit here, with me, Giulio," she said.

He obediently turned me a bit and, with a hand to my lower back, guided me to an open chair. Once I was seated, he took the chair on my left.

Adri leaned in from my right. "Tiliani and Valentino are across from you," she whispered. "Ilaria is beside Valentino and your brother next to her. So you only have confidants within reach of your voice. Think of the trencher before you as a clock face, even though it's a bit of a rectangle. You have a roasted hen's leg on your trencher—the bone reachable at eight o'clock—as well as a hunk of bread at ten. I'll put a bit of stew on a spoon, resting at four o'clock before you. A maid is about to reach between us to pour you a bit of wine."

I obediently leaned back and a bit to my left, giving the girl room to see to her task. Once she was gone, I leaned back in and whispered, "I wish you could always be at my side, giving me such instructions."

"Ask Giulio to do so. He is eager to be of aid. Your brother and friends too. However, he is not quite as used to clock faces as we are in modern times."

A man cleared his throat, and his chair scraped across the tiles as he presumably rose to his feet. The room stilled.

"Beloved family and friends," Marcello intoned. "Today we were caught unaware by our enemies. While I am thankful that our knights were spared on the field, I am sorry that it took a pledge by three of our daughters to avoid massacre."

I could feel the heat of the room's attention turn toward me and Tiliani.

"Rest assured that this is not the end," Marcello went on.

"Not by any means!" growled Luca, shoving back his chair too. "Because Lord Ercole does not know yet *who* he has allowed inside his walls."

"Nay, he does not." Tiliani rose too. "For too long, Ercole has underestimated me. But I intend to find every weakness that man has and discover a way to bring him down for good."

Men shouted their approval and began to slap their hands against the wooden tables, the rhythm gathering in speed.

Did they expect me to rise and say something valiant too? I hesitated, too overwhelmed to move.

"And while my niece and Lady Betarrini work toward that endeavor," Marcello said, graciously covering me, "we shall be solidifying support from Siena and establishing additional allies. So that when we establish a new border, it shall again be on the *far* side of Castello Paratore."

The pounding on tables resumed, and cries of hope and encouragement arose.

"Firenze believes this is the end," Luca shouted.

"But it shall prove to be the end for them!" Marcello yelled. "Now eat and drink, my friends. Toast to the betrothed. For in the weeks to come, we shall *fight*."

Then the room truly erupted, men cheering and pounding one another on the backs, from the sound of it. Clay goblets clacked together, and I grinned, looking back and forth as if I could see it all. I so *yearned* to see!

Adri squeezed my hand under the table. "You are a big part in these men finding their hope again," she said in my ear. "What you did today was very brave."

"Or very stupid," I returned, rueful.

"I am glad you and Til will be in there together," she said, no semblance of a smile in her tone.

"Me too," I said. I reached for my chicken leg, thinking about Marcello's words of eating now, so I could fight in the future.

"Any change in your vision over the last day?" Adri asked quietly.

"None." I paused. "But my headaches have abated, thankfully." I paused. "I think my only chance is another round in that tomb. Or the one further in, nearer Firenze. Can you tell me more about that one?"

"It's far more exposed. That makes it more likely that you shall be seen entering or exiting. And ever since our other Betarrini cousins arrived, the villagers are highly suspicious of it. We narrowly saved them from being tried on charges of witchcraft and executed."

I thought about how Giulio had voiced those very same fears. "Great," I said. "So our choice is either villagers on a witch hunt at one end or Manero on the other, huh?"

"That's about the size of it." She dropped her tone. "There's no guarantee that if you go, you shall return to us, here. *Now.* If you are delayed . . . When Gabi and Lia and I went back for Ben, we were gone for a couple of hours or so. When we returned, more than three *years* had elapsed for the Forellis. I have no idea if that rule still is in play, or if it fluxes, but you need to know it's a risk. If you're caught in contemporary times for a day, does that mean a decade passes here? It's entirely possible."

A decade. Giulio would be thirty-two instead of twenty-two. Some of these people I had come to love might even be dead.

"If you manage it," Adri said, "if you go at all and return—it would be best if you return and pretend you are still blind. Give me a few days, a week, to see if we can come up with some sort of 'cure' for you. The people will need to tie your healing to me, not anything with the tomb. Understood?"

I nodded. She meant everyone, whether Sienese or Fiorentini. This was a time steeped in superstition. The last thing I wanted was to take the chance at the tomb healing me, only to find my neck encircled by a rope. I shuddered, remembering Rosa dangling from the gallows. How close we had been that day to capturing Ercole! If only Nico and I had succeeded, we could have stopped so many bad things from happening.

"Hey," Adri said, taking my hand again. "I know you are doing all you can. The fact that you volunteered to help aid Celeste is admirable. Father Giovanni has taught me to not fret over what lies behind us. Only to look ahead for what God has for me to do next. You are doing just that, yes? Taking the opportunity to aid our cause—and yours—by helping Til look after Celeste. Right?"

"Right." I forced a bite of bread into my mouth, but it took a hefty swig of wine to get it down.

6

LUCIANA

"Of what were you and Lady Adri discussing?" Giulio asked me as we walked around the courtyard during the hour between the end of supper and the start of Til's wedding.

"Of the tomb, and what might transpire if we ventured through it again," I said.

"I expected as much." He sounded resigned and yet fearful.

I rested a hand on his arm. "Giulio. What if you knew of a healer in Siena who had a reputation for curing blindness?"

"I would take you to him. Immediately."

"That is the tomb. Every time an injured person has traveled, they have been healed. Your very own sister experienced it." I could almost hear him thinking on this comparison. "Do you see now why I cannot rest until we at least try to travel back and forth?"

Domenico and Ilaria joined us just as I finished saying this.

"Travel? *Via la tomba?*" Ilaria repeated in a whisper.

"If you go, you shall not go without me. And Ilaria," Giulio said, his tone growing more confident. "My sister and I have agreed. If the Betarrinis are *traveling* again, then so shall we. You asked me to think. And I have done so. Your sight is precious to you, and so I shall do everything in my power to help you get it back. Turn over every stone. Try every healer. Even get you to the tomb."

I held my breath, wondering if I had misheard him.

"And if this villain Manero gives you trouble, his neck shall meet the end of my sword."

I was speechless. Giulio had thought about it and done a one-eighty. He was totally with me. And if we were going, so were they.

"That said, 'twill take a great deal for even you and Nico to get together long enough to approach one of the tombs," he said somberly. "So if you have the opportunity, you must take it, with or without me."

"But what if we get waylaid? What if Manero captures us?" Back and forth I went with my plan, every day. Five times a day. It was one thing to ask him to take me to the tomb so we could all travel together. It was another to risk leaving him. Possibly forever.

"My sister reminded me that you and Nico did *everything* to save her," Giulio said, turning to face me. "We owe you a life debt."

"It was no more than you would have done for us," Nico said.

"Exactly." Ilaria turned in to make our foursome a circle. "So if we have the opportunity, we shall all do so again."

I still couldn't summon a response. My mind was still stuck at the prospect of traveling through the tomb without Giulio. I had spent so much time arguing for the potential of travel that I had not adequately weighed the risk. Now that he had stopped blocking me . . . was I ready to cross a bridge that might altogether disappear?

He reached up and caressed my cheek with a knuckle. "Caring for someone, loving them, means you do everything you can for them. Every day. I want to be that man for you, Luciana—even if it means risking letting you go."

I said nothing. Was I truly ready to risk that? He had said they would come with us to the tomb. Help us fight to return. But if the opportunity presented itself to make the leap—just Nico and me—would I take it?

"You may need to travel via the tomb near Firenze," Ilaria said. "It all depends on which one you first can enter."

"I may have a way to connect with you in Firenze," Nico explained.

"You do?" I could hardly keep up with the turns this conversation was taking.

"Marcello and I have been talking. Who is the greatest ally we could get?"

I considered the question. "Pisa? Venezia?"

"They would be good," he said, and I could hear the grin in his tone. "But think, Luci. Who is more powerful than either of those cities? Any city, for that matter?"

"The Church," Giulio said.

"*Yes*," Nico whispered excitedly.

"But the Church is not fond of Siena," Ilaria said. "She excommunicates us every time we cross purposes with her."

"And yet she has a weakness," Nico said.

"Money," I said.

"Exactly. She is hungry. And Marcello knows an influential cardinal with old ties with the Forellis and Grecos in the eastern part of Firenze. He has been trying to build his own cathedral for the last ten years. Her walls are built, but she lacks a roof."

"The most costly aspect," I said, remembering my studies.

"Indeed," Giulio said. "Only so many florins can be squeezed from her parishioners' purses."

"And yet to leave it half built is an affront to his power," Ilaria said.

I shook my head. "The Church was notorious for not being able to pay her bills," I said to my brother in English. "It almost took down the Medicis. That's seriously dangerous territory. Is it Forelli money you would lend him?"

"Sienese," he said. "The Nine see the necessity of an advocate in the Church that has pull with other republics. Mayhap this cardinal could eventually welcome us back into the 'fold.' But in the meantime, he could certainly dissuade Firenze, Arezzo, and Perugia from attacking us. Or at least some of them."

"One cardinal can do all of that?" I asked, switching back to Tuscan.

"Which cardinal?" Giulio asked.

"Cardinal Borgio," Nico whispered.

Giulio let out a low whistle of admiration.

I turned toward him. "He truly has the power to save us?"

"In more ways than one," Ilaria quipped.

"He would like to believe that," Giulio said, "but Padre Giovanni assures us it is untrue. The keys to our salvation are held in Christ's hands alone. However, we shall pretend a desire to shelter under the Church's wing."

"Whatever it takes, eh?" Nico said to him. I could tell he was looking at me.

"Whatever it takes," I repeated. But, for the first time, I wondered what exactly that would require.

7

TILIANI

We elected to wed at the top of the wall, surrounded by torchlight. My father wanted Ercole's spies to witness and testify to the truth, when he learned of it. I could see the wisdom of it, but tonight, I did not want one more single thought to be captivated by Andrea Ercole or my imminent future at Castello Paratore.

Tonight, *tonight*, belonged solely to me and Valentino.

My heart soared as I emerged from the turret to see the vast canopy of stars stretching above us. With no moon in sight, the Milky Way shined like a billion distant flames. Firelight danced from twelve torches, held by knights behind my family on the far side of Valentino. More light hovered overhead as Papa and I walked past other knights, who closed the circle behind us. Between the heavenly light above and the earthly light around us, I felt both more protected and yet more free than I had in years.

I smiled at Valentino as we neared him. Papa turned toward me and kissed both cheeks. "You are certain, my sweet?" he whispered. He reached back for Mama's hand, and she stepped forward to join us.

"Very much," I assured them both. Everything in me told me that this was right and good. It was as if I had lived my whole life entirely so I could come to this moment, this precipice. On the other side of the mountain, life would change. But it would still be the same mountain. I felt both assured and excited.

"He is a good man," he said.

"He is."

"Not perfect," Mama warned.

"Nor am I," I said with a grin. Was it not a bit late for parental advice? Still, they hesitated, glancing from me to Val and back again. Mayhap it was because I was their one and only.

Zio Marcello stepped forward and put a gentle hand on Papa's shoulder. "'Tis time."

Zia Gabi wrapped her arm around Mama's waist. "This is a good thing," she assured.

"Indeed." Papa's eyes never left mine. He gave a tender, encouraging smile, and Mama hugged me. "We are always here for you," she said, hands on my shoulders, "even married."

"Thank you," I whispered. But even as I said it, I was turning to Valentino. How long I had made him wait! I did not want him to think for a moment that I doubted this.

His warm hands reached for mine, and I eagerly placed my own in his. The feel of his touch! A jolt shot up my arms to my shoulders, my neck, and up over my scalp. What was it about him that affected me so? Did every bride feel such things for their intended?

Padre Giovanni took a stole from around his neck and wrapped it around our entwined hands, speaking words I did not quite comprehend. All I could see was Valentino's steady gaze. The promise in his soulful, hazel eyes. The silent vow that he was mine, as I was his. The formal words hardly mattered as we uttered them. Everything that mattered silently passed between us.

It all felt so . . . *inevitable.* I had fought against it. So had he, knowing 'twas best if I was Aurelio's match. But what had started that first day on the field—when we first came across Aurelio, Valentino, and the squire as they surveyed Castello Greco— seemed to be reaching its culmination. Our eyes had locked that first moment, and in it, I'd felt like I'd known something about him, just as he did me. How was that possible? Was that God?

As much as I was fond of Aurelio—and other friends—I had never experienced anything like it. Nay, I had been Valentino Valeri's from the start. And now, I would forever be his.

Giovanni went through the liturgy, making the sign of the cross over us, over the rings, speaking in Latin as I slipped Val's ring on his finger and he slipped a thin gold band over mine. It was a bit big—there being no time to reach a goldsmith this afternoon—but we would resolve that as soon as we could.

We knelt on the stones of the parapet, and Giovanni prayed over us both in our own tongue. For understanding. For love. For prosperity. For many children. For peace and joy.

As he uttered the words, I kept asking myself if this was truly happening. But as the men around us—and the courtyard full of others below—erupted into cheers when our priest declared us husband and wife, permitting Val to kiss me—and he did so—I decided nothing had ever felt more real in my life.

Mama and Papa distributed paper lanterns, while others distributed more below. Father Giovanni began to hum a hymn of praise, which others picked up. Eventually, all hundred and fifty or more in the castello were humming the same tune as all lanterns were lit.

"Father in heaven!" Papa called to the stars. "Watch over our precious daughter, Tiliani, and her new husband, Valentino. May their life together be long and full of joy!"

"Hear, hear!" called some.

"To their health!"

"To their love!"

"To their children-to-be!"

One by one, as each whispered or shouted their well wishes, they released their paper lanterns, filling the sky with more than fifty of them. Rising, rising, until they disappeared into the stars themselves.

And never, ever had I felt so blessed.

LUCIANA

"Well, that's going to be hard to top," I muttered to Nico as he described the lanterns disappearing into the spectacular night sky.

"Yeah," he said. "We might as well not even try." He turned toward me, and I imagined his head appearing as nothing but a silhouette against the canopy of stars and lanterns. "Unless you just want to piggyback on this feel-good moment and drag Giulio to the altar. He's only twenty paces away. And there's still like a minute or two left of this cinematic moment. If you're gonna make your move, make it now."

I shook my head, smiling ruefully. "I'm not in a place to drag *anyone* to the altar."

"That's fair." He put an arm around my shoulders, and I wrapped an arm around his waist.

He led me along the allure, and in our measured, familiar, twin steps, my pulse steadied. Here was the one person I could always count on. He seemed to intuit my need for some space from the others after such . . . closeness. I was both drawn to the Forellis' intimacy and wary of it. I knew I should not be repelled— that it was likely a self-protective, defensive reaction. A lot like how I had kept our extended New Jersey family at bay. If I didn't attempt to enter their closest circles, I could not be hurt if they did not always invite me in.

When they shared inside jokes, I could smile in appreciation that they knew one another so well, but not be offended. Because I did not expect to be in that inner circle. Only in the outer orbit.

But what if I always kept myself on the outside? What if I never found myself in that precious, inner circle, with people who loved and knew me, and I, them? Was it truly a choice to step inside, to risk loving on that level?

"I just need to see again, Nico," I said. "I know I should be bigger than that. Deeper. That I should know that I could have a life of value, regardless of what I can take in through the old orbs. But I *miss* it. To not see the night sky and those lanterns tonight . . . You have no idea what you miss until it's gone. I'd rather lose my hearing. Or feeling in my fingertips. Or my sense of smell. But then every sense—*every* one—is so vital. Yes, I can make it without my sight. Yes, I can find a life of value and purpose and love without it. But if I can get it back? If there's a *chance?*"

He took that in as we continued to walk the perimeter of the wall. "I understand," he said. "I think I'd want the same."

"Would you? Even if getting to the tomb and going through meant you'd never see Ilaria Greco again?"

He contemplated that for five steps. Then ten.

Until I knew that neither of us had an answer to it. And we would not until the moment of decision was at hand.

8

TILIANI

As lovely as the ceremony was . . . as lovely as it was to return to our new, shared quarters . . . as lovely as it was to kiss and not have to stop . . . as lovely as it was to come together fully as man and wife . . . I believed that waking up in Valentino Valeri's arms was the loveliest part of all.

I moved my cheek against the smooth, olive skin of his chest and ran my hand across the breadth of his fine muscles. His arm tightened around me—pulling me closer—and he sleepily moved to tenderly kiss my forehead. He reached for my hand and interlocked his fingers with mine. His long, thick lashes blinked and slowly opened until he stared at me in silent wonder.

"Good morning, husband," I said, trying the title for the first time.

"Good morning, wife," he returned.

We grinned at each other, and my stomach flipped at seeing pure, unadulterated joy in his eyes. For the first time, there was not a trace of sadness. Only peace and contentment and happiness. Still smiling, I tried pulling him closer. Would I ever get enough of this man? I wanted to be with him every minute I could—and we had only two days.

A pang of sorrow at the thought made me inhale quickly.

"What is it, beloved?" he asked, his brows instantly furrowing.

"'Tis nothing," I said, regretting that I had robbed him of his moment of pure joy. I lifted my head to bestow tiny kisses along his jaw.

He rolled over, pinning me softly. "Nay. What is it?"

He seemed genuinely concerned.

I sighed. "I lament that while I wish to spend weeks in this bed with you . . ."

"We have only two days," he finished for me soberly. He released one of my hands and traced my face from temple to chin, as if memorizing it. He bent to kiss me softly, gradually becoming more intent.

"Then I believe," he said between kisses, "that we must fit a week's worth of loving into the days to come." He paused and looked up at me. "Are you amenable to that, wife?"

"Most amenable," I assured him with a grin.

TILIANI

We left our marital bed sooner than we liked to make some plans. By midmorning we had conferred with Captain Pezzati, Giulio, and Ilaria about potential strategies. What they could do to weaken the wall further in the midst of battle. How we might escape if necessary. A signal to indicate we needed immediate extrication and another to tell them we needed an escape soon. As a gesture of good faith, both Siena and Firenze had pulled back their troops, reestablishing camps two miles distant from the border. The result was a sense of tenuous peace that I was sure both sides fought to trust.

I invited Valentino to join us, but he hovered outside of our circle in the solarium, leaning his back against the wall, arms crossed, head bowed. He listened intently but said nothing. We then took a leisurely walk along the allure and heard the report that not one Fiorentini had been found within two miles. 'Twas a relief—to see that our enemies seemed to want to honor this tentative peace agreement—both for these days and mayhap for the days and weeks to come. Once we returned and broke bread at noon, Nona paused beside me and asked me and Val to search for herbs typically found only near the border creek.

We both agreed to it, knowing her request was likely more to give us time alone, but also borne out of a need brought on by all the wounded still arriving from Castello Romano. Many were fighting infection, and my grandmother was trying to save both limbs and lives. Mounting up, we wordlessly left the stables again, armed, but alone.

"Lady Tiliani," said a knight by the gates, "allow me to summon more men to accompany you."

"That shall not be necessary," I returned. "The Fiorentini shall not assault us. Not at this juncture. Be at peace and open the gates."

"Yes, m'lady," he agreed reluctantly, studying Valentino as if he did not quite trust him yet, then looking past us both as if to see if another superior might be within reach. But he dared not disobey my command.

I proceeded through the gates in the lead, reminding the men that I had the power to command them all. And after all, was I not about to voluntarily enter an enemy castle to help protect little Lady Romano with no aid but one blind friend? Valentino followed on my left flank—the Fiorentini side. We rode east for a mile along the creek and then headed north along a narrow tributary that was fed by a spring. We clattered over a rocky field and paused at the top of a hill, but still saw no sign of enemies. I knew that with so many knights within a five-mile radius, any bands of robbers would have fled too. I took a long, deep breath.

For the first time in years, I felt a definitive sense of peace and security. It would last only for a bit, but I was determined to relish every moment.

"This is what we might have felt like, had Aurelio lived," I mused to my husband. "This freedom. This tranquility. This ability to ride out, where we wish, only the two of us. 'Tis what we must fight for in the future."

He contemplated my words a moment. "Aurelio would celebrate that. But do you believe attaining it is truly possible, Tiliani?"

I urged Cardo around a boulder, and Valentino followed me. When he was able to pull alongside, matching my mount's gait, I said, "I must believe it. At least that *portions* of our lives shall be lived out in peace. We enjoyed some months of peace when Aurelio was lord of Castello Paratore. Years of peace before that, when Giulio Greco was lord."

"But we shall not with Ercole as lord," he said lowly.

"Nay. Not for long," I agreed.

"What if—what if we do not find a way out for you and Luciana? What if you are held captive for years to come, tied by your vows to protect Lady Romano?"

"That shall not happen," I said. "It cannot. We are simply buying time in order to make a plan. We have to find a way to best Ercole—forever."

"Domenico's plan is clever. Incorporating the Church might be the only way out of this."

"The Church is a fickle friend."

"Indeed. Yet we need only persuade them to be *our* friend until we secure Castello Paratore again."

"Although men of the Church could open many other gates to us. And barricade others."

"I would rather see through my battles on the field than behind closed doors with men of their ilk."

"They are not all bad," I said. "There must be some good men among them."

"There are," he admitted. "I know of some I trust. But it is a sore temptation, such power."

"As it is in any sector," I said.

We continued to climb, and when it became too dangerous for our mounts, we hobbled them beneath two ancient oaks that would provide adequate shade. We went on, scrambling up rounded granite rocks that held one gentle pool after another, carved from centuries of water making its way. When we reached the fourth pool, I glimpsed a bit of bright gold in the crevice ahead. I grabbed Valentino's arm and pointed. "Is that lungwort?"

He ducked and searched for the same view. Then his face split in wonder. "I believe it is!"

The golden lichen was famous for its ability to treat breathing ailments. Even a tiny portion worked miracles for those cases my grandmother and Chiara despaired healing. If we could bring home some of that, might we save one or two men on the brink of death?

I edged closer to the pool, going on my belly to try and reach it. I stretched as far as I could up and into the water streaming into the pool from above but could not quite touch it.

"Can we reach it from above?" Valentino called, raising his voice over the rush of the water.

"I do not think so. It looks as if it is only growing here in the shadows between the rocks. Grab my hand—hold on to me!"

"Tiliani, allow me."

"Nay! I have it! I am almost there!"

My left side was partially submerged as I stretched, my right wrist held firmly by Valentino's two strong hands.

"A little farther," I grunted. "Only a bit more!"

When he gave me that bit, I felt the moment of hesitation and then a release as he slipped on the wet rock. I tumbled into the pool and struggled to gain my footing on the mossy stone beneath. I came up sputtering as Valentino fell in, almost on top of me.

I was laughing before he even rose to the surface.

He emerged, gasping for air. Apology etched across his forehead's wrinkles, but when he saw me laughing, he gradually allowed himself to do the same. He pulled me into his arms, and I wrapped my arms over his shoulders and looked into his eyes. He turned me around in the water, both of us gasping at the cold but still laughing. "Do you think you might be able to reach that lungwort now, wife?" he asked.

"Most likely," I grinned, tipping my head up to kiss him. He looked so handsome with his dark hair slicked back, droplets of water running down his olive skin.

He smiled and met my lips, softly at first and then increasing in intensity. My skirts billowed in the water. He pressed one hand against the small of my back, and the other between my shoulder blades, pulling me closer. He carried me backward until the tiny waterfall was running down my hair while he pressed a row of tiny kisses from my temple down my cheek and then down my neck, following the stream of water. At last he returned to reclaim my lips.

In the heat of his arms, the cold of the water was forgotten. The precious lichen was forgotten. All I could think about was Valentino Valeri and how it felt to be in his arms. Together at last, *at last*. Together as man and wife. I wished I never had to leave him.

He pulled back and gazed at me, running his fingers down my cheek. "I love you, Tiliani. I am grieving, so my heart feels torn in two. Half in sadness over Aurelio, half in wonder that you—a lady such as you—might hold a portion of the love for me in your heart that I do for you."

I put my hand against his cheek, willing him to understand that I spoke truth. "I do not think I could love a man more than I love you, Valentino. You have captured me. Wholly. Like no other man ever has. The thought of separating from you, now, is utter misery."

All trace of humor left his face. We stared into each other's eyes as if we could not see the other enough. As if we had to memorize this moment. And mayhap we did, for there were days to come when we would not be able to be together. Let alone together like this.

With one last, searching kiss, full of longing and hope, he took hold of my waist. "We had best get to drying out. If we return to the castello like this—"

"We shall never hear the end of it," I agreed reluctantly. He bent and then lifted me to the rock, placing my rump on the same small ledge that he had used for a foothold. As I pulled myself back up, he moved to the waterfall and reached past it, using a rock to scrape off a wide patch of lungwort and turning to me in triumph.

I smiled with him, fighting the urge to jump back in and resume our kissing. I wished we were past this quagmire with Ercole. I wished we could move on to exploring what it meant to live life together as a married couple.

I sighed heavily as he clambered up the rock. His shirt had come untied at the neck and his wet tunic hung low, exposing a glimpse of his finely muscled chest. He offered his hand. "Come."

I took it and he helped me rise, then move across the boulder toward a broader rock face more exposed to the sun. He pulled off his tunic and spread it over some bushes to dry. I did the same, leaving my shirt on. It was a thin fabric and would likely dry within an hour, even though the band that bound my breasts was wet too. Valentino, on the other hand, did not hesitate to take off his shirt and spread it across the bushes. While his back was turned, I reached under my skirts and pulled off my undergarment, wringing it out and hanging it to dry too. We stretched out on the sun-warmed dark rocks, the heat at our backs warding off the gooseflesh that rose on our skin.

His hand found mine between us as we lay there in the sun, hearing nothing but the rush of water to one side of us and the calls of starling and finch in the woods. The sun was warm but not overly so, and in minutes, my skin was dry. "How long do you suppose it shall take for our clothing to dry enough for us to return?"

"If God smiles, hours," he said, contentedly pulling my hand to his lips. "Here, now, I can forget about everything but you. This is utter *respite*." He turned to his side, one hand and elbow holding his head up. He traced my profile with a slow, featherlight touch, from forehead to the base of my throat. "You are beautiful, wife."

I turned to look at him. "As you are handsome, husband."

He gave me a small smile, and I hoped he would lean in for another kiss, but he rolled to his back again and groaned. "I want to do nothing but kiss you. But if we do not stay apart, we shall never dry out. And then your father shall send a search party after us."

"Indeed," I said with a grin. "And Giulio and Ilaria are gifted trackers. 'Twould take them minutes to figure out all that transpired here."

"And we must look for more lungwort before we return."

I squinted up at the sun, gauging the time. "We shall accomplish our mission. And mayhap still manage to make our way into the castello without our secret being exposed." It was not as if we could not stand by the truth that we had simply fallen into the pool—the ribbing we would receive from the men would never abate. We would hear about it for years to come, especially any time we neared a creek. I had spent enough time in the company of men to know how it would transpire. So did Valentino.

And yet it was so warm and relaxing on the rock, so lovely to be in each other's company, holding hands, such a relief to be away from the intensity of the castello, that we eventually gave into slumber.

I awoke to Val shaking my shoulder. "Tiliani!"

I blinked and sat up, my hand going to my head. I could feel the heat of a burn on my face. "How-how long have we been asleep?"

"Far too long," he muttered, and as I gazed around, I realized he was right. The front of my skirt was dry, but the back was still damp. I could explain that I had slipped, the burn due to too much time in the sun, foraging for herbs. But we needed to find more herbs in order to make that story ring true.

"You said we would likely find tansy ahead? Up there?" he asked with a nod, slipping his tunic over his shoulders.

"And vetch."

"I will go ahead of you. Come behind me, yes?"

"Agreed." I watched as he scrambled up and over the face of the boulder, then put my hand to the top of my head, feeling as if I might have dreamed all of this, rather than actually lived it. But no, I remembered his kisses too well. Those exquisite, searching kisses, promising so much more.

I pulled on my tunic and undergarment in a hurry, settling my skirts back in place as I gazed out and over the canopy of the woods. We had to find those medicinals and return before sunset. So that we could quietly slip back into the castello and take our supper alone, in our room. Which would be far preferable to enduring a bunch of laughing knights, sent to find us.

9

LUCIANA

Nico and I took to the sparring yard as the sun rose. I was one day closer to entering Ercole's keep. One day closer to potentially regaining my sight. But also one day closer to being parted from Giulio.

I had nervous energy to burn.

"Okay, sis. Are you sure you're ready for this?"

I heard the pivot of his foot on dried grass and turned my head. "Are you kidding? I've been itching to move. There's been far too much sitting around of late."

"A serious head injury kinda demands it. Are you sure Adri would approve?"

"Lady Adri wants me to be safe. Able to defend myself. Blind or not. Now come at me."

He didn't pause. He grabbed my arm, twisted, and brought it up behind me.

Grimacing, I slammed my boot back. As he moved to keep me from striking his shin, I stepped out with my opposite foot to untwist, grabbed Nico's wrist with my free hand, rolled toward him, and threw him over my shoulder.

He laughed quietly from the ground. "Well, that's embarrassing."

"Because I'm blind or because I'm your baby sister?"

"Both," he said, rising. "Let's pretend someone jumps out

and grabs you with no warning, like this." He wrapped me in a headlock and began to roll me.

"Then I'd have to. . ." I posted my right foot in front of him, placed my right hand on his thigh, knelt, and used his momentum to pull him all the way across me. I pretended like I was about to slam his nose with the flat of my palm.

"Nice," Nico said, deflecting my hand. "You still got it."

"So much of it is muscle memory," I said, relieved to feel it coming back.

"Luciana!" a man shouted. *Giulio.* He reached us seconds later, breathing heavily. "What are you doing?"

"*Stiamo combattendo.*" I tried to answer simply and calmly, knowing where this was going. *We are sparring.* I released my hold on Nico. "Let's go on," I said to my brother in English. "You're holding back on me."

"Nay, m'lady—" Giulio protested.

"I must," I hissed. "Do you not understand? I must be able to defend myself, at least in some measure." I turned and squared off with my brother again, listening to his boots scraping across the dirt and gravel, bending my knees and bringing my arms up in a protective stance. "My goal is to protect myself from blows," I explained, "and in doing so, find an opportunity to go on the attack."

"This is madness," Giulio said.

"This is necessity," I returned.

Nico sent soft jabs and thrusts that I narrowly fended off. But I heard the pivot of his foot and knew a chest kick was coming my way next. I leaned back, feeling the brush of his boot near my breast. I caught his leg and, with a growl, shoved him back to his butt.

"Nice," Nico said in admiration. "How did you do that?"

"I could hear your pivot in the gravel and guessed what was coming."

"Impressive," Giulio admitted with a grunt.

I smiled, in spite of myself, finding it impossible not to take it as praise. "Do you feel better about me sparring with Nico now?"

"A bit," he allowed. "But mayhap I might have a turn with him. Have you a handkerchief, m'lady?"

I frowned, confused, but felt for my tunic pocket. I found the small square of cloth and felt him tug it from my fingers. "What are you doing?"

"He's tying it around his eyes," Nico reported in English. "This is gonna be fun."

"You do not need to do this," I said to Giulio. "I need to be ready for sighted opponents. 'Tis why I am sparring with Nico without aid."

"But I wish to experience what you are," Giulio said quietly, with great care in his tone.

"Nico is a skilled fighter. You are signing on for a thrumming."

"So be it. You held your own with him. Let me try and do the same."

I shuffled backward, stunned, as I heard him tentatively step forward.

"Mayhap this shall be added to our sparring regimen for all," Giulio said. "'Tis a boon to note signs of your attacker's next move through hearing alone."

"Yes, but nice if you do not *have* to use hearing alone," Nico said.

I heard soft blows and Giulio's soft grunts. And when Nico delivered a roundhouse kick—this time, connecting with Giulio's body somewhere—my man went down.

"I pulled it at the end," Nico assured me, taking my arm and leading me to Giulio. I felt him bend and help him up.

"Clearly, my hearing skills are not as attuned as Luciana's," Giulio lamented.

"When you are forced to use it, you discover how valuable hearing is," I said, pleased by this show of care—and bruises—from the man I loved. "I find I am discerning direction—of voices or movement—faster than before."

"I have noticed that," Nico said. "You're getting better at looking at my face when I'm talking, rather than over a shoulder."

"If only fists made sounds moving through the air," I said. "But the creaking of leather armor and belts do. And footsteps are most useful."

Giulio and Nico went a few more rounds, each one ending with Giulio in the grass. "Enough for now, or I'll not be able to lead my men in training today." A grunt and stretch of fabric told me Nico helped Giulio back to his feet. "But now I have gotten a glimpse—if you will pardon the phrase—of what it is like to be sightless."

Giulio drew close enough that I breathed in his scent of clean sweat and grass and sage. He gently tucked my handkerchief back into my pocket and brushed his lips across my cheek. "Thank you, m'lady."

There was the scattering of grumpy chickens as a person walked through a flock, the creak of the well crank and distant splash as the first water bucket of the day was lowered, and somewhere near, the crack of someone splitting wood for Cook's fire.

The rest of the castello was rising.

"Shall we go to the Hall to eat?" Nico asked.

"Yes," I said. "But first . . ." I turned to him and raised my brows.

"Say no more, sis," Nico said in English, already backing away. "You two need a little alone time. Got it."

"Thanks, Nico."

I reached for Giulio's hand. His strong, warm palm met mine, and he squeezed my fingers. "Thank you for that," I said. "Letting me spar with Nico. And wanting to spar with him yourself."

He hesitated. "I want you prepared for Ercole's castello as much as he does. And I shall be more successful at that if I can better understand your strengths and your obstacles. You shall need every edge to negotiate the jackals in that castle, as well as to make your way to the tomb tunnel."

"When it comes time, you will be there to travel with me?" I asked, hating the needy edge that crept into my voice.

"I shall do everything I can to be with you." He leaned back and took my face in his hands. His meaning was clear. He'd try. But if he couldn't pull it off—

"I cannot leave you behind, Giulio." I put my hands atop his.

He stood there, saying nothing, and even though I could not see him, I could feel his emotions warring within him. "You can. You will."

"You are certain 'tis the right choice?"

"'Tis certain that you want to see again, and if you find the opportunity, you must seize it. If I am waylaid, beloved, you *must* go without me."

But now I doubted the plan. "If Nico and I are detained, I would abandon you here, alone . . ." I stopped, hardly able to finish such a horrid thought. "There is a chance I never return in your lifetime." I bit my lip and swallowed hard.

He drew me close, cradling my head with one hand, the other pulling me into him. "I have waited all my life to meet a woman like you, Luciana. No one else has ever been close to claiming my heart, while you . . ." He huffed a laugh and heaved a sigh. "You, my love, have so thoroughly claimed it that I cannot imagine ever loving another so. I will wait for you. Even if our reunion is in heaven alone."

His hands moved to my face, cradling my cheeks, tipping my face up. "But you do everything you can to get back to me, yes? As fast as possible?" His hands pressed, as if willing his sense of urgency into me.

"I will do everything I can, as quickly as possible," I whispered. "But I do not want you to wait—"

He hushed me with a kiss so deep, so full of longing and pain and wanting, that when he released me, I was a bit short of breath.

"There is only one woman for me," he said, bestowing tiny kisses from one temple, across my brows, to the other, then back to the center of my forehead. "And that shall forever be you and you alone, Luciana Betarrini."

LUCIANA

As the heat of the afternoon eased, Giulio took me for a walk outside of the castello. I could hardly believe my luck at claiming more of his time for yet another portion of the day, but instead of resuming sparring, talking—or kissing—he sadly insisted on telling me every little detail about Castello Paratore, once Castello Greco. He wanted to prep me. I reluctantly asked him more about the dungeon, thinking that if Ercole caught us doing anything out of line, either Tiliani or I might end up there. I had seen it when we had taken that tour in the final days that he had been lord of it. Solemnly, he told me everything he knew.

"But we removed every chain and torture device," he tried to assure me.

Inadvertently, my hand went to my chest. Weeks after Ercole stabbed me, the wound had healed over, but deep inside, it still ached. And as I sparred with my brother each day, learning to anticipate moves I could not see, it felt like I ripped it open a bit each time. Knowing that both Giulio and Nico would put a stop to the sparring if they knew, I kept it to myself.

"I saw the dungeon that day," I said. "But I confess my mind was more on the handsome Lord Greco than my environs."

"Remember that if you go to the rear-left portion of the left cell, you should be directly above the Etruscan tunnel. If you can find a way to remove some stones, it could be a potential escape route. Or an access route for us, if we are on the attack. But if we are in all-out battle, our men shall try to set it afire and bring down that part of the wall."

"So it could aid my escape or kill me," I said. How long would it be until Ercole discovered the weakness in his new fortress?

"Yes. 'Twould be best for you to stay out of that dungeon, Luciana." He paused and turned toward me, taking both of my hands in his. "May I embrace you, beloved?"

I swallowed a smile. Ever since I'd been blinded, he had been terribly cautious with his touch, as though he might somehow harm me further. "I would very much like that."

Tentatively, he pulled me into his arms, and I relished the feel of my head tucked underneath his chin, the sound of his heartbeat. It had been too long—ever too long. He rubbed my back and kissed the top of my head, pulling me even closer. "Ahh, Luciana. I do not know if I can bear it, seeing you disappear behind gates that I once held myself. Cut off from me."

"I pray it shall be only for a bit. Thank you for allowing me to help Tiliani, as well as little Celeste."

I had never, ever met anyone like Giulio Greco. And I knew without a doubt I'd never meet anyone like him again. How could I? And could I truly do what he asked—potentially leave him behind and risk it being forever?

Was my sight worth that?

The same thing that drew him to me—a strong, independent, modern woman—drew me to *him*—a medieval man with a thing for a "different" sort of girl. I was not a metro-male kind of gal. Nor was I a fan of mindless, macho jerks. I loved that the men of Castello Forelli were unapologetically manly, but still fans of strong women like Gabi, Lia, Tiliani, and me. My distant cousins had laid down a firm foundation for the kind of guys that would draw me, and whet Giulio's appetite for a different sort of woman altogether.

Suddenly, I had a vision of a very long, very single life in contemporary times. Maybe like Giulio was envisioning for himself, here. He'd just come to it before I had.

"I shall do everything I can to travel with you," Giulio said, breaking the silence as though sensing the depth of my very thoughts. "Even if it means remaining with you there." His breath washed over my cheeks. I recognized that the heat of the day ebbed, and sunset was likely upon us.

"You would do that? Stay with me? In our time?"

"Luciana Betarrini," he pledged, kissing my forehead. "I want to be with you here." He kissed my right cheek. "Or there." He placed another on my left. "As long as I am with you, I shall find a way to peace and contentment. Can you say the same?"

"Wait," I said, backing up a step, sliding my hands down his arms until I could hold his hands. "You would truly come to my time with me?" I tried to imagine it. This big, handsome knight making his way there. "It is vastly different."

"Any more so than this time has been for you?" he asked, leaning away.

"Well, nay. There has been much for me to take in here. But your time is simpler, more straightforward. 'Tis difficult to describe. There are benefits to life in my own time, but definitely others to life here, now." What would he do? For work? Enter the military? Become a police officer? How would he handle the onslaught of sensory overload, technology, the numbers of people? Congestion, traffic, vehicles themselves? I could not imagine it.

"Which do you prefer, my love?" he asked, gathering me in his arms again.

I rested my cheek against his chest a moment. "I prefer to be where you are. And my brother. If you two are with me, I could be happy anywhere."

"Even blind?"

I paused. "May-mayhap."

He squeezed me. "Let us leave it to God. If he makes a way for you to get to the tomb and find healing, so be it. If not, we shall learn to negotiate life together as you are."

As you are. Was I truly okay with it? Could I leave it to God?

I realized, belatedly, that he had gone on speaking while I was lost in my own thoughts.

". . . as my wife?"

I inhaled sharply. "Wait, what? Are you proposing?"

"*Proponendo?*" he repeated, confused over the word.

I huffed a laugh. "Are you asking me to be your *wife?*"

He laughed in kind. "I thought you were going to ask me to be your husband? Is that not what we discussed?"

I laughed for real but tried to pull away. I did not want to joke about this. He allowed me to wriggle free of his arms but held on to my hand. When he did not release me, I turned back and quieted, wondering what he was doing. He laid his cheek against the back of my hand for a moment and then turned it to kiss my palm reverently. "I should not jest, Luciana. For this is no laughing matter for me."

He shifted before me, kneeling, I realized. My heart paused a second and then pounded. Was this real? Was this really happening?

I went to my knees too. "Nay. Please, Giulio. Not now. Not here. Not when I am blind."

His hands moved to my face, cupping either side. Again, he leaned his forehead to meet mine. "Blind or not, I want you, Luciana Betarrini. Here or there. Forever. Please say you shall be my bride. Let us wed this very night. What is to hold us back?"

"Is-is that allowed?" I stammered, trying to catch up. How I wished I could see! "I mean, can I marry and still be Celeste Romano's tutor?"

"I do not see why you cannot. It shall afford you further protection inside Castello Paratore, as a married woman, just as Tiliani is now better protected. And allow me increased access as well."

I blinked, as if it might help me think better.

"Say yes, beloved," he said, wrapping one strong arm around my waist and cupping my face with his other. "Please say you shall be mine. Forever."

"I want to say yes, Giulio. I want to be with you forever. You must believe me. But right now, in this moment. . ." I shook my head sorrowfully, begging him to understand.

The sound of hoofbeats met my ears, and I felt Giulio rise, his hand on mine, helping me up too. I rose, jarred by the interruption, as well as the proposal.

Together, we turned toward the approaching rider, and I gasped. Flashes of light filled my eyes, like lightning in the dead of night. And what I glimpsed made me cry out.

"Luciana, what—" he began.

"'Tis Ercole! Coming toward us!"

He moved me behind him and drew his sword. "The riders are not yet in view, beloved—"

"Right there!" I pointed to the contingent of horses cresting the hill before blackness flickered back into place. "He is coming fast! And he is not alone!" I blinked furiously, waiting for more of my sight to return, to solidify from flashes, glimpses, to full-on view.

My sight. I could see! Or at least, I had seen for a moment . . .

But now it had returned to solely shadow. The sounds of horses drew closer, and I clung to Giulio's waist, praying he could defend us both from two intruders.

"'Tis well," Giulio said, patting my hand. "They are ours, Luciana. *Our* men. Not Ercole."

Still, as they reached us, I cried out and clung to Giulio.

"Forgive me for the intrusion, Captain," said a man on horseback, slightly out of breath as he pulled up. He paused, probably noting Giulio's drawn sword and me cowering behind him. "Forgive me! I did not intend to alarm—"

"Nay, we are well. Only a bit . . . startled. Tell me what you must."

"Lady Tiliani has not yet returned from her ride with Captain Valeri."

Giulio hesitated. "When were they expected to return?"

"Some hours ago," the man returned.

I rubbed my bare arms, feeling the relative cool of late afternoon. Was the sun soon down?

"I must get Lady Betarrini to safety," Giulio said.

"I can see her safely home, Captain."

"Nay. I shall see her back to the castello before I go after Lady Forelli." He turned to me. "He has a mount for us," Giulio said. "I shall lift you to the mare's back now."

His broad hands encircled my waist and lifted me. I did my best to aid him, moving my left leg across the haunches of the mare, making room for him to sit before me and trying to settle my skirts in some sort of dignified manner.

My mind struggled to catch up. Tiliani and Val were missing? What might have transpired? Weren't we temporarily at peace?

Giulio mounted before me and touched my hands after I wrapped my arms around his waist. "Ready?" he asked.

As soon as I indicated I was, he took off, and in minutes, we were down the hill and at the front gates of Castello Forelli. He pulled up, and the horse wheeled around in agitation.

"Escort Lady Betarrini to safety!" he bellowed, obvious in his agitation to get on with his task.

Another horse clattered to a stop beside us.

"How long have they been gone?" Giulio said, dismounting and grabbing hold of my waist to lower me down.

"Hours," Ilaria said, from atop her mount. "She and Valeri should have returned by now."

"Where were they headed?"

"Due east. In search of medicinals for Lady Adri."

"Medicinals," Giulio repeated drolly. He and I both knew Tiliani and Val hungered for time by themselves, just as we did.

"Adri is in need, given the new patients on her hands."

"Yes," Giulio said. "So many patients. Have you called for patrols to join us?"

"Three," Ilaria returned. "Lord Forelli wants them found before nightfall."

Giulio was handing me off to another knight when we heard the approach of other horses. A pair of them, from the sound of it. I turned back and found Giulio's shoulder, then stood behind him.

"Lady Tiliani!" Giulio declared, his voice betraying his relief, and I released a deep breath too. She was here. Safe and sound. It was all a false alarm?

"Captain Valeri," he said afterward, not nearly as warmly. Clearly he blamed the man for their delay.

I winced, knowing Valentino needed no further strikes against him. Was his lot not yet challenging enough? A "traitor" Fiorentini amongst our ranks? Every Forelli knight doubted him, despite how he had risen to our defense at Castello Romano. And every Fiorentini knight he would meet would want him dead. As much as I felt a bit lost between two worlds, how much more lost was he?

"Forgive our tardy return, Captain," Valentino replied. "We were in search of some very elusive medicinals for Lady Adri."

"Of course," Giulio said tightly. He took my hand from his shoulder and led me along with the others, between the open gates. "And were you successful?"

"We were," Tiliani responded brightly. "We even found some tansy!"

This news hushed the chatter around us. Apparently tansy was some sort of hot commodity.

"How fortuitous," Giulio said wryly.

"Indeed," Tiliani returned. If I was guessing right, she did so with a barely concealed grin in his direction.

I stifled a sigh, longing to see what was playing out before everyone.

Seeming to sense it, Giulio leaned toward me and whispered as we walked. "They are both well but appear to be a bit . . . *umido*."

"Damp?" I asked, confused. "Meaning . . . they took a swim?"

"*In* their clothing," he said, and I could hear his amusement.

"Now that is a story I shall want to hear," I said.

"As will I." He paused and turned toward me. "Luciana. What transpired out there? Obviously, 'twas not Ercole. But you behaved as if you could . . ." His voice trailed off.

"As if I could see," I finished for him. "Yes." I shook my head. "I cannot explain it. But it was as if I *could* see." I reached for his hands, and he took them. "I do not know if it was only in my mind or if I only mistook who approached us. For the moment, I would have sworn that my vision had returned." I swallowed hard. "'Tis gone now."

He squeezed my hands and pulled me closer to kiss me tenderly on the forehead. "Shall you wish to speak to Lady Adri?"

"Very much so."

"I shall take you to her now."

We found Adri in the eastern wing, tending to the wounded from Castello Romano. All around us men moaned or cried out, and I fretted about pulling her away from their obvious needs. We waited a few minutes as she changed a dressing, and then the woman approached us.

"May we have a brief word, Adri?" Giulio said. "Something has . . . transpired."

"Of course, of course." She took my hand.

We followed her out of the room and down the hall to a quieter one. Giulio shut the door. "We are alone," he assured me.

Quickly, I told her what had happened.

She took my hand again. "Look, I am obviously no doctor. But I have treated many people—the best I can—while living here. And I have had several elderly, nearly blind patients over the years who had something similar happen. One saw patterns. The other loved ones. And the third saw animals—some he had only read about."

"Animals, huh?"

"Animals. Zebras were his most frequent 'friends' to visit. We got a great laugh out of that every time it happened."

"You laughed with him?"

"You must laugh anytime there is the opportunity, yes? Life is serious enough."

"I wish I could laugh about seeing Ercole."

"That is definitely not a laughing matter."

I sighed heavily. "Why do you think it happens? Do you think it will happen again to me?"

"For these others, I think it may have been their minds, bored and wanting to engage again. Without visual stimulation . . ."

"The brain fills in the gaps?"

"Could be. As to if it will happen again, that remains to be seen, if you'll pardon the expression." She squeezed my hand. "If it helps you to know, they seem harmless to me."

We could hear a man cry out, even through the closed door.

"Thank you, Adri," I said, eager to free her to return to her patients. "Speaking to you has relieved me."

"Of course. Come to me any time you wish to explore it further." She squeezed my hands. "You are grappling with a great deal, friend. And you are not forgotten. Everyone in this castello is praying for your vision to return."

"There might only be one way for me to see again," I said meaningfully.

"Mayhap. Just do your best to follow where God leads."

And with that, she left me.

"If only God led like captains in a castello," I said to Giulio.

He took me in his arms and kissed my forehead again. "I would not mind that either." He paused and I braced myself, wondering if he would revisit his proposal.

Thankfully, he only sighed and pulled me closer. But as I listened to the steady beat of his heart—a heart he so freely offered me—I wondered if I had made a terrible mistake in saying no.

10

LUCIANA

The next morn, Nico and I took to the old clearing in the woods to do some more sparring. It was a bit distant from the border, and we hoped to evade any Fiorentini spies. If Andrea Ercole and the other knights of Castello Paratore thought me nothing but a wounded wolf—incapable of defending myself— mayhap they would leave me alone. Or would that encourage them to torment me further?

"So did you convince Giulio that you have to get to the tomb?" Nico asked, as I tried to strike him and missed repeatedly.

"No. I mean, our little blindfold experiment seemed to make him more empathetic. It helped him understand why I need to go if I get the chance. But he did offer to go with us, if he can get there. Even if it means forever."

He paused. "Whoa. He'd go with you to *our* time? To stay?"

"That's what he said. But he also said to go, if I had the chance. With or without him."

He shifted, swung, and this time, I blocked his strike. "Are you really willing to risk it, Luci? Leaving forever? Losing him forever?"

"I don't know. Especially since he just asked me for forever."

"Meaning . . . ?"

"He asked me to marry him." Using his momentary surprise, I twisted and landed a knee to his chest.

"Cheap shot!" he groused, staggering back. I imagined him rubbing his ribcage and frowning.

I grinned. "When operating with a disability, one must utilize any opportunity one finds."

"True." He feigned, letting me feel the brush of one fist before softly landing a blow with his other. I grunted and took a step back. "Sorry," he said.

"No," I returned. "Keep it coming."

We resumed our circling, and I managed a glancing blow to his shoulder.

"So what did you tell him?" he asked. "About the marriage thing?"

"I said that I want to marry him, just not now. Then we got interrupted."

"Why not now? Like Val and Til did."

"I kinda have a lot on my plate at the moment. And I'm not going to get married just to keep me safer while in Ercole's keep. Giulio deserves more than that. Til and Val have their own issues. We have our own *unique* set."

"That makes sense."

A shiver ran down my neck as I remembered the vision of Ercole riding toward us at top speed. I had been so certain . . . it had been so clear in my head. But I had "seen" nothing since. Was it a hallucination? Had I eaten something bad at lunch? I cocked my head to the left, then right, trying to get back in the moment.

He landed another soft blow to my shoulder, then spun away before I could recover. "You're going to do best trying to grab hold in a wristlock, sis, so you can take your adversary down."

"Agreed. But I might have to take some hits before I manage to *find* that wrist."

"True." He stepped to the side and punched me in the abdomen, pulling his punch at the end so it wasn't too painful. "So Giulio realizes that if only we two are able to travel, he might be a gray, old man before you come back?"

"We gotta get back faster than that." I dropped my arms,

signaling to him that I needed a break. "I mean, will you not want to too? With Ilaria . . ."

"Yeah," he said, slowly. "We're not as far along as you guys, but I have to admit I'd be pretty bummed if she was old by the time we got back. I've never been into the cougar thing."

I laughed softly. "So we have double the reason to get back fast. Right?"

"Right."

"Are you sure *you're* willing to risk it, Nico? With your investments and all—besides Ilaria? The Forellis have come to rely on you, and now with this potential deal with the cardinal—"

"To get your eyesight back? Heck, yeah. The Forellis can continue to build on these investments. And that dealio with the cardinal might get me closer to that tomb outside of Firenze. If Ercole decides to take a trip about the same time and hauled his 'guests' with him . . ."

"That could work out," I agreed. "Though Adri said it would be harder for us to enter and exit without being seen."

A trumpet blared from Castello Forelli.

"What's that for?" Nico asked.

"Probably word of the Romano family approaching."

He groaned. "Best get you back, then, and into a proper gown. The Romanos might not be keen to see their daughter's tutor in boys' clothes."

I smiled. "But you'd better believe that girl is gonna learn some jiu jitsu alongside reading and math."

He took my hand, and we set off across the meadow. "I'd expect nothing less of you, baby sis."

I changed my clothes and freshened up as best as I could in my quarters, determined to do it without help. The maid—bless her!—had set out an undergown beside my skirt and bodice on the bed, as well as a cloth on the edge of a bowl of water. She had chosen a bodice with stays along my lower torso rather than in back, allowing me to tie it myself. As the guards announced the arrival of the Romanos at the gates, I met Domenico outside my door.

"Hey, not bad," he said. "You did all that by yourself?"

"For the most part. Margarete set me up for success." I took his arm, and we moved down the corridor, thinking I needed to get ahold of about four more dresses like this, since I doubted Ercole would allow us to bring our own maidservants or insist upon hiring his own. We were going to try, but knowing him, it would not be an argument we could win. Besides, we needed to save our chips for bigger bids—like allowing Giulio in to see me, and Valentino, for Til. Or better yet, allowing us out.

The knight at the turret opened the door for us just as I heard horses and wagons rumbling inward. From the sound of it, there were a fair number of men before the family entered.

"Oh no," Nico murmured. "No, no, *no*."

I gripped his arm. "What is it?"

"I thought her father said she was eleven."

"He did," I said. Tiliani and I had spent some time talking about her and retrieving books from the library that we thought might best help us tutor the girl.

"Luci, she's so *small*," he whispered.

"Tiliani says her mom is small too."

"She's beautiful. All big curls and big, brown eyes. I would've guessed she was more like eight or nine." He leaned in. "How can they do it? Pledge a girl that young to a man like *him*?" he asked, that last word strangled.

I heaved a sigh but steeled myself within. "Welcome to a darker side of medieval times. Think of how it is in some countries in our time. Countless children are married off to old men. And here, given that battle is around every corner? In this time, women hunger for established security most. And men need heirs to keep what is theirs in the family."

He turned away to stand beside me again, I assumed to nod and greet those passing by. "Regardless of the era, I am not a fan."

"Nor am I," I said. "We gotta find this kid a way out of that castle as fast as possible. Or you and Marcello find us another escape route?"

"You mean with the cardinal in Firenze?"

"Yes."

"We intend to rendezvous with him in ten days."

That news both encouraged me as well as sent me sinking. Ten days was good—it couldn't be easy to manage a clandestine meeting with one such as him. But that was also nine days after we would have been living in Castello Paratore.

What havoc could Ercole stir up over the course of nine days?

TILIANI

I had steeled myself for the Romanos' emotional arrival—and impending separation—but still, I was not ready to see Lady Romano, eyes ringed with dark circles and wiping away constant tears. Little Celeste was seated between her parents on the elegant wagon's seat. She was round-eyed and clinging to her mother's hand, constantly looking to her for reassurance and clearly finding none, then to her father, who managed only a brief, faint smile.

On the bench behind them in the wagon were the next three siblings, ages nine down to four, with a slight nursemaid holding the youngest and wiping her own tears away. All seven of them looked wan and drawn. Their driver pulled the wagon to a halt, and my mother, father, aunt, and uncle strode toward them.

"Welcome, my friends," Marcello said, lifting a hand up toward them. "We are so glad to see you safely arrived."

"Thank you." Lord Romano wearily climbed down and reached up for his eldest child. He lowered her to the ground, then did the same with his wife, as the others scrambled out and assembled behind them. "May I present my daughter, Lady Celeste Romano?"

Marcello and my father each took a turn bowing over the little lady's hand, and my mother and aunt bobbed a brief curtsey. Each murmured, "Lady Romano."

I remembered similar greetings for me at such an age from men of maturity, but it was not treated with such gravity as this.

Papa turned to me and then looked over the crowd, searching for Luciana. "M'lady, you shall want to meet two of our own, my daughter, Lady Tiliani Valeri, and ahh, there she is. Lady Luciana Betarrini."

Lord Romano leaned down beside his daughter as Lady Romano remained stiffly standing, wiping away tear after tear with a handkerchief. Nico led Luci to me, and I took her hand to go and greet the little girl. "She stands about as high as your chest," I whispered to her. "I shall position you directly in front of her."

"*Grazie*," she whispered.

"May I present Lady Tiliani Valeri," Papa said to Celeste. "And her good friend and cousin, Lady Luciana Betarrini."

"I am so pleased to meet you." I bent and offered my hand.

The child took my hand and squeezed it as she gave a quite dignified curtsey, bowing her head in sweet deference. She turned to Luciana.

"And this is Lady Luciana," I said.

Little Celeste offered her hand, then pulled back. "Can-can you not see?" asked the girl, looking confused.

"Ahh," Luci said smoothly. "I had an unfortunate accident in which my head hit a rock. We are hoping and praying that my sight shall return in the coming weeks. But for now, my eyes are not cooperating as I wish."

"That is most dreadful," said the girl, giving her a curtsey too. "The only blind people I know are the beggars at the gates of Siena."

"Celeste!" said her mother, aghast. She wrapped an arm around the girl's shoulders, shaking her a little.

But Luciana smiled and straightened. "Fear not, Lady Romano. She is but a child, and children say exactly what they are thinking, yes? I think we shall get along well. I myself am rather direct."

"I can attest to that," quipped Domenico, making the crowd ease with a bit of laughter.

"One cannot be a She-Wolf of Siena if one does not speak her mind." I winked at Celeste. "You shall be a She-Wolf pup, in our company. Would you like that?"

"Oh, yes!" Celeste clasped her hands together. "Shall I be as famous as you, Lady Tiliani?"

I cocked a brow and folded my arms. "That depends on how you progress with your training. What say you, m'lady? Shall you train with a bow or sword?"

"A bow," her mother answered for her. "'Tis more ladylike." Catching herself, she wrung her hands and glanced at Zia Gabi. "Present company excluded, of course, m'lady."

Zia Gabi grinned. "I like it when men do not expect me to attack with a sword. Gives me an element of surprise."

"Be that as it may," Lady Romano said, seeming a bit cowed, "I believe Celeste shall favor bow and arrow."

"Then a fine archer she shall be," I said, resolved to ease any concern I could in the young mother. I smiled at Celeste. "I shall teach you myself."

The little girl grinned. "Are you as good an archer as people say?"

"Well, not nearly as good as my mother. But mayhap we shall *show* you after you settle in and we sup."

11

TILIANI

Luciana was so natural with little Celeste, allowing her to lead her around the dining hall after they supped, then patiently awaiting the child as she shut her eyes and tried tapping about with her stick. I admired her for rising above, ignoring the jibes and whispers of the knights. Those nearest them kept it more subdued, of course, with Giulio cross-armed and leaning against a wall near the two of them. Periodically, he cast a warning look across the room and all hushed under the heat of his gaze.

I giggled under my breath and shook my head. He was going to be a beast pacing the cage every day Luciana was separated from him. Valentino leaned toward me and interlaced his fingers with mine below the tablecloth. "I do not know what Giulio or I will do without our ladies."

I smiled at him. "Nor do I, without my lord," I returned. "It shall be my daily prayer that it shall not last long."

"Daily?" He cocked a brow. "It shall be hourly from me."

I squeezed his hand. "May God hear us both and reunite us far faster than we hope."

"At least as my bride, I can demand to see you. Giulio made no progress in convincing Luciana to do the same?"

I bit my lip. "Nay. She likely cannot commit until she attempts to regain her sight."

A twinge of guilt went through me. Valentino knew nothing

about the Betarrini twins' ability to travel through time. What would he say if he knew?

A knight entered the Hall and shouted to my parents, "M'lord! M'lady! All is prepared!"

Men in the far corner began hitting the table with their palm and chanting, "She-Wolf! She-Wolf! She-Wolf!"

Papa rose at once and offered Mama his hand, grinning. She demurely took to her feet and allowed him to escort her off the dais, then paused to turn toward me. "Daughter," she said, a smile making her lips twitch. "Shall we?"

"Oh, yes, Mother," I said, invoking a title for her I rarely used, "we most certainly shall." Valentino rose and pulled out my chair. I took hold of my skirts, and together we made our way after my parents, Zio Marcello and Zia Gabi right behind us. More tables joined—and adapted—the chant. "She-Wolves! She-Wolves!"

I smiled to see Celeste clapping, joining in the excitement. She grabbed hold of Luciana's hand and pulled her toward the door, eager to not miss a moment.

I joined Mama in the armory, closing the door behind me, while Val, my father, and uncle and aunt urged everyone in the Great Hall to come out into the courtyard for the best view. Mama had asked Captain Mancini to stage fifty targets about the castello, where we would expect them—and where we would not. She called it *andando al freddo*—going in cold—which by now we all knew meant that we would not be told where to expect the targets.

"We want the Romanos to know that Celeste is in good hands," she said, staring at me. "And shall gain a valuable new skill while in your company."

The passageway grew quiet, and we could hear nervous laughter and shouts out in the courtyard. We had asked that for their safety, the people be gathered into groups. Neither my mother nor I feared striking any of them, but we did not want to frighten a one. A maid handed us our royal-blue tunics, which we slipped over our heads, then our first quiver of arrows.

"Thank you, friends," my father called. "On this eve of saying a temporary farewell to our daughters, we thought you all might need a reminder of just what the She-Wolves of Siena can accomplish. As you can see, fifty targets are about the castello, some visible now, some visible in time. We ask that no matter where my daughter and wife walk—or run—that you remain where you are."

Three men began to pound on drums, slowly. As the beat picked up, Mama and I smiled at each other, grabbed hold of an extra quiver of arrows, and together rounded the corner, already nocking arrows. The people erupted into thunderous applause, but our attention was solely on locating our first target. Mama let her arrow fly a breath before I did. Together, we turned back-to-back, each sighting and striking targets in opposite directions. We kept on, drawing and striking, over and over again.

A horse ran between the groups of people, a straw man tied to his saddle. Along a corridor devoid of people, Mama sent her arrow into the straw man's chest. When there was another clear shot, I struck him through the head. The people exploded with cheers, raising their hands in the air. But we were still on the move. Twenty targets were soon hit, then thirty.

Three chickens were set out on a run, Cook shooing them before her apron. Each had a tiny target tied above her back. Mama and I shared a quick glance and then set off around the groups of people. I hit the first one, ripping a hole through the target and sending the hen skittering in the opposite direction. And by the sound of the applause, Mama had hit the second.

I took a knee and, in quick succession, struck one target after another on the wall. Within another minute or two, we thought we had them all. Mama returned to me, and we circled, arrows nocked, searching every bit of the castello. Then, knights took off running along the allure—one along the south wall, the other along the north. They were behind massive, long shields with additional straw dummies pinned to the front. They'd made masks for each, with their tongues hanging out, as if taunting us. The crowd dissolved in laughter—until Mama and I struck each of them simultaneously.

"Is that it?" Papa cried. "Have the She-Wolves of Siena struck every target?"

The drums came to a sudden stop as all eyes moved over the targets again.

"The rooster! The rooster!" shouted a group on the far side of the courtyard.

People laughed and took up the chant. *"Gall-o! Gall-o! Gallo!"*

"I shall get it." I set off at a trot to intercept it.

People shivered with excitement as I passed them, and I had to admit, this rooster was more challenging than his hens. Every time I rounded one group of people, the bird took off around the next, as if he understood I hunted him.

This amused the people greatly. "Shall a bird best a wolf?" called one.

"Never!" cried another.

"Some adversaries are more canny than most!" I called. "Like our new neighbor to our north!"

"That is it!" shouted Giulio. "May we forever refer to him as Lord Gallo! Nothing but a proud rooster!"

"Destined for the chopping block!" I yelled after him.

"And a good plucking!" Ilaria added.

Groups of people shied backward as I passed, wanting to see what happened next, but leery of my sharp arrow. I scurried forward to scare the rooster into a run past them, then turned on my heel and ran the other way. I took a knee as he entered the next path devoid of people and, after gauging his speed, let my arrow fly.

The arrow lodged into the target this time and dragged the rooster twenty paces. When he regained his feet and ran off, the arrow still across his back, everyone laughed and cheered, moving in on me and my mother to pat our shoulders.

But then Domenico and Luciana appeared, both dressed in leggings and a Forelli tunic. I lifted my brows in surprise toward my mother, silently asking if she knew what was about to transpire. Mama gave her head a little shake.

"You, there," Nico said, pointing to two knights, "pretend to be her foe! And you as well!" He pointed to a third.

Some gasped in the crowd, others whispered, before growing silent. There was not a one that did not know of Luciana's infirmity. I swallowed a slow smile. I knew she had been training relentlessly with her brother and Giulio.

"We cannot fight a blind wo—" started one, hands up.

But Luci's roundhouse kick cut off his last word, sending him staggering back. The crowd gasped as the second and third knights crouched, arms up in defense. They moved to either side of her. Pointing and mouthing their plan of attack. The crowd hushed again, somber and respectful as Luci cocked and moved her head, clearly listening.

As one lunged toward her from the right, she rammed her palm into the chest of the one at her left. Surprised, the man paused. Luci ducked her attacker from the right, swept around, and took out the left man's legs from under him with her own leg. The right man grabbed her shoulder and managed to come up behind her, arm under her neck. He hauled her backward with a victorious smile. But as soon as he let her gain her feet, she gripped hold of his arm and twisted. His smile evaporated, and he faltered, clearly in pain.

Gaining a better hold, Luciana stuck out her hip and brought the man over her shoulder and to the ground before her.

The crowd was utterly silent, shocked at her ability, despite her infirmity.

"*Lu-pa!*" a lone man in back shouted, lifting a fist. *She-wolf.*

"*Lu-pa! Lu-pa!*" the crowd chanted, growing in strength as

more and more joined in. The castello walls reverberated with their cries, so loud that I hoped it carried on the wind to Castello Paratore. Many of our people lifted their chins in a howl, and Mama and I smiled at each other.

The entertainment over now, people retreated, some back to the Great Hall and others circling to several small bonfires about the courtyard.

Mama and I joined hands with Luciana and went to our family and the Romanos. It was the first time I had seen genuine smiles on them all.

Celeste looked from Luciana to me. "I might learn to shoot an arrow as well as you, Lady Tiliani?"

"Of course. We shall practice daily."

"And will you teach me to defend myself as well as you, Lady Luciana?" she asked.

Luci smiled. "In time, yes."

Lord Romano nodded in approval and slipped an arm around his wife's shoulders. "Clearly our daughter shall be in good hands."

"There are none better than these two, friend," Papa said proudly, gesturing to me and Luciana. "They shall be fierce protectors as well as guides, for as long as your sweet girl is sequestered."

"You have our word," I said, promising them both. "We shall do everything we can to keep her safe."

Lady Romano visibly swallowed, wringing her hands. "That is most appreciated, m'ladies. For I fear that as much as we jest, Lord Ercole is more snake than rooster."

"Mayhap," Luciana said. "And mayhap not." She lifted her chin. "This shall not be the first time we tangle with the man. And each time we become wiser to his ways."

I turned as they went on talking, suddenly aware that my husband was absent . . . and I had not seen him since we'd supped.

12

TILIANI

I wove my way through the crowd, still smiling smugly over our success with the revelers, but gradually sobering as people began to retire—and I still could not find Valentino. I resisted the urge to shout for my "husband"—as good as it sounded to my own ears—knowing I would receive an impossible amount of teasing from the hordes of knights within earshot if *they* heard it too. *A hen chasing after her rooster!*

I circumvented the entire courtyard—including behind the kitchen building and stables. Two knights passed me by and gave an obligatory nod, arm to chest. But one glanced up to his left and quirked his lips. I followed his direction and saw the silhouette of my husband's back.

I hastened to the south tower and climbed the turret steps, inclining my head toward the guards at top and bottom, but thinking only of Valentino. He was there before me, arms akimbo on the wall, staring out into the dark.

I paused a foot away. Surely he had heard me approach. "Valentino."

His head dropped, but he did not look my way. I stepped to his side and wrapped my hands around his broad, muscular arm. That was when I felt him trembling. "*Valentino,*" I said again. "What is it?"

He heaved a sigh and straightened, rubbing his face with both palms as if scrubbing it. He left one hand on his head, pulled back his dark hair, and stared down at me. He took my hand and laid it upon his heart. It pounded beneath my palm.

"Val, you are frightening me," I whispered, looking up at him. "What is it? Please."

"Seeing you again," he began, putting a broad hand on either of my hips, "with bow and arrow . . ."

I frowned, wishing I could see his face better. Against the torchlight beyond him, he was little more than a silhouette. Something about seeing me with my bow upset him? Why?

He heaved another heavy sigh. "It reminded me too much of that terrible day," he murmured and pulled me into his arms, his actions urgent, as if he could not get close enough.

That terrible day, I thought. *On the field before Castello Romano.*

"I-I thought we were watching you die," he confessed. "I urged Aurelio to come to your aid." His voice cracked on that last phrase, and his trembling turned into sobs. "'Twas my fault," he said as I clung to him, willing him to borrow my strength. "I should have urged him to come to your aid sooner." He brought a fist to his lips. "And mayhap we could have saved Lady Luciana from her terrible blow." He turned slightly, and twin tracks of tears glistened in the torchlight. My own tears ran in tandem with his. "Or I might have . . . urged him to stay out of it . . . and saved him."

I lifted a hand to his cheek and waited until he looked me in the eye. "My aunt says that your only responsibility is to make the best decision you can in any given moment, with the information you have at that moment. You cannot control what you do not know. And you cannot control the consequences." I took a deep, heavy breath. "As much as I lament that Luciana was so gravely injured, as much as I lament that Aurelio was so callously murdered, I cannot regret that you saved us. I cannot regret that that decision allowed us to be together at last."

I turned more fully toward him. "'Tis terrible and wonderful and horrifying and miraculous all at once. But hear me on this." I put my other hand on his other cheek and tensed my fingers, willing him to understand. "There was no way to save us all.

That any of us lived is a miracle. And Aurelio—I am confident he would want us to live without guilt, without second thought to our decisions. He would want us to embrace the gifts of our lives every day. To not let his sacrifice go to waste."

He nodded, and I released his face, then wrapped my arms around him and laid my head on his shoulder. Gradually, his weeping ceased, and he calmed.

"Seeing you with bow and arrow reminded me that you are going to have to defend yourself in Castello Paratore," he said, "behind walls I cannot scale."

I smiled and wiped away my own tears. "Were you not encouraged, husband? I struck every target."

"I do not doubt you, *wife,* when it comes to shooting your opponent. But Ercole has proven himself a formidable adversary in hand-to-hand battle, even managing to stab Luciana."

"Through a wall of a tent," I said. "A very underhanded blow."

"He shall use every angle he can to best you, underhanded or no."

"True. The man is wily. But we have learned much of his ways. In time, Luciana and I shall puzzle out how to best him."

He leaned back and stared down at me intently. "I do not wish to spend any more time thinking of Ercole. Not when I have precious moments with you."

I wrapped my arms around his neck and ignored two guards passing us by, laughing and whistling lowly. "I think that wise." I ran my fingers lightly along the open vee of his shirt collar, tracing the olive skin beneath. "There are much better things to occupy us this night, yes?"

I could see the white flash of his smile just before he growled and bent, lifting me in his arms and carrying me down the allure— which set the guards all around to cheering. I buried my face in his neck, kissing him, even as I laughed in embarrassment. "Must the whole castello know we are returning to our chambers?"

He laughed, too, as he set me down before the turret doorway.

"Frankly, my dear wife, I care not who knows. I merely want to get there in all haste."

Then he took my hand and hastened me down the stairs.

LUCIANA

Giulio laughed, and for the twentieth time that night, I wished I could see. Captain Greco was a rather stern man, and maybe because his smile was infrequent—and laughter even more rare—each instance was all the happier. Even if I could not take it in with my own eyes, the sound of it warmed me from head to toe.

"What is it?" I asked as the guards erupted in laughter and cheers.

We were seated on a bench beside the chapel, wanting every last minute together we could grab. "'Tis Valentino and Til," he said.

"Oh?" I leaned a bit away, without moving so far that he dropped the arm he had wrapped around my waist.

"After what appeared to be a *spirited* conversation, he picked her up and carried her to the turret, presumably to . . . retire."

"Retire, eh?" I grinned.

"Retire," he repeated, a smile still in his tone. He caressed my cheek, and I shifted to face him. "I wish we were man and wife and about to *retire*," he said, tracing my jaw with his calloused fingers, then my neck, sending shivers over my shoulders and down my arms.

"In this moment, so do I."

It was his turn to lean away. "Shall we raise Padre Giovanni? We could make these hours before sunup all the more memorable."

I laughed and leaned into his shoulder. "Not *this* night, m'lord. Our time shall come, should God smile."

"Oh, and how I hope he does," sighed Giulio.

We sat there together for several minutes, and I thought about how I might not have ever talked about God, in my own time. This place, this era, was changing me in so many ways. Some for good, and some not so good . . . like my blindness. But this relationship with Giulio? It was a hundred-percent good. "Tell me what you see." I leaned my head against his shoulder.

"What I see? Well, there are the guards on duty, settling back into their rotations along the wall. The courtyard torches are sputtering, some dead, due for a change."

"But that allows for better stargazing, yes?" I asked.

"Yes," he said, and from the sound of it, he was looking upward.

I was so taken by the vast night sky when I first saw it in this era, laden with stars and so visibly showcasing that Milky Way! This land, without any light pollution, offered a mesmerizing star-scape every single night. Even on full-moon nights, the major constellations—and many of the lesser—were still visible. I missed seeing it so much that it almost made me sick with longing.

"What do you see? Do you know the names of any of the constellations?"

"Know them?" he scoffed. "Aurelio and I had a tutor who was rather enamored by Ptolemy and his forty-eight constellations. He made certain we learned each one."

"Oh, that is good," I said, squeezing his arm. "Tell me of them. Then I can ask Celeste to do the same."

He hesitated at my mention of Celeste, reminding him of our departure come morn, but he cleared his throat and said, "Ahh. I see my favorite."

"Which is your favorite?"

"The Romans called it Lupus, or the Wolf." He kissed my temple.

I grinned. "Oh? I do not know that one. Describe it for me."

"Nine fairly bright stars, with a great number of lesser stars about too. She appears to be a wolf reclining on her back."

I smiled as he nuzzled closer and kissed me lightly right where my neck met my shoulder. I shivered and shied slightly away. "Has that always been your favorite?"

"Ever since I met you," he said, pulling me close again.

I turned my face away as he tried to claim my lips. "What else do you see? Tell me."

He let out a beleaguered sigh and looked up again. "There is Pegasus, the Winged Horse. And Leo Major, the Lion. Ahh, and there is Sagittarius, the Archer."

I thought back to my astronomy class in college and how I loved to make out various constellations. "Back home," I said quietly, "we did not call them by more than their names. We do not use titles like 'the Lion,' or 'the Archer.' Astronomers likely do, but not the common people."

"Why not?"

"I don't know," I muttered, in English. Why had my professor *not* shared them? Or maybe she had. When we had looked up into the night sky just outside of the city, precious little was visible other than the brightest stars. Maybe the city lights had made it impossible to see the lesser stars that helped the ancients sketch objects and, therefore, name and remember them as such. In modern skies, figures were hard to make out. "We could not see as many stars as you do here."

"Why not?" he asked, sounding confused.

"There are big buildings in our time. Very tall. And they hold many people."

"How tall?"

"Some buildings are about twelve or fifteen stories tall. So think of this castello—" I said, waving to the far side, "but with four additional castellos on top."

"You jest."

"Nay. Some are more than a *hundred* stories tall. The tallest building in the world measures somewhere around half a Roman mile, if I remember it right."

He seemed to stop breathing. "Why would one need a building so tall?"

"To house all the people," I said with a shrug.

"How many people?" he whispered.

"Billions," I said softly, knowing it was a lot to take in. "There are eight billion people around the world."

"Billion," he said, trying out the word. "How many is that?"

"A thousand million."

"I see." A million was a term he apparently had heard before. "And how many people live in the world today? My day?"

"Somewhere around three hundred million. Around the whole world. And just in case you wonder, it is most definitely round."

"So the world's population—how did it grow so quickly?"

I paused, knowing this would be hard. "There is exponential growth, especially in later centuries. There is more food available. Work. Housing. Medicines to prevent disease. Excellent medical care to treat those who are hurt or ill. It all builds the population. And all those people, in all those homes, produce enough light in the cities that it makes it hard to see the stars at night."

"No stars at night," he mused. "I would think that the world was coming to an end."

"There are some in my time who think the same."

He leaned back against the chapel wall, and I leaned against his chest, nestling my head between his shoulder and neck, my arm hooked around his torso. After a while, he asked, "How do they all not kill one another?"

"They do," I said with a sigh. "In scuffles on the street, in vying for power, and between countries vying for more power."

"Countries?"

"There are few kingdoms or republics in my day. No more empires. Most unify with others inside major land masses—they are called countries."

He mulled that over. "People then are the same as they are now."

"In some ways, yes."

"So it never changes?" He stroked my hair, toying with a tendril that had come loose from my braid.

"Never," I returned sadly. "Until we die, everyone always wants what the other has. Greed, envy drives us all."

"I do not want greed or envy to define my life."

"I know. I believe that is part of what made me fall in love with you. Your selfless heart. Your desire for peace, even if it meant turning Castello Greco over to Aurelio Paratore. I shall never forget that day, Giulio."

He let out a long, exasperated breath. "'Twas all for naught. Look at us now. The castello in Ercole's hands. You and Tiliani, about to be captives inside her walls." His body tensed as he said it.

"Not captives," I corrected. "Guardians. And if God smiles, liberators."

Across from us, I could hear men emerging from the Great Hall, laughing and speaking quietly.

"Ladies Gabriella and Evangelia have just emerged," Giulio told me.

"Heading to bed?" I asked.

"Nay. They approach us." He straightened and allowed his arm to slip down from my shoulders to my waist. I straightened too.

"My sister and I were talking," Gabi said in English as she neared. "And we decided that if you are to enter that castle, you'll need every edge you can get."

"Agreed," I returned evenly, waiting.

"Come along," she said in Italian. "You as well, Giulio."

He rose and took my hand, leading me to the southern turret and what I assumed would be a private conversation in the solarium. But we entered and climbed to the top, emerging on the allure.

"Leave us," Gabi said to the guard, and I heard the turret door shut behind us. "Good," she said. "Now there are about five minutes between two guards patrolling the wall. But the night is calm. They will not be as alert as if, say, battle was upon them."

I waited, tense, wondering where this was leading.

She put a hand on my shoulder. "You are blind, Luciana, but you are quite strong. Remember that, no matter what comes. Remember what your body is capable of. How you have brought down one man after another in battle, many much bigger than you. Right?" she added in English, when I didn't immediately respond.

"Right."

"Now Evangelia and I have both been in Castello Paratore and held against our will. We freed Lia from the dungeon."

"I removed all the chains and torture devices," Giulio said.

"But that does not mean Ercole has not replaced them," she countered.

"Or will," Lia added.

I shivered, thinking of movies with those horrible stretching devices. Was that what they were talking about?

"You saw me rappel down from the castello wall in Firenze, yes?" Gabi asked.

"Yes."

"I have done the same off of this wall, and again off Castello Paratore."

I held my breath, guessing where she was going with this. I remembered the great height of Castello Paratore's far wall—about twenty feet higher than Castello Forelli where the valley and old Etruscan village intersected with it. Would the rope even reach to the bottom there? I wouldn't be able to see if it did!

Lia came to my other side. "The power of the mind is as great as the power of the body. You must not doubt you can do this. You must simply do. Have you entered jiu jitsu matches and faced an opponent that made you doubt yourself?"

"For a moment," I allowed, thinking back. "But then I switch to thinking about how to use their size to my advantage."

"Exactly. Remember that. There is always another way to look at it."

"Now Castello Paratore—like our own here—shall have a length of rope set on a hook every twenty feet or so," Gabi said. "Knights use them to haul up buckets and supplies, for the most part. It will likely be at least as deep as the courtyard floor."

"But maybe not as deep as the ground outside the castle," I finished for her, slipping back into English.

"Mayhap," she allowed. "Find your way to the next hook and take the length of it on your shoulder. I want you familiar with the weight."

I followed her instructions and found the hook, lifted it, and grunted. "It's heavier than I guessed it'd be."

"Here," Giulio said, "allow me to help."

"Nay, Giulio," Gabi said, switching back to Italian. "She needs to do this herself."

"But you do not intend to—"

"We do," Lia said. "You want her to do so too, yes? It may be her only means of escape."

"But-but she is blind."

"That does not make her helpless."

He went silent. They wanted me to do this. Right now. Rappel off the side of the castle wall. My heart skipped several beats.

Gabi took my hand. "Tie the rope to an outer parapet. It will not be seen by anyone from the courtyard, at least, but it will be immediately obvious to the next guards on patrol. That is why you must time your descent between them."

"Understood." I ran my hand over the pointed rise and fall of the parapet and envisioned the rope going around one. I dropped the rope—maybe fifty pounds—at my feet and stretched the end around the small tower before me.

"Tie it with a flat overhead knot," Gabi said. "Do you know how?"

"I do." As a college freshman, I had dated a guy who was into rock climbing and gone with him several times. But it had been more of an interest in *him* than dangling over rocks that could kill me, so when the relationship fizzled, so did my interest. But I remembered several knots, at least. I quickly tied it.

"Now your gown," Gabi said.

"Sumo style, right?" I asked.

She laughed. "Right."

I bent and grabbed the back of my skirt, pulled it between my legs and tucked it into my waistband. I could feel the evening breeze on my skin.

"Excellent. Now toss the rope over and climb onto the wall, keeping hold of the top of the rope. There is a space between each rise that is just big enough for your foot. 'Tis the same at Castello Paratore."

I did as she asked, ignoring Giulio's quick inhale of fear for me. I sensed the chasm beyond the wall, the great height, but concentrated on the firm feel of the stone at my feet and hand, the rough weave of the thick rope.

"Take a length of rope, pass it between your legs, up across your chest, and then over your shoulder. Fist it firmly beneath you. That is your 'seat,'" she said. "One hand above you and one below. You cannot go very fast or you will arrive at the bottom with burned palms."

"Ahh, for a belay device, eh?" I quipped.

"Indeed." I could hear the smile in her voice. "But it still works the old-fashioned way. Just take your time."

"As long as nobody is shooting at me."

"Well, yeah. If somebody is shooting at you, you're going to need to risk the burn."

"Better sore palms than getting captured by the enemy," Lia said.

Worried I'd second-guess myself, I grabbed hold of a length of rope, stretched my hand above, and stepped out against the wall. My feet slipped, and I dangled there for a heart-stopping moment as Giulio cried out my name.

But then I pushed off my slippers, used my toes to find purchase against the wall, and took my first breath. "I'm okay."

My heart was pounding out of my chest, but I was okay. Alive. Not falling to my death.

"Under no circumstance release the rope from beneath you . . . unless you intend to fall," Gabi coached. "Lower your top handhold by your belly. Your bottom hand will control your descent."

I did as I was told.

"Good. Now allow the rope to gradually slide through both hands."

I did as she asked. And then again. In moments, I dangled maybe a dozen feet below them. The rope pinched my chest and rubbed my neck and palms with its rough fibers. "It'd be better if I had rags tied around my palms."

"Agreed," Gabi said. "Then you could slide more. But I wanted you to feel what it is like if you have no time to wrap your hands."

If I was fleeing, she meant. I descended another length.

Men shouted. We were discovered. How many now watched me? I put them out of my mind, concentrating only on the cold, rough stone against my toes, the prickly rope in my hands, and getting down, one length at a time. I would have to be faster than this if I tried it at Castello Paratore. Men there would not be cheering me on. They might be shooting at me. Or worse, sawing the rope to send me hurtling to my death.

In another few minutes, I reached the ground. My knees trembled so much that I collapsed to my butt and gasped for breath.

But above me, both women and men howled their praise. The sound of it made me laugh until I cried.

I'd just rappelled down a castle wall. *Me.* A blind woman. If I could do that, what else might I accomplish? For the first time, I decided I just might be able to stay in medieval Italy forever. Blind or not.

13

Tiliani

As we gathered to break our fast in the Great Hall the next morning, few spoke. No one laughed. I had always considered the hall a warm place to gather. Today, it felt empty and cavernous, even full of people. Everyone knew what was about to transpire.

Our clothes and belongings were packed. Even now, servants likely carried them to a wagon. We brought with us enough for the season, but not for the winter. *Please, God, that you shall not let us languish in the enemy's lair through winter! Pray, show us the way out!*

Valentino had said little more than a mournful "buongiorno" to me, more a farewell than a morning's greeting. I had felt the same grief—how long would it be until we once again awakened in each other's arms?

After forcing a bit of bread and cheese into my mouth, we followed the others, solemnly processing out into the courtyard as if we were about to attend a funeral. As expected, our belongings were packed, and knights in their midnight-blue Forelli tunics stood side by side with the Romano knights in green.

The Romanos had taken their meal in the guest quarters, likely to avoid curious eyes. They emerged from the southern turret and walked toward us, Celeste between her parents. The other children walked hand in hand behind them. A lump formed in my throat, even as I forced a smile for Celeste.

"Here we are," I said to her. "Are you ready for our little adventure?"

She nodded but did not return my smile. Her mother sniffed, trying to hold back her tears. Celeste looked dolefully up at her and then to her father. Lord Romano managed a wan smile of his own. "Up you go, my darling," he said, lifting her to a small mare's saddle.

I turned to my family, kissing my aunt and uncle, then doing the same with Mama and Papa.

"Watch your back, She-Wolf," Papa said. "As well as Luciana's and Celeste's."

"Every moment of every day," I promised.

"We shall find a way to free you and liberate the castello posthaste," Mama promised.

"I know." I held on to her hands as I stepped back. "I shall convince Ercole to hold a feast and invite you all. By then I shall have learned a few key aspects of their defense."

"That's my girl," Mama said.

Zia Gabi and Zio Marcello joined us. "He shall likely ease his watch in time, if you prove not too much trouble," my uncle said.

"Make him believe that you are there to do naught but watch over little Lady Romano," my aunt added. "Fulfill your duty."

"I shall do my best," I returned, thinking of Andrea Ercole and his lecherous ways. He likely still blamed me for having him dismissed after I'd caught him with the chambermaid. My nuptials with Valentino would afford me some protection, but my gaze moved to Luciana saying a tender farewell to Giulio. Ercole would delight in trying to seduce her, especially if he knew she was Giulio's intended.

I squeezed Mama's hands and let her go. Even though I was a woman grown, I had rarely spent more than a few nights away from my parents. Rarely more than a few nights away from the castello, for that matter. A few sojourns to Siena, a number of summer months in the country villa to escape the heat—but all in their company. Even when we were prisoners in Firenze, they had been with me.

I swallowed hard and pulled my shoulders back. 'Twas time to be a woman. A She-Wolf as I had been raised.

Valentino awaited me beside Cardo, holding the gelding's reins, as well as his own mare's. He gave a low whistle and shook his head a bit in admiration as I approached. "You are a sight to behold, beloved. And I shall thank God day and night that you are mine, even while parted."

"I am forever yours." I looked into his eyes and tipped up my chin. He kissed me, tenderly, caring not if others looked upon us. I pulled away slowly, wanting to memorize the feel of his kiss, the smell of him—this morning, all sage and leather.

Everyone else mounted up, and we moved toward the opening gates of the castello. I looked about at the long-familiar stones, knowing I would miss these walls every day I was behind another's. *Please, Lord, make a way for us. Help us!*

Our procession wound through the dense forest and to the creek and over it. Ercole had but two patrols positioned at the temporary border, obviously lulled by our agreement and wanting to show trust. They did not shout or cast jibes our way, merely watched with barely concealed glee. We ignored them, staring straight ahead.

We passed the tomb field and turned toward Castello Paratore, her long, thin, crimson flags waving in the wind from each corner. The castle had been built several decades after Castello Forelli, and her gates positioned to the far side—ostensibly to protect her from enemies easily observing who came and went. It was with some pleasure that I noted that the tunnel we had reestablished under her back wall seemed undisturbed. With luck, they had not discovered the breach and been able to fortify under cover of darkness. No reports had reached my ears of them doing so by day.

As agreed, this was our last-resort plan. If negotiations did not free Lady Celeste—and therefore us—come spring, Siena would attack when least expected, and the Forellis would bring down Castello Paratore's wall. Luciana, Celeste, and I would hole up somewhere we could defend ourselves until others came to our aid.

The plan comforted me, as fraught with weakness as it was. At least it was some sort of tangible crack in Ercole's armor, some way we were ahead of the man. We passed the trees where Ercole had forced me and Otello to surrender, after showing us whom he held captive. Bitter gall rose in my throat as I remembered that fateful moment. We had almost captured the castello that day, with precious few knights left to defend her. Now knights lined the allure above, too numerous to count—when we had once been down to fewer than a score! They, like the others, uttered nothing, but their gleeful expression said it all. They considered themselves victors, and we, the vanquished.

We turned onto the entry ramp that led into the castello. The gates were open before us, and men lined both sides of the ramp, inside and out. How many Fiorentini were still encamped in the hills beyond the castello? The hair on my neck rose.

It would take some time, settling into enemy territory. I *had* to settle—at least ostensibly—for little Celeste's sake. I wanted the child to find some ease in their company. Luciana and I would bear any burden to make this lighter for her.

Ercole, dressed from broad hat to pointed toe in finery, awaited us before the keep. We circled around and pulled to a stop before him.

"Welcome!" he said, stepping forward and clapping his hands. "Welcome, my friends."

I bit my cheek and dismounted before my husband moved to aid me. A groomsman took my reins and led Cardo off to the stables. Something about him taking my horse, and not Valentino's, struck me. This was it. We were separating again. We had not been apart for weeks.

I willed myself not to look at him as I placed my hand on his. Together, we strode forward after my parents, the rest of our group falling in behind.

Ercole went directly toward the Romanos. "Welcome to Castello Paratore."

"Castello Paratore, not Ercole?" managed Lord Romano.

Andrea let a sardonic smile slide across his face. "My lawyers are solidifying the paperwork in Firenze even now. By birthright, I am a Paratore and shall take the name. Thus there shall be no need to change the name of this fine fortress yet again." His eyes flicked over to Giulio for a telling moment and then dropped to Celeste. Her parents visibly stiffened. He bent down and offered his hand. "You are more beautiful than reported, my little lady."

She dutifully put her small hand in his and curtsied prettily. "Thank you, my lord."

He bent further and kissed her hand, still holding it. "I shall make every effort to make you feel at home here. Your parents may visit you on occasion."

"Truly?" the girl asked, eyes rounded.

"Truly," he said magnanimously and straightened. He turned toward Lady Romano. "I know this must be a trial for a mother."

"Indeed," she managed to utter, hands clenched together.

"In time, you shall see that this shall benefit all."

"Mayhap," Lord Romano said.

"It has already saved countless lives," Ercole said. "For both Firenze and Siena." He turned toward me. "Ahh, Lady Tiliani. The guardian-governess."

"M'lord," I forced myself to say, barely inclining my head.

His eyes flicked over Valentino dismissively and moved to Luciana. "And the 'tutor,' Lady Luciana. Still blind, my dear?"

"Indeed," she said, lifting her chin. "But I have found my way at Castello Forelli, as I shall here."

"Ahh. And has your shoulder mended fully?"

She paused, her lips drawing into a thin line, nostrils flared. Domenico stepped to her side, hands fisted, but she stopped him with a flat hand to his chest. She lifted her chin. "It continues to heal."

"'Tis a good thing," Ercole intoned, lifting his voice and looking to his men, "for I could not in good conscience invite two perfectly hale She-Wolves into my home unless both were tethered. It eases my mind to know that one of them is yet maimed. I have been called many things, but never foolish!"

The knights laughed as if he had uttered an uproarious joke, but we remained sober. *Let him believe Luciana is so weakened,* I thought. She would show him in time. 'Twas part of our plan. Making him think she was no longer a threat, for as long as possible. But she and Domenico and Giulio had been training every day. She was not nearly as formidable as when she had her sight, but she could certainly hold her own.

Andrea glanced over the remaining people assembled. "So then, say your farewells. We must see that our new ladies are well settled."

My father stepped forward. "We require daily missives from our ladies, verifying that all is well."

"Morning and night," my mother added.

Ercole cocked his head. "It is in *my* best interest, Lord Forelli, to make certain they are content. For it is in Firenze's best interest that all goes well here."

"Be that as it may, we shall still require daily missives. And as you have mentioned the Romanos might visit their daughter, we ask the same accommodation."

A muscle in Andrea's cheek flexed as his eyes shifted over Papa's. "Lady Celeste is not yet a woman grown. She shall have need of her family to provide succor and ease her transition into my household." He lowered his head. "Lady Tiliani and Lady Luciana are no children in need of the same. Nay. You shall see them in a week's time, and not before. After that, I shall consider what I shall allow."

I tried to ignore the ball growing in my throat. I had assumed I might see Valentino when I wished. I was not a prisoner here, merely trying to lend aid in an impossible situation. But I could see the cold determination in Ercole's stance. This was not the time to press.

My father seldom backed down, but he clearly recognized the same. Papa was less hotheaded than my uncle, better at reading people and anticipating their actions, and therefore better at politics. Zio Marcello willingly took a step back here, by design. "In a week's time, we shall agree on it *together*," Papa said. "If it is not mutually satisfactory—and if we do not receive daily missives from our women that all is well—we shall consider this agreement null and void and come to collect them."

"Even if that brings war down upon you?" Ercole lifted his chin.

"Even if it brings war down upon us *both*," Papa returned evenly. "This agreement works only as long as it benefits all." He raised his voice. "And if any of the ladies are abused, we shall take it out on you and your men tenfold. See that you and your men treat each of them as honored guests."

"You may be assured that it shall be so."

"Nothing about you assures me, Ercole," Papa gritted out, glancing to me.

I widened my eyes, trying to signal him. We were to be playing the game. Making Andrea think we were coming to the table. Fully invested in this truce.

"We shall find our way in time," Ercole said soothingly. "It is likely a significant adjustment to look upon me as fellow lord versus your knight to command. A shock to think of me as a neighbor versus your enemy."

Papa took a concentrated breath through his nose. "Indeed."

Andrea clasped his hands and gave him and my mother a

genteel nod, then another to my uncle and aunt. "I beg you to say your farewells, ladies," he said to us.

Celeste turned to her mother and threw her arms around her, weeping openly. Lord Romano enfolded them both in his arms. Luciana kissed her brother on both cheeks and then went to Giulio for a few last, tender words.

Valentino took my hand, and I turned to him. He looked over my shoulder. "I do not trust any of them. I would not, even if I were yet a loyal Fiorentini."

"Nor do I." I put my hand on his chest. "Do not fear for me, beloved. I see them for who they are. The danger they represent. Luciana and I shall be vigilant."

"And yet Luciana cannot help you keep watch."

"She picks up things we might miss. She has become more attuned to what she hears, senses. Together, we shall piece it together."

"I will be a lion pacing the cage until we receive your missive each morn and eve."

I gave him a gentle smile. "Assume we are well until you hear otherwise. And I shall convince Ercole, in time, to allow us outings. Rides to the hills, hikes in the glade. Places you could join us."

"I pray it shall be so."

"I shall miss you every hour, beloved."

"As will I, you," he said, pulling me close and kissing me tenderly on the forehead.

Men on the ramparts hissed down at us, calling him foul names.

"Cease!" Ercole thundered.

The men reluctantly looked away and resumed their patrol of the wall.

"Ignore them," I told Valentino.

"I hear and see nothing but you," he lied, tracing my cheek and pulling me close. Then he kissed me, knowing that we were certainly watched by Ercole, if no one else. Making his claim.

I laughed under my breath and gave him one last, quick kiss

before forcing myself to turn away and reach for Luciana's hand. Giulio reluctantly turned her by the shoulders and whispered in her ear. She strode forward, and I caught her hand.

"We wait yet for Celeste," I murmured to her.

"Is it quite terrible?" she asked.

"Worse," I said, watching as Anselma Romano visibly strived to keep back what must be sobs in her throat. A fist was to her mouth, and she turned away as Lord Romano hugged their child one last time and then ushered her to me, even as twin tear-tracks streamed down his face.

"Off you go, now, Lord Romano," I said brightly, taking the girl's hand. This would become altogether unbearable unless they all left at once. Better for us to face the hardships ahead than continue dragging across the jagged crags of this farewell. "We shall see you in time, for a feast. And Lady Celeste shall have ever so many tales to tell!"

Luciana leaned down and offered her hand. "We are embarking on quite the adventure together, are we not?"

"S-sí," the girl sniffed, trying to put on a brave smile.

"Wave one last time," I said, "then let us find out what our new quarters look like, shall we?"

The girl nodded, waved half-heartedly once more to her parents as they mounted up, then allowed us to stride toward Lord Ercole. Or Lord Paratore? What were we to call him?

"It has been quite the trying morning for Lady Celeste," I said to him. "We must take our *riposo* early this day and take some time to unpack our trunks. Might someone see us to our quarters?"

"Of course," he said, snapping his fingers at a slim servant and waving him forward. "Please show our guests to their quarters, Eduardo."

"At once, m'lord," he said.

The child set off after the man, Luciana in tow, but as I moved to follow them, Ercole grabbed my arm. "You truly wed that foul traitor, Lady Forelli?" he asked. "I thought it nothing more than a ruse."

I looked over my shoulder at him, then over to Valentino, who had pulled up on his reins, watching us. "That fine man is my husband," I said, wrenching my arm away. "And you may refer to me as Lady *Valeri* from now on."

With that, I took hold of my skirts and went after Luciana and Celeste—the only friends I would soon have in this castle.

14

TILIANI

Eduardo was a little younger than I. He seemed both fervent to serve Lord Ercole and nervous, like he was still proving himself. Every servant here was likely on a trial basis, since a few weeks ago there had been but a cook, a few maidservants, and forty-eight knights.

"This is where Lady Romano shall abide." Eduardo gestured through an open door to rather opulent rooms. Lush Danish tapestries hung from the walls on all three sides—depicting three scenes of a nobleman's hunt—as well as a carpet on the stones at our feet. The four-poster bed was elaborately carved and draped with fabric, and the feather bed was mounded with beautiful coverings.

I finished my turnabout and looked to him, hands on hips. "Where Lady Romano shall abide," I repeated flatly.

"Yes, and you and Lady Betarrini shall be right through here," he said, scurrying to the wall and pulling back one of the tapestries to show us a door.

"Nay." I shook my head. "There shall be no door between Lady Romano and at least one of us at any time."

"But Lord Ercole—"

"I care not for what Lord Ercole told you. My word shall prevail. Now you may take that door from the hinges and remove the tapestry, and either Lady Luciana or I shall sleep in the next room. But day and night, one of us—always one of *us*—shall attend our charge, including sleeping with her. Thankfully, there is ample room for two in a bed that large. If this is the accommodation of the lord's intended, how elaborate are his own furnishings?"

The young man colored and wrung his hands, uncertain as to what to do now. He knew—as did I—that Andrea would not welcome this report.

"His are . . . that is, I find . . ."

"He finds my quarters rather utilitarian," Ercole finished for him. "Any finery has been reserved for my lady."

I turned and saw him leaning in the hallway doorframe, arms folded. I swallowed my dismay that he had followed us upward. I had hoped to be free of him for several hours yet.

He strode into the room and waved about. "Is it to your liking, Lady Celeste?"

"I have not seen a room as pretty in all my life!" the child said honestly, clasping her hands in delight.

"Good, very good," the man said with a smile. He walked over to a settee and opened a chest before it. "In here you shall find all manner of games to help occupy your time. Do you play backgammon?"

"I do," she said.

"You shall find me a formidable opponent," he promised lightly. "What of chess?"

"My mother was teaching me." She hurried over to the chest and lifted a beautiful chess piece carved out of ebony.

"Then I shall pick up where she left off," he promised.

Luciana stepped forward. "We shall see how much time Lady Celeste has. We have quite a bit to cover in her studies."

"Ahh, yes, the blind *tutor* has much for her to learn." He moved over to my friend and slowly circled her. I clenched my fists as he looked her up and down, eyes lingering overly long at her bosom and rear. "Pray, what do you intend to teach her, lovely Luciana? What *can* you teach her, without the benefit of sight?"

"It does not require eyes to pass on knowledge. And Tiliani can demonstrate forming letters and numbers and check her work each day."

"Luciana has had more education than ten noblewomen put together," I said.

"That was before she sustained her head . . . injury. Are you certain she is capable of clear thinking?"

"Quite," I bit out.

"Together we shall see to Lady Celeste's formation," Luciana said.

"Indeed." He paused before her. His eyes drifted to her cleavage again. "And who better to see to her formation than two formidable women? But hear me on this. I intend to keep my future little bride in every comfort." He turned to wink at Celeste, and she gave him a tentative smile. "She need do nothing but learn how to run a household and direct servants. So reading and arithmetic are good subjects on which to concentrate. In her spare time, to embroider well and mayhap spin or weave, if it pleases her."

"We shall see to those duties too," I said soothingly. "But until she reaches womanhood and takes your hand, Lord and Lady Romano demand that she learn all she can, including French and Latin, science and history. Would this not make for a more winsome hostess and dinner companion?"

He pursed his lips, tapping them. "Mayhap. But I have never turned away a comely maid unable to spell her own name." He had the audacity to wink at me.

"Nay. You have turned away precious few," I gritted out. "And have gone after others who did *not* seek you out."

"Ahh, but that was in my youth," he said, stretching out his hands. "You cannot hold it against a young man, exploring his boundaries, right? Now here I am, lord of this fine castle and a man happily settled with my intended and her . . . *ladies*. You shall see it in time, Lady V—nay, I shall not utter the traitor's name," he muttered. "Lady *Tiliani*," he finished. "Tiliani is such a lovely name," he said, coming closer to me. "And so fitting for a beauty such as you."

I stared up at him, refusing to back away.

"Did you really feel as if you must wed before you came to me?" he whispered. "Did you doubt yourself in my company?"

"Never," I said, without dropping my gaze. Could he see in my eyes how much I loathed him?

"Come now. Mayhap you reported to your father about me being with that maid simply because you were jealous."

Behind him, I saw Celeste nervously take Luciana's hand. They could not hear us but sensed the tension rising.

"I can tell you quite honestly that it never made me jealous seeing you with a maid. Only sick at heart for her. As I was for Rosa."

He feigned a smile and took my hand, then leaned down to kiss it. But as he did so, he squeezed it painfully. Still holding it and partially turning it in order to hide his action from our companions, he leaned his head toward mine. "Poison the child against me and you shall find poison in your own cup, m'lady. This can be a tolerable arrangement, or quickly become intolerable."

"Make it intolerable," I said, digging my fingernails into his hand, "and all of Siena shall be upon you."

He released my hand and casually fished a handkerchief from his pocket to wrap the bleeding half-moons I had left. "I confess I have only dreamt of one Sienese upon me." He gave me a long look before he glanced back at Luciana and Celeste, quirked a half smile, and put his wrapped hand against his chest. "But mayhap 'tis time to make room in my mind for another."

I stared after him. What did he mean? Was he turning his attention to his young bride? Or . . .

LUCIANA

"Lady Luciana." Ercole drew near and took my hand. I struggled not to pull away. "I trust you did not rush to wed Sir Greco as Lady Tiliani did with Valentino."

"I . . . nay. I have not yet wed Giulio."

"Good, good," he said, brushing my hand with a kiss and tucking it in the crook of his arm. He opened the door—creaking on its hinges—that I assumed Eduardo had referred to. "Come this way, ladies. See if this is to your liking."

"We shall need this door removed," Tiliani said, following closely behind.

"Yes, yes," he said dismissively. "I heard your demand. Eduardo shall see to it at once."

I could tell from the increased warmth of the room that it must be smaller.

"There is a large bed," Tiliani said to me, "as well as several wardrobes. Our room enters Lady Celeste's about midway down the wall between us."

"All is satisfactory?" Ercole asked, but I could tell he looked in my direction, not hers. "Is there anything else we must change or acquire to make you feel at home?"

"Lady Celeste shall need a writing desk," I said.

"Make a note of that, Eduardo," he directed.

"And is the room well lit?" I asked Tiliani.

"'Tis all the brighter with you in it," he murmured, close to my ear.

I frowned in confusion. Was that directed to me? Bile rose in my throat, but I knew I could not alarm the child.

I could hear the swift taps of Til's slippers as she rushed to come to my side. "Say the word, and it shall be yours, m'lady," he said, squeezing my hand.

"Allow us a day to take stock, and I shall inform Eduardo of anything we further need, m'lord." I gave him a brief curtsey and wrenched my hand away.

"For now, you have several hours before we sup. We shall send maidservants to attend to you. My cook has planned a very special menu in anticipation of your arrival." He turned away, and I felt the brush of his tunic.

Celeste squealed with delight.

"He has gifted her three toy tops," Tiliani explained quietly, "and set them to spinning."

"I shall eagerly await your company, m'ladies," he said, backing away, by the sound of it. "See if you can get all three spinning at once," he said to Celeste. "Should you succeed, I shall tell Cook to serve you an extra helping of pudding after we sup."

Celeste clapped her little hands and set to her task. The door clicked shut.

"Are we alone?" I asked lowly.

"For the moment," she said.

"What just took place?" I whispered, shaking my head in confusion. "Was he . . . *flirting* with me?"

"That man flirts with every woman he meets."

"Even women he has *stabbed*? Women he thinks addled by a head injury?"

Tiliani laughed mirthlessly. "Every woman he meets."

"Look! Look!" Celeste cried in delight. "I did it!"

"Very good!" Tiliani praised. "Now count how many seconds all three *stay* spinning at once. One, one thousand, two, one thousand . . ."

She turned back to me. "Andrea Ercole relishes a challenge," she said soothingly, stroking my arm. "And he might have made you his newest target. Celeste shall never wed him, nor shall you warm his bed. But in the meantime, we must play this game, my friend. Bide our time. Find his weaknesses. And if he begins to relax in our company, we may find the means to lay him and this castello low. Forever."

"You want me to flirt with him?"

"Nay," she said slowly. "Just not be quite so caustic."

"He shall not buy me acquiescing to his charms. He knows I'd like to see him dead."

"Agreed, and yet he puts great stock in his ability to woo. You have only recently come to abide at Castello Forelli. And you are different than many of the women he has known. But you must tread carefully. He is crafty. Take your time. Make him think you are, at first, repulsed but then gradually charmed. *Gradually.*"

"Or does he merely toy with me, well aware that there is no chance? Men like him are like cats with mice—idle, bored, seeking distraction."

I turned as the child laughed and clapped her hands again in delight. "Ten seconds that time! I shall try again for twenty!"

"Let us shield our little sister from his attentions as long as we are able. Agreed?"

"Agreed," I said grimly.

I understood what she was after. I wanted to keep the creepster away from little Celeste as long as I could. If he molested chambermaids, would he go after a child? There was a reason Til wanted one of us with her twenty-four seven.

But would Giulio get it, me playing this gradual flirtation game? I could picture his face if I tried to tell him.

Nope. He would not get it—or like it—at all.

15

"Lord Ercole seems kind," Celeste said. She was still sprawled across the tile floor, setting one top spinning after another.

"Does he?" I asked, trying to keep my voice light. Lady Romano said she had told Celeste very little about Andrea Ercole—only that she must be brave and get to know him over the coming months, in case they had to wed for the sake of all.

"I only wish our courtship could have waited until I was of age. That I was still at home with my family." She shook her head, and her brown curls bounced around her shoulders.

"As do I." I crouched beside her and set a top to spinning myself. "He is trying to win your favor, I believe. With this beautiful room, the toys, and all."

She nodded.

"Do you think you might come to like him in time?" I asked carefully.

She shrugged.

"All you must do is your best, dear one. Only try and be polite to him, yes?"

"Yes. I promised Mama to do that."

"Very good." I rose and went to Luciana, who stood beside a window, looking to the light. Mayhap she felt the warmth of the sun streaming in.

"Do you think the child knows he was instrumental in the attack?" she asked quietly.

"Children learn many things, overhearing castello chatter. But I believe the Romanos shielded her from such things."

"Children simply *know* sometimes," she whispered. "They have an instinct about people."

I glanced over at the girl, who was now trying to spin all three tops on a small table, but they kept falling off the edge.

"Must we sup with Lord Ercole this eve?" Celeste laid the final top to rest and moved idly toward the bed.

"Yes. According to Eduardo, he expects us to break our fast with him each morn and dine with him come suppertime. The rest of our days are free for us to fill."

"With anything?" the child asked hopefully, dragging her hand along the ornately embroidered coverlet of the bed.

"Within reason," Luciana said. "And with your studies in mind."

"May we walk outside the castello?" she asked. She wrapped her small hands around the carved post of the bed and hung backward. So young, so innocent was she!

I cleared my throat. "I certainly hope so. In time, I shall teach you about different herbs we can find in the forest that help us to heal. It can be a part of your education and serve you as lady of the castle."

"I would like that." She climbed up onto the bed and then let herself fall back against the feather-filled coverlet. "And I shall learn archery from you and how to flip men to their backs from Lady Luci!"

I smiled. How long had it been since I had spent time in the company of a child? None of my cousins or closest friends yet had children. Only villagers and servants, but those were often shy and retiring. Not as forthright as this one. My hand went to my belly. How long would it be before I carried Valentino's child? Might I be carrying a babe even now? We had had only a few short nights . . .

"Come, Celeste," I called. "'Tis time for us to change into gowns suitable for Lord Ercole's table."

"You mean that old, threadbare gown I used to clean the pigsty?" Luciana whispered.

I laughed under my breath. "What color is yours?" I asked Celeste.

"Red! Mama told me to wear it to the supper table or when m'lord is entertaining nobles."

"Very good," I managed to say. I could not stomach wearing anything close to the Paratore crimson, but Lady Romano had advised her daughter well. It would please Ercole.

"Should we all wear a version of red?" Luciana murmured. "Give the illusion of falling into line at least?"

"I shall not," I whispered. "What is the opposite color of red?"

"Green."

"You look well in green. Did you bring that pearl-lined gown?"

"I did," she said, but she remained staring in my direction. "I know this feels wrong in a hundred ways, Til, but should we not wear red or burgundy? Or mayhap purple? Give him a nod? Soothe tensions? Are we not trying to convince him that we come in peace? So that we can fight him on *our* terms?"

I wanted to deny her, but she was right, of course.

"I hate being here," I whispered. "Under his thumb. Forced to go to him whenever he wishes."

"As do I. But wearing a green gown will not take him down," she said.

"Here it is!" Celeste shook out a blood-red bodice. A pile of other bodices and skirts were cast over the trunk's lid.

"Very good! Find the skirt!"

"Tiliani—"

"Very well," I grunted, moving toward the child and away from her. I did not want to hear one more irritating word from her, even if I knew they were words of wisdom.

Sometimes the wise way costs you something, Nona had said

to me often as a child, knowing I had the propensity to choose selfishly.

Grace. Mercy. Direction, I prayed, falling back to my old prayer, as I went to my own trunk. *Grant me the grace to deal with Ercole when I only wish to throttle him. Grant us mercy and protection, here in the devil's lair. And grant me direction, day by day, hour by hour, Lord. I need you. More of you, less of me, Father. Lead us all.*

I shook out a beautiful, deep-blue gown that complemented my eyes and reminded me of our Forelli tunics. I longed to wear it. But then I spied the corner of a burgundy gown and knew it was right. At least on this first night. To start us off as well as possible, I could do it.

Pretend to be cowed.

Falling into line, as Luciana put it.

Which I would continue to do, until the fine day we brought Andrea Ercole down, once and for all.

LUCIANA

We entered the Great Hall arm in arm, with me between Til and Celeste. We followed Eduardo, who had come to fetch us, and heard raucous laughter and bawdy conversation as we drew closer to the doorway.

Upon seeing us, someone clanked a knife against a glass goblet, signaling for attention, and the room quieted. A chair pushed back against the tile floor, ostensibly for a man to rise, then a number of others followed suit.

We paused at the table. "Ercole is at the end of the table," Tiliani hurriedly whispered. "An empty chair to his right. There are two empty chairs on this side, for us, I assume, separated by a man." I pictured the long, hand-hewn table that could seat twenty-four from my tour with Giulio, as well as the barrel-vaulted ceiling above and massive fireplace at one end.

"Welcome, my ladies!" Ercole called. "Come, come and join us. Lady Celeste, please join me here." The change in the direction of his voice implied he gestured to the lone chair on his right.

Tiliani pulled us forward. "I need to sit nearer to Lady Betarrini," she said, "in order to . . ." I assume she made a motion of helping me figure out how to eat. My face burned as I imagined all eyes on me.

"Oh, quite so," he said easily, as if he had forgotten my disability. "Sartori, would you be so kind as to switch your seat with Lady Betarrini?"

"As long as I may take my wine goblet with me," the man said with a smile to his tone.

"Take it and the jug as well," Ercole returned. "If you are to sit next to a She-Wolf, you shall need more fortification." The table erupted in laughter.

"Gentlemen, this is Lady Tiliani Valeri, new bride to Sir Valentino Valeri." All laughter and chatter was quickly quelled by their combined dismay. "And this is Lady Luciana Betarrini, gravely wounded in battle and now lacking her sight."

In battle. I noticed he did not mention *which* battle in front of Celeste.

"The only thing fiercer than a wolf is a *wounded* wolf," muttered a man, clearly having had one too many glasses of wine already. "Thanks be that she is not sitting next to me."

"Hear, hear," laughed two others, clinking their goblets together.

"I do not know," Ercole said. "While she is undeniably a She-Wolf of Siena, she appears much like a tranquil lady of Firenze this eve. I appreciate your choice of colors this night, ladies."

A man—the Sartori dude?—to my right brushed my arm lightly. "I have pulled your chair out for you, Lady Betarrini," he said. "You shall find the back of it right before you."

"*Grazie*," I said gratefully. It felt better to have something firm and stable before me, when I felt a bit lost at sea in this room.

"And this precious young woman is my intended, Lady Celeste Romano."

"To her good health!" cried a man, and others repeated him in the toast.

"Sit, ladies, sit," Ercole enjoined, and we did as he asked.

The man who had pulled out my chair helped me scoot in, then took his seat to my right.

"I do not care for sitting this far from Celeste," Tiliani whispered.

"She is what—but three people away?"

"Far enough to not hear all their conversation," she returned. But there was little to be done. To take issue at this point would cause a scene.

Introductions were then made to the men at the table. Three were captains of his guard—Captain Robostelli, next to Celeste, Captain Verga, beside Til, and Captain Sartori, the man to my right who had pulled out my chair. Four were nobles from Firenze. Nine were other knights. Seventeen men in total, and the three of us.

"May I pour you some wine, Lady Betarrini?" asked Captain Sartori.

"Yes, please." I could smell that servants were carrying in the food. From the scent, I guessed poultry of some sort, and my mouth watered. We had not eaten much since breakfast. None of us had been interested at noon when a servant brought bread and soup to our room. There had been too much going on, too much upset, to think of our bellies. But now, here, I was suddenly ravenous.

"Your goblet is above two of the clock," Tiliani said. "On your plate before you, I shall place a roast pheasant leg at three, some vegetables at six, and some bread at nine."

"Thank you," I whispered. I prayed I could get through the evening without pushing the food off my plate or spilling my wine.

"You are rather new to Siena, as I hear it told," Captain Sartori said to me. His tone was careful but amiable.

"Rather new, yes." I tentatively felt for my goblet, worried I'd tip it. "I come from Britannia."

"Allow me," he whispered. He picked up the vessel and put it in my hand.

I gave him a tentative smile, relieved to have a firm hold on it. I took a sip. "And you? Were you born and raised in Firenze?"

"Born and raised?" he said, repeating my odd phrase. "Born and reared there, yes. As were my parents and grandparents before them. My great-grandparents, however, were of Bologna."

"Oh? And what brought them south?" I managed to find the pheasant leg and took a bite.

"Work. My great-grandfather was a stonemason. He came to work on an addition to the Duomo and never left."

"Were your father and grandfather stonemasons too?"

"They were."

"Why did you not become one?"

He paused, and I could hear him tearing his crusty bread into pieces. "I was one of eight children, the second eldest of three boys. My elder brother is a mason, my younger brother, a priest. I was sent to a noble family as a squire." He sounded proud of it.

"I see." I thought of the young boys who were squires at Castello Forelli. Some were as young as six or seven. Valentino had sent Aurelio's squire back home when he came to abide at Castello Forelli. Was it any wonder that a family could send off a daughter to be groomed for marriage, if they sent their young sons off to be reared by the Church or to be honed into knights? Sometimes the differences of this era were startling. But I had to pretend they were not.

"You are Lady Romano's tutor, I hear," he said.

"I am."

"You have had the blessing of studying with a scholar yourself?"

"Many," I said, taking the last bite of meat from the bone. "In Britannia, I primarily studied history."

He paused over that. "A woman both learned and adept at fighting." I heard him swallow and set down his goblet. "I saw you myself, out there," he said quietly.

I took another sip of my own wine. "Oh?"

"You killed one of my friends." His tone was steady. Not accusatory, simply relaying a fact. "As he was about to kill you," he added.

"Battle is beastly, no?" I said stonily—not knowing if he was sharing my sorrow or casting blame.

"Indeed." He paused again. "But I have never seen a woman in the midst of one. And Castello Forelli fields not one woman, but five among their fighters, yes?"

"When we are all together, yes. The battle at . . ." I paused, not wanting my words overheard by Celeste. "That battle called for us *all* to be present. For it was unjust, that attack. Lord Romano had nothing to do with Lord Beneventi's missing treasure."

"So you say."

"So I say," I said firmly. I bit the inner side of my lip. What was I doing? Trying to win him over? This man had *been* there. He was a captain of Ercole's guard! Maybe he had even been in on setting Romano up. "We lost many dear to us as well. But I am truly sorry for your losses."

"As I am for yours," he said, so faintly I wondered if he had truly uttered the words.

"Emanuele!" called Ercole. "Are you attempting to woo the only eligible lady among us?" he teased.

"Nay!" returned my companion good-naturedly. "For you know well that my wife would throttle me should she discover it!"

Others around us laughed, as I absorbed the fact that he was married. Why did it surprise me? Because he had seemed genuinely open to me? Warm, even?

One called, "You can count on us not to tell her!"

"Indeed," Ercole said. "Anything that transpires in Castello Paratore stays within her walls. Agreed, gentlemen?"

"Hear, hear!" thundered the men, clinking goblets again.

A musician began strumming his mandolin from a corner. A fire crackled. On the day that Giulio had given me the tour, the massive fireplace—big enough to stand in—had been cold, the ashes swept out. I doubted the room had been used in years. Tonight, it felt warm. Like Castello Forelli, even. But not quite.

A castle is just a fortress without a family to warm her. Giulio had said something like that. That was the difference. Castello Forelli was filled with family—and friends that were *like* family. Castello Paratore was filled by men bound by taking up arms together. Some were clearly friends. But it wasn't quite the same.

A servant leaned between us to refill our goblets. When he finished, Captain Sartori said, "I hear tell that another who once was lord of this castello has your heart."

"Indeed he does," I said. There was something freeing in confessing this. The man was married—and he knew I was with Giulio. Somehow it put us on an even playing field. Like we understood each other somehow. "But Giulio freely gave up this castello to Lord Aurelio Paratore, in the desire to establish peace."

He sat back in his chair. "So many attempts at the same effort. Mayhap this one, with Lady Romano, shall finally achieve it."

"Mayhap," I repeated, forcing some hope into my tone.

He leaned forward again. "You are a fine fighter, m'lady. But you are a poor liar."

"Oh?"

"You do not believe this union might work?" he whispered. Obviously, he referred to Ercole and Celeste.

"It could. It has before, has it not?"

"Many o' time."

"Then may it do so again," I said without commitment.

"What are you not telling me, Lady Betarrini?" I could hear a teasing smile in his voice.

I squinted and pursed my lips. "I know not of what you speak."

"Of course not," he murmured. "I believe I shall enjoy getting to know you over the coming weeks."

"I would welcome a friend here," I said, wanting to establish the ground rules. He was married, and I was Giulio's, heart and soul.

"In me, you shall have it."

We'll see, I thought. But I smiled and hoped my face told him I believed it, bad liar or not.

16

TILIANI

Three days after our arrival, I handed my morning missive to Ercole—I could not bear to call him Paratore—after we broke our fast. He unfolded it and read it over—the only way he would permit me to send daily word to my family. He then handed it to an attendant. "See that this is delivered to Castello Forelli straight away."

"Yes, m'lord."

He looked back to me, wondering why I still hesitated beside him. "You wonder why I must read it over?"

I lifted my chin. "I assume you are checking for any sort of intrigue. But our family—and Lady Celeste's—only wishes to know we are well."

He took a long, slow sip of his watered wine. "Do you believe we might make it to weekly missives instead of daily? Especially *twice* daily?"

"Nay." I looked him in the eye and strived to soften my tone. "That is, you and we," I paused to look over my shoulder at Celeste and Luciana, "may come to be at peace, in time. But it shall take years of proof for the rest of the family."

He let out a little dismissive sound and said, "Lady Celeste, I had Cook make you a treat I have loved all my life."

She came around me and waited expectantly. He reached to the center of the table and took a small box and handed it to her.

"Oh, 'tis like a present!" she said with a smile. "I love presents!"

"As do I," he said.

She opened the box, and inside were some honey-and-nut confections. Her eyes widened.

"Go ahead! Try one," he said.

She eagerly scooped one out and popped it into her mouth, then closed her eyes in appreciation. "That," she said, covering her mouth as she still chewed, "is heavenly. Try one!" She offered me the box. "You as well, Lady Luciana!"

We obliged her, and I had to admit that the sweets were indeed delicious.

"Thank you, m'lord," she said to him.

"Of course, m'lady," he returned, inclining his head. "If you favor them as much as I do, I shall have Cook prepare a fresh batch each day. I find the honey has a pronounced lavender flavor here to the south. In Firenze, one detects more rosemary in such treats."

I took that in, that Ercole might have refined tastebuds—at least in the realm of sweets.

"You are wise in the ways of flowers and herbs, I hear tell," he said to me. "Is there more lavender growing here than in Firenze?"

"I do not know," I admitted. "But we do have a great deal, both in castello's gardens and in the wild."

"Hmm." He turned his attention back to Celeste. "Your governess has expressed her desire to get you out of the castle each day. Captain Sartori and I were about to peruse the perimeter of the castello and make notes of improvements we must make. Would you three ladies like to accompany us? We shall take our time, walking it rather than on horseback."

"Certainly," she said, while I willed my heart to cease pounding. Would they discover the old Etruscan roadway and our preparations to bring Castello Paratore's wall down?

"The chance to stretch our legs would be most welcome," I managed.

He rose. "Then come along. I must see to other matters in the coming hours. We expect a contingent of dignitaries from Firenze this afternoon."

"And Luciana shall want to see to Celeste's studies before we rest," I said.

He offered his arm to the girl, and I followed behind, looping my arm through Luciana's. She kept her face carefully devoid of emotion but appeared a bit wan. Did I too?

Captain Sartori opened the door for us and held it. He was tall and broad shouldered, with rounded features—nose and chin and cheek—made more apparent beside Ercole's more angular lines. There was something about it that made him appear more friendly. The servant girls of Castello Forelli had all twittered over how "handsome" Ercole was, but I never understood it. Mayhap it was because his angular looks were so unique.

Sartori followed after us, and Captain Verga joined us outside, taking Ercole's arm in morning greeting. "All quiet out there?" Ercole asked, apparently asking after a patrol.

"Indeed," Verga said. He was a man of about forty, graying at the temples. "Mayhap having their womenfolk here shall keep it so for some time."

"Mayhap," he mused, smiling over at us. "The benefits abound! Open the gates!" he shouted to the guards.

"Open the gates!" repeated the knights.

"Eight more to attend us," Ercole said to Captain Verga, with a wave of his hand. "Four before us, four behind."

"Straight away, m'lord." The man turned to the group of knights awaiting him.

Together, we moved as a group, walking beside the castle wall. The front gates and portions of the wall had been repaired decades ago—likely in a battle with my kin and Siena—but seemed to be holding strong. Captain Verga pointed them out as well.

Luciana pulled on my arm, reminding me to play the role of

lady-of-leisure rather than knight-on-guard. "Mayhap you two can gather some flowers for our room?" she suggested.

"Oh, yes," Celeste said, breaking from Ercole's side with a brief bob and coming over to us. "Mama always liked us to do the same."

"You must write to her this evening and tell her of every flower you picked," Luciana said. "Lady Tiliani shall help you with the names, and we shall write down the scientific names when we return, and sketch each one. Your first lesson in botany."

"That shall be great fun!" she enthused. "Let us gather a big bunch of flowers!"

"Indeed." I watched the girl scurry to the side of the road that circumvented the castello. In moments, she had picked five stems of lavender and five more of ragwort.

"*Senecio jacobaea*," I said, when she brought them to me. "Very useful in treating wounds."

"As well as pretty in a bouquet?" Luciana asked.

"Indeed."

"Get some greenery as well—whatever you think suits your flowers."

Ercole stopped when we were a quarter way around the castle. He waved to the forest, encroaching on the road. "I want this all cut down," he said to Sartori and Verga. "Have the men chop the wood up to dry. It shall keep us warm, come winter. It shall also free us of any enemies who wish to shoot at us from a bird's perch." He leveled a gaze at me, and I remembered that fateful day—when we had almost wrested Castello Paratore from the Fiorentini. "And clear out the underbrush as well."

That fateful day. Before Ercole showed up with Luciana, my grandmother, and Domenico as prisoners. And the weight of power again swung to Ercole's shoulders.

I told myself not to sigh in exasperation as he continued on, demanding his men take out one copse of trees after another. It rankled, watching the man make plans to make it all the harder to win the castello back. Otello and I had been so close . . .

Celeste pushed her way through some underbrush and returned in a few moments with a few delicate, pink-red sprigs. "Ahh, honeysuckle," I said, leaning in to inhale deeply. "Do you smell their sweet scent? The botanists refer to them as *Lonicera periclymenum.*"

"*Lonicera periclymenum,*" the child repeated.

"The berries are poisonous and can induce vomiting, but the plant in proper doses can treat asthma and constipation. I know you are gathering a bouquet, and it shall be most pretty. But in the future, never harvest these with their roots, agreed? We would like the roots to remain so that they can produce more blooms in the future. And when we harvest, we always leave one flower in order that it can go to seed and propagate."

"Yes, m'lady," she said.

Ercole leaned over and smelled the bouquet. "Tradition says that if a girl places honeysuckle in her bedroom, she will dream of love. And if it is brought into a home, there shall soon be a wedding."

I gazed at him with some surprise. "I never thought of you as one who holds with tradition," I said lightly.

"Mayhap you do not yet truly know me at all."

He was right, of course. I knew much of him, from the outside. I needed to learn what truly drove him, inspired him, discouraged him. And what might bring him low.

Celeste left us with a bob and ran off to search for more flowers. The child seemed free in this moment, having forgotten the separation from her home and family.

Ercole watched her, too, and gave me an appreciative nod. He walked alongside us, hands behind his back. "She flourishes out of doors."

"As do we all." I turned my face up to the sky. "My grandmother says we all need a portion of sun each day. To stay indoors all the time is to invite poor health."

"Your grandmother still practices the healing arts?"

"As does Giulio's sister, Chiara Greco." But then he might remember that, after his brief time as a knight of Castello Forelli.

"Is it your grandmother who taught you about medicinals?"

"'Twas. I greatly enjoy foraging in the woods and gathering herbs and bark, leaves and flowers. Much of our natural world can be utilized in the healing arts. My husband enjoys it too."

The muscle in his jaw twitched at the mention of Valentino, but still I pressed. "I shall need to see him. Mayhap we may have your permission to forage in the glen on the morrow? We have had good luck of late in finding some rare specimens—medicinals that would be a boon for both of our households."

He considered this. "In the spirit of our newfound conviviality, and in light of your newly anointed marriage, I shall allow it. But some of my men shall accompany you."

"There is no need to—"

"You intend to take Lady Celeste along? To instruct her further?"

"Yes."

"Then you shall take some of my men."

I swallowed my protest. Valentino and I had run into brigands in that glen, and as much as I knew they were long gone—and unlikely to return with both Sienese and Fiorentini soldiers combing the hills—I could not risk little Celeste. And I had permission to see my husband, outside of the confines of a crowded Great Hall or a courtyard full of nosey nobles and servants!

But had he also seemed to intimate that he might allow Luciana or I to leave the castello on our own, as long as we did not have Celeste in tow? My heart leaped with hope. Mayhap one of us could escape, occasionally, to see our loved ones without escort.

"'Twould be good to see to her horsemanship as well, m'lord,"

I said. "And she has expressed interest in learning the art of wielding a bow."

"Intent on training up yet another She-Wolf?" he asked lightly.

"Would it not benefit you, to have such a woman by your side?"

He lifted a wry brow. "Indeed. Did I not consider you yourself?"

I gave him a small smile. Altogether, this was an entirely different conversation than I had ever had with the man, and I found it jarring. Had becoming lord—as much as I wished it to be temporary—grounded him in some way? Ercole seemed in measure a new man.

"You shall have escort for a daily ride, and you may teach her the ways of bow and arrow. It shall be a joy to observe." With that, he strode forward to rejoin Verga, who had stopped and was contemplating a long crack in the southern-facing wall, which extended from the foundation to nearly the top.

Captain Sartori stepped up beside me and Luciana.

"You have no input on the masonry, given your upbringing?" I asked.

He smiled, and I saw his teeth were even, except for a slight gap between his front two. He put a hand to his chest. "Alas, there was a reason my father chose me to become a squire rather than work among the stones with him." He looked on as Ercole and Verga conferred, waving upward and considering their options. I did as well. Could this be another place my family could target to bring down a portion of the wall? How long would it take them to make repairs or fortify it?

We resumed our walk, and by now, both Luciana and I were holding some of the flowers for Celeste as she continued to hunt and gather. With each one she brought, I named it and told her how it might be utilized. Luciana repeated the name of each, as if memorizing them for a test for the child later. A few were weeds, worthless in terms of medicine, but beautiful in the growing bouquet.

"My lord truly wishes this to work well, between us," Captain

Sartori said, keeping pace with me. He gestured after him. "As evidenced by his agreement to your every demand."

I took this in. Was he trying to convince me too? "How did you become acquainted with Lord Ercole?" I asked carefully. Did Emanuele know the depths to which the man could sink?

"Lord *Paratore*," he corrected me gently, "and I were squires for a time for Lord Berucci of Lucca. But then his father arranged for him to go to Castello Forelli after a year, when we were about ten and five."

"Lord Berucci," I repeated. "How did he come, then, to serve a Sienese lord afterward?"

Sartori lifted a brow. "In those days, we enjoyed a long stretch of peace, did we not? Do you remember all those summers without battle?"

I inclined my head and moved around a sawed-off stump in the road. Those were summers of bliss and play. Of freedom and laughter, training without any inherent threat, solely for the joy of landing an arrow or sword well. Many were spent at the manor house, taking dips in the pools with Ilaria and Giulio and my cousins, Benedetto and Fortino. This also explained how Ercole came to serve my father at Castello Forelli, highly recommended from a trusted friend. He had spent a good portion of his youth in Sienese lands. How then had he come to prey upon us? When he discovered his grandmother had Paratore blood?

Had that been a latent discovery? Most families I knew could recite their genealogy for generations. "Is our lord's family still in Firenze?"

"His parents and brother died in the plague," he said. "'Twas an aunt who sponsored him as a squire, but she died soon after we were with Lord Berucci."

I thought of Valentino, and how he, too, was orphaned as a child. But he was on the streets when Lady Paratore rescued him and later made him a squire, leading to his knighthood. Ercole's path had been far more straightforward, a nobleman's path.

"Did your parents survive the plague, Captain Sartori?"

"Call me Emanuele, if you please," he said, putting a hand to his chest. "And yes, as well as my five sisters."

"Five!" I said. "Plus two brothers. You are blessed."

"Indeed. Do you have any sisters?"

I smiled wistfully and pulled Luciana closer. "Only friends like Luciana and Ilaria Greco, who are like sisters to me. My two brothers also died at a young age."

He crossed himself. "May they rest in peace."

We neared the Etruscan thoroughfare, as well as the hidden apse in the wall. My heart began to pound as I watched Ercole climb atop a discarded stone, hands on hips, surveying the path of it. "What is this?" he asked, glancing toward me.

"'Twas once an Etruscan settlement," I said lightly, waving in the direction of the tombs. "They buried their dead, there, outside the walls. This," I said, taking my skirts in hand and climbing to a neighboring stone, "was once their main street."

His keen eyes followed it to the castle wall and narrowed. "It extends beneath the castle?"

"Indeed. Your forefathers filled it and built atop it, likely wishing to take advantage of a natural spring that feeds your well, and once fed this town."

He nodded, still looking back and forth. "See to it that this brush is carted away and bring me a report on the stones. Mayhap it needs further reparations."

"Yes, m'lord," said a knight.

But Ercole did not head onward. He began following the line of the Etruscans' main road, until he reached the end. He hopped down and crouched to look inside the bricked-in tunnel. Verga did the same.

"This mortar appears fresh," Ercole said, looking up at me. "No more than a year old."

I shrugged. "I believe Aurelio made some reparations. He said something about strengthening the foundation. He had visions of inviting villeins to lay claim to plots of land about the castello again, create a village as the Etruscans once had." I looked around as if wistfully remembering the vision. "He thought that more people here, between the castellos, might solidify our peace."

Ercole squinted at me. "A fanciful thought. At times it takes fewer people, not more."

"At times," I agreed.

His eyes moved to Luciana, as if he thought to question her, but she was in conversation with Celeste.

"See to it that this stonework is thoroughly examined," he said to Verga. "I want verification that this cannot be used by our enemies."

"Yes, m'lord."

I prayed that they would stop after one or two layers in that process of verification. I could not remember how many layers deep the men had added to erect the false wall. It mattered little at this point; what was done was done. We could only cope with whatever came of it.

We continued around the castle, and I could feel Luciana lagging. I looked to her and found her face turned toward the tombs. Was she thinking about how she might make her way there with Domenico? Was it possible that Lord Ercole would grant her permission for a ride with her brother, much as he seemed amenable to me taking time to be with my husband? How long would it take them to go . . . and return?

I put a hand on hers, silently reminding her to focus on the moment, not the future.

LUCIANA

Tiliani inhaled sharply as we walked, but only I seemed to notice.

"What is it?" I whispered.

"'Tis Giulio and Valentino, along with six others on patrol. They have paused on a hill to watch us."

I lifted an arm, my heart in my throat. How I longed for Giulio to be here now, beside me. To take me into his arms. To hear his voice. We'd never been apart for this long. "Does he see me?"

"He sees you, m'lady," Captain Sartori said. "He, too, raises a hand in greeting."

"Come along," Ercole said, passing by us. "I have told Lady Tiliani that she may steal away with Valeri on occasion. I shall consider your request to see Greco, should you wish it too."

Should I wish it. What did that mean? But I felt both relief and surprise. Had we miscast Ercole as nothing but the evil villain? Or did he wish to make amends for attacking me? Or . . . did he attempt to lull us into a sense of complacency? I had heard Sartori speak of him and his childhood. Losing a mother somehow bonded me to them both. I was only thankful that I had not lost mine until I was nearly an adult. *So many motherless sons and daughters in this era,* I thought. How did that shape a society? Few lived beyond fifty, and with their penchant to go to battle, our current world was filled with the young. Medieval Italy was not a place for the infirm. The weak died on the daily.

We finished our circle of the castello and reluctantly entered her gates again. Tiliani made our excuses, and we retired to our quarters to begin Celeste's studies and take our *riposo*—the afternoon nap. I had begun by taking an inventory of what the child knew of numbers—she knew how to add, subtract, multiply, and divide, which Tiliani confirmed was sufficient. "What of language and reading?" I asked.

"I am proficient in Latin," she said, shyly digging the toe of her slipper against the edge of a stone in the floor, by the sound of it. "But I prefer the Normans' novels!"

Tiliani laughed. "Do you? Who shared such a thing with you?"

"My mother and tutor," she admitted, sounding sheepish. From my history studies, I knew that books in this era were rare indeed, and novels all the rarer. There were a number of books dedicated to philosophy and religion, some to poetry. Dante's *Inferno* was the most widely published, I guessed, beyond the Bible. And most tomes were on chains in libraries. This child had had access to French romances?

"What do you like best about novels?" I said, sitting at the end of her bed.

"I like imagining that I am the character, doing what they do, saying what they say. They are all so terribly clever!"

I smiled. "I like that too. But what about when things happen that are hard or sad?"

"I do not like those chapters as well," she said. "But it makes me hopeful for what shall come next."

"Indeed," I said. "I heard once that novels make readers more empathetic, because we feel what the characters feel. We experience what they experience—good or bad—and learn from it."

It sounded like Celeste fell back among her pillows. "I do so wish that I should experience love like those I have read about." She paused. "Do you think Lord Paratore handsome?"

Tiliani coughed. "I know many women do," she said diplomatically. "Do you?"

"I think he is terribly handsome," the girl said dreamily. "I know Mama and Papa did not want me betrothed to him, but could it not be so much worse? He is not all that old, and I shall have you as neighbors as I grow and have children."

My mouth went suddenly dry, and I longed for a tall glass of ice water. *Ice.* How I missed ice! Somehow, Lord and Lady Romano had completely protected their daughter from the fact that Ercole had been instrumental in the attack on their castle. Should she be forced to marry him, I supposed that was just as well.

"I know Papa wanted you two with me, to protect me from Lord Paratore and others. But he seems nothing but kind."

"Yes," I managed. "I believe he is trying to make this as easy as possible, given that we all had to leave our homes."

"Do you intend to wed Sir Greco, Lady Luciana?" the girl asked brightly. "*He* is ever so handsome! Handsome in a different way than Lord Paratore."

"He is handsome, indeed. And I hope to, in time," I said. "I-I hope that my vision shall return in time too. Before then . . ."

Celeste scooted over to me and took my hand. "You are quite beautiful too. I do not think that Sir Greco would care whether you can see or not. He looks at you as if you were the rarest flower in the forest!"

"The rarest gem in a mine," Tiliani added.

"Yes," I said, grinning. "He does." I sighed, missing him again, missing *witnessing* that look for myself. "And while he might not care whether I can see or not, I do. I am praying that my sight shall return soon."

The girl squeezed my hand. "I shall say prayers for that too."

17

LUCIANA

Late the next morning, we set out for the glade, where Tiliani was intent upon collecting usnea lichen, a kind of medieval antibiotic useful for treating wounds. But I knew she was even more hopeful that Valentino would have received our morning missive and come to meet us there. Would Giulio too?

Ercole sent us off with eight men to guard us, one of them Captain Sartori. "See to it that they come to no harm and do not deviate from the path, Captain."

"Yes, m'lord," Sartori returned.

Did he fear for our safety? Or did he fear we were up to some scheme?

I shook my head as we walked, thinking it through again. The man was not behaving anything like I anticipated. When we had asked to go, I assumed he'd block our way. And yet here we were. Could we trust it? Or was it all an act? Did he hope that we would report back to the Forellis and Grecos how nice he was behaving? Engender more good will? Could he possibly, truly want long-term peace between us?

"Do you trust your lord, Captain?" I asked Sartori. I held on to his arm with one hand, following where he led, trusting him to get me around obstacles. Tiliani and Celeste were ahead of us.

"I do," he said.

I considered that. "Is anyone else within earshot?"

"Nay."

"You seem an honorable man," I said. "But your lord has been less than honorable in recent years. What say you to that?"

He paused. "I am aware that my lord has made some . . . questionable choices."

"He told you of his escapades?" I asked. "He has been instrumental in numerous battles that have cost the Forellis—and their friends—dearly. I myself overheard him involved with intrigue in Firenze. I believe he misled a few other Fiorentini lords, as well as Lord Beneventi, in his attack on Castello Romano."

He paused. "There are usually two sides to any story," he said at last.

"True. But I believe your lord skews *his* side of the story in order to personally gain."

He was silent for several paces. "Politics in Toscana contain many levels. Every single nobleman I know struggles to gain in position. Lord Ercole has spent years finding his way to this, and in many ways, as a Paratore, 'tis his birthright."

I considered his words. "And you support him in his efforts? No matter the cost?" I knew I pressed, but I couldn't resist the opportunity. When next might we speak in private?

"He is my lord," he said. "I cannot unearth what has happened before I accepted my position. Only make decisions on what I know today."

I pulled him to a stop. Felt others pausing behind us. "And yet now you know more, today, than you did."

He said nothing for a moment. Then, "Come along, Lady Betarrini."

I fell into step with him, aware that I'd already pressed more than I should. I needed time, days, weeks, to truly make friends with the man. At this point, Andrea Ercole Paratore was poised to benefit them all. And what was I but a sort of penniless hostage along for the ride with his lord's lady?

But I felt hesitation in his silence now. Noticed his short answers to his men, as if he was thinking about other things. *Good,* I thought. *Let my words wiggle into the cracks of his conscience. Let him wonder about Ercole and have new eyes and ears as he witnesses his actions.*

"Val!" Tiliani cried ahead of us.

I heard swords drawn immediately around me, including Captain Sartori's.

"Hold!" cried a man, and my breath caught. Giulio? "Hold!" he cried again, and then I knew it was him. "Be at ease! We are unarmed, solely here to see our ladies."

"Giulio," I said, hating that my voice cracked, unable to stop myself from pressing forward, blind or not. But Captain Sartori held me back.

"Sir Greco," he said, gripping my elbow. "We were not expecting you."

"Be at ease," Giulio said, boots moving toward us through underbrush. "We received word that they were out to collect herbs for your lord's medicinal chest, and we thought to join you. There is no harm in that, is there?"

"Lord Paratore seemed amenable to it," Tiliani said. "He read over my morning missive himself."

"Would you not take any opportunity to see your woman, Captain?" Giulio said.

Sartori paused, and I wondered for half a second if he missed his wife. But my mind was on Giulio, only steps away. Here. Now.

"So be it," Sartori muttered, releasing me.

I stumbled forward, reaching for Giulio, wondering if he was farther than I thought, but then I was in his arms, and he was lifting me, kissing me, as if we were the only two in the woods. I ignored an off-color remark from an Ercole knight, unable to think or focus on anything but the breadth and height of Giulio, the strength in his arms. We had only been apart for little more than a week, but somehow, it felt like a month.

Finally, Giulio set me down and wrapped an arm around my

waist. "Take your ease," he again encouraged Sartori and the men. "We are alone. Our sole purpose is to spend time with our ladies."

"It is terribly romantic, Captain!" enthused little Celeste. "Is it not? These beautiful woods and, now, my ladies with the men they love."

I heard a pent-up sigh from the captain behind me. "Quite," he said. "Be about it, then. But mind that you return to the castello with every required herb, yes? I do not want to be questioned by my lord."

"Of course," Tiliani said. "We shall bring home a bounty. Thank you, Captain."

"The ladies shall be well guarded by these men," Sartori said to his own. "Giuseppe, remain here, at the base of the glen. Sound the horn if anyone approaches. Two of you follow the Valeris, two Lady Betarrini and Sir Greco. Three of you are with me—we shall head up the glade ahead of them to scout out the path. We shall turn back when they do."

"Yes, Captain," said one.

Giulio's arm around me tightened. "This way," he said.

How I longed to be alone with him! Away from prying eyes. Even though I couldn't see, why did I feel everyone staring at us? Only Til and Val would be looking away, I knew. And likely some of Ercole's knights were gazing after them, but it still left me feeling vulnerable. Yet another way my lack of vision weakened me. But I endeavored to concentrate on the fact that I was with Giulio, for what? A precious hour or two? I didn't want any intrusive thoughts to rob me of this treasured time.

"So you decided to collect some medicinals with Valentino, eh?" I wrapped my arm around his waist, while his was around my shoulders. "I never knew you had an interest."

"If I knew there were maids like you amongst the trees, I would have been here ahead of him." He pulled me to a stop. "Hold. A tree has fallen."

Before I knew what was happening, he swept me into his arms and deposited me neatly on the other side. He hopped across.

"You could have simply told me," I said. "I am blind, not helpless."

"And miss the opportunity to hold you?" he whispered in my ear. "I am no fool."

I smiled as he took my hand, leading me up the increasingly steep path.

"What are we seeking?" he asked.

"I heard Til mention feverfew," I said. "A small white daisy sort of flower. And a light-green moss?"

"Usnea?" he asked.

"That is the one." I brushed against tree trunks and bushes and knew we were winding our way up a narrow path.

He pulled me close. "Are you well, Luciana? Truly?" he asked under his breath.

"I am," I answered, breathless. "He is treating us well. Fine quarters. Good food. And permission for this excursion, which was a bit of a surprise."

"As it was to us," he returned.

"Ercole—or rather, Lord *Paratore*—seems different. Mayhap 'tis his new lordship. But he seems—at least on the surface—more settled. Confident. Less wild. Less . . . desperate."

"He has a castello to call his own," he said, and I didn't miss his droll tone.

I winced. "Your castello."

"My castello, once. 'Tis no longer mine to give or wrest away. 'Tis for the Fiorentini to figure now. At least for a time," he added, so quietly I almost missed it.

"He spotted the Etruscan tunnel," I warned as Giulio pressed nearer, squeezing between two rocks and pulling me through.

"Oh?"

"He intends to remove a few layers of the rocked-in work," I said.

"If God smiles, he will not go farther," he said. Then he pulled me around, making me gasp and gently pressed me backward until my shoulder blades touched the arc of a wide tree. Before I could catch my breath, he leaned in, said only my name. *Luciana.*

Then he gave me a long, searching kiss. Before I could return it, he again had my hand and was pulling me along. I heard the crack of a twig and rustle of leaves and knew two Ercole knights had followed us through the crevasse of rocks.

But the way he'd said my name, *Luciana*, rolled through my head again and again. He'd said it with such reverence. How long were we to be apart? For weeks or months?

"Here is some of your usnea on a fallen log," he said, his voice near the ground as he presumably bent to harvest some.

"Excellent," I said. "Now we only need to find a few sprigs of feverfew"—I paused to drop my voice—"and we might find another moment for another stolen kiss."

"Why, Lady Betarrini," he said, "methinks you are distracted from your task."

"Only while you are about."

He laughed under his breath, and the sound of that deep rumble in his chest, the radiant smile I could imagine spreading across his face, made me smile too. His hand felt warm and strong in mine, our fingers interlaced now. I wished for the thousandth time that I could see. I could feel him, sense him, hear him—but I longed to see him. To see all around us in this beautiful glade. I could smell the rich, moist loam of the earth. Hear the crackle of dead leaves at our feet. The rustle of leaves still clinging to the branches high above us. But I longed to *see* it all.

Please, Lord, let me see again.

It was a simple, but earnest prayer. Had I been missing that piece all along? Did God want me to ask before I received?

There was no rumble of thunder, no crack of lightning in response. I could feel the warmth of the sun on my head when it broke through the forest canopy, but I could not see it. Again, I thought of the tomb, of how it could heal, but the risk . . .

I tightened my grip on Giulio's hand, feeling every inch of his skin against mine—the tender flesh between his fingers compared to the rough callouses of his palm.

Did you bring me all this way only to leave me with a disability forever? What do you want me to learn from this? I thought about it as we walked. I had learned to depend more on others these last weeks. I supposed I had learned to rely on more than my physical abilities, out of necessity. And I had discovered that I could negotiate more than I ever imagined.

But could I settle into the gift of those discoveries? Rest in them? Come to peace, as a blind woman?

"Over here," Giulio said, pulling me to the right. "A patch of feverfew. Tiliani and Valentino walked right past it."

"They must be as distracted as we are."

"Likely." His hand tightened around mine. He paused and turned toward me. "Gentlemen, give us a moment of privacy, would you?"

The two knights behind us paused in their movements. "We are to keep our eyes on Lady Betarrini at all times."

"Only a moment?" he pressed.

"Very well," said the reluctant knight.

He must not have waited until they had completely turned their backs, but I didn't care. I cared only that he was pulling me closer, one hand pressed between my shoulder blades, the other cradling my face as he bent to kiss me.

I kissed him, too, my hands roaming the breadth of his strong back, feeling every muscle. *Is there not an ounce of fat on this man?* I supposed not, with all the hours of training and horseback riding. People in my day were always after a core workout; people in this day survived by developing and keeping a strong core. A strong person had a far better chance at making it through the day to day, let alone a battle. It wasn't only the knights—maids carried heavy buckets of water. Cook kneaded six dozen loaves of bread a day. Life was *physical* here, which I supposed made us all sleep better. Since my blinding, my sleep schedule had been all wonky. My brain didn't know the difference between day and night, making it harder. *Circadian rhythms,* I thought they were called. And while I had been training with my brother and Giulio, learning how to use at least some of my skills without the benefit of sight, it wasn't like the regular days of going on patrol and training with the knights at large.

Just another reason to regain my sight.

"Luciana?" Giulio said, pulling back from his kiss.

I startled in his arms. Guilt shot through me. My mind had been a hundred miles away—even while he was *kissing* me.

"Forgive me," I said, pulling him closer again and resting my head on his shoulder. "I was thinking again of my sight."

"You miss it," he said simply.

"Every moment of every day. Giulio, I *want* to see."

He pulled back slightly and traced the line of my jaw. "Then we shall find a way to recover it."

The tomb, he meant. For the hundredth time, I wondered if we could find a way to go together. It relieved my mind to think of that—that any time I missed here, he would too. I was terrified that I'd be waylaid, and by the time I got back, Giulio would be old and gray. And if we ran up against trouble on the other side, he'd be there to help me fight my way back. Who knew if my vision would return instantly or bit by bit? Ilaria had left here unconscious—on the verge of death—and rose on the other side of the time jump, so it seemed pretty much instantaneous.

"Here is more lichen." Giulio moved away from me to pick it. Did he put it in a sack on his belt? I assumed so.

"Lady Luciana!" Celeste said from above us. "Come and see! We found a whole treasure trove of all kinds of herbs!"

"A treasure trove? Sounds like a pirate's loot."

"It is, in a way. Come!"

I heard others around her and knew she, too, had guards

watching her every move. Those assigned to us returned to their station. "Show us the way," I said to the girl.

She took my hand, and Giulio fell in behind me, still holding my fingers at the cradle of my back. The path was too narrow here to do anything but follow the one ahead of you, but I just couldn't let him go.

"There is a big step up here," the girl said. "Careful."

Giulio's hands went to my waist and lifted me as I stepped forward.

"I can manage," I said.

"And well I know it," he returned in my ear, before giving me a whisper-kiss where my shoulder met my neck. It sent delighted shivers down my arm. He'd moved so fast, I doubted either the girl or knights had seen it.

Tiliani

Valentino handed me a clump of lichen and then took both my hands in his, pulling me closer. He laid them on his chest and covered them with his own. He gazed down intently at me, ignoring the two knights who watched us. One had the sense to at least pretend to look away; the other openly stared with hostility. Valentino seemed not to care.

"He is treating you well, beloved?" he whispered. He lifted a hand to tuck an errant strand of hair behind my ear.

"As well as can be expected," I said, smiling sorrowfully at him. "Even better than I expected, actually."

His eyes narrowed and I raised a hand. "Be at peace. I understand. It may well be part of his strategy. I proceed with my eyes open."

He nodded approvingly. "Do not be lulled. Look to ways he might betray you. Or Celeste and Luciana."

I turned to follow his gaze to the girl and my friend, slowly making their way up to us. Celeste's basket overflowed with lichen and feverfew—which was a blessing since Val and I had failed to gather little in our arms but each other.

Luciana suddenly became rigid and splayed her hands wide, eyes rounded. "Giulio!" she said, her voice breaking.

Ercole's knights closed in, concern etched on their faces, but Giulio waved them back and held her waist. "Beloved? What is it?"

Luciana closed her eyes and rubbed them, then opened them wide, looking up into the trees. "Do you see it?"

Giulio frowned, but we all looked up in the direction she seemed to be looking. "What do we seek?"

"There! High up in the tree!"

"Luciana." He spun to face her, taking both her hands in his. "Are you telling me you *see* something?"

"Yes." She laughed, tears streaming down her face. A knot immediately formed in my own throat. She could see? "Do you not? He's right there." She pointed, but with a sinking heart, I noted she pointed toward a gap in the trees.

"What is right there?" Giulio said, frowning.

"A monkey! Look! He's moving! Where did he come from? Might he be some lord's pet that managed to escape?"

Giulio frowned, glanced around one more time and then put his hands on her shoulders. "Luciana, you have seen nothing in weeks, except . . ." He paused, frowning. "Now you see a monkey?"

"She has gone mad!" muttered a guard in disgust.

"Shush!" Captain Sartori said to him.

"What else do you see?" Giulio said. "Describe it to me."

She frowned and blushed, as if caught in a lie. I stepped toward her, but Valentino took my arm. "Let them resolve it, love."

"I-I am unsure," she mumbled, looking wildly about. Her blush spread up her neck to her cheeks, splotchy red with patches of white. She covered his hands with her own. "He was right there, Giulio. But a moment ago!"

"And now?"

"Now," she said miserably, looking as if she wanted to cry, "I see nothing. Just as it was before."

Before? She has had other visions?

"Mayhap you have simply overtaxed yourself," Giulio said tenderly.

"Nay!" She swept his hands from her shoulders and half turned, chin in hand, the other arm across her belly as if she sought to protect herself. "He was there."

"Very well," he said, placating her. "But he is not there now. Trust me. Do you see anything else?"

She looked around, slowly turning in a circle, wide-eyed, and put her hand to her head. "Was it all in my mind again? Truly, none of you saw it?"

"Nay," I said, after momentarily thinking of lying to ease her pain and humiliation. But why was she seeing anything at all? Was it a hallucination? "Luciana, does your head pain you?"

"Y-yes." She turned her face my direction. Never had I seen her look so forlorn and lost. "I would like to see Lady Adri," she said with a tremulous voice. "And my brother."

I went to her. "Luci, I am here," I whispered, taking her hand. "Your headache . . . is it quite terrible? Did it come on suddenly?"

"I . . . do not know." She appeared dazed.

I glanced to Giulio, sharing a look of concern. I had known a man who died suddenly, weeks after a battle and head injury, and who had encountered blindness too. Like Luciana, he had a vision—his of his wife, in a doorway, before all became dark again. Adri had guessed that it was a clot which cut loose and blocked some critical pathway. He had seized, flailing about the floor, before lying terribly still. When I had bent to check his pulse, he was gone. Thankfully, while Luciana appeared distraught over her vision, she did not appear ready to collapse.

Giulio turned to Captain Sartori, fists clenched in agitation. "Tiliani's grandmother is a healer. May I take her to her?"

"Nay." Sartori shook his head in apology. "But I believe my lord will allow her to come to Lady Luciana."

"And her brother?" Giulio pressed.

Sartori hesitated.

"Please, Captain," Luciana said, turning toward him. "He is my twin. Only for a brief visit. *Please.*"

Sartori's lips twitched as he thought it through. "I shall ask Lord Paratore for his permission," he finally said.

With that, Giulio swept Luciana into his arms and carried her down the path.

"I can walk!" she protested.

But he ignored her—seemingly not hearing her—and I knew why.

He was terrified he might lose her.

As was I.

18

"Giulio, please put me down," I said. He was huffing and puffing after bringing me out of the glade. "I am all right. I simply had a . . . moment. Like before," I added in a whisper.

"And yet your head still pains you?"

"Yes," I said reluctantly.

"Then you are not to take a step. My gelding is right over here. I shall set you upon him." In moments we were beside the animal, and Giulio slipped my left foot into the stirrup. I felt around for the horn of the saddle, then stood and straddled the horse. Giulio set to pulling down my skirt, covering my legs, and his action made me teary with gratitude. He was a fierce warrior on the battlefield and a firm commander to his men, but with me, he was all tender and caring. I knew this second "vision" had spooked him. That he was scared. I was too.

What was causing this? Was it something more than phantom visions—my brain trying to answer my longing for visual stimulation? Had I thrown a clot? Suffered a ministroke? I hadn't had a headache come on like this, last time. Thinking about it made it pound all the harder.

Valentino and Tiliani were beside us. "I shall go for Lady Adri," he said.

"And my brother?"

"And your brother, if he is about. He mentioned something about visiting a client with Lord Marcello."

I said nothing more as he galloped away. I knew I needed to see Lady Adri. But if something was going very wrong, I would need to get to the tomb. *With* my brother. I prayed we could wait until the cover of darkness, at least.

Captain Sartori hurried alongside us as we approached the castle. "Sir Greco, I shall need to escort your lady inside the gates. Lord Paratore shall not welcome you within our walls, without some warning."

Giulio pulled the reins and stopped our progress. "But your lord invited us to a feast in time."

"Yes, you, among *others*. You, alone . . ." He paused, as if measuring his words. "Your presence might agitate the men. If you were a part of a crowd, it would diffuse some of what might irritate."

"I see," Giulio said coolly. "I shall remain outside your gates. But I shall require frequent reports about my lady."

"You shall have them," Sartori said with some relief.

I heard the slide of the metal crossbar, the creak of the massive gates as they opened. Giulio took my hand, kissed it, then laid his cheek against it for a moment. "I shall be praying for you constantly, beloved. Lady Adri will know what to make of this. Take comfort."

"Thank you, Giulio. I love you."

"As I love you."

With that, Sartori led me into the courtyard and helped me down. Ercole was there beside us. "What has transpired?"

"Please, m'lord, let us get the ladies to their quarters, where we may tell you of it in private."

"Has something happened to them?"

"To Lady Betarrini," he said.

And then I found myself not in Giulio's arms, but in Lord Paratore's.

TILIANI

I followed them up the stairs and down the hall to our quarters. Celeste clung to my hand, looking anxious, as Andrea laid Luciana on the edge of her bed.

"Really, m'lord," she protested, trying to sit up, "I do not need to be abed."

"Rest is likely necessary." He pressed her shoulders back against the pillow. "At least until Lady Adri arrives and gives us her opinion. Now quickly. Someone tell me exactly what transpired."

I glanced at Captain Sartori, who closed the door behind him and stood by it, hands clasped.

"Lady Luciana thought she saw a monkey!" Celeste said with a giggle, half amused, half frightened.

"*Saw* a monkey?" Andrea pulled his chin back, raising his eyebrows. "Can you see anything at all now?"

"Nay," Luciana said with a heavy sigh and sat up higher, pulling her knees to her chest beneath her skirts.

"My lord," I said carefully, "mayhap she simply needs some quiet."

He seemed to remember himself, sitting there, on the edge of her bed, and rose. "Come, m'ladies. Let us all give her quiet and rest until Lady Adri arrives."

I watched with some dismay as he led Celeste out of the room.

I hurriedly pulled the covers up and over Luci's knees and said, "I shall return as swiftly as I can. Captain Sartori has left, too, but I imagine a maid is just outside your door."

She nodded, looking pale and worn. There was no evidence that she had been out of doors, the sun on her face. 'Twas as if the vision had drained her of blood. I reluctantly left, closing the door quietly behind me, before setting off for Andrea's private parlor, guessing that's where he had led Celeste.

I stiffened when I saw them over by his desk. He was sitting on his chair, knees akimbo, with the child between them. He held her hand between both of his, as if comforting her. My skin crawled. "My *lord*," I said, sharply enough to make them both start. "Come to me, Lady Celeste."

She glanced back at Paratore and then hurried over to me. I put a gentling hand across her shoulders. Before I could find the appropriate reprimand for him, he was speaking.

"The men say Lady Betarrini has gone mad." He rolled the stem of his quill back and forth across a writing pad.

"She is not mad," I said. "'Tis merely a complication from her injuries."

"Mayhap," he said. "Still, if she should have visions of monkeys, what shall be next? Elephants?"

"I have no idea," I responded honestly. Where was he going with this?

"Were you frightened, little love?" he asked Celeste.

I bristled at his familiarity, but the child seemed to be warmed by it. She nodded somberly. "More out of fear for Lady Luciana than for myself," she said.

"Of course, of course," he said.

"May we return to her now?" I asked. "She may well be anxious as she waits for Lady Adri."

"You may go. But leave Lady Celeste with me. We can play a round of chess or backgammon. *Lady's* choice." He tipped his head and waved his hand as if formally bowing to Celeste, and the girl giggled. I fought the rising bile in my throat. Was there not a female alive this man could not charm? Could no one else see him for the snake he was? But she was only a child . . .

"I fear that is not possible," I said, keeping her close. "For she needs a chaperone at all times. The Romanos trust that it shall always be either me or Luciana."

"How much can Luciana keep an eye on her anyway?"

Celeste giggled nervously at his crass joke.

"Better than most," I said benignly. "Mayhap we can join you on the morrow for that game. For now, we must attend our lady."

"Very well," he sighed, flicking his fingers.

We hurried down the hall toward our quarters. I could feel the heat of his gaze long after we had returned. What had that been about? And was he already flirting with his little intended bride? I had hoped he would be nothing but cordial until she came of age. Watching him with her left me feeling as if I had bathed in an algae-choked pond.

Celeste put a finger to her lips, and I saw, with relief, that Luci had fallen asleep. It was only midday, but the poor thing was already dead tired. I paced at the foot of her bed until we heard the sound of boots coming down the hallway. I went to the door and opened it.

My grandmother, flanked by Chiara, took me under one arm, and I melted in relief. "Nona," I whispered, "I am so glad you could come."

She hurried to the side of the bed as Luci awakened, sheepish to have been found slumbering. "Domenico?" Luci asked, sitting up and rubbing her face.

"He is away with Marcello," she said.

Luciana nodded forlornly. Had she grown even more pale?

My grandmother felt her forehead for fever, then felt along her jaw for swollen lymph nodes. "Any symptoms of illness?"

"Nay, m'lady. I was feeling fine—happy to be outside, picking flowers and herbs—"

"And spending some time with Giulio," Nona teased.

"Well, yes. That too," she admitted, some color returning to her face.

"And then?"

"I saw a monkey this time," she said simply, switching to

English. "Clear as day. Full-on Technicolor," she said. "I heard him screech, Adri."

I did not understand all her English words, but enough. "And then?"

"And then he was gone."

Nona turned Luci's head toward the windows, covering them and uncovering them to observe the pupils. "You said Technicolor. Did you see him in the trees? Blue sky beyond?"

"Yes. Vivid greens, and blue-blue. Last time it was more like black-and-white. This time, I looked that monkey in the eye, Adri. He had such human-like eyes!"

Nona took a deep breath and then took her hand. "Did you see anything before? Anything after?"

She shook her head and bit her lip. "Nay. Back to the dark I went. It was like that monkey found a rip in the canvas and tore open a window to the world of sight. And then the headache began. I didn't get such a headache last time. Adri," she said, covering her eyes with her palm, "what do you think is happening? Did I throw a clot? Am I about to die of an embolism or something?"

"I hope not," Nona returned. "Maybe the strain is just kicking off a migraine."

Luciana leaned back against the pillows and rested her head against the decoratively carved wooden headboard behind them. Celeste drew closer, curious about this conversation, largely spoken in English. She wound her small hands around the twisted post at the foot of the massive bed.

Nona perched her hip on the side of the bed. "Luci, how else was this different than what you experienced before?"

Luci paused. "When I thought I saw Ercole coming at us," she whispered, "it was far more brief. More like theatre curtains, opening and closing. Lightning flashes." She blinked several times, and I wished it was to clear her vision. "How did this go with your other patients? Did it just end in time?"

"When *their* time was done, yes. But they lived with it until the end." She squeezed her arm and brightened. "But only one of them died of an embolism."

"No strokes?"

"No strokes."

"Good," Luci said, putting a hand to her chest. "Give me a good heart attack any day over a stroke."

"Be careful what you wish for." Nona looked about our quarters and then to me. "Everything is well here?" Nona asked.

"We are well." I moved over to Celeste. "We are learning our way around the castello and her woods, as well as her people."

"Take care, in that," Nona said to me meaningfully.

"Of course," I said. "Now there is nothing more we should do for Luciana? Should she rest or—"

"I leave that to Luciana," she said, turning back to her. "Do not tax yourself, my friend, for a few days. After that? 'Tis up to you."

She moved to go, but Luciana held on to her hand. "Lady Adri, tell Nico to watch for me at the southwest tower each night at midnight," she whispered in English. "I may need to make my move sooner than later."

I frowned. Her *move*? What did that mean?

Nona nodded. "I shall. But are you certain you cannot wait until you are closer to the one in Firenze?"

"Not if I keep seeing monkeys," she said with a shake of her head. "This . . . What if it gets crazier than that?"

Oh, the tomb, I thought. *Why, Lord, why? Why press her to leave when you know how we need her here?*

Giulio needed her here. Marcello and Ilaria needed Domenico. The thought of them both disappearing, never to return, made me ill. They were a part of us now, part of our family. To lose the Betarrinis would be to lose a significant portion of our family's heart.

Nona left then, promising to return on the morrow to check on her again.

Ercole, outside, overheard her as the door opened. He

straightened. "Ahh, but there shall be no need for your trouble, m'lady," he said with a slight bow. "I have sent for a proper Fiorentini physician to come and examine my lady's tutor. He shall attend us as quickly as possible."

"There is no need for that," I tried to intervene. "My grandmother is—"

"He shall arrive soon," the lord interrupted, lifting a palm to me. "But rest assured, should something else transpire before his arrival, we shall send for your grandmother at once."

19

LUCIANA

Ercole strode into our room as if he owned the place—which, I had to admit, he pretty much did. Still, it grated how he had dismissed Adri outside our door—sounding so smug and patronizing—knowing none of us could argue with his plan. I felt sick at the thought of being left to the choices of some medieval quack. I shivered, remembering the pain of the one in Firenze who had sewn me up with what felt like the thickest needle possible pulling through thick sinew as "thread." There was no "going to sleep" during surgery in this era—you simply passed out when you couldn't take the pain any longer.

The barber-surgeon had sewed up my shoulder wound—a wound Ercole had given me. Andrea had not just stabbed me through that tent wall. He had stabbed and dragged the blade down to inflict maximum damage. He had not cared if it was me or Domenico. Only that he had the chance to kill me . . . or at least make sure I wasn't coming after him again.

And now he was in a room with me, and I was in his castle.

"I . . . I think I am going to be sick," I said, not lying. My head ached so badly and was starting to spin.

"I thought Lady Adri said—"

"Celeste!" Tiliani interrupted. "Fetch that pot for Luciana!"

The child had only just slipped the vessel into my hands when I vomited up the little lunch we'd had. As the nausea passed, I heard the click of our door. "Let me guess," I muttered. "He could not tolerate it?"

"Nay," Tiliani said. I could hear the smile in her voice. "'Tis useful information. When we wish for him to go away . . ."

"Go away?" Celeste repeated. "Why would you want him to go away?"

"When we need some privacy," Tiliani said soothingly. "There are times a woman does not want a man around. But *you* must change into your dressing gown for riposo, little lady. When you rise you may choose which gown you wear to the Hall for supper."

The girl skipped across the stone floor. I could hear the sound of bare feet sticking upon cold tile. I leaned back into the pillows again, exhausted. How long had it been since I had skipped? I could not imagine skipping while blind. *Just a faster way to take a spectacular fall,* I thought. But the thought of how long it'd been since I'd skipped—plus the loss of the chance to do so again—made me unaccountably sad.

Did every adult think of such things? Or was it my injury, making me feel so melancholy? "She still skips," I said to Til.

"Yes."

"How long has it been since you skipped?"

She thought about that. "Ten years. Mayhap more."

"Do you think a person who still skips is ready to wed?" I whispered.

"Not at all."

LUCIANA

Several days later, we were exiting the Great Hall after breakfast when we heard the gates opening. The clomp of horses' hooves on the cobblestone, followed by the creak of wagon wheels, greeted me.

"'Tis a fine wagon," Tiliani whispered.

I frowned. A dignitary from Firenze? Most men rode astride their horse, noble or not. Wagons had no shock absorbers. I remembered well the painful bumps and jolts as a prisoner in the back of the wagon in Perugia.

"Ahhh, 'tis Sir Cafaro," Ercole said as he exited the hall. He paused beside us. "The man of medicine I sent for on Lady Luciana's behalf."

"But he . . . he arrived so soon!" I said, mouth dry.

"God be praised, I sent for him as soon as I learned of your new ailment. For my own peace of mind, you see. It does not set well with me to have one infirm, such as you, tending to Lady Celeste. As much as Lady Adri is heralded as a fine one to attend an injury, I wanted a Fiorentini's opinion." He moved away from us, presumably to greet the man.

Tiliani leaned closer. "He must come from a rich family, to travel in such a wagon. I have only seen the like in Siena. It is drawn by a pair of matched, black geldings. And here he is," she said, as I could hear the men greeting one another. "About thirty years of age. He knows Ercole well. He has brown hair. Trim, but he wears his tunic wide at the shoulder to give him what he does not naturally have."

"Height?"

"Shorter than Ercole. A little taller than you. His manservant is reaching for two big bags. Ercole is gesturing toward you. They are coming our way."

I waited, so glad that Tiliani was by my side. Celeste, seeming to recognize my fear, came around to take my free hand. Why did the man need to bring *two* bags to examine me? I tried to school my expression into one of ease and self-confidence but had no idea if I was successful. Inside, I was a wreck. My head started throbbing anew, after easing over the last few days.

It just brought back too many memories of that wretched table in Firenze. Being strapped down. The taste of the dirty leather in my mouth. My stomach roiled.

"Do you need me to fetch a pot, m'lady?" Celeste whispered. "You do not look—"

"Ladies," Ercole interrupted as he approached. "This is Sir Cafaro. He has been a teacher at university in Bologna for some time, but fortunately for us, is visiting family in Firenze for the year. He has studied the brain and vision for some time. Sir Cafaro, this is my intended, Lady Celeste Romano, her tutor—and your patient—Lady Luciana Betarrini, and Lady Romano's governess, Lady Tiliani Valeri."

"Tiliani *Valeri*," the man sniffed. "I have heard of a Lady Tiliani *Forelli* in these parts."

"I am one and the same," Tiliani said. "I am newly wed."

"To Valentino Valeri?"

"*Sí*, Sir Cafaro. To Valentino."

"He is a good man! As was his lord, Aurelio, may he rest in peace."

"Indeed," Til returned. I relaxed a little, hearing his praise of the two men. Maybe they had been friends in Firenze?

"Well," Sir Cafaro said, "where shall we see to Lady Betarrini's examination?"

"In her quarters is likely best," Ercole said.

"Please," I said. "I would feel better if you would send for Lady Adri to attend us too."

Ercole let out a scoffing laugh. "There is no need for her here today. As I said, I have sent for the best." He took my arm from Til and pulled me to his side. "Now come along."

He hustled me into the keep and up the steps to our quarters, chatting with Sir Cafaro, who followed behind with Tiliani. I assumed Celeste trailed behind and that Til was keeping track of her. The doctor spoke excitedly of having some success with spectacles that he had crafted by a glass artist from Venezia. It *was* pretty exciting, I decided—the birth of glasses to a world full of people who probably needed them. Most in this era just made their way through life the best they could. Many, as they aged, lost the ability to see anything close-up but a blurry mass, given that there weren't readers on display at every drugstore in town.

The door closed behind us. "Please, sit, Lady Betarrini," the doctor said. "Tell me how you came to be injured so."

I glanced to where I thought Tiliani might be. "Mayhap Lady Celeste should go to the next room and begin her studies for the day? Maria can watch over her."

Tiliani hesitated, but I knew she'd understand. I didn't want Celeste to hear about the battle. "I shall get her settled and return straight away."

When we could no longer hear them, the doctor led me to a horsehair-covered chair. I perched on the edge. I thought he took a seat on the corner of the side table—in order to more closely examine me as I spoke? "Tell me of it, m'lady, all you can."

"I was in the battle at Castello Romano," I began.

"*In* the battle?"

"In the battle," Ercole said. "She is the new She-Wolf of Siena."

"Ahh, yes. The newest Betarrinis. Go on."

"A knight much bigger than I disarmed me. He wrestled me back, took hold of my head . . ." I tried to swallow but found my mouth dry. My head started swirling at the memory.

"He rammed her head against a rock several times," Ercole finished. There was neither joy nor lament in how he related it, purely fact.

"I see. Did you lose a great deal of blood?"

"I do not remember," I managed. "Please, may I have a sip of water?"

"There was a great deal of blood," Ercole said. I heard a pouring sound. "Most thought she was dead when her brother escaped with her on horseback."

A goblet was placed in my hand—by Ercole?—and I took a sip. It was cold, and I took another sip.

"You lost sensation?" the doctor asked, referring to my unconsciousness. "Go to sleep?"

"Yes."

"For how long?"

"A day? Two?" I wished Domenico was here with me, able to answer. It made me breathe easier when Tiliani slipped back into the room and came to stand beside my chair. I felt the rustle of her skirts against my own.

"May I examine you, m'lady? Place my hands on your head and face?"

I inclined my head, giving him permission.

His fingers were long and thin, but strong. He used a pincer movement to stretch open one lid and then the other. He asked me to open my mouth and stick out my tongue; I had no idea how it related, but I complied.

To my surprise, he grabbed hold of the tip and pulled it left, right, and upward. "Mm-hmmm," he murmured, as if that told him something. "Now your head, if I may." His fingertips slowly traced over the entirety of my scalp, from my temples to the top, then around the back. "You are running quite warm m'lady. Is that normal for you?"

"I suppose so. I do not feel . . . overly warm."

"You are much warmer than the average female. It is likely indicative of an imbalanced humor—mayhap due to your ventures out on the battlefield. Women—She-Wolves or not—were not meant for such strain."

You have no idea of the "strain," buddy, I thought. He'd likely never been on a battlefield in his life.

He straightened and moved behind me. "May I?" he asked, unpinning my knot before I gave him permission. My hair fell down and across my shoulders, tickling the bare skin, but he was lifting and moving sections, intent on discovering the entirety of my wound. It did not take long. Adri's sutures—and the resulting jagged scar—was a good five inches across.

"This is Lady Betarrini's work?" he grunted.

"Yes," Tiliani said.

"'Tis most impressive," he said. "Does she have formal training?"

"Nay. 'Tis all self-taught."

"I would like to speak to her," he said.

"That can be arranged," Ercole said. "Do you wish to confer with her out of idle interest or to aid you in treating Lady Luciana?"

"Both. Mayhap she could sup with us?"

"We shall issue an invitation."

"Did she bleed you, Lady Luciana, as you recuperated?"

"Nay," I said carefully, knowing this would likely be unwelcome news. "In the early days, we were still in the midst of battle. And I had already lost a great deal of blood. Once back at Castello Forelli, I seemed to recuperate well without further treatment."

"Hmmm," he said doubtfully. "Please, m'lady, will you kindly move to this stool over here?"

I took his hand and followed him, sitting as he requested. He leaned down and placed what felt like a cup against the top right of my back. "Take a deep breath in and out." I did so, and he moved to the other side. "Another."

"Good." He rose. "The lungs are clear. Now I must ask that you urinate in this bowl."

"Urinate," I repeated.

"Yes," he returned, unfazed. "I must examine your bodily humors to determine why you have not regained your eyesight, as well as why you have this new malady."

"Lady Betarrini attributes her blindness to her battle wounds, of course. But she is uncertain as to why she is having visions," Ercole said. "Yesterday, she believed she could see. And when she did, she saw a monkey."

"A monkey!" the doctor repeated with a laugh. Belatedly, he remembered himself. "That must have been, err, quite startling."

"Quite." Of my earlier vision of Ercole, I said nothing.

"Well, we shall give you a bit of privacy and return in a few moments to continue your examination." They moved to the door and out.

I turned toward Til. "What will he *do* with my urine?" Surely they had no sort of urinalysis in these days. At least the kind I was—

"He shall taste it."

I choked on another sip of water. "Wh-*what*?"

"He shall taste it. 'Tis part of his examination."

"And what does the taste of it tell him?" I had a hard time not gagging as I asked.

"I do not know. I have only heard tell of it. Nona puts no countenance in such practices, but she will look at a patient's urine on occasion. Smell it at times." She sighed. "Zia Gabi often says, 'No way through but through.' May as well get it done." She led me over to a chamber pot, handed me a cup, and lent me a hand to help me to squat. Was there no end to the ways I could be humiliated, given my new disability? I just hoped I wouldn't get any pee on my undershorts or skirt. It was hard enough to do this on a toilet in a well-lit doctor's bathroom . . .

But I managed and stood, awkwardly holding the bowl.

The men knocked at the door, and I heard Ercole flop onto the horsehair-covered chair with a sigh as the doctor returned to my side. "The bowl?" he asked.

I handed it to him, trying not to gag again.

He took a sip and—God help him—actually swished it around his mouth a moment, then bent and spit it out, presumably in the chamber pot.

"All is well?" I asked, hoping that was over. But no, he took a second sip, swished, and spit.

"Most curious," he said thoughtfully.

"What is it?" Ercole asked.

"A bit of melancholia, I think. Your black bile must be unbalanced, Lady Luciana. Have you felt a bit out of sorts of late? Prone to sorrow over joy?"

"Well, yes," I admitted. "But then I am adjusting to being *blind*."

"Right. There is that," he admitted. "But does it seem as if you are overwhelmed by it?"

"Mayhap. 'Tis a great deal to manage."

"Hmm. What of your dreams? Any nightmares?"

I hesitated. "Some. But that is to be expected after enduring such an attack, yes?"

"To a certain measure." His tone told me he doubted. "I must examine you further. Lord Ercole, may I ask you to please vacate the room? I must ask Lady Luciana to disrobe and lie down upon the bed."

"Disrobe?" I repeated. "I think not. This is a head injury, Sir Cafaro. Anything you must discover is from the neck up."

He laughed dismissively. "What a peculiar idea! Everyone knows that the body is complex. One humor can easily affect another."

"Well, that is not happening in my body," I said.

"I believe it is. I must insist you do as I say."

"I shall not."

I heard the creak of the chair as Ercole rose. Felt Tiliani tense beside me.

"You are under my care in this house," Ercole said. "And as lord of the castello, I insist you do as Sir Cafaro says. I will depart and you may do so in privacy."

"Nay." I shook my head. "I shall not." This was ridiculous. There was no way some creepy medieval doc was going to "examine" my belly or more private parts. At this point, I doubted there were any limits, especially if he was chalking up my lack of recovery to being a woman and having spent some time on the battlefield.

"You are giving into hysteria," the doctor said, laying a hand on my arm. "Further evidence of an imbalance of the black bile."

"I am not. And this examination is done." I pulled my shoulders back and widened my stance.

"*Luci*," Tiliani whispered in warning.

"Simply do as he says, and it will soon be over." Ercole laid a commanding hand on my shoulder from behind. He leaned closer. "Slip out of this gown," he whispered in my ear suggestively, "and take your ease atop the bed."

I reacted before I'd thought it through. I took hold of Andrea's hand, bent and sent him over my shoulder to the floor. When the doctor cried out my name and grabbed my arm, I put him in a wristlock, twisted, and waited as he gasped and fell to his knees before me.

"I told you," I panted. "This examination is done."

20

LUCIANA

"Luciana," Tiliani grunted. "'Tis all right. Release him now."
Knights from the hallway—hearing the commotion inside—rushed in.

Celeste called out to Tiliani. She had come in, too, and was witnessing all of this.

I bit my lip and flung the doctor's arm away. Ercole gasped for breath—the wind clearly knocked out of him.

"Lord Ercole!" the doctor cried. "You are bleeding!"

I frowned. How? From hitting his head? A man on either side grabbed my arms. I lifted a foot and kicked away the one on my right, but another rushed to take his place.

"Lady Betarrini!" cried the doctor. "Cease! Cease this at once! You only do yourself further harm!"

I paused, panting.

"This is far worse—far worse than I first thought," the doctor said. "We must get her to Firenze on the morrow and call upon my colleague, Sir Langoni. He is adept in relieving pressure on the brain, which might well be instrumental in Lady Betarrini's malady."

"It is not a malady," I said, trying to wrest myself free. "I am but blind!"

"Clearly, the first step is relieving her excess of blood," he went on, as if I had not spoken.

"No," I said in English, shaking my head in terror. "Nay."

"'Twould be best to remove her to a more secure location," the doctor said. "Away from Lady Tiliani or Celeste. We do not want to further upset them."

"I will remain with her," Tiliani said.

"Forgive me, m'lady, but I think not," said the doctor.

"We shall take her below," Ercole said wearily.

"Your wound, m'lord—" the doctor began.

"Think not of me," he said, as if shaking the man off in agitation. "'Tis but a minor gash. You know how head wounds tend to bleed. I am quite well. 'Tis Lady Luciana that is most *unwell*."

"Quite," replied the doctor. "She cannot be trusted, especially during such a delicate procedure."

"Nay. We must restrain her." Was there a note of glee to his tone?

"Where is that best done? Here? We could utilize the posts of this bed."

"Nay," Ercole said. "Take her to the dungeon. Anyone who dares to attack me, in my own home, is to be treated as an enemy. Until she is in her right mind again, all shall treat Lady Betarrini as such."

"You cannot take her there!" Tiliani cried. "She is a patient, not a prisoner!"

"Remove them," Ercole shouted. "Take them back to their quarters."

My heart sank as Til's voice grew muffled as she and Celeste were hastened to the other room and the door shut. I remembered the cold, dark chambers of the dungeon beneath this castle. They would take me there and bleed me? Using leeches? Or simply cutting open my veins? I struggled again, but the guards had an iron hold on me now. A third had his hand tangled in my hair, tugging painfully on it every time I tried to free myself.

"Send me home. Home to Castello Forelli," I said, as the men began dragging me to the door. "Lady Adri shall see to my recovery."

"Lady Adri is clearly out of her depth," Sir Cafaro said smugly.

"And if you leave, so shall my intended, as per our agreement," Ercole added. "Nay, we shall see to your complete recovery. In time, you shall thank us."

"I . . . think . . . not." I used my feet and legs to stop our progress, knocking over a chair and then pinning both my legs against the doorframe.

Two guards outside simply took hold of my legs, and the four of them carried me down the hallway. "Release me! Release me, at once!"

"Let me attend her!" Tiliani cried from somewhere distant. But then a door slammed, and I could no longer hear anything but the stomp of the knights' boots, their various grunts as I writhed, trying to free myself. If I could manage to get away, to bring a few of them down, could I get to the wall? Find a rope and rappel my way to freedom?

"Cease!" said a knight.

"Lady Luciana," said another—not one holding me, but one walking alongside us.

"Sar-Sartori?"

"Yes, 'tis I. You shall make this far easier on yourself if you comply."

"Alas, I cannot," I grunted, writhing again. I was so close to breaking the man's hold on my right leg!

We moved into the turret, and the men were forced to release me to but two of the knights, given the narrow stairwell. I let them think I was giving in, afraid to fight on the incline, but after about ten steps, I writhed again, and the bottom knight fell, swearing. Gathering my legs beneath me, I rammed upward, my head hitting the knight's chin, and he fell back with a cry, against others. I leaped forward, scrambling over the knight below me— still apparently dazed—and down the turret stairs as fast as I could. Men shouted.

The turret door below me slammed open, and I barreled into

the person who had opened it, landing on top of him. I scrambled up and tried to think how far the next turret was across the courtyard, and where the doorway was exactly. I could hear the sound of men running toward me. *Please, God. Help me!*

I ran, my hands outstretched, wanting to rush, and yet anxious not to break my wrists by slamming into a wall. If I could just find that next turret . . .

I partially turned, hearing men closing in from either side, gravel scattering beneath their boots. But the one from my left surprised me with a full-on body tackle, taking us both to the ground. He landed on top of me, and the weight of him kept me from taking a deep breath. "Bind her feet!" he cried, and it was then that I knew it was Captain Sartori. "And her hands behind her!"

I writhed again, trying to get him off me, but another leaned painfully on my legs while a third wound a leather rope around my ankles. He let me rise only when two men again had a firm hold on my arms. They wrenched my arms back painfully and swiftly tied my wrists too—so tightly, I feared for my circulation.

"You have just made this," Captain Sartori said, taking me over his shoulder like a heavy sack of grain, "far harder than it needed to be."

"Oh?" I struggled to breathe with my diaphragm pressed in half by his shoulder. "I should have simply submitted to the ministrations of a man who intends to slowly bleed me to death?"

"Not to death," he said, waiting for a guard to open a door for him. "To *life*. You shall see. Bloodletting has saved many of my loved ones. Do you Sienese have something against it?"

I said nothing in response. It was too much effort. And what would it gain me? I had to reserve my strength for what lay ahead. We entered the narrow hallway that I knew led to the dungeon, and down the steps. This time, I did not struggle, well aware that a fall down this staircase—situated as I was upon his shoulder—might well break my neck.

It was a good twenty degrees colder down here, and the sweat swiftly evaporated from my forehead and neck. He set me down on the cold rock slab that I remembered at the center of the room that had once been used for torture. Would this serve as my "examination" table? At least the torture devices that had once been here were gone.

But even as I thought it, I felt them releasing the binding at my wrists and feet. A man on each limb kept me from escaping. Not that I tried—the chances of getting free of them again and upstairs? Through the courtyard and up to the wall? *Slim to none.*

"Sir Cafaro shall need her gown off for his examination," Captain Sartori said. "Disrobe her."

"What? Nay!" I cried, even as rough hands fumbled at my bodice, untying it.

"He shall need access to your skin, m'lady," Sartori said placatingly. "See to your task, men, and *nothing* more."

I bit my lip as another untied my skirt and let it fall to the floor. I was wrestled out of the bodice, each man careful to not give me an opportunity to lash out. Now solely in my underdress, I was lifted back to the rock slab. A cold ring of metal was clamped down on each wrist, each ankle, and I heard the clatter of chain as each was tightened, leaving me spread-eagled on the table. The rings were loose enough to avoid chafing, but not loose enough for me to pull free.

"The prisoner is secure," Captain Sartori said, slightly out of breath. "Leave us, and one of you, alert Lord Ercole and Sir Cafaro that she is ready."

I heard them clamber out obediently.

"Why did you struggle so?" Sartori asked, when we heard the click of the door atop the stairs. "Why not simply submit to the procedure?"

"Because bloodletting can be fatal," I said, wrenching at my wrist chains. "I know of a man who died of it!" *His name's George*

Washington, and it won't happen for a few hundred years, but still . . .

"Many more survive and improve."

"Because they are strong. In spite of the bloodletting, they survive."

"As are you, m'lady. Never have I met stronger women than those of your family."

I stifled a sigh, exasperated. He did not understand. No one would understand. Not only was the bloodletting risky, but if the doctor did not properly clean his instruments, or my skin . . . would I die of infection?

We heard the door creak open and then boots along the stairs. "Return to the men, Captain," Ercole said, arriving alone. "Tell them to continue on, as normal. Our enemies must not know that something . . . *adverse* might have transpired."

"Yes, m'lord," he said slowly, as if hesitant to leave. I fought the urge to call after him. As much as Ercole had shown me a different side of himself, I did not want to be alone with him, completely at his mercy.

Too late for that, I told myself. *Because you already are.* I bit my lip, waiting for him to speak, act, but he seemed to simply stare at me. I could feel the cool air on the skin at my knee on one leg, my thigh on the other. Goosebumps rose along my bare arms.

"Luciana," he said wearily. "You try me most thoroughly. I call for a man well trained in the medical arts to attend you, and you bring him to his knees?"

"You both laid hands on me without permission."

He laughed softly at this. "You have mettle. And pride. I admire that. But if you ever dare to try and take me down again, there shall be repercussions."

"Release me," I tried. "Send me home to Castello Forelli if I displease you so."

"Nay. I think . . . not. We both know that that might jeopardize my agreement with Lord Romano. But I have another idea. Something that might soothe the heat in your blood."

He settled a broad hand on my thigh.

Wait. What? Is he making a move on me?

"Get your hand off of me!"

"Come now. Might we not be companions rather than enemies, Luciana?"

Companions? He wanted me to be his girlfriend? I remembered Rosa's battered and bruised face, the bruises on her neck, her forearm. And she *had* been his girlfriend, not a captive in his dungeon.

"My blood, too, runs hot."

"Get your hand *off* of me! You are fortunate I am in chains or I would make you pay for daring so. I shall never take *Rosa's* place."

He leaned even closer, as if examining every inch of me. I could feel the warmth of his breath on my lips as he hovered there, then my chin, my neck. I imagined him as I might Dracula, about to take his fill of my blood. And was he not about to? If he allowed Sir Cafaro to do as he wished?

"Rosa was a simpleton," he breathed in my ear, gently pushing a stray lock of hair out of my face. "I like a woman of strength. And of sound mind, which Sir Cafaro—or his compatriot in Firenze—shall restore for you."

"You are betrothed to Lady Celeste," I tried.

"You and I both know that it might take years for her to reach womanhood. As we await that momentous occasion, why not keep ourselves . . . entertained?"

I laughed mirthlessly and shook my head. "You are mad! You attempt to seduce me while I'm *chained in your dungeon*? You are truly so full of yourself that *you* are the one who is blind. My heart belongs to Giulio Greco."

"Giulio Greco," he scoffed. "In time, I shall teach you how to forget him."

I swallowed back bile rising in my throat. He really thought he was impossible to turn down! "You tried to *kill* me."

"Only because you tried to kill *me*," he said lightly. He moved above me and took my hair in both hands, tenderly stroking the length of it and laying it above my head. "Surely we can put that behind us now."

"There is no putting it behind us. I shall carry the scar to my deathbed," I said.

"Oh? I think scars are fascinating. They tell stories." He ran a light finger along the lace of my underdress then along the bumpy line of the scar on my chest. Along the wound he'd given me.

"Cease!" I demanded.

But he ignored me, running two fingers down the length of my bare arm.

"Leave me *alone!*" I growled, wishing I could scratch his eyes out. I could *feel* his leer.

"I fear I cannot," he said. "I must make you presentable for the surgeon." Carefully, he straightened the thin fabric of my underdress over my legs—as if only wanting to protect my modesty—but he completed his task by touching every inch of me that he could.

I shivered with rage and he paused. "Does my touch please you, m'lady?"

"I tremble with the desire to *choke* you," I said, wishing he would come closer again so I could spit in his face. "You want a strong woman?" I lifted my head. "Release me from these chains."

He laughed mirthlessly. "I am a man of strong passions, but I am not a fool. When you are again in your right mind, I shall unchain you. Not before."

The door opened above. "Lord Ercole?" Sir Cafaro called.

"All is well, my friend!" Ercole returned. "I have prepared your patient for your examination and the procedure."

I battled the desire to scream. But such an action would only make the doctor all the more convinced that I was not in my "right mind." *Oh, God,* I prayed. *Oh, God, oh, God, oh, God . . . what am I supposed to do?*

"We shall resume our conversation later," Ercole whispered in my ear.

The doctor reached the bottom of the stairs and approached us. "Lord Ercole," he said, and from the sound of his voice, I guessed he was looking around. "Must we truly see to the lady *here*?"

"The lady attacked my men. She attacked *us*. She shall remain here, until you are sure she is sound and stable."

"I see. I shall need more light. And some blankets to keep the patient warm."

Ercole left my side, and I heard the rustle of a basket, then strike of flint. I could hear new torches crackling and imagined the cavernous room illuminated, as well as their faces in deep shadow.

I gasped as the doctor pressed on my belly. "Does that hurt, m'lady?"

"Nay," I said, feeling a bit foolish. "You only startled me."

"Ahh, forgive me for that. I should have warned you." He patted my arm and resumed probing my belly. "'Tis a shame we ended up in this dismal place. After we finish, if you are stable and calm, mayhap Lord Ercole shall allow you to return to your quarters."

"We shall see what good the bleeding does," Ercole said. By his tone, I knew it would be his call, not the doc's. And he was getting a thrill, seeing me chained up.

"Have you had any terrible gas?" the doctor asked.

"What?" I sighed. "Nay."

"Any diarrhea?"

"Nay."

"Vomiting?"

"Nay."

"She vomited in my presence," Ercole said.

I inwardly groaned.

"You must tell me the truth, m'lady."

"That was not related to this, sir."

"You might be surprised," he said. He moved to palpate my lymph nodes beneath my jaw, then under my armpits. "A preponderance of black bile sometimes walks hand in hand with cancer." I vaguely remembered that medieval physicians were obsessed with bodily functions, especially urination and defecation, as it helped them discern when some internal disease was occurring. "Now let us see to the bloodletting and on the morrow—"

"Please, do not let my blood, my lord," I begged him. "Do you not see? I am not ailing! I am strong!"

"Too strong, I would say," he responded. "I believe you now carry too *much* blood. After your injury, your body likely became imbalanced. Was your last monthly bleed heavy, normal, or lighter than usual?"

He was asking about my period? "It was . . . normal."

"Hmm," he said, as if my memory did not square up with his thought process. "Now, this shall not hurt a bit, m'lady. Cease your fretting! I am quite good at what I do."

I was panting, trying to shove down the need to weep, straining at my bonds. I felt so helpless! "Nay!" I cried. "I demand that you stop this at once!"

"This is for your own good, Luciana." Ercole grabbed my hand and pulled my arm straight. "Proceed," he directed the doctor.

I felt the hot slice of a sharp, thin knife at my elbow and, immediately, the trickle of warm blood. "There it is," Sir Cafaro said. "What did I tell you? 'Twas perfectly executed. You did not feel a thing, did you?"

To be honest, it hadn't hurt much. What hurt most was the fact that they had totally ignored my demands. Made a move on my body of which I did not approve. I closed my eyes and tried to get ahold of myself. *It's over, Luci. The deed is done. Now how can you best maneuver?*

It came to me at once.

Work the doc.

Because the last thing I wanted was to be left alone, chained and weak from blood loss, with Andrea Ercole Paratore.

21

TILIANI

"Let us out!" I cried, ramming my fist into the door again. I had done it so many times over the last hours that my hand was bruised. "Take us to Lady Betarrini!" Celeste cried behind me, and I was clearly not convincing the guards outside our door, so I turned and took her into my arms. "Shhh," I soothed, stroking her hair. "Come." I led her to the edge of the bed and held her until her tears eventually abated.

"Why-why would they take her away?" she sniffed, wiping her nose with a handkerchief.

"They wanted to let her blood, and she did not want that. In Britannia, it must not be common."

"Why is Lady Luciana so against it? Mama has had it done many times and made a recovery each time. Papa too. A barber-surgeon came to bleed me when I had a terrible fever, and I was quite small."

I wrestled with how to answer. "Our family simply does not believe it aids us. Lady Adri says that it harms more than helps, so we do not do it."

"But could Lady Luciana not have allowed it, only this once?"

I lifted my brows. In retrospect, it might have saved us from much angst. But once the Betarrinis got an idea in their heads, they were as stubborn as any Forelli. Zia Gabi was a perfect example. Nona, too, in her own quiet way.

A knock sounded at the door. The bar was lifted, and in walked Andrea Ercole, followed by two maids. One carried a platter full of food, the other a pitcher and three goblets.

I rose and Celeste followed.

"Remain where you are," Ercole demanded. "I do not care to assail either of you as we did Lady Luciana."

"That was most dreadful," Celeste said, sounding small and frightened.

"I agree." He gave her a sorrowful look. "But we did it solely to aid Lady Luciana. At times, we must face the dreadful in order to get beyond it to something better." His face brightened. "You shall see. In a matter of days, Luciana shall be much improved. Mayhap Sir Cafaro shall even help her regain her sight—or at the very least, curtail her visions."

"My grandmother said it was merely her mind, searching for stimulation while grappling with her blindness."

"Yes, well"—he poured us both a goblet of watered wine—"I prefer that does not occur while she is in my care." He handed one to me. "I do not want the Forellis claiming that she suffered here and this is the result."

"So you took her away and restrained her," I said bitingly. "Where is she? Did you take her to the dungeon?"

"She is safe and well cared for. You need not fret over her, either of you." He reached out and stroked Celeste's hair like he might a treasured little sister.

I pulled her closer, out of his reach, and he frowned at me. "I am not the enemy, Tiliani. I wish only to aid your cousin."

"Do you?" Or would it be better for him if one of us was out of the way? "Your agreement with Lord Romano and my family is null and void if anything unsavory happens to me or Luciana. I think this qualifies as something unsavory. We were to remain together at all times."

He topped off his goblet—this time, straight wine from a jug—and considered me. "They shall not hear of it."

"Oh, yes, they shall. I shall report it this evening when I send my missive, and we three shall depart by nightfall."

"Nay, you shall not." He looked not at me, but the window. He took another sip. "This shall be our secret." His tone was deadly calm. A shiver ran down my back.

"Why would I keep your secret?"

"Because if you do not, I shall separate you further." He gave me a meaningful look. Did he mean that he would take Celeste from me? Send Luciana to Firenze? What?

I squared off with him, tucking Celeste behind me. "In a matter of hours, my family will know that something is not right. They shall demand to see us. Storm the castello within days. And what would that achieve? Was this all not meant as an attempt at peace?"

"Which is why this shall remain between us."

He said it in a tone like he was sharing a mindless pleasantry, not as the threat it plainly was. So as not to alarm Celeste?

"This castello," he went on, patting the rough rock of the wall, "can withstand weeks of attack. We have supplies, water, and weapons. But Firenze would rise to our defense long before we would have to resort to our stores."

I threw up my hands. "So we are back to where we began! Why bother with these games? Celeste may not reach womanhood for a year—even three."

"I am aware. That is why I am toying with the idea of taking Luciana as my consort. It shall afford me . . . patience."

I paused, fighting for a breath. "Luciana?" Had I misheard him?

"Consort?" Celeste asked, forehead wrinkling.

A close-lipped smile spread across his face. "I beg your pardon, Lady Celeste. It only means that Lady Luciana and I would form a strong bond and spend time together. 'Twill keep me entertained and allow me to await you, my little bride."

She took my hand and glanced warily between me and Ercole,

her brows still knit in confusion over the word *consort*. "Whatever would please you, Lord Ercole," she said, with a dip of a curtsey.

"Lady Betarrini's heart belongs to Giulio Greco." The burn of righteous anger rose along my jaw. "She shall not consent to this." *To say nothing of how she loathes you!*

"I believe she shall. You all are dear to her. She was willing to risk her life before to save you. Why would she not pledge her . . . companionship?"

I laughed. "She would not have you even if Giulio did not hold her heart."

"I disagree." A slow smile spread across his face. "I shall persuade her in time. She may be a She-Wolf, but I have never met a woman who refused me for long. And once she sees how it will serve us *all*, we can resume our life together in peace."

I bit my tongue, seething. There was no reasoning with a man as mad as Ercole. As soon as I thought I understood where he was headed, he changed course. Where was Luciana? What had he done? Drugged her? Chained her? Bled her until she was senseless? "Allow us to attend her."

"Nay," he said, draining his goblet. He strode over to the door, and I followed him.

"Allow me to see her. Even for a moment."

"Mayhap on the morrow. Tonight, you all have need of a good meal and a solid slumber."

But as he left us, I feared he would not allow Luciana the same.

LUCIANA

The first thing I noticed as I roused was how cold my nose was. I tried to lift my hand to cover it, but felt the weight of the manacle, heard the chain, and remembered.

"Ahh, there you are," said Sir Cafaro from somewhere to my left. "You needed that good rest."

Good rest? I didn't remember falling asleep. More likely I'd succumbed to unconsciousness after losing a fair amount of blood. I shifted, my back aching from too long in one position—and on a stone slab, at that. But he'd covered me with several blankets at least. My nose was the only part of me that was chilled.

"How do you feel, dear woman?"

"Weak from blood loss, you idiot," I muttered in English.

He *tsked*, as if my use of English meant I was not in my right mind. My earlier thought—*work the doc*—came back to me.

"I feel . . . curiously *restored*," I said in Tuscan.

"Ahh, yes," he said, clearly pleased. "You see? I knew it was what you needed!"

"I should have listened to you from the start. Forgive me?"

"Of course, of course, my lady." He patted my shoulder. "You are not the first to resist and later find you were in error. I have been seeing to the infirm for some time."

"I feel much calmer now. Might you release me from the chains?"

He hesitated. He may be pleased with his results, but he clearly remembered I had him in a wristlock and on the floor only hours ago. And he'd seen me flip Andrea to his back. "I-I think that I must wait for Lord Paratore to decide on that."

"Please. Call some guards down if you must. I need only to be free. My fingers are numb!"

He examined my fingers—checking to see if they were going blue? The temperature? And then made a concerned sound. "I see, I see," he muttered. He made more sounds under his breath and seemed to be talking to himself. Did he fear Ercole's rage? I knew I would, if I were in his employ.

"Do call some guards down," I said again. "I want you to stay in our lord's good graces."

I could feel his stare. "You *are* quite restored, are you not?

M'lord shall be most pleased! Let us set you to rights and back into your gown." He went to the base of the stairs and rang a metal bell.

We heard the door creak open above. "Sir Cafaro?" called a man.

"Yes! Please send down four guards to tend to Lady Betarrini."

The man agreed and shut the door. I wondered if I had time to sweet-talk my way out of my bonds, lock the doctor in a cell, and prepare to fight off four armed knights, but knew it was hopeless. Hearing I'd roused, Ercole might return, and then I'd have to deal with him too. My goal was to get to the wall and escape, but could I leave Tiliani and Celeste behind? Was my priority to save myself, now that Ercole had set his creepy sights on me?

When the door opened again, it was Ercole who came down first, followed by what sounded like knights and a maidservant. "The lady has recovered?"

"She is most different!" said the doctor. "Acting more the genteel lady."

"Do not be fooled," Ercole said. "The lady is a good actor."

"Like you act the nobleman?" I said, before I thought it through.

He let out a laugh. "Exactly so." He leaned closer to me. "Another way in which we are well suited." He straightened. "Unlock her chains. Help her to dress."

"Very good," said the doctor. "She would do well to take supper with us, up by a warm fire."

"Ahh, I think not," Ercole said. "Lady Betarrini shall remain down here for the night, if not for the next few days."

"Down here!" said the man. "But 'tis far too cold."

"Send for more blankets," Ercole demanded. "And some soup. A bit of warmth in her belly shall be restorative."

The lock sprang open on one heavy manacle and then the other at my wrists. A guard moved to my feet, as I sat up and rubbed my aching wrists. My ankles were freed in short order, and I quickly slid my legs over the edge of the table. The movement seemed to make me dizzy.

"Easy now, take care!" said the doctor, grabbing my arm as I swayed. "Take a deep breath, m'lady."

I did as he asked, in through my nose, out through my mouth, and again. Gradually, I felt steadier. Maybe it was late? Who knew how long I was out? Maybe I was hungry, as well as suffering from blood loss?

"I have your bodice, m'lady," a knight said, touching my arm. Sir Sartori.

"Thank you." I lifted my hands so he could guide my hands into the sleeves. If it had to be a man, I was glad it was him. He laced me up from the back, his movements perfunctory.

"Your skirt, m'lady," Sir Cafaro said gently, placing it in my hands. "You feel steady enough to stand?"

"I think so," I lied. I edged off the table, stepped into my skirt, and tied it myself. Just being dressed again made me feel more myself. "May I return to my quarters, Sir Cafaro?" I asked sweetly, pretending like I hadn't heard Ercole's directions. I rubbed my hands together. "'Twill be good to sit by a warm fire."

"Mayhap on the morrow," Cafaro whispered, patting my arm. "Tonight, we shall do our best to make you as comfortable as possible here."

I blinked back tears. "What if I catch a chill down here?"

"You shall have plenty of blankets," Ercole said. I could picture him leaning against the wall, arms crossed, totally unmoved by my act of weakness. The doctor was my only chance.

"If she does catch a chill, she might develop a fever, m'lord," the doctor tried.

"Then you shall deal with that on the morrow. You can stay with us for another few days, yes?"

"Yes, but I do think—"

"Hold that thought, friend. I have had more experience with this one. She seems the innocent, suffering maiden. But she is clever and using your compassion for her own purposes."

I frowned and shook my head, as if totally confused by what he was saying.

"Remember this—all of you—there is a reason she is called the newest She-Wolf of Siena." He took hold of my arm and hurried me across the floor. He flung me forward, and I took several steps before I stopped and straightened. The iron door of a cell clanged shut before I understood what he had done.

"M'lord, there is no need for this," I said, moving toward him. "We have done all you asked of us since we arrived, have we not?"

"Until I asked you to submit to my authority."

"And I was wrong in that, obviously. Sir Cafaro has come to my aid. I shall not fear the bloodletting next time."

"You dared to put me on my back," he bit out.

"I reacted without thought—"

"And tonight you may give it more thought, here in this cell. On the morrow, we shall discuss the future. Ways in which you might work your way back . . . to a much nicer bed."

I swallowed hard, ignoring his innuendo. "If Tiliani does not send the evening missive, telling our family that all is well, they shall surround the castello this very night."

He paused. "With you down here, Tiliani shall write the note as I dictate it."

I clenched my fists. "They shall demand to see us in time."

"We have invited them for a feast. They shall have no just cause to attack us before then. And much, dear woman, much can be accomplished in the span of days."

I swallowed hard. He spoke of me. What did he intend to do?

He instructed everyone to go.

"You cannot leave me here!" I cried, hating that I sounded more a little girl than a grown woman.

"A servant shall be along shortly with soup for your belly and blankets for your bed," he said from across the room. "In the morning we shall see if you are further . . . improved."

22

LUCIANA

The door clanged shut behind him, and I felt the chasm of the dungeon anew. I shivered as the knights' footfalls faded, and I heard nothing but my own pulse in my ears—and the skitter of a rat. I hugged myself. *Now what, Luci?*

I leaned against the wall and sank to my haunches, wondering if I could have done something differently. I mean, besides flipping Ercole on his back and bringing the doctor to his knees. Yeah, that hadn't been the best call. I'd reacted, rather than responded. Fought, since fleeing wasn't an option.

Would Nico know something was up when I didn't appear on the wall at midnight? Or would he figure that I was merely unable to get there? I wished we had super-twin telepathy, and he could feel my stress through the five-foot thick walls.

The door creaked open above, and I listened. A maid—or two, from the sound of their slippers on stone rather than the heavier clomp of boots.

"We have your blankets and some soup, m'lady," said one. I didn't recognize her voice.

"Thank you," I said wearily, forcing myself to rise.

"There is an opening down here, m'lady, where we can pass them to you."

I ran my fingers over the cold, rough metal bars until I reached them.

"There are three more good blankets here, m'lady," the girl said. "Make certain you have enough on the ground beneath you to ward off the chill and put the others on top."

I nodded. "Have you tended to prisoners down here before?"

"No, m'lady." She sounded embarrassed. "You are the first. 'Tisn't a place for a lady, if you ask me."

"Nay," I shivered.

"Here is some soup," said another girl, timidly.

"'Tis full, so mind yourself," said the first.

I set down the blankets and reached for the bowl. "*Grazie*," I said. "I am very hungry. What time is it?"

"The sun has set, and we must be off to serve those about to sup in the Hall. We shall say an extra prayer for you this night, m'lady. Be well, and on the morrow, m'lord shall surely allow you to return to your quarters."

I wasn't so certain. He might keep me here, thinking he could force my decision to be his mistress. Could I outlast his brand of crazy? I sat on the stack of blankets and ate every bit of my soup straight away, conscious that if I didn't, the rat would happily do so. My mind whirled, but my body felt like I'd gone ten rounds in a ring, probably due to the bloodletting. I settled on the blankets, as the maid had suggested. The chill of the stones beneath still permeated upward, but huddled beneath the thick woolens, I got modestly warm. I turned to my side, resting my head on one arm, and heard the torch sputtering in its holder.

At least I didn't have to watch it go out and witness the dungeon go completely dark. I let out a sarcastic laugh. *The upside of being blind.*

I thought about seeing the monkey and how good it felt to think I was seeing anything again. How hope had warred with confusion in my mind and heart. And if I had to imagine seeing anything, I wished it had been Giulio instead of Ercole. How I longed for him! The feel of his strong arms around me, the warmth of cuddling against his chest. I went to sleep, praying that somehow, some way, we would soon be reunited.

I awakened some hours later, hearing footsteps on the stairs again, as well as the crackle of a torch. I blinked and frowned. My vision was blurry, but I could see! *I could see.* Light cut through deep shadows. I rose, stumbling, my knees shaky. "Who is there?" I asked.

The stairwell was illuminated and my visitor's shadow grew larger as they neared.

"Tiliani?" I whispered. "N-Nico?"

My fingers clung to the iron bars, and I swayed. Why did I feel like I might faint?

I saw his boots first, and I dragged my eyes upward, unable to believe what I was seeing. "Giulio?" I gasped. I leaned closer, wishing I could somehow melt through the bars. "How-how is it that you are here?" I smiled, and tears ran down my cheeks in sweet relief. "Giulio, I can see you!"

"You can?" he asked.

"Yes! Could it have been the bloodletting? Did it heal me?" I asked. There was no way, was there? But what else could explain this, my vision's sudden, miraculous return?

"Mayhap." His voice sounded strange, but I couldn't get over the joy of seeing him again—let alone the fact that he was here! I wasn't alone! He had come to rescue me!

He smiled at me and tentatively covered one of my hands with his own.

His action seemed odd, but we had no time to mess around. "Do you have a key? Can you get me out of here?"

"Oh, yes." As if remembering himself, he pulled the key from somewhere, slipped it into the lock, and pulled the door open.

"How did you get in here? Are you alone?" I asked, rushing into his arms.

"Yes," he whispered. Belatedly, he pulled me closer and stroked my back.

"I missed you so!" I said, wondering if I had forgotten exactly how it felt to be in his arms in the short time we were apart. He felt . . . different. I blinked. My vision was still blurry—as if I had slipped underwater.

"As I did you," he said.

I lifted my chin, eager for a quick kiss, the reassurance of it before we found our way to Tiliani and Celeste and made our escape. Or were our people already collecting them?

He leaned down and covered my lips with his own, demanding, hungry. His hands pressed against me, and he eased me backward until I hit the stone wall.

I frowned. He did not taste like Giulio. Smell like Giulio. Feel like Giulio.

Nor was he acting like Giulio. Desire I had known with my beloved, but this was more like . . . wanton *lust*.

"No, wait," I said in English. I tried to push him back and instinctively knew this man was a bit taller, a bit lankier. I blinked and my vision grew murkier. "Giulio. Help me . . . I-I am losing—"

"Oh, I shall," he said huskily, kissing my neck as he leaned in again.

And as my vision became utterly dark again, the lightbulb turned on in my brain.

This was not Giulio.

It was Ercole.

It was just another figment of my imagination, thinking Giulio was here now. A vision. But Ercole thought he could fool me. He thought he could have me, compromise me, use me, while I thought him to be Giulio.

What he did not know was that Giulio Greco would never compromise or take advantage of me.

I forced myself to let him go on kissing me, making sounds as if I were enjoying it, trying to think my way through. He was alone. It was late. Mayhap most of the castello slept. Had he left the key in the lock? I couldn't remember the sound of it slipping back out, only the creak of the door opening.

I lifted the hair off my neck and stretched languidly. "Oh, Giulio, please," I said, as Ercole's hands roamed. "Will you not lie back on my blankets?"

"Your blankets?" he said in confusion, leaning away from me.

"Yes," I said with a grin. "I have something special in mind for you."

"Do you?" he asked wickedly. "How delightful."

"Mmm-hmmm," I said with a half smile.

He backed up, pulling me with him until he could kneel on the blankets. I knew where we were in the cell then. Could imagine the door, wide open behind me. He kissed me on the belly, tugging at the ribbon that held my bodice closed. I put a hand over his. "Not yet, beloved. Lie back."

"I wish I had brought a second torch for this," he said, releasing me.

I whirled and reached for the door, blessedly passing right by it. The tips of my fingers touched a bar, I grabbed and pulled, my heart racing when it clanged shut. He cried out in anger. I reached desperately for the keys, praying they were still in the lock. He grabbed my left arm and rammed me against the bars.

I hit my forehead and groaned, but my right hand had found the keys. I turned it in the lock and then flung the keys to the floor behind me. But now Ercole had a grasp on my arm and his other hand tangled in my hair. We stood there, grunting and gasping. I reached through the bars with my right hand and clawed at his face, his eyes. I managed to scrape one cheek before he let go of my hair. I turned, grabbed hold of his wrist and used my full body weight to ram it backward.

He screamed as the bones broke, and he fell to his knees, gasping.

"Do not fear," I said. "I hear the lord of this castello called in a most excellent practitioner of the medical arts. He shall tend to you, when? Come morn?" I assumed he had told others not to disturb him down here. Who knew what he had intended to do with me even before he found I was having a hallucination?

"What . . . have you . . . *done?*" he screamed. I backed away from the cell as I heard him rise. "Release me now," he said. "You cannot escape the castello. And my fury only rises by the moment."

"What have *I* done?" I repeated incredulously. "At least I did not take advantage of a woman! I did not pretend to be someone else!"

"You knew it was me. I felt you melting into my touch."

"When I thought you were my beloved. Not my sworn enemy."

I was wasting time with him. Who knew how long it would take to get to Tiliani and Celeste and for us all to escape?

"Guards!" he screamed. "*Guards!*"

I felt my way forward, going as fast as I could, praying the men wouldn't hear him above. Stone was soundproof, right? Or at least a great muffler? *That's why they have the bell!* I hurried up the stairs, hoping that if they did hear him, I could at least surprise them. At the top, I pulled my skirt between my legs and tucked it in the waistband. If I couldn't see, I wanted full freedom to move, at least. I listened against the wooden door. Was it unguarded? Ercole would not have expected trouble from me, locked in the cell, but was he so arrogant as to come alone?

He's totally that arrogant.

I felt along the door for the handle. This one likely wouldn't be barred on either side—after all, any prisoners would be kept behind iron bars or in chains below. I unlatched it and let it creak open a few inches, widening my stance and lifting my arms in preparation, but no one reacted. Quietly, I eased out the door and closed it behind me before anyone patrolling the courtyard heard Ercole shouting below.

Once shut, I was relieved that I could barely hear him—and only right by the door. I stood there a moment, trying to remember the structures about me. Was I hidden in shadow, or standing under a torch? I could not hear the crackle of one burning, nor smell any smoke. *Please, God, hide me!*

I heard men approaching and quickly slid to my left, reached a corner, and rounded it. I stilled, waiting for them to pass. They were laughing, distracted, and passed by without notice. I heard them reach a door—the castle keep?—and go inside. The door seemed to be unguarded. Were the only guards on the wall, as they were at Castello Forelli?

I tried to figure out what to do. Could I truly manage to enter the keep, get to Tiliani's room, and free her and Celeste? Or was my best chance to try and escape to tell our family what was transpiring inside Castello Paratore? What if it was way past midnight and Nico wasn't near the wall? How would I cover the distance to Castello Forelli without getting lost or captured again?

My mind whirled and my heart pounded. Standing here, doing nothing, was not going to help me at all! I would neither escape nor help Til and Celeste.

A distant clanging jolted me out of my indecision.

Ercole had somehow managed to reach a metal bar of some sort and was banging it against the bars of his cell. It was distant, but would gradually draw someone's attention, like an alarm clock going off in the next room.

"Do you hear that?" a guard asked, pausing on the allure, not far from where I stood. "What is that?"

"Wait here. I shall go and find out," said a second guard.

Hearing them speak gave me my bearings. I was almost directly below the western stairwell to the wall. I took a long, slow breath, knowing the choice had been made for me. *In minutes, Ercole will*

be discovered and the alarm sounded. My only chance is the wall. If
he gets his hands on me again, he might be mad enough to kill me.

I slid toward the stairwell turret—praying the guard above
would not notice me—found the door and went to the far side.
In seconds, the guard came through the door and left it open
as he stood, quietly listening, then took off at a trot toward the
dungeon's entrance. I hurried up the stairwell, knowing the guard
would likely proceed at a similar pace, even if he paused at the
end, unsure of what was about to greet him below.

I felt much the same. Would the guard see me? Or was his
attention solely on the courtyard below? By now the dungeon's
door was open and Ercole's screams all the clearer. Surely every
guard on the wall had to be on the interior, awaiting news. I heard
one call to the other, wondering what was up. *Please, let them all
be watching for Ercole.*

I could hear the man swearing and screaming to be *after the
woman* as I rounded the stairwell's top and scurried along the
allure, praying I would run into a rope and not a knight on duty. I
made good progress, five seconds, then maybe ten passing without
a further alarm sounding. They all seemed to be trying to make
out what Lord Ercole was saying, a most excellent distraction.

And then I stubbed my toe and knocked over a bucket,
almost falling.

I stifled a groan and immediately dropped into a ball. If the
guards were looking along my expanse of wall, hopefully they'd see
nothing. When no shout arose, only Ercole's screams becoming
ever clearer—*The woman! Lady Betarrini! Find her!*—I felt out and
forward for the bucket. It was about five feet away, on the other
side of a mound of rope! Had they been using it for repairs? Or to
haul up rocks to use as weapons?

Whatever the cause, I was not complaining. I rose, dropped
it over the side, and crouched again as it clattered against the
rock wall.

"What was that?" cried a guard, maybe fifty feet away.

I didn't have time to think. I couldn't see, which in this case, was a blessing. Maybe if I was my normal, sighted, sane self, I wouldn't be doing this.

I prayed that the bucket was somewhere near the bottom.

And then I hauled myself over the edge of the wall, took a good grip on the rope, and dangled, abandoning the majority of Gabi's rappelling instructions. I slid for a few feet, anxious to put some distance between me and any grappling hook. Then a few more for good measure. I bumped against the castle wall, turned, and put my feet against it. I hauled myself upward, held tight with one hand, and pulled the rope around my thigh and over my shoulder, then fisted it beneath my butt. Wishing I'd remembered to wrap my hands, I slid again, trying to ignore the burn. But more men were shouting above. I slid a good distance more, the fibers cutting into my neck.

I felt a tug on the rope and looked up by reflex.

"There she is!" yelled one. "I see her! 'Tis the lady on the rope!"

"Do not cut it, you fool! He wants her alive!"

"Torches! More torches!"

I felt the whir of a falling torch and smelled it as it passed—then heard it land below. I imagined it made me all the easier to see. I bit my lip and slid down farther.

"Lord Paratore! M'lord! She is here and attempting escape!"

"Knights to arms! To the gates! Perimeter check at once!"

I concentrated on their words. Imagined their faces. Imagined Ercole's face when he learned I was over the wall. I could not hear his shout, among the others.

Did that mean he was heading for the gates himself?

Preparing to ride around and capture me, even as I reached the end of the rope?

I slid some more and tried to stifle a cry as skin tore. How much farther? Could my hands even hold out that long?

I thought about switching hands, but I feared my bleeding palms would slip. They were already slick. I gritted my teeth and forced myself to release the tension on the rope below, as well as a bit of the rope above. And then again—this time giving voice to my cry.

"Luciana! Luci!" cried my brother, forcing me to concentrate on something beyond my own scorching palms. "I am here! You are almost to the bottom!"

Nico! Nico was here! Relief and hope made my heart pause and then pound anew.

"Intruders! Knights to arms!" I heard men shout above. An arrow whizzed by me and hit stone below.

Below. Nico had said I wasn't far, but the arrow told me I was within what? Ten, fifteen feet? Someone scrambled across stones below me.

"Hurry!" he said. Nico again. This was our chance. To escape. Get to the tunnel. Regain my sight.

But where was Giulio?

"Only a little farther, beloved," Giulio said, and a cry of relief broke through my lips at his very real, very close voice. My Giulio. Not another hallucination. "Slide a bit more."

We all heard the creak of the massive gates on the far side of the castello.

"Make haste!" Giulio cried.

I dropped for a span, but when it came time for me to stop, I had not the strength. I went barreling down and, with a cry, landed half on Giulio.

23

LUCIANA

I groaned and rose, rubbing my stinging elbow and apologizing to Giulio. "Are you all right?" I asked when my brother arrived. Another person panted beside him—female. Ilaria.

"Epic dismount, sis," Nico said with a laugh, grabbing my shoulder and urging me behind him. "But we gotta go!" He bent and lifted me, piggyback style, and hurried over the rock bed as fast as he could. Giulio and Ilaria flanked us, and then I felt the brush of leaves and knew we were in the woods. With horses! They'd brought horses!

They mounted and Giulio said, "Your arm, Luciana."

I'd no sooner lifted it than I felt his gelding brush by and Giulio grab hold of my forearm. He swung me up and behind him, the horse surging into motion. The other two followed us, but I knew Ercole's knights were not far behind.

Giulio bent lower and I with him. I thought he was breaking for the road to Castello Forelli, but then he whirled and made a broad turn to the right. I heard the others following us, urging their mounts to an even faster speed. Where were they going? Were other knights closing in on us somehow?

But then Giulio pulled up on his gelding's reins and rapidly dismounted, urging me to follow. "Come! Come quickly!"

I dropped down into his arms, but he did not embrace

me. He slapped the horse's rump, sending it away with a command for *home.*

As did Ilaria and Domenico . . . What was happening? Weren't the bad guys—

"C'mon, Luci." Nico grabbed my elbow and rushed me along. "We're *here.* At the tomb. We're going to make the leap. Right now."

"Right now," I said, feeling as if this was a dream.

"Right now."

"Giulio? Ilaria?" I needed assurance. I couldn't risk Giulio staying behind. I knew he was willing to sacrifice himself for me. But I wouldn't allow it.

"They're coming with us! Now duck your head and crawl." Nico shoved me downward. "Fast."

I did as he said, ignoring how pebbles and rocks scratched and pierced my already-raw palms and tender knees. I had to move— make way, so the rest weren't caught! I scrambled to my feet once I was clear of the entrance and edged along the wall.

"Luci?" Nico asked.

"Over here. Near the prints?"

"Feel for them. They'll be hot."

I began feeling for them, finding old, dead stone, wondering if I was leaving a twenty-first-century person's DNA in streaks of blood deposited in the fourteenth century. What would Manero make of *that* carbon dating? "Giulio? Ilaria?" I asked anxiously, even as I heard them rise behind us. They froze, and we all heard multiple horses racing past. Chasing the mounts to Castello Forelli?

I giggled, feeling a tad manic. "Well done."

"Don't congratulate us yet," Nico groused. "They may come back around. Let's be gone when they do." He felt around the wall, too, in the dark.

"Here," I said, finding the source I'd just passed over.

Nico moved to my left. "Over here," he directed Giulio and

Ilaria. "Grab hold of us, and no matter what, do not let go. Luci and I will free ourselves of the wall when it is time."

"Free yourselves?" Giulio grumbled. "It holds on to you?" He wrapped his right arm around my waist, the other around Ilaria, I guessed. She likely held on to my brother and Giulio.

"Ready?" Nico asked in English.

"Let's go," I returned.

"Three, two, one, now!"

Together we settled our hands on the prints. I moved to match the heat signature, praying I was doing it right, praying that my bloody palm would not impede our progress. But even as I did so, I felt the heat rising, the searing sensation as if my skin was becoming part of molten rock. Felt my body spinning deep within, as if from the belly outward. As if I was becoming smaller, ever smaller, then bigger, ever bigger.

I fell away from the wall, once again on top of Giulio Greco in the most embarrassing sort of way—for the second time that night. But as we maneuvered away from each other, I plopped on my butt, mouth agape.

Because it wasn't night.

It was day. Light streamed in from the tomb raider's hole above us. Over my brother, brushing dirt off Ilaria, laughing. Over Giulio, looking at me in fear and then wonder. I rubbed my eyes and looked at them all again. There was no way I was having a hallucination with all four of us in it, was I? Seeing this whole tomb?

Was the whole thing a hallucination? My escape?

I turned and was sick.

Giulio put a gentling hand on my back and bent over with me. "Beloved, are you overcome? Please. Rise. Look at me."

I rose, still feeling queasy, afraid this was all going to disappear in a moment. That I'd find myself back in Ercole's wretched dungeon, him laughing at me.

Giulio gripped my upper arms and stared into my eyes. Even

in deep shadow and a bit blurry, I knew this was different than my last vision. I took a deep breath, daring to hope.

"Beloved, can you *see* me?" he asked.

I nodded. "I-I think so." I lifted my hand and traced his face, feeling his whiskers along chin and cheek. He *felt* like the real Giulio.

Nico wrapped an arm around Giulio's neck. "How many fingers am I holding up?"

I blinked, and my vision cleared a bit more. "Three."

"Now?"

I lifted a brow. "None. Your hand is fisted."

Nico whooped and then dropped his tone to a whisper, glancing over his shoulder. "Sorry. Forgot," he said to me in English. "Let's get back, eh?" We could hear two men talking, not far from the tomb entrance. Manero's grad students? Then a shout of alarm.

"Let's go." I reached for Giulio and pulled him close. Just to make sure. And to my relief, he smelled like the man I loved. I turned in his arms, pulling him closer as we resumed the position to make the leap home.

Nico and I were just reaching for the wall when a net fell down upon us.

"What the—?" Nico said.

I tried pulling it off me but seemed to just entangle myself further.

And that was when an alarm began shrieking.

TILIANI

I paced the room barefoot, trying to keep Celeste asleep, while wondering how the child slept through the commotion clanging through the castello. What had happened? Were we under attack?

It made no sense. My family would not attack, not with us inside. And I had sent the evening missive, exactly as Ercole had dictated.

Was it Luciana? Was she in danger? Were they bleeding her again? Why had they not brought her back to us? Was she ailing?

I wrung my hands and continued to pace and, for the hundredth time, tried the door latch, only to find it still locked. I patted on the door again. "Please," I said quietly, loud enough to be heard by a door guard, but hopefully not wake Celeste. "Is anyone there?"

No one responded. Were they all on the wall, defending the castello?

I went back to the tiny window—nothing more than an arrow slit—and moved about, trying to see all I could down below in the courtyard. I managed only to glimpse knights rushing about, some with swords drawn or carrying bows in their hands. Some carried torches as they ran, quivers of arrows on their shoulders. Something was most assuredly happening on the wall or at the gates. I had heard them open earlier, and now, they were opening again.

Was that a call announcing Lord Paratore?

I could not be certain.

But in minutes, I was certain of one thing. He was coming my way. I could hear him screaming at men as he passed. Blaming. Belittling. Sending furniture crashing against the hall walls.

I backed up and climbed onto the bed before Celeste, shielding her. "Celeste, wake up. Get behind me," I said as she roused, delicate brows arcing in fear.

"Open it!" Ercole screamed. "Make way!"

The latch on our door was unfastened, and the door rammed against the wall. Celeste gasped. Ercole strode directly toward us, paused and took a deep breath, as if attempting to regain his composure. His right hand was clenched awkwardly against his chest. Blood ran down his cheek from a deep scratch—Luciana's doing? He pinched the bridge of his nose for a moment and then spread out his left arm.

"Lady Betarrini is not to be found. She managed—" He broke off, noticing his voice rising. "She managed to make her way out of the castello. Outside, she was aided by others. While in pursuit, she and her companions disappeared. I beg you, Lady Forelli, for the sake of our tentative peace, please disclose the location of their hiding place. We intercepted their horses en route to Castello Forelli, but their riders are absent. The only place they could be is somewhere in the forest. Is there a glade or a rock formation that makes a good hiding place?"

I smiled, hope washing through me. *Their riders are absent.*

There was only one explanation. The tomb.

My smile aggravated him, and he lashed out, grabbing hold of my neck.

"M'lord!" Celeste cried, yanking at his arm.

He ignored her. "You *know*." He pulled me closer to his face. "You know where they are. Tell me."

"N-nay," I choked out in defiance, clawing at his fingers.

"My *lord*!" Celeste screamed.

His face flushed red with fury. And then he abruptly released his hold on me, flinging Celeste back to the pillows. He whirled away, his good hand on his hip. Had Luciana broken the other? He lifted his head to the ceiling—as if beseeching God? His forefather, Cosimo Paratore?

Andrea half turned. He waved at me, ignoring Celeste quietly weeping behind me. "You realize what Luciana has done, do you not?"

"Escaped you and your wretched bloodletting, at the very least," I said.

"That was done for her own well-being," he bit back.

"In the dungeon? In shackles, I presume?"

"You saw her! She was unreasonable."

"And keeping her there, afterward? How did you know she was gone, Lord Paratore? Given the hour?" I narrowed my eyes at him, remembering the Forelli chambermaid and Rosa. Had he gone down to abuse Luciana? Make her his "consort"? Few things would make her run and leave us behind.

His eyes shifted over mine, and he leaned closer again. "I went to make certain she was well. And she threw herself at me as if she meant to embrace her new role as my consort."

I puzzled over his words. "Luciana would never do that. With you, of all people." *Unless she used his own game against him . . . pretended seduction in order to escape.*

"With me," he said tonelessly. "Is it so difficult for you to see what most women see in me?"

"Most women do not see anything in you. They see only what you portray on the outside. If they knew what was inside . . ."

"My goal is peace and prosperity for all of us, as quickly as we can obtain it," he said wearily. "Apparently, we must return to our first plan and await Lady Celeste's maturity to see it through."

Understanding dawned. Luciana had bested him. And that enraged him. What had he done to her before she broke his hand? How had she managed to escape both the dungeon and the castello itself?

I was glad she was free. Safe, with our family. Finding healing through the tunnel passage. *Please, Lord, bring them home to us.* Who knew how long they would be gone? Zia Gabi and Mama and Nona were gone for years when they'd left in search of my grandfather.

So we might have to see this through without the Betarrinis.

"We need to return to the table with Lord Romano and my family. Without Luciana, your agreement with them all is void."

"You are still here. And I still intend to find Luciana. Tonight."

"You will not find her."

"You *do* know where she is, then."

"Nay. She could be anywhere in the woods between us. But

she is good at hiding. And I would wager that Giulio Greco and his sister are with her. They are the best trackers I know—and therefore, the best at hiding their tracks."

"We shall see," he said

I wanted to laugh. He thought he could find them when they had likely disappeared altogether!

"Send us home, Lord Ercole. Tonight. Or at first light. If you want to preserve peace, that is the first step."

"Nay." He shook his head. "I shall wait for Lady Celeste to come of age. And we shall find a new tutor, from Firenze."

"That was not the agreement."

"I did not fail to hold up my side of the agreement," he gritted out. "Lady Luciana was the one who flung herself over the wall!"

"You must have done something that forced her to flee."

"*She* was the one who kissed *me*."

I frowned. "She loves Giulio Greco. Why would she do that?"

He let out a scoffing laugh and lifted his hands. "I believe she had another of her visions. She thought me to be a man who gave up *everything*. I thought I would give her a taste of a real man who now *has* everything and see if she might consider me as suitor."

She thought he was Giulio. My heart sank. "She chose a selfless man who truly had peace in mind when he gave over the castello keys to Aurelio. But he held on to everything that truly mattered."

He laughed and gave me a dismissive wave. "She chose a fool. They deserve each other."

I said nothing. They did deserve each other. For all the best reasons.

He turned toward the door. "Bring them both. Lady Valeri shall show me where they hide. Or Lady Romano shall bear the consequences."

LUCIANA

"A knife!" I cried frantically, trying to lift away the cloyingly sticky net. It was a fine weave but weighted on the edges. Every time we pulled, it further entangled our companions. "Who has a knife?"

"*Lasciarli cadere,*" said a voice, telling them to drop the knives. "To your feet, now."

I glanced up and my heart dropped. Dr. Manero.

He had set this up! To trap looters? Or us?

He came closer, slowly, and two broad-shouldered grad students followed him in. Manero held a gun. "Shut off that alarm!"

"There is no need for a gun, Doc," Nico said. "You could kill somebody."

I knew he said that for Ilaria and Giulio's benefit. They had to know the danger we faced.

"Your companions have swords," he said.

"Props," Nico lied. "We just popped over from a reenactment party over at Castello Forelli. We thought we'd show our friends, here, the tomb. I know it was stupid, but—"

"Try another story," Manero interrupted. "I *saw* you disappear. I bet my cameras picked up your *reappearance* just now too. And you've been gone for hours!"

I looked up and saw the camera on a tripod in the corner and grimaced. It was hooked up to a hard drive, probably to record continuously. *Gonna need to take that with us.* I forced myself to breathe normally, not hyperventilate, with the need to return home.

Return home, I repeated in my mind. Because it was home, now.

This time, this place, felt foreign. How could that have happened so quickly?

"Disappear?" Nico said to Manero with a laugh. "Did you find some odd mushrooms in the woods, Doc? Last I checked, disappearing is not humanly possible. Luci and I ran out of here, not wanting *these* sort of unpleasantries."

"You lie," he said, advancing. "I saw you." The two grad students flanked him now, encircling us. "Who are these people?" He checked out Giulio and Ilaria from head to toe.

"Our friends, reenactors from Milan."

"Do they speak for themselves?"

"We do," Giulio said.

"Ahh, good. Tell me what year it is," Manero said. I could see him taking in the hand-stitching on Giulio's shirt and tunic, the soft boots.

"What do you think he will say?" Nico scoffed. "1492?"

"Nay, earlier," Manero said, moving on to Ilaria.

I heard a quiet sound and saw Nico still had a knife. He was sawing at the net in front of him, making a hole. "What year do you want it to be, Doc?" he asked over his shoulder. He passed me the small dagger. "If we tell you what you want to hear, will you let us go?"

"No." Manero laughed. "The police have been called. They shall collect you on charges of trespassing, and in time, we shall have every bit of the truth."

Precious minutes were passing as we bantered back and forth! What was happening back home, with Tiliani and Celeste? How many hours were already gone? But as they talked, I kept cutting through strand after strand of the net. We now had two holes. We could put our hands to the wall. But if they reached for us, would we bring Manero and these two young men with us? And what of the camera?

Giulio made the decision for us. He rammed his elbow up, sending Manero's gun flying, and then scrambled for it, while still under the net. The rest of us pulled and pulled the endless net away from us. The grad students tackled Giulio, still in the net, and Ilaria, just as she escaped it. I pulled the last of it from my head and ran for the camera. I thought about grabbing it and taking it with us, but then how would I explain it back in medieval times?

Nico sent one grad student flying backward, right beside me, who hit his head on the wall and slumped to the ground. Giulio and Manero were still grappling, as were Ilaria and the other grad student. Another man came in through the tunnel. Nico went to meet him. "Hurry!" he said to me, understanding what I was after.

"I'm *trying*," I muttered. I took the camera, pulled out the memory card and then smashed it against the wall, again and again, hoping I'd killed any internal drive. Then I grabbed the hard drive, figuring I'd best bury it back home, rather than leave it for some computer genius to recover "damaged memory." A crazy story from one or two archeologists was one thing; cold, hard proof another.

A young man had Ilaria in a chokehold from behind, his burly arm around her neck. She clawed his skin, drawing blood, but he stubbornly held on.

"Use that hip," I said to her, reminding her of our jiu jitsu training.

She didn't hesitate to do as I said, and I made way for the man coming over her shoulder. My brother pounced on top of him, muttered an apology, and then knocked him out cold. He rose, shaking his stinging hand.

"You didn't break it, did you?"

"I don't think so."

A gunshot deafened us all.

I whirled in time to see Giulio drop to his knees, hands over his chest. Gaping at the blood. So much blood . . .

"No!" I screamed, falling to my knees beside him. I eased him to the ground, instinctively pressing my palm to the wound, then watched in horror as blood seeped up through my fingers. "Nico . . ."

Manero stood there, gun still raised. He seemed just as shocked as I was.

"What have you done?" Ilaria screamed. She lunged for Manero, drawing her sword.

"Nay, Ilaria!" Nico barked. "You cannot kill him!"

Ilaria grimaced and managed to hit Manero with the flat of her sword, knocking him to the ground. She pounced on him, and he gazed up at her as if in wonder, as if seeing a vision from history—which, of course, he actually was. She grabbed hold of his shirt with one hand, and with three punches, his head lolled back, unconscious.

Nico grabbed her arm. "Time to go," he said.

Giulio was already pale. Unmoving. Was he even breathing? Was I? "Nico . . ."

"Get up! Get your hand on the wall!" Nico said with force. "If there's hope at all, that is where we'll find it."

Numb, I put my trembling hand near the print and grabbed one of Giulio's limp, heavy hands with my other. There was so much blood! Had he risked it all to help me find healing through the tunnel only to be killed? *Oh, God. Oh, God,* I prayed. *Please, please, please . . .*

Giulio's breath was raspy and irregular. Was he dying even now?

I gaped at my brother. "We don't know if it works the other way!" I choked out, tears running down my face. "Should we get him to a hospital here?"

He turned to grip me with both hands. "The nearest hospital is a good forty-five minutes. This is his *only* chance, Luci. Now put your hand on that print and don't let go of Giulio!"

Ilaria wrapped her arms around his waist, and Nico pulled me closer to him. "Let's go." Nico slapped his hand on top of his print.

I glanced down at Giulio, growing more pale as the pool of blood spread beneath him. *Oh, please, God. Please, please, please!*

I pressed my hand to the print.

But I didn't feel the heat as I usually did. I frowned, shifted it a little, but still, there was nothing. My heart raced. What was this? What was wrong?

"Are you on it?" Nico cried.

"Yes! Yes!" I checked again, but my hand perfectly matched the print. Frantic, I glanced at Giulio who was so deadly still . . .

"It's the dried blood on your palm!" Nico said. "Or maybe the blood you left behind? Water. Get water!"

I turned away from the wall, searching for a canteen or flask. One of the guys had brought in an old green Stanley thermos. I raced toward it, praying it wasn't empty.

Another young man peeked into the tunnel, but seeing Manero and the other guys out cold on the floor, rapidly reversed. "Police! Over here!" We heard him scream.

"Maybe it's because it's Giulio's blood on your hand?" Nico asked.

"Maybe!"

Manero roused, grimacing and rubbing his head. With trembling hands, I unscrewed the thermos top and poured hot coffee on my hand. "Ouch!" I cried in surprise. I rubbed it dry on my skirts and hurried back over to the wall and grabbed hold of Giulio's hand, so dreadfully cold. "Let's go! Fast!"

My brother lifted his hand in tandem with mine.

And this time, the heat surged.

"W-wait!" called Manero. "Stop!" But the room started to swirl, and his call was swallowed by time itself.

24

TILIANI

Ercole rushed us out of the keep, Celeste in one hand, me held between two knights—who half dragged me behind them. I dared not complain or try and negotiate with him, given his rage. "Fetch Lady Valeri her mount," he said, once outside.

Knights scurried to do what he bid.

He turned to Captain Sartori. "I want two patrols with us. We are going back out to find them."

"If we wait until sunup—"

"Nay. We shall locate Lady Luciana while still covered by darkness and kill anyone who dared to try and spirit her away. Their mounts are in our stables?"

"Yes, m'lord."

"Good." He awkwardly lifted Celeste to the front of his stallion with one arm.

"Shall I awaken Sir Cafaro to see to your hand, m'lord?" tried a man, watching him.

"When I return," Andrea snarled. "For now, we must retrieve Lady Betarrini. Open the gates! A torch for every man!" He dropped his voice. "We shall set the woods themselves afire, if necessary. Burn them out."

I pictured my beloved trees burning, as well as all the important herbs and medicinals with them. Given the shorter days of autumn upon us, it would not take much to set the summer-scorched forest ablaze.

Captain Sartori tied my reins to Andrea's saddle.

"Bind her hands too," Ercole said, wheeling his mount around. "We do not need the Lady Valeri going missing this night as well."

"But, m'lord," Sartori began.

"Tie them!"

Sartori's lips clenched, and he waved to two men to bind my hands behind my back. I was only thankful that I was not on a sidesaddle. Otherwise I would likely fall if something spooked my horse—and heading off at night, with twelve men all carrying torches? The horses were already skittish.

Andrea watched as they bound my wrists. He bent and pulled Celeste closer to him, moving somewhat suggestively as I observed them. 'Twas for my benefit that he did so, of course. He wanted me to remember that the child was still firmly in his control, and if I tried anything, she would pay for it.

We both knew I could easily disappear into the woods as Luciana had, bound or not, since I had the benefit of sight. It was dark, but there was enough starlight for me to navigate my way home. And yet I could not make a move without the girl. The only way I could escape was if I had Celeste Romano with me. I had promised her parents I would see to her, as had Luciana. Luciana would have left only if she had no other choice.

Whatever had propelled her out of the castello, I was glad she was free. And if they had reached the tomb and healed her eyesight? 'Twas worth any cost that Celeste and I had to now bear. But as we set off, Ercole acting so frenzied, I braced myself for a long night ahead.

We rode toward the woods, looking to the castello where guards above indicated Lady Luciana had met the others. We saw arrows scattered about the rocks—but guards had likely been wary of shooting the prized prisoner. Two torches still smoldered where they had been tossed in order to better see Luciana and the interlopers.

"They came from the forest, right here?" Andrea called up to the knights on the wall.

"Right there, m'lord!"

His stallion danced beneath him, unnerved by the late-night action, torches, and tension of his master.

"We searched these woods, m'lord," Sartori said. "They had horses hobbled within, and when we approached, they took off west, toward the tombs. When we caught up with them again, the horses were riderless and drinking at the border creek."

"So they must be between the tombs and the creek," Ercole said.

"We have men guarding the road, others on the western path," Sartori said. "But why abandon their mounts?"

Ercole perused me. "They had to know our men pursued them. By abandoning their mounts, they diverted their pursuers. They are holed up for the night, awaiting daylight—and mayhap, reinforcements."

"My people would not be planning an attack. Not with Lady Celeste and me still in your keep! They merely were alarmed because Luciana had disappeared. You had not kept to the agreement, with us viewed on the allure each eve."

He let out a scoffing sound. "Leave it to me to discern what is transpiring here. We shall capture Luciana and every one of the interlopers who illegally crossed the border and interrogate them all. Now tell me where they are." He wound his good hand in Celeste's long hair until the child cocked her head in pain.

"M'lord!" the child squeaked. "You are hurting me!"

"Am I?" he said, feigning surprise. But he did not release his grip. He glanced down at the girl's thin, exposed neck and then back to me. "Tell me, Lady Valeri. If it were you in these woods this night, where would you seek cover?"

I hesitated, trying to come up with an option that would

distract them. "When we were children, we used to hide in a cleft in a boulder along the road."

"A cleft in a boulder," he repeated doubtfully. "Is it wide enough to hide four adults?"

"Mayhap. Two, at least."

Still staring at me, he asked his captain, "Did you check the tombs?"

"The tombs, m'lord?"

"Yes, the tombs, the Etruscan tombs!" he said in disgust. "Two of them are open, largely empty. Could they not have crawled inside after sending their horses toward home?"

"Mayhap," Sartori allowed, grim-faced. "We did not stop to search them, given that they would so easily be entrapped there."

"Or easily outwit their enemies," Ercole growled. "And by now, be on the run again. Why do you wait? Let us go and see!"

Sartori took off with one patrol. The other stayed with us, moving at a slower pace. If my companions were truly in the woods, we were making quite a tempting target. Every man besides Andrea held a torch. I itched for a bow and arrows myself. If I were in the woods, I could take out three before they determined where I was and scattered. Was someone out there right now, thinking the same? Or did they hesitate, fearful they might strike me or Celeste?

I tensed as we neared the tombs but pretended not to care when we saw knights exiting the two open tombs and move on to check the perimeter of the other buried mounds. They had found no one. If Luciana and Domenico had made the leap, they obviously had not yet returned. I had to get us moving again! If Luciana had made it this far, only to be apprehended again . . .

"Shall I show you that boulder, my lord?" I asked.

He grimaced. "You toy with me. You know they are not there. You would not so freely give up your friends."

"To protect Lady Romano, I would. Did Lady Luciana and I not volunteer in order to help keep her safe?"

"Lady Luciana risked Lady Romano's safety by electing to *run*," he sneered in disgust.

"Because you pressed her."

He lifted his injured hand. "She shall pay for her choices." He turned to surveil the silhouette of the dense woods that lay between the castellos, then back to Sartori. "Take your men and search the vineyards and homes that lay along the border, making certain they have not sought shelter with any villeins. If you find them sheltering in one, burn the home and barn to the ground."

"Yes, m'lord."

"I will take one patrol and return to the castello. We shall depart again at sunup."

"To resume our search?"

"Nay. I am taking the ladies to Firenze."

Sartori's brows lifted in surprise as my stomach flipped. I had not been in Firenze since I narrowly escaped death in her cages.

Ercole smiled. "Yes. I must seek counsel on how to proceed with our *neighbors*. And removing these two from the premises shall remove further temptation to try and free them."

I considered rolling off the saddle and running for the forest right there and then, but I would not make it far before knights apprehended me, nor could I leave Celeste. I sighed. Luciana had escaped, but how were we to escape without her?

LUCIANA

We fell back, and once again, Giulio took the brunt of my weight. I caught my breath and looked about the tomb—dimly lit with dawn's peach hues.

Dimly lit with dawn's peach hues. I can see hues. I can see I can see I can see . . .

But then my heart skipped a beat in panic. *Giulio.* He'd been shot!

I scrambled off his still body and immediately turned to press my palm into the gunshot wound. "Giulio!" I cried, shaking him. It hadn't worked. Was he still bleeding out? It didn't seem like it was gushing like it had before. *Was* it bleeding at all?

He groaned. "L-Luciana?"

"Giulio?" I breathed.

He sat up, wincing. I laughed and threw myself into his arms.

Nico whooped and thumped his back, hurriedly examining his wound. His eyes met mine. The bleeding had stopped.

Thank you, Lord. Thank you thank you thank you.

"That was harrowing," Ilaria muttered, leaning down to kiss each of Giulio's cheeks. "I do not think I care for weapons of that sort."

Still holding his hand, I looked about. There were no cameras, no net, no grad students. We were back—all four of us. And I could *see* every one of them.

Domenico hopped to his feet and brought a finger to his lips, reminding me to take care. He gave Ilaria a hand up, then put a palm to either side of her face. "*Stai bene?*" he whispered, asking if she was okay.

She nodded and looked to us. "Luciana, your eyes?" she whispered.

"Better, still," I said with a grin. "Completely healed."

She put her palms together and glanced upward, as if shooting a prayer of thanks to God. But Giulio stepped between us, his deep-blue eyes searching mine. "Truly?" he asked, lifting my chin with one knuckle. "You can see, beloved?"

"Yes, yes." I wrapped my arms over his shoulders and kissed him. I pulled back in order to look upon his handsome face, making sure I wasn't having a hallucination. But it was him. It was all of them. "We did it," I whispered. "Made it there and back!"

"As fab as that is, baby sis . . ." Nico said, then crouched and glanced down the tunnel entrance. "Now what? Do we make a break for it? If knights on watch see us, they will try and intercept us before we reach Castello Forelli. We don't know if we lost the night or several days, or what's happened while we were gone."

"Time it," I said. "Watch for the guards to pass the point they'd be looking our way, then run for the hill above. There is enough brush and trees to hide us there, right?" I stared at him, and I knew he was remembering the night we first came to the tombs, stealing into them right under Manero's nose. The night this whole mad adventure had begun.

"That could work." Nico nodded in approval. "Are you ready now? Are you feeling steady on your feet?"

"I am."

"Giulio?"

"I am hale." He took my hand and led me behind him as Nico and Ilaria crawled toward the entrance. I suspected he would be as reluctant to let me go as I was with him. I had my sight back. Could we find our way out of this mess and rescue Tiliani and Celeste? Then we could wed. I would be his wife. He would be my husband. The thought of it made me giddy.

Because I absolutely, positively now knew that I never wanted to be without Giulio Greco and the rest of our family.

The sound of my brother and Ilaria scrambling outward and away brought my mind back to the present. I bent and crawled toward the entrance. The next two knights on patrol on the allure made their way around the western turret door and onward. No alarm arose. I paused, wondering if we should wait for the next pair, but that might be another five minutes. Biting my lip, I scrambled outward and yanked up my skirts, scurrying around the mounded tomb to join the others hidden in back. Giulio was right behind me. We were just sharing a smile of silent glee when we heard the shout. Then another.

Domenico dared to peek over the mound. Had they spotted us or had something else alarmed them?

"Tell me it's not what I think it is," I said in English, as he slowly sank back to his haunches.

"Wish I could," he said to me. "We need to move," he said to the others. "*Now.*"

I pulled the back of my skirt between my legs again and tucked it into my waistband so the folds would not catch in the sagebrush and I'd be free to move. Ilaria was in the typical patrol dress of tunic, leggings, and soft boots. Her tunic was not the Forellis' royal blue, but neither was it the Paratore crimson—chosen to blend rather than stand out. And regardless of how I wore my skirts, it would be clear to them that I was female. My hair had long fallen from its knot, the pins gone the night before. Giulio took my hand, and we set off at once, directly behind Ilaria and Nico.

More shouts came from Castello Paratore, and I put more effort into every step. We reached the top of the hill and moved into the trees, then ran as fast as we could south. If we could just get to the far side of the creek before Ercole's knights intercepted us, we would be safe! But that was still a half-mile distant, and they would likely be coming on horseback. I prayed that the Forellis had a patrol nearby and they would come to our aid.

Because there were precious few places to hide between us and the creek.

25

We arrived in Firenze under cover of darkness. We spent the night in a villa outside the city, the gates closed until morning. The next day, Ercole and his knights ushered us into the city and directly toward Castello Paratore, where, after an awkward moment, we were allowed entrance. It was clear to me that Ercole planned to claim this property as well, usurping all that had once been Aurelio's as the heir apparent.

Returning to the city that had nearly taken my life—and now, to Aurelio's home—set my hands to trembling uncontrollably. I tried to hide it from Celeste, not wanting my fear to frighten her, and from Ercole, who would likely revel in it. I was reasonably successful until we entered the courtyard. I looked around at the colonnade and remembered coming here with Forelli and Sienese knights. Of fighting our way through an angry mob when I was recognized. Of how Aurelio had taken us in, and I saw—finally saw—my Valentino again. How he had avoided me, still denying our love, feeling it as a betrayal to his dear friend, Aurelio.

How I longed for my husband now, especially here. He would have helped me to find my way. He would know people, still . . . fellow Fiorentini who might lend us a compassionate ear. Who might aid us. I thought of the kindly lord who had held my family under house arrest, and turned a blind eye when my aunt, uncle, and cousin escaped from his rooftop. Val had heard he had paid a dear cost for aiding us, so I doubted he would do so again.

"M'lady? Are you unwell?"

It was Captain Sartori, who had come alongside my horse to help me down. I had entered the city with my wrists unbound, but I trembled so much that I doubted my own ability to dismount. I had not eaten that morning, my stomach queasy on the outskirts of the city. And now I was at her very heart.

"I–I . . ." I could not even form a sentence in my head.

"Here. Allow me." He reached up, took hold of my waist, and lowered me down.

I faltered, one knee giving way. I gasped, but he caught me, one hand at my waist, the other gripping my upper arm. "Are you unwell?" he repeated.

"Only a bit faint," I managed.

He raised a hand and snapped at a manservant. "Send a maid!"

His action drew Ercole's attention, and I inwardly groaned. Thankfully, Lady Celeste was already being ushered inside the palazzo. Distantly, I remembered I needed to stay with her, protect her. But I wavered, feeling my head spin.

Sartori bent and lifted me in his arms. "The lady is unwell," he said briefly to Ercole as he neared us.

"Bring her." He turned on his heel and led the way. "Inform Sir Cafaro that he should not return home as of yet. The lady is in need."

I grimaced. Would Cafaro bleed me as he had Luciana? I took heart in the fact that Luciana had survived his ministrations and been strong enough to rappel off the castello wall and escape. But I had to admit that I already lacked the strength to consider such a feat. What was wrong with me? Was I simply famished? Or was it merely returning to this place—this cursed city—that almost claimed not only my life, but Mama and Papa's too?

Captain Sartori was a bit short of breath when he reached the top floor of the castello. Ercole turned back, clearly irritated at the slow pace, and I saw he was ghostly pale. Because Andrea did not want us out of his sight, we had been forced to bed down on straw ticks, hastily brought into his room, and listened to his screams as Cafaro straightened his broken wrist and tied his hand to a carved board. Then he had wound the whole hand in bandages and given Ercole a tonic that soon had him blessedly snoring. Celeste crept onto the mattress with me, and when I pulled her close, we both finally slept.

Were Luciana, Domenico, Giulio, and Ilaria back yet? The only thing I celebrated in being spirited off to Firenze again was that it took Ercole away from obsessively seeking them out. The last thing they needed was a patrol at the tomb. But I knew from the stories that they could be gone for days, if not weeks or more. Had not Zia Gabi, Mama, and Nona been away a couple of years in seeking my grandfather?

We had left under cover of morning darkness. Did my family yet know that they had taken us away? I had not sent a missive in more than a day, and the last had been dictated by Andrea. When my family sought the next, they would be met with the unwelcome news that we were gone, off to the city.

It was one thing for my family to storm the gates of Castello Paratore. They could not take on Firenze herself—not until Siena had the backing of Cardinal Borgio. I swallowed back the bile rising in my throat as Captain Sartori laid me upon an opulently covered, four-posted bed. Celeste hurried over to me, but Sir Cafaro pushed her into a maid's arms. "Take the little lady to the kitchens for a bowl of hot soup and bit of bread."

I knew I should object, insist she remain with me, but had not the strength.

"Are you weary from the travel, m'lady?" the barber-surgeon asked, setting the back of his hand against my sweating forehead.

Captain Sartori backed up to the far wall but did not exit. I found comfort in that. Ercole pulled up a chair and wearily sat down on it.

"Most likely," I said. "I have had precious few hours of sleep of late."

"Understandably," he said kindly. He took my hand in his, and his fingers probed my wrist, counting my heart rate. For a moment, I wondered what was truly wrong, for I had not felt this ill in some time.

"Your pulse is very fast." He fished a ceramic cone from his bag and bent to listen to my heart.

"I-I have not been back in the city since I was . . . detained," I said when he rose.

He studied me. "So this may be naught but a bit of hysteria?"

I frowned. "Nay." I did not want to admit to such a cavalier diagnosis. And yet, if it was that at its root, could anyone blame me? When they brought down that cage, when they opened the doors, they had meant to strangle us when they found we yet lived . . . Even now, I felt like I could not take a full breath. "Please. Might you open the shutters? Allow in a bit of breeze?"

The room felt stifling. Suffocating.

"She needs to be bled, m'lord," he said to Andrea. "She suffers female melancholia."

"Nay." I tried to rise. "No bleeding. I need only rest and a bit of food."

Cafaro pressed my shoulder back, and I sank into the pillows. I was embarrassed that the thin man could do so with such little effort. But my head was spinning again, as if I were in an eddy in the river beside our summer villa. We had played there as children each August, escaping the heat, and delighted in that portion of the river that doubled back on itself, sending us in an endless circle as we floated on our backs.

But this eddy was taking me under.

"Lady *Tiliani*," Sir Cafaro said, holding my hand and staring down at me with some intensity. "More light! Bring candles! And water! And retrieve my chest!"

Luciana

We were running for our lives, and I was the last in line. I panted with the effort of keeping up with the others. Nico tripped and we slowed, but he waved us on angrily, knowing there was not a second to waste. "Go! Go!"

The creek was within sight, but Ercole knights on horses closed in behind us. Would they capture us and drag us back to the castle? Or simply kill us as we ran?

I heaved for breath, my arms pumping, willing my feet to fly over the earth. And then, blessedly, twelve men emerged from the forest at a gallop. Six of them dropped from their saddles, taking a knee and drawing arrows from their quivers. *Forelli knights.* Never had I seen something so welcome. I continued to run, gasping for air, praying my brother was behind me. Giulio ran beside me. Ilaria was in front.

She dived—literally dived over the creek—rolling onto her back and leaping to her feet as men closed around her. I hurtled over, too, not nearly as graceful. I landed in a heap and rolled, thinking at once that I was safe, and at the very same time, thinking that I was a fool to think I was.

I turned and forced myself to my feet, watching as Nico jumped the creek at last, and enemy arrows narrowly missed him. I ran to help him up as archers on our side let loose their own arrows.

Horses on the far side scattered, circled, and rejoined at a safe distance.

We were panting heavily, gasping for breath, clinging to one another. When they had gathered themselves, a man shouted, "Send back Lady Luciana! She is all we need to hold on to this tenuous peace!"

The men around us laughed in amazement and looked at us,

then back to their enemies. "I think not!" called Captain Pezzati, stepping in front of me. "If the lady finds she must run from you, she must not have found your hospitality satisfactory!"

Giulio stepped forward. "Take word to Lord Ercole—"

"You shall refer to him as Lord Paratore now!"

Giulio grimaced. "Take your lord word that he must sit down with Lord Forelli and Lord Romano to discuss the return of the Ladies Forelli and Romano!"

The man lifted his chin. "My lord has departed for Firenze."

I squared my shoulders and stared back at him. Had he just said . . .

"Firenze!" Giulio barked, hand going to the hilt of his sword. "Did he leave our ladies ensconced at Castello Paratore?"

The Fiorentini grinned. "Nay. Do you object to that?" Others around him laughed.

Giulio seethed and turned his back on them, refusing to give them the satisfaction of a reply.

"We shall get them back," I said, half in encouragement to myself, half to him, even as guilt washed through me. Firenze? He had taken them to *Firenze*?

Otello, the closest knight, turned to face me. "M'lady! Are your eyes . . . improved?"

I nodded. "A bit," I fibbed. "My vision seems to be returning."

"That is grand news!" said another. "Lady Adri's visit to see to you made us concerned."

"Her skill as a healer surpasses all," I said, latching on to the opening and remembering Adri's advice should I use the tomb for healing. "Soon after she departed, I began to improve."

"As you say!" said Captain Pezzati. "Improved enough to escape the castello? That shall be a tale we shall all wish to hear."

A third said, "If you can escape Castello Paratore and live to tell about it, we shall live to keep you safe, m'lady."

"And make them regret it," said another.

I smiled with them but inside, felt sick at the news. What did they face in Firenze? What sort of vile treatment? Had he taken them there out of fear of losing them too?

I deeply regretted leaving them behind as I went over the wall, even if it was the only choice I had. But now . . . to know they were deep within the enemy city?

How were we to aid them in escaping the city herself?

TILIANI

I screamed, more in frustrated complaint than in pain, as Sir Cafaro sliced my arm at the elbow.

"Truly, m'lady?" he asked dryly, hovering over my arm with a tiny, bloody blade. My arm was bound to a plank, my body pressed to the bed by servants.

"You did not have my permission to cut me." I shook my head to emphasize my dismay.

"Nay," he said lightly, reaching for a cup and watching—with some satisfaction—as my blood ran off my arm and dripped into it. "But I had Lord Paratore's."

"Lord Paratore does not have say over what happens to my body."

"On the contrary," Ercole said, rising from his chair. "We are now in the heart of Firenze. And if I ever had a say, I do so now."

I watched as his eyes strayed down the length of me.

"I am Lady Tiliani Valeri. A married woman. I ask that you—an unmarried man—remove yourself from my private quarters."

He returned my gaze, leaning against the post nearest my pillow. "I wish only to ascertain that you shall survive until morn."

"I shall survive, m'lord," I said tiredly. "Kindly remove yourself."

"As you wish, m'lady." He gave me a brief wave and left the

room then, as if relieved to be done with me. Mayhap he was ailing from his own injury.

Celeste returned, then, curling up beside me like a frightened stray dog.

I looked up into Sir Cafaro's eyes as he bound my elbow, curtailing the bleeding, and set my arm on the bed.

He took my hand and looked down at me with kind eyes. "You shall feel better come morn. The road has sorely taxed you, m'lady."

"Is that truly all?" I whispered, wishing for a drink of water. My throat was terribly dry. "I confess I have not felt such weariness ever before. 'Tis as if the weight of the world is upon my shoulders. And I am both famished and nauseated at once."

He frowned and looked me over again. "May I?" he asked, gesturing to my body, asking permission to examine me.

I was at a loss. Something was terribly, horribly wrong. I had never felt so ghastly. Surely, this was not all due to my last horrible experience here? "Please."

He gently probed my belly. He moved around my lower abdomen. He eventually took a step back, tapping two fingers to his lips.

"What is it?" I dared to ask.

"When were your last monthly courses?"

I flushed at the personal question. My mind spun, thinking through the days and weeks. As the calculations came together, my eyes went wide, and I looked to him, startled. "Oh."

He met my gaze. "I believe you might carry a child. 'Tis too soon to be certain, but your nausea, your weariness, might indicate it."

My breath caught. "A child?" I huffed a laugh, incredulous. Valentino and I had shared but three nights as man and wife before I was away to Castello Paratore! Was it possible? That I carried his child in such a short period of time? Did not some couples long for a child for years?

And in the same moment, I recognized that Andrea Ercole would not welcome such news. He already found my marriage to Valentino distasteful. I grasped Sir Cafaro's hand in both of mine. "Please, do not tell the lord. At least not yet. Please?"

He frowned. "What you ask of me . . ."

"I know what I ask. I am asking for my preservation," I whispered. "Tell him I only need to break my fast and have a bit of rest, which is true, yes?"

"Well, yes, but—"

"Please, sir. Only for a few days." I did not know what Ercole would do with this information, but I knew it somehow made me more vulnerable. I put a hand protectively over my belly.

He considered me a moment, then gave a brief nod.

I relaxed against my pillow, relieved. Given a few days, I prayed God would show us some way to escape.

LUCIANA

We sauntered into Castello Forelli upon the knights' horses as if we were conquering heroes, men cheering us from either side, as well as along the walls. The archers—those who had held our enemies at bay—followed us in. But I felt like a failure—an utter failure—leaving Celeste and Tiliani behind. And the knowledge that they were now in Firenze? It stabbed me like a hundred knives, even as I raised a hand to faintly accept the men's praise.

Fake. Fool. Failure, my mind called.

But still I raised my arm and pretended to smile because they were so glad to see us.

I dismounted and took Giulio's hand as he led me to the lords and ladies. They all embraced us. Adri took me by the shoulders and waited until my eyes met hers. "Did you do it, then?" she whispered. "You can see?"

My smile was genuine in response as I nodded. "*We* did it," I whispered. "Manero almost trapped us, but thankfully, Giulio and Ilaria helped us fight our way free."

"Manero." She said his name like a curse word. "Even separated by seven hundred years, that man continues to plague the Betarrinis." She shook her head and then smiled. "But you can see. God bless that tunnel and its healing properties! Remember to pretend gradual improvement over the coming few days." She squeezed my shoulders and then walked me toward the Great Hall.

"We could say that a physician from Firenze treated me while I was at Castello Paratore. That it furthered my healing that you began."

She narrowed her gaze at me. "Were you?"

"Yes," I said. "He bled me."

Adri groaned. "Why is that always their first recourse? Is that why you fled?"

"That and Ercole imprisoned me in the dungeon and was making moves on me. He suggested I become his mistress, Adri! And I-I had another hallucination." I faltered, humiliated at the memory. "I thought Giulio was in the prison cell with me. I-I kissed him. And it was Ercole all along."

"That cad takes advantage of every opportunity." She patted my arm. "Now that you're healed, the hallucinations will stop. You'll see. You mustn't blame yourself."

I shook my head as if I could shake loose the memory. "But now he has taken Til and Celeste to Firenze."

She grimaced. "He likely knew that with you gone, we and the Romanos would demand our daughters be returned, so he fled north. To regroup, we suppose. Figure out what to do next."

"The Romanos must be beside themselves with worry."

"Indeed. Luca accompanies them to Siena even now to meet with the Nine."

"How are we going to get them out?"

"We shall arrive at a plan."

"Good." I dropped my voice. "How long were we absent?"

"Two and a half days. The castello knew the Grecos were on a special mission, but no one was told where they were going and what they were up to. Figuring out how to bring you home is explanation enough for most."

I glanced over her shoulder to Giulio in deep conversation with his sister and Domenico, and I thought I'd never seen a finer man in the entire world. As if sensing my perusal, he looked over at me and smiled.

"I have not seen a smile on that man's face since you left," Adri said, following my gaze. "And now that you're home, I expect he's going to want to be with you twenty-four seven."

"Which is totally fine with me."

"So this is it?" she asked in a whisper. "You're set to stay with us forever?"

"As soon as we get Tiliani home and Celeste back to her parents."

"And we will go to Firenze herself to make certain that happens."

26

If I could not stop vomiting, how was I to find a way out for Celeste and me? Was it better to tell Ercole of my pregnancy? Use that as an excuse to send us home? Or would he use it somehow against me? I shoved myself up in the bed and pushed back my hair, breathing slowly and steadily through my nostrils to try and settle my stomach.

"Are you still feeling ill, my lady?" Celeste asked, rolling over to look at me. After threatening every servant and knight in the palazzo with corporal punishment if they permitted either of us to escape, Andrea had allowed us to share a bedroom away from him. And after watching him seduce a lady at the dinner table last night, I assumed he might have had an overnight guest. I was thankful for his distraction, though I pitied the woman. Even if the man eventually married, I doubted he would be a faithful husband. His eyes were forever on the prowl, and now that he had means, he would consider himself unstoppable.

"I am much improved," I lied to Celeste, practicing. Sir Cafaro would likely return for his morning visit—as he had for the last four days—and I knew my only chance to escape another bleeding was to tout my improved health. After all, I was not truly sick—I was merely possibly pregnant. But if he continued to insist upon letting my blood, I might soon *truly* ail.

A knock at the door announced two maids, who came in,

wished us a good morning. One went to the shutters to open them, the other set down a tray to break our fast. "You have more color this morning, m'lady," said the girl approvingly as she delivered our food. "Sir Cafaro is down in the hall with Lord Paratore. Shall I send him up to you?"

Lord *Paratore*. It still grated at me that he had succeeded in taking the name. Somehow hearing it used here made it all the more final. I swallowed back my resentment as I felt the last of Aurelio's hold slip away. Ercole had assumed everything once held by Aurelio as the rightful Paratore heir, even including the name. Why did I doubt his claim? Was this what Luciana had heard him scheming about? He could not have accomplished it without some very powerful friends. The castello was but one aspect—had he managed to usurp everything that belonged to the Paratores?

"You may inform him that I am much improved," I said, swinging my legs out from under the covers. "Lady Celeste and I would like to walk about the colonnade to get a bit of fresh air today."

"M'lord will be most pleased. He intends for you and the little lady to accompany him to a ball tonight."

"A ball?"

"Yes, 'tis a masquerade. It shall be most thrilling." The maids shared a smile of glee.

"A masquerade?" Celeste bounced a bit on the bed. "What is that?"

"'Tis when people attending the ball wear masks, so you have to guess at each one's identity," I said.

"The doge of Venezia is in the city, and Lord Garamondi is hosting the feast," a maid informed us. "Given that Venetians are so fond of masquerades, he decided to host his very first. And when the doge learned that you were in the city, he insisted you accompany my lord."

I took in that news. Would I have the chance to speak to the doge? Attempt to try and secure his favor for Siena? A previous doge had been rather fond of Mama and Zia Gabi, even hosting Mama and Papa's wedding. Could I garner similar favor?

"Everyone wishes to meet a She-Wolf of Siena," said the other maid.

"Especially one that survived the cage!"

So I was to be paraded about. I doubted Fiorentini lords and ladies would treat me with anything but contempt. But mayhap with a costume, I might mingle in disguise and manage to speak with Lord Garamondi as well as the doge.

"And you are to be introduced to your new tutor, Lady Romano," said the first maid. "Lord Paratore came to an agreement with him last night."

Last night? Whom had he found? "What are his qualifications?" I asked.

"He is most learned. He delighted one and all with tales of his travels as they dined."

I moved behind a dressing screen and pulled off my nightdress to don a soft, white undergown for the day. "Will you please fetch my light-blue gown?" I asked the woman on the other side of the screen.

She coughed nervously. "Lord Paratore asked that you wear your gold gown." She set the bodice on the top of the screen, then shook out the skirt. I took it in my hands. It was lovely, with a beautifully embroidered swirled pattern all across it, as well as on the bottom edge of the skirt. But now the man was dictating what I wore? Was the gold a nod to the color we once flew from our towers? Was he taunting me, reminding me of how he had stolen Forelli tunics and used them to frame my father and uncle?

I clenched my fists and considered denying the request, insisting I wear any other color but what he had asked to see me in. But I wanted Andrea to believe I was falling into line, content to look after my little charge. Lull him into a sense of complacency so when we had the chance to escape, he would not see it coming.

I rubbed my flat belly, thinking of the babe only now potentially taking root, growing day by day. For the child's sake, and Celeste's, I had to make clever decisions—clever enough to outsmart the lord of this house.

Dressed and ready, we descended the staircase and entered the main parlor, where people chatted. There were mayhap twenty in attendance, conversing in small groups around the grand room. Andrea turned to glance at us as we entered.

"Ahh, at last. My ladies!" He strode toward us. All conversation ceased, and everyone watched as we curtsied to him. He took Celeste's hand and turned to the room. "May I present Lady Celeste Romano? And her guardian-governess," he said with a nod to me, "the lovely Lady Tiliani Valeri."

As ladies bent to whisper among themselves, Andrea smiled. "Yes, 'tis true. Tiliani Forelli took the hand of Aurelio Paratore's former captain, Valentino Valeri. They wed nigh a few weeks past or I might have persuaded her to take my hand instead, ending this strife between Siena and Firenze."

"So Valeri has thrown his shoulder behind the Sienese cause?" asked a man.

"So it appears."

"Traitor!" called one.

"Dog!" yelled another.

"Now, now," Andrea said. "Those of the Forelli and Betarrini bloodlines have long entranced men." He looked me up and down and circled me. "Look upon her! Can you entirely blame Valeri? I have half a mind to call upon my friends of the Church to see about annulling her marriage and taking her to wife myself."

I pretended to laugh with the others, pretended to smile as if flattered, but a cold shiver of fear ran down my back. Could he do that? Nay, not if I carried Valentino's child. And yet Firenze had far deeper ties to the Church than Siena did. More often than not, my people were excommunicated, refusing to do what we ought to garner the pope's favor. Every pope for decades had favored the

Fiorentini because they frequently supported the Holy Father's pet projects and purse.

How had Domenico and Zio Marcello fared with their cardinal friend on this side of the border? Were they making headway? Might Cardinal Borgio be a friend to me too? Could financing the roof of his cathedral seal the deal for us all?

I reminded myself that not every priest or man of the Church was swayed by coin or other payment. I remembered the priest who had dared to stand up to the lord in the piazza that fateful morn my parents and I were almost murdered. Had it not been for him . . .

He was proof that one needed only one decent friend in any given situation to stand against the tide. The thought of it strengthened me. Even here, in the heart of Firenze, there were certainly good people. *I need only find them.*

I smiled and turned to my captor. "I thought it would be bolstering for Celeste to take a turn around the colonnade. Given my ill health, the girl has spent far too many days indoors."

"By all means," he said magnanimously, waving toward the doorway. Giving me permission to stroll along walkways that had belonged to Aurelio Paratore only a few short months before. How had he managed it?

"Lord Paratore," I said, "the maids told me you have found a new tutor for Lady Celeste. She would very much like to make his acquaintance." I glanced around the room, wondering if he was here.

"He plans to join us for the ball this evening, and I shall introduce you then. Did the maids tell you of those plans too?"

"They did. There is to be a masquerade?"

"Indeed."

"What shall Lady Celeste and I do for masks?"

"Do not concern yourself over that. All shall be provided for you." He looked at me, catlike, and I again pretended not to notice.

"Very well. Thank you, m'lord. Now with your permission, we shall go for that walk."

"By all means."

I took Celeste's small hand and turned.

"Lady Tiliani."

I glanced back to him. He took my hand with his good one, and I fought to not pull away. "It is most gratifying to see you making yourself at home here." He bent and kissed my knuckles softly.

I did not know how to respond. I inclined my head toward him and then turned again to go, suddenly wanting nothing but a quick escape. Away from the curious eyes of those in the drawing room. Away from the whispers and ill will. *One good person,* I prayed. *Or two, Lord? We need some friends in this enemy territory.* How I missed Luciana! Her company had been such a blessing to me. I had not been alone, solely responsible for Celeste, as I was now.

Could she see now? Had they made their journey and returned?

Celeste pulled on my hand. "My lady."

"Yes, my sweet?"

"Am I not to wed Lord Paratore? My mother told me that I must prepare myself for that, when I came of age. But he speaks of taking others to wife, even you! And I . . . I saw . . ." Her eyes drifted to the intricate frescoes that adorned the domes above our walkway.

"You saw what, dear one?"

"I saw a lady leave his rooms this morning, and she was in naught but a dressing gown," she whispered. "She passed me on the way to the garderobe."

I considered how to answer her. "Lord Paratore is looking for the fastest way to expedite his goals to establish peace between Firenze and Siena. And peace is a good thing, yes?"

"Y-yes," she said.

"Your father's castello—so close to the trade route with Firenze—and ours, the most eastern outpost in the republic, are logical lynchpins. Firenze wants to either claim them for herself or establish a firm kinship with both."

"Making you and me logical targets as well. To wed either of us would accomplish his goals. And you are a woman grown."

I lifted a brow in surprise at the child's astute and mature summation. "Exactly right." I tucked her hand in the crook of my elbow as we walked. The fresh air and morning sun felt good on the bare skin of my arms. "But I am already wed to Sir Valeri. You must not take it as an affront, his casual mentions of wedding another."

"I understand. Truth be told, I would much rather see someone else marry Lord Paratore."

I laughed under my breath. "I do not blame you."

"I want to choose my husband, as you did."

"That is why I only recently wed. It took me a long time to find a man worthy of my love."

"Do you believe Lord Paratore worthy of love?"

I shrank within. How was I to answer that, truthfully? This girl could very well be forced to wed him within a few short years. Even with us pursuing every avenue to free her, I had no idea how this might turn out.

"Everyone deserves love," I said carefully. "Lord Paratore has long pursued what he thought he deserved. Mayhap now, with all of this to call his own"—I waved about at the palazzo—"he shall begin to accept what we all inherently crave, which is love."

Who knew? I thought. If Saul became Paul, mayhap even a damaged soul like Ercole's could be redeemed. Thankfully, God himself could muster more grace and mercy than I could for the man.

Luciana

We entered Firenze the way we had months before, disguised as merchants, here only to trade for the day. We had promised the Romanos we would find out how their daughter fared, and Domenico and Marcello hoped to arrange for a clandestine meeting with Cardinal Borgio. Giulio and I set off for the market and tavernas, steering clear of Palazzo Paratore, where we feared we might be recognized by some of Ercole's knights. Ilaria accompanied Nico and Marcello. They would call upon the cardinal at his villa on the outskirts of the city, and we would meet up with them there come morn.

The market was a feast for my newly healed eyes. Giulio had to pull me away from gorgeous tapestries imported from the Netherlands, bright pottery vases and plates, and colorful bolts of cloth. It was as if my eyes were hungry to take it all in after the long famine. *Thank you, thank you, Lord, for restoring my vision!*

I paused before a fruit and vegetable vendor's stand, admiring fat green artichokes laced with purple and orange squash blossoms on leaves of green. And as I did so, I eavesdropped on two chatty kitchen maids. Soon, I'd learned all about the masquerade that night at Palazzo Garamondi, and of Ercole's claim to the Paratore name and palazzo. She went on to talk about the new tutor he had hired for Lady Romano, as well as Lady Tiliani Forelli being in residence.

"I heard Lady Forelli wed the traitor, Valeri," returned the other maid.

"That is what she claims. But I heard Lord Paratore speaking with another in his study yesterday—m'lord believes it a lie to keep him at bay. If you ask me, he aims to woo the lady while here in the city. And what woman in her right mind would deny him?"

She gave a little shiver and widened her eyes. "So handsome, as well as rich! If she does not take to him, he could have me for the asking."

I asked the merchant for a bundle of onions, even as my stomach turned. What was it about Ercole's power with women?

"I wish such drama were unfolding in m'lord's palazzo! He is old and dull! What of the little lady? Romano, is it? Is *she* not his intended?"

When the vendor turned toward me, I pointed to a bunch of carrots.

The maid cocked her head and lowered her voice as if to share a confidence—but still loud enough for me to hear. "Patience does not sit well with one such as Lord Paratore. He needs a bride now. He wants peace with Siena, so that he can begin filling his coffers."

"I see. Well, mayhap he shall discover the gem waiting for him in his own kitchens," the girl said with a wink at her friend.

"From your tongue to God's ears!" said the girl with a big smile. "I have half a mind to purchase a mask and gown and sneak into the ball tonight!"

"Can you imagine?" her companion said. "What if he asked you to dance?"

She squealed and moved on to the next stall in the market to purchase fresh fruit and trade more gossip with the vendor. But she had given me an idea. What if Giulio and I sneaked into the ball in the same way? Given that it was a masquerade, few would be stopped by guards to give their names. But would they require an invitation to enter? Most likely.

Giulio rejoined me, and as we walked down the nearest street, I told him all I had learned. Giulio stopped and put his hands on his hips. "A marriage contract with the Romanos was his idea." He shook his head and frowned. "Now he has not the decency to wait for her to come of age?"

"He has never been a patient man," I said. "He wants what

he wants, as quickly as he might obtain it. And with me gone, he knows the agreement with the Romanos is null and void."

Giulio huffed a laugh. "But Tiliani is a married woman." He paused and lifted his brows, as if remembering something. "I trailed two priests for a couple of blocks. They spoke of a noble trying to find a way to annul a marriage. Do you think they spoke of Ercole?"

"Annul?" I tried to remember what that meant.

"It is when the Church declares a marriage invalid—as if it never happened. Tiliani would have to claim coercion. Or that they did not consummate their marriage. The Fiorentini would be quick to believe it. But the Sienese would not."

"Nor would Til do such a thing. She loves Valentino with all her heart."

He turned toward me and took my arms. "Did he attempt to convince you to marry him? Is that why you fled?"

"Not to wed. Given my blindness, and my visions, he considered me damaged. But that did not stop him from suggesting I become his *consort*, nor from taking advantage of me that last night," I confessed.

"*Consort*." He pulled me into an alley, his brow furrowed. "And how, exactly, did he take advantage?"

Quickly, I told him of that terrible night, and how I believed Ercole to be Giulio. "I am fairly certain I broke his hand. After that, I knew two things—I had to get away from him before he hurt me in response, and I had to get to the tomb to try and heal my sight. I could not tolerate any more visions. And Ercole and Sir Cafaro talked about bringing me here to Firenze to see a barber-surgeon that specialized in treating maladies of the brain. I knew that likely meant certain death. I had to leave. But I feel terrible for leaving Til and Celeste behind, Giulio. We have to make certain they are all right. We have to help them find their way out too."

"I shall not rest until you *all* are safe." He pulled me into his arms.

Please, God, make a way, I prayed silently. *Help Nico and Marcello. Give them favor with Cardinal Borgio. Bring us again to times of peace, and Tiliani and Celeste safely home. Amen.*

27

I laughed, aghast, when I saw the mask and gown spread across the bed. Celeste's was more what I expected—a lovely pearl-colored gown and pearl-and-black split mask.

"You do not care for it, m'lady?" asked the maid, looking confused.

"This is not a disguise! 'Tis a costume, yes, but everyone shall know who I am."

She glanced dolefully down at it with me. "And yet, have you seen anything so beautiful?"

I picked up the mask. It was elaborate—with what appeared to be real gray-and-black fur glued to the face. Pointed ears, slanted canine eye sockets, and a long nose. Clearly a wolf. The matching gray-and-black gown only made the illusion more obvious.

"'Tis not to your liking?"

I glanced over my shoulder to the doorway and saw Ercole leaning against the doorframe, one arm in a sling, the other hand on his hip.

"This is not a ball gown, my lord," I said in a measured tone. "'Tis a She-Wolf's flag."

"I thought you would enjoy it." He moved into the room. "A chance to thumb your nose at every Fiorentini present."

"I think my gown is lovely, m'lord," Celeste tried.

"Good, good," he said absently. But his attention was solely on me.

"You believe thumbing my nose at your fellow citizens would be wise? You forget that the last time I was here, I very narrowly held on to my life. As did my parents."

He let out a dismissive noise and flicked his fingers. "That is in the past. Firenze is ready to embrace a new era. You and I represent the bridge that shall be forged."

"You mean you and Lady Romano."

He stared into my eyes and a thin-lipped smile spread across his face. "Yes. Of course. You, *Lady Romano,* and I form the bridge that shall end decades of strife. But without you, Lady Romano would not be present."

His words said one thing, but his eyes said another. The hair on the back of my neck rose.

"I am married to Valentino Valeri," I said.

"Oh?" he sniffed, bending to stroke the fingers of his good hand across the fur of my mask. "And did your father hand you over to him? Proper *tradere filia sua* was performed?"

"Of course. We did so on the allure of Castello Forelli so your spies would be certain to see."

He pursed his lips and cocked his head, as if this was the first he had heard of it. "What of *usorem ducere*? How did Valeri lead you to his home, with no home of his own to go to?"

"He has made his home with us, now."

"Hmm," Ercole said dismissively. "And who conducted the ceremony, Lady Forelli?"

I frowned at his use of my maiden name. "Our chaplain, Padre Giovanni."

"I see. And your chaplain is in good standing with his cardinal in Siena?"

"He is."

"Ahh, but your cardinal in Siena . . . he does not fare as well with the pope, does he?"

I leveled a gaze at him, wondering just what he was insinuating. "The pope is angry with our cardinal because he does not force our people to fill his coffers with gold."

"So he excommunicated everyone in the republic."

"Which he shall rescind in a year or two when he has need of us again. Such are the games that churchmen play."

Andrea took a couple steps toward me. "Some say that ceremonies conducted by the excommunicated can be declared null and void." He arched a brow. "That is what my cardinal tells me."

I laughed. "And *you* are suddenly in good standing with the *Church*?"

He lifted his hand and smiled. "The Lord moves in surprising ways."

I gripped the folds of my skirts to keep from slapping him. "In Siena, by law, we can simply marry before other witnesses. No priest is needed in order for it to be lawful."

He smiled. "And you wonder why you continue to incur disfavor with the Church."

"If the Church bestows favor upon only those who pander to *her* favors, then I am with my fellow Sienese in ignoring her. God knows our hearts."

He let out a long sigh. "Alas, so shortsighted! I fear you are not nearly as clever as you are beautiful. We shall have to work on that."

"There is nothing for you to work on. I am not your charge."

"You are my charge. For as of this morning, you are to be my bride."

I stared at him, blinking slowly. "Nay," I said slowly as I shook my head. "I am Sir Valentino Valeri's wife. I shall take no other to husband."

"Come now, m'lady. Even you can see how this shall settle things at once. Disavow your false nuptials and take my hand.

There was a reason that your union with Aurelio was to work so well. Both Firenze and Siena wanted it."

I glanced around the room, wondering if I suffered a nightmare, and discovered Celeste and the maid, both gaping at me. "Maria, please take Lady Romano for a walk in the courtyard garden."

"Yes, m'lady." The maid took the child's hand. Celeste looked over her shoulder longingly as they disappeared. Curious.

I looked back at Andrea. "I am here only to watch over Lady Romano. To keep her safe in our enemy's household. You must be aware that that was why I offered my service."

"Or was it," he asked, taking my hand, "to make me consider you anew?"

I laughed without mirth and snatched my hand away. I took a step back, but he followed. Again I stepped back, and again he followed. "Cease," I said.

"Why?" he asked, his voice a bit ragged as he stared at my lips. "Do you not trust yourself when I draw close to you?"

"I do not trust myself to not *kill* you."

"Is it rage you feel or desire? Both can make a person not think straight."

"This is not *desire*! I loathe you!" My back hit the wall.

He pressed against me. "Are you certain?" he whispered, bending his head as if to kiss me.

I slapped him, and he acted as if he barely felt it. "Such passion," he whispered again, close enough that I could feel his breath on my cheek.

I tried to strike him again, but he caught my wrist and put it on the wall above my head, pinning it painfully with his splint. I attempted to hit him with my other, but he ducked so that my hand merely glanced off his head.

"Such exquisite, fiery passion. My own little She-Wolf." He bent to kiss my neck. I tried to knee him in the groin, but my skirts impeded the impact. His lips touched right below my ear and trailed downward.

"I . . . am . . . with child," I gasped. I was not certain, yet. But there was a chance.

He paused, his lips hovering over the damp skin of my neck, and I felt a chill for more reason than one. This was most unwelcome news. But I took a breath. At last, at last, this would bring him back to his senses.

"'Tis Valentino's child," I added. "My *husband's*. Now get away from me."

He straightened but did not release me. He looked down at me for a long moment. "You are not the first woman to present such a problem to me. Sir Cafaro shall see you rid of it."

I gaped at him. "Nay! I do not wish to be rid of it. This child is already treasured!"

"You shall have others. Handsome sons and beautiful daughters bearing the Paratore name." He sniffed and then abruptly released me. He took a step away before I could lash out. "'Tis a good omen, as I think of it. Clearly, you are fertile."

I trembled in my fury.

Half of me could not believe what I was hearing.

Half of me did.

"You cannot force me. I shall not submit to Sir Cafaro's ministrations."

"Yes, you shall," he said soberly—as if he were a bit sad to make me do this. He went back over to the bed and lifted the wolflike mask.

A chill ran down my neck. Had he not dragged Luciana to the dungeon to submit to Cafaro's treatment? What would keep him from doing the same to me?

"I shall not take another bridal oath. I belong to Valentino Valeri alone."

"As discussed, your false oaths shall be dismissed."

"They were not false. They are legal and binding in Siena."

"But we are not in Siena, my love."

I stared at him. My *love*? I gaped at him. He was utterly mad.

No wonder Luciana had to flee! He belonged in an asylum. "You cannot force me to take the oath, to take you as husband. Even here, in Firenze, they shall not honor a marriage not freely entered into by both husband and wife."

"You shall take the oath and do so freely."

"Nay. I shall not!" I shook my head with a laugh. How could I make it more clear to him?

"I can think of a few ways to make certain you do." He stroked the fur of the mask.

"Such as?" I said with a laugh.

"Lady Celeste—she is a dear child, is she not? So tender, so sweet. So earnest in her desire to please."

I stared at him, waiting, before understanding dawned. "You would not dare." He would not harm her! Threaten her!

"Ah, yes. You see the way of it." He gave me a small smile. "'Tis all over your beautiful face."

My mouth was dry. Celeste was away from me, even now. I had sent her away! Yes, he could have dragged us apart at any moment, but I had allowed her to part from me. Something in that made it feel like I had somehow played right into his hands.

"Good." He gave me a crooked smile. "Comprehension dawns. Do not fret overmuch. I shall return her to your side in time. When our vows are spoken and our marriage consummated. And once all that is accomplished, we might happily send her *home*, yes? The Romanos would be glad for that. Yet another act of goodwill to solidify the new bond between our republics for years to come, yes?"

I could not answer him. Not a word came to my mind.

"Wear the costume this night, my love." He tossed my mask to the bed and gave me a long, languid look. "I am most eager to see you in it."

28

TILIANI

I paced for hours, hoping that Andrea would relent. But Celeste was not returned to me.

I turned hopefully toward the door when the latch opened, but it was a kitchen maid, not Maria. She set a small tray of bread, cheese, and wine on the table and turned back to the doorway to take a pail of warm water from a manservant. He closed the door behind her, and I watched as she poured it into a basin. Steam rose with a sinuous curve. "For you to freshen up, m'lady," she said, waving toward it. "Other maids will arrive soon to help you dress."

She turned to go, taking up Celeste's small dress and mask.

"Wait." I strode over to her and placed a gentle hand on her arm. "Please. Might you tell me where they took Lady Romano?"

"She is safe, m'lady. In her own room. Her new tutor is teaching her numbers."

New tutor? I had not even met the man! And now he was alone with her?

"Does she have a maidservant with her? She should not be alone with a man, even a trusted man such as this new tutor."

"Of course, m'lady. Lord Paratore saw to that himself. He sent Maria to chaperone."

"Oh, good, good," I said, partially mollified. At least the child was not in some dank dungeon. I wanted to believe that Ercole's threats toward Celeste were empty but could not quite do so. Nothing about Ercole had ever been idle or empty. The man was single-minded, and now his mind was set on succeeding where Aurelio had not . . . securing a Sienese bride.

The maid disappeared through the door again and the latch slid into place. I went to the basin and splashed my face, then took the cloth and rubbed my neck and chest, thinking. Ercole could not be trusted, ever. Not even if he managed to make me his wife. He would forever be motivated by furthering his own goals, no matter who it cost—whether that be Siena or Firenze herself. Once established at Castello Paratore, both sides would find difficulty in keeping him in check.

There was no way I would wed him, nor let him take this child from my womb. I had to escape and find a way to take Celeste with me. Might I run across a friend at the ball? The lord who had aided us under house arrest before? Other, more moderate Fiorentini who had been sympathetic to Aurelio's cause? I remembered him mentioning several, but none had risen to our defense when we were sentenced to the cages.

Nay, I had to get Celeste out of this city.

But as I thought about how—solely on my own, surrounded by so many of my enemies—I sank to the bed in tears.

LUCIANA

"H-how did you get *that*?" I asked Giulio, when he let me peek at the invitation to the masquerade that night.

He pulled me into a small alcove in the taverna and gave me a shy grin. "At times, God redeems the sins of our youth."

I smiled at him, pulling the invitation from beneath his tunic. I gazed at it in awe. "He redeems slip-gibbets?"

He looked back at me from beneath furrowed brows. Such handsome brows! I marveled at how gorgeous he was, but knew I was irritating him.

"Pickpockets?" I tried, wondering if *slip-gibbets* came into use in another hundred years or so. Maybe two . . .

He shook his head, making me concentrate again. I leaned close to whisper in his ear. "Thieves and rogues?"

He grinned and leaned back, looking down at me. His warm hand drew me close, perched at my lower waist. "You say that in a way that makes me believe you fancy thieves and rogues, m'lady."

I wrapped my arms around his neck and gazed up at him in silent adoration, marveling again that I could *see* him. "I love a man with a noble's heart, good sir," I whispered. I took hold of his tied collar and pulled him closer. "But if he had a *brief* history in thievery and rogue-dom, he might find that he understands me all the better."

He raised one of those handsome brows before he kissed me. "Truth be told, my moments as a thief were refined when I aimed to steal a sweet from the kitchen as a child. Once a man, I left such sins behind me. That said, I was rather good at it. And today proved I have not lost the touch."

We smiled together. When he pulled away, he grabbed my hand and said, "We need to find the proper clothes for this night, yes?"

"Yes! Masks! A new gown for me. A new tunic for you."

And we hurried down the street to find what we could.

TILIANI

I stood by the door, waiting for my escort. With the help of two maids, I had donned the gray-and-black gown. It took some effort to get the tight sleeves up my arms, as well as another tug on the laces of my bodice so that it was modestly closed behind me. I shut my eyes and gritted my teeth.

I did not doubt that Andrea Ercole had designed this—either he wanted me to endure the implicit shame of a too-small bodice, or he wished for this too-small bodice to show off . . . larger parts of me. And the skirt had a small train—I would need to hold it or endure other guests stepping on it all night. When I examined it over my shoulder, I understood why. While the majority of the skirt was gray, at the center was a swatch of black. I shook my head. *Giving the illusion of a tail, of course.* It was even more taillike when I picked up the skirt and hung it over my forearm, giving it a curl.

I put my hands to my cheeks, wishing I could wipe away the kohl and rouge the maids had applied to my face . . . a face that was to be covered by a mask! Why had they bothered? And yet as I stared at my reflection in the polished brass—bringing the mask before me and then away—I knew they had accomplished what they were after. The deep coal that lined my aquamarine eyes emphasized the slightly haunting effect of the wolflike mask.

I was further troubled when I removed the mask. With how the maids had applied the coal, my eyes continued to look completely foreign. As if I were truly half human and half wolf. A knock sounded at the door, and I rose from my small stool by the window, setting aside the burnished mirror and mask. The door swung open.

My adversary marched in and came directly toward me. He looked me up and down and his men at the door froze, clearly taken aback by his brazenness. After all, for weeks he had told them over and over that they must respect Lady Celeste and me as *ladies.* After finishing his circle of appraisal, he lifted my mask and passed it to me with a wink. "Come," he said. "All is prepared."

"I do not wish to don that mask, m'lord," I said.

"And yet don it you shall," he returned.

I blinked once, twice. "Mayhap there is another I might wear?"

"None that serve us as well as this." He lifted the mask in his good hand. "Enough chatter," he said, his tone chilling. "Don it, now."

I took a long, deep breath and took it from him. I sat down on the stool again and waited for the maids to pin it to my elaborately braided hair.

Lord Paratore looked down at me with utter pleasure and offered his hand. "Come, She-Wolf. Let us give Firenze that for which she hungers. We shall be the talk of the city!"

LUCIANA

We, unfortunately, did not appear in finery anywhere near what the nobles of Firenze wore that night. With word about the masquerade flooding the streets, mask-makers and dressmakers alike popped up like lemonade stands on a streak of hundred-degree days, back home. Giulio made the mistake of thinking the nobles would all be shopping in the same place. Turned out, the nobles had access to some other shopping district.

While our outfits looked like Internet knockoffs that took a month to receive in the mail from China, theirs looked like they had been planning with their private tailors for months. I heard it from the fishmonger—who had a brother who was a tailor—that he'd received a whole month's worth of engagements in one week. But they all had to be completed this very morn.

I had hoped he'd spoken of a small minority, but it appeared we were in the minority. And we were in such rare company that we drew disapproving stares. My mother's old advice came to me as clear as if she was whispering in my ear. *Own it,* I heard her say. *Stare right back at them. Make them think they are the ones who need to reexamine their choices.*

I smiled and did what she suggested. And magically, women stopped staring, and men stopped sniffing as if smelling something foul. Maybe they all weren't as self-confident as they pretended. Maybe they were now wondering if all their gold florins had not gone to waste. *Own it,* I thought with an inner laugh. That would pretty much have to define my entire night.

Still, there was a serious difference between bravado and blending in. And we needed to blend in to avoid discovery. If Ercole discovered *I* had stolen in? A shiver ran down my back. "Think we might trade our invitation with a couple of servants for the night?" I asked quietly. "Tell them we will do their jobs, and they can simply enjoy the celebration for once?"

"You think we can find such servants? They would risk dismissal."

"Indeed," I said with a sigh. "Or mayhap we can simply steal a couple of those cloaks."

Even as I said it, I knew I had convinced him. Because to lend an air of mystery, all the male servants passing out wine—and all the females, appetizers—wore long, dark cloaks with deep hoods. One of those would help hide my golden-brown hair and Giulio's dark, famously handsome looks.

"Clever." He steered me to a corridor to the right after we had passed the knights assigned for guard duty. Thankfully, neither of them looked us over for more than a cursory glance at our clothing and masks. Spotting far more elaborate and intriguing specimens behind, they had hurried us through—a Lord and Lady Spamotti, I think they had said. I thought of the poor Spamottis, madly searching for this invitation. Giulio had slipped it from the lady's purse after she'd shown it off to a companion, also shopping for masks. When it was disclosed that she, too, was attending the same masquerade, the conversation had dwindled as both women turned to opposite sides to peruse the inventory.

Giulio had taken that opportunity to lean toward the back wall and point to the red-beaded mask I now wore . . . and then to pilfer the invitation from the lady's forgotten parcel. After rapidly choosing the black-beaded one for himself, he paid the man and slipped from the milliner's shop before Lady Spamotti had finished trying on her tenth mask, still vacillating between two others.

I was just wondering how many florins it would take to convince a couple of servants to risk them losing their jobs— undoubtedly, challenging to replace without references—when we spied four cloaks on hooks outside a room. We could hear voices inside—were they changing? Without pause, we slipped two from the hooks and hastened away.

TILIANI

"Welcome, my fine friends!" Lord Garamondi shouted to the vast room as I entered through the wide, tall doorway on Paratore's arm. "Welcome!" He smiled at us and took several steps forward as the room quieted. He was a handsome, slim man with wavy brown hair tied at the nape of his neck.

"I offer a special welcome to our esteemed guest from Venezia, His Serenity, Doge Contarini, as well as his dogaressa." He bowed to the nobles as they inclined their heads. "Despite his clever disguise, I am certain you know my honored guest, Lord Andrea Ercole Paratore, back from his post along the border, along with his most intriguing companion."

Ercole gave an elegant, deep bow as the room erupted with cheers at mention of his name—even more so when he mentioned the border and me. He rose, smiled—visible even beneath his mask's mouth opening—and then gestured to me with a wave of his hand.

When the crowd quieted, Lord Garamondi went on. "And

to Lords Vanni and Piccolomini, two of the esteemed Grandi honoring us with your presence this night, I offer a special welcome."

I froze at the sound of their names. Ercole glanced at me after they inclined their heads toward him as well. I grimaced at how he wielded his newfound power with such ease. Seven years ago he was naught but a knight-at-arms in our keep; now he was a deadly enemy with significant power.

"Tell us, Lord Paratore," Garamondi said when the crowd quieted. "Did you bring a newly captured creature for the doge's menagerie?"

Ercole took my hand with his left and lifted it. "Nay, my lord. I fear I must keep this She-Wolf for my very own." He turned to the crowd again, still holding my fingers tight. "For she is the promise of our future filled with prosperity and peace. With her at my side, and Castello Paratore firmly secured, we shall insist our neighbors finally bow to our pleasure."

I tried not to wince as he clenched my fingers. Did he intend to send me to my knees, dramatizing his last statement? I refused. He could break my fingers before I bowed before him. Or I would break the rest of his.

"Your wolf needs a taste of a whip!" yelled a man, already feeling his wine.

"Or another turn in a cage!" shouted another.

"Mayhap," Ercole said with a grin at me. "Although I hear told that some animals can be made to heel with far kinder methods."

"Bring her to me, Lord Paratore," the doge bellowed. Ercole immediately complied.

I curtsied before the gray-haired man—the highest-ranking noble in Venezia—and inclined my head toward his lady before rising.

"I hear you came with Lord Paratore under your own volition," Doge Contarini said. He took a deep drink from his goblet and lifted it to a steward to refill.

"Yes, Your Eminence. To look after the young Lady Romano."

"Oh, yes, the Lady Romano! Where is she?" said the duchess. "We must have a look at her as well!"

The doge tiredly snapped his fingers and Ercole did the same. "Bring Lady Romano!"

The crowd parted, and I finally saw little Celeste, practically skipping toward us. Maria held her hand, but she was followed by two knights in Paratore-crimson tunics.

"Lady Romano," said the doge, leaning forward in his seat. He was a bulbous man, so the effort was no small one. "What do you think of this fine city?"

"I think it lovely, Your Eminence," she said with a bob of her skirts. "But I have not seen much of it since I arrived."

"Well, that should be remedied." He frowned at Ercole. "You cannot keep one so young cooped up in your confines, man! Take your guests out for an afternoon ride! Picnic along the River Arno, or better yet, drift along on her current!"

"The Venetians have always best understood the art of leisure," I dared to add.

"Quite so!" said the doge. "Have you visited us, Lady Forelli?"

"Regrettably, not since I was a child," I said. "But my mother and father shall always remember it fondly."

"As they should!" laughed the doge, lifting a hand. He leaned toward his wife. "My predecessor hosted their nuptials!"

The room erupted with excited chatter. Mayhap the Fiorentini did not know this tale as well as the Sienese.

"How do your mother and father fare?" asked the doge.

"They eagerly await my return," I said. "As does my husband, Sir Valentino Valeri."

The room erupted again, this time half with boos and hisses at the mention of his hated name. To them, he was the worst—not only had he betrayed the Fiorentini, but he now lived with and served the Sienese.

"She persists in thinking she wed him," Ercole said, shushing the crowd. "But Cardinal Argono shall help her understand how Valeri failed her. She is not the legitimate bride of the traitor!"

"Is she his *illegitimate* bride?" cried a boisterous man in the back of the room.

Any trace of a smile left Ercole's mouth. I could feel quiet rage begin to build in him, as did the people around us. A hush fell over the room.

Cardinal Argono intervened. Wearing his broad-brimmed red hat and ermine-lined red robe—seemingly impervious to the heat of the room—he stepped forward. "Lord Paratore sought out my counsel, and we discussed the issues at length this day. I have cast away any commitment he had to Lady Romano. It shall be under my authority that Andrea Ercole Paratore take Lady Forelli to wife! Saint Peter himself shall smile over their union and bring peace and prosperity to our fine republic through their union."

The crowd applauded slowly and then gradually gained in momentum. Ercole pulled me closer. "Smile at me now as if this is welcome news," he hissed in my ear. "Or Celeste will be taken from your sight immediately. And she shall not be skipping into the next room."

29

LUCIANA

I gasped as I finally made my way through the crowd and glimpsed Tiliani. She reminded me more of an actress in "Cats" than a She-Wolf in a ball gown, and Ercole seemed to be smiling down at her. Odder still was that *she* seemed to be giving *him* a pained smile. What was this about being a bride? What had they said? All around me, the crowd buzzed with chatter, many of them asking my same questions, no one seeming to know.

I carried a large jug of wine and refilled guests' empty goblets as I passed, affording me better access to eavesdropping. In short order, I understood the gravity of Tiliani's situation. We had to find the child, free both of them, and escape this palazzo and city. *No problem,* I groaned inwardly. Just another impossible-odds scenario. Again I prayed for Nico and Marcello and their progress with Cardinal Boeri. Because the cardinal present here was all kinds of bad news if he'd hooked up with Ercole.

When did I become a praying person? I wondered with a smile. Faith had snuck up on me as surely as my love for Giulio had. And both felt right. I guessed nearly losing my life, sight, and newly discovered family had all combined to teach me who I was meant to be. *Funny how the threat of loss can lead to magnified gratitude.*

"Lord Paratore!" cried the doge from his perch on the dais at the end of the grand salon.

"Yes, Your Holiness?"

"Permit me to escort the She-Wolf for the first dance, and I shall give you a fine ship!"

Ercole smiled and cocked his head, while putting his good hand to his heart. "Far be it from me to decline such a handsome offer, regardless of how it pains me to give her up."

Music rose above the din of conversation, and guests all around me moved to clear the center of the floor for dancers. I offered a tall man near me some more wine when I unexpectedly had a too-clear view of Ercole, and he of me. Had he recognized me?

I shivered at the thought. I could not be captured. Because I had no doubt he would break every finger of my hand as retaliation for what I had done to him. Or worse.

TILIANI

I was as eager to dance with the doge as he was with me. Here, here might be an opportunity to win his favor and persuade him to help us. *Grace, mercy, direction, Father!* I prayed as I made my way to the center of the floor to meet him. The musicians began with a song appropriate for an *estampie*—a couple's dance—and the man offered me his left hand and placed his right on my hip. With my train circling my forearm, I placed my right hand over his.

Thankfully, his touch was polite, not wandering.

"You are as lovely as they say, my dear," he said. "You must take after your mother."

"My father would say my good looks all came from him," I quipped, and that made the doge—about twenty years my senior— laugh. He was a gifted dancer, easily leading me about the floor and among other couples as they joined us. "Are you as gracious and strong a leader as they say *you* are, Your Reverency?"

"I like to think so." He paused in time with the music, lifted my left hand, and watched me as I turned under his arm in three measured points. We resumed our steps together again. "Why do you inquire?"

"Because I am in need of a strong and gracious friend. All of Siena is."

"I have heard of your plight. What would Venezia gain in coming to your aid?" he asked in a whisper as I passed before him to the other side again, paused, then returned.

"The Nine would certainly compensate you handsomely. Mayhap lumber for your shipyards? Leather for your cobblers? Sheep and cattle for your kitchens? Wine for your tables? Siena is rich in resources, which she eagerly trades with friends."

"We already trade with you," he grunted, "and have all those goods."

"Mayhap we can grant you more favorable terms," I said.

"Why not wed Lord Paratore and bring peace to your republic?"

"Because my heart belongs to my husband, a man I wed a little over a month ago."

"Ahh, love," he said. "I, too, have shared it with only one woman—the dogaressa." He paused and nodded his head toward her, and the pretty lady smiled in turn. Ercole stood beside her, and his brow furrowed in concern. Then the doge smoothly returned to our dance. "I do not wish to lose trade with Firenze."

"I do not ask you to divide from Firenze," I said. "You clearly have good friends among the Fiorentini. What we most need is for Perugia and Arezzo to cease their threat in joining Firenze against us."

"Ahh, yes. It was not a fair fight, was it?" He worked his lip as if thinking. "I might be of some assistance with Arezzo."

My heart pounded with hope. If he could block Arezzo from joining the Fiorentini against us, and Cardinal Boeri could persuade the Perugians, mayhap we could battle our way back to freedom.

"Could you reach out to them at once?" I dared to press. "Send an emissary?"

"Mayhap," he allowed. As the dance came to an end, he bowed, and I curtsied, wishing we could continue to speak in private. "There are nobles from Arezzo in this very room. I shall see what can be accomplished." He took my hand and kissed it.

"How ever might I repay you, Your Holiness?" I whispered.

"Bring your family and grace us with a visit to Venezia. You have been away far too long."

"With pleasure," I said, even as Ercole came to stand at my side again.

The doge moved to sit beside his wife as guests assembled into lines for the next dance.

"What was that?" Ercole asked. "He has invited us to Venezia?"

"Indeed," I lied. He could assume we were the family the doge referenced.

But Andrea Ercole Paratore would have a hard time going anywhere after I sent an arrow through his throat.

LUCIANA

While Ercole led Tiliani into a dance, I gestured to Giulio and went to the kitchens to fetch a full jug of wine. Our plan was to have at least one of us close to Tiliani at all times, looking for an opportunity to speak with her. But while I was out of the grand salon, I thought I'd try and see if I could find Celeste—or at least where they were keeping her.

When two Paratore knights came my way, I turned and picked up an empty tray, put my jug atop it, and lifted it to my shoulder. That afforded me the chance to turn my back as they passed—a relief, since I had never *seen* any of these men before. Only heard their voices. If they were the same guys who had served at Castello Paratore on the border. Had most been left behind, the city palazzo manned by different knights? The thought of it relieved me, since I'd be less likely to be recognized by the new crew. Regardless, I again gave thanks for the cloak and deep hood.

My eyes traced the beautiful frescoes along the hall as I peered into one doorway after another, wondering where they'd stashed little Celeste. Were they not intending to allow her to take part in the ball? The girl would love an event like this! But Ercole would likely prefer she be absent, especially if he had set his sights on Tiliani now.

A shiver ran down my back at the thought of it. Could he really manage it? Get her marriage to Valentino annulled and force her to marry him? Tiliani could refuse to utter the vows. Fight with everything in her to not even be present for a ceremony. Only one thing might persuade her: If Celeste was threatened. Both of us had volunteered to accompany the child out of a desire to protect her from Ercole. And well he knew it.

I heard voices up ahead and, with some relief, heard Celeste's sweet laugh. She was clearly with people who relaxed her, for she never laughed when stressed. I passed by the door with my tray and glanced inward, glimpsing a maid—maybe Maria—and a thin, young man on the ground, rolling dice with the child. The new tutor? He had a kind, smiling face, and I thanked God that the girl seemed to be in good hands . . . for the moment, at least. My heart went out to her anew—she was as darling as I had imagined. And she had the most adorable dimples when she smiled! There was no way—simply no way—we could leave that precious child to Ercole's whims.

The room was the second from the last, and at the end of the hall, I noted a window, barred from within. *Barred from within but with a door that opened to a small balcony.* I paused and studied the bars, the thick lock. Who held the key to that? I glanced outside. We were one floor up from the ground—above an alley. *Jumpable.* If we could only get through the door. On the horizon, a full moon rose. It would help if we were fleeing. Or be a hindrance if we were chased.

"You there! What are you doing?"

I winced in surprise and—mouth dry—turned slowly to face the two burly guards who sidled up to me, hands on the hilts of their swords.

"Forgive me," I said with a bob, tucking my chin. "The moon was simply so beautiful, I got lost in it for a moment."

"Should you not be about your duties in the grand salon?" asked one, lifting a hand to tip back my hood.

He did not sound familiar, but I batted his hand away when our eyes met. "Leave me be," I groused. "I shall return! Does not a girl deserve a moment's reprieve? I have been working since sunup!"

"Not if that girl is employed to serve the lord's *guests*," said the second. "Get back where you belong. And no more staring at the moon!"

"Hmmph." I pulled back my shoulders and sashayed down the hall, as if they were nothing but meddlesome fools. Not potential jailers. Memories of the dungeon at Castello Paratore were all too fresh. The scrape of metal at my wrists. The cold of the stones that sent my teeth chattering. But I aimed to walk as I thought a normal, innocent servant girl might. Not a twenty-first-century time traveler who had recently escaped their compadres in the country.

My next task would be to find the key for that lock. The knights behind me wore no keys at their waist. Who held them? Ahead of me, four knights entered the hall and carefully closed the door behind them. A moment later, two went through the same door. Did that lead to their quarters? Most palazzos had wings to house their knights, and that was where their armory was usually located as well.

I turned to enter another door that led to the kitchens, wondering if I had the courage to follow through with my plan. If I were discovered, all might be lost. Ercole would have me to abuse in compelling Tiliani to submit, as well as Celeste. But if I knew one thing about a group of bored knights, it was this: A full jug of wine could buy a whole lotta love.

30

Tiiliani

I sensed someone staring at me. Truth be told, I was under the scrutiny of many in the salon, but it was a servant that I spotted looking my way, again and again. His face was in such deep shadow, I could not make him out. But his mouth—his mouth and dimpled chin reminded me of Giulio Greco.

Which was ridiculous. Giulio would not be so reckless as to enter this palazzo. Would he? My eyes searched the room, studying each servant anew. Was Luciana here too? Had she now returned for me and Celeste? I could not imagine Luciana allowing Giulio to come alone.

Half of my heart hammered with hope, half with horror. I did not know how I was going to escape the palazzo with Celeste, but could they aid me? We had to flee in as quiet a manner as possible or we would have all of Firenze after us. And yet if he could get word to my elders about what the doge had said, mayhap that would be the best aid of all. A plan began to form in my mind.

I moved toward the servant, now praying it was indeed Giulio, when Ercole approached. He was accompanied by the young Sirs Rondelli and Donati. I froze at the sight of the Sienese men.

Stefano Rondelli grinned over my surprise, took my hands, and kissed both cheeks. "Friend, how lovely it is to see you!"

"Wh-what are you doing here?" I asked, while inside my mind

I screamed at them. *Traitors! What are you doing across the border?* Sir Donati took his turn, taking my hand and kissing it.

"I invited them here, my lady. In the spirit of our impending peace, I thought we might make inroads for renewed trade between our republics."

I frowned. These families already did a significant trade in weapons. These two had objected to a union with Aurelio Paratore and me because it might impede trade! Or was it because Aurelio had been the wrong sort of Paratore, with his heart and mind set on true peace rather than continued warfare? I angled a glance at Ercole. What had he negotiated with them? How long ago had his friendship formed? My skin crawled.

"I am certain you would not wish to sell weapons to our enemies," I said in a hushed voice, hating how my voice shook. How could they? How could they even consider it? How many Sienese would die when a Donati- or Rondelli-forged sword or arrow pierced their flesh?

"Nay. But do you not see?" Donati said. "With you and Lord Paratore soon wed, we shall become a sister republic to Firenze. Our weapons shall go to fight anyone who attacks us."

"But who would dare attack?" Andrea crowed, patting their shoulders. "Together we shall form a well-supplied, unified front that shall rule Toscana and beyond."

I almost laughed aloud. The animosity between our republics ran deep; the most Aurelio and I hoped for was tentative peace. What they spoke of now was impossible. Nay, Ercole simply wanted his hands on as many weapons as he could find before he led the Fiorentini in vanquishing the Sienese once and for all. I knew from my mother and aunt that Firenze would succeed, eventually, in doing so. But we wanted to lay a foundation for our family to survive when that occurred a couple hundred years henceforth.

"You are fools to believe him," I said to them. "You cannot trust him! Surely your fathers do not abide by this plan."

"Our fathers want us to build upon our family fortunes," Rondelli said with a frown. "They shall stand aside if they must."

"Stand aside?" I said. "The Nine shall hang you if you go through with this."

"Oh, I think not," Donati said, with a catlike smile. What did he mean by that? Had others in our ruling council already been bribed to support them? Did my father know?

"I believe your She-Wolf may require a muzzle," Rondelli said, crossing his arms.

"You there," Ercole summoned a servant.

The man turned toward us, and I sucked in my breath. It was Giulio. It had to be him. Even without seeing his nose and eyes. "Yes, m'lord," he said, with a lowered, humble tone. "How may I be of service?"

"Fetch the little Lady Romano. Bring her to us at once."

"As you please," he said and turned to go.

"Lady Romano?" Rondelli asked, shifting uncomfortably. "I thought you set her aside in favor of Lady Forelli."

"I have. But the child shall serve me in her own way." He sidled a glance at me. "I find that the Lady Forelli is more compliant when the child is within reach."

"Lady Valeri," I gritted out. "My name is Lady Tiliani Valeri. And no one shall 'muzzle' me."

Ercole's face split into a closed-lip grin. "You may be surprised," he whispered in my ear. "Now come. I believe the crowd requires a bit of entertainment." He lifted his head. "Bring my lady her bow and a quiver of arrows!"

LUCIANA

Having just made it into the knights' hall, I almost yelped in surprise when a servant pushed in the door I was trying to shut. "Lady Tiliani's bow and a quiver of arrows!" he shouted, passing by me. "Lord Paratore has asked me to fetch them!"

A knight appeared in the doorway to the left. "The lady's bow?" he frowned. "Did it come with us from Palazzo Paratore?"

"He seemed to think it was here," groused the servant. "It probably does not matter. Just give me your finest."

I peered over their shoulders as they searched the wall. It would matter to Tiliani. And if she was going to shoot, I wanted her to have the best possible outcome. "'Tis that one, on the upper right!" I said, pointing at the one that held a carving of a triangle on it—a nod to her father, uncle, and friends who carried a similar tattoo. "That is Lady Tiliani's."

"How do you know?" asked the servant.

"I was given it to store when they arrived," I lied.

"Hmph," he grunted. "How fortuitous! So fetch that one, man. And a quiver of arrows." He turned back to me. "Unless she had her own quiver too."

I searched the wall for it, but did not see it. "Simply send your finest. M'lady can shoot with most anything."

"That she can," the knight said. "Why does he send for it?" he asked the servant who handed them over.

"I can only guess that Lord Paratore wishes to show off her prowess with the bow."

I narrowed my eyes. That could not be all he wanted. But before they shooed me away, I saw ring after ring of keys. My heart sank. We would likely not have time to try one after another. Which one could it be?

"Did you need a sword or shield, girl?" scoffed the knight gruffly, hands on hips.

"Nay, of course not," I said with a laugh. "I simply wished to admire your fine armory. Palazzo Garamondi appears prepared for battle!"

"As it should. An unarmed lord is soon a dead lord."

"Quite." With a quick bob I turned to go, carrying my jug of wine.

"Girl!" barked the man.

I froze and slowly turned. Had he recognized me? My voice? "Yes?" I asked sweetly.

"'Tis no skin off the lord's nose to leave that jug with us, is it?" He gestured to the wine.

"Of course not," I said, handing it over. "I shall simply go and fetch another."

He smiled as he took it but then narrowed his gaze at me. "What were you doing in this hall?"

"I-I became a bit lost. Forgive my intrusion."

"Well, if you intrude with wine jugs in your arms, come again. And bring some friends." He grinned and then used his finger to poke back the top of my hood. I gave him a tremulous smile when his face didn't contort with outraged recognition. He did not know me.

"I shall look forward to it," I pretended to flirt. "After we see the last guests out."

As long as the last guests are Tiliani and Celeste.

31

TILIANI

As Andrea left my side to clear the dance floor, I understood what he wanted. He wanted to show off my skills with the bow and arrow. As if they were now his.

"Wine, m'lady?" asked a man at my elbow.

Even before I turned, I knew it was Giulio. "Yes, please. I am quite parched."

He poured slowly.

"I need to get out of here," I whispered. "He plans to threaten Celeste to get what he wants. Me."

"Agreed. But how?"

"I do not yet know. But stay alert." He handed me the goblet of wine, and our eyes met for a moment. "The doge shall call off Arezzo. See if my uncle can persuade the cardinal to dissuade the Perugians."

He nodded and turned away to offer wine to another guest as Andrea strode back toward me. If Giulio was discovered here, in disguise . . . and Donati and Rondelli would know him in an instant! *Grace, Lord. Mercy. Please direct our way out of this city! Away from Ercole!*

I saw that Maria had entered the salon with Celeste and brought her over to Ercole. A knight followed them, carrying my bow and a quiver of arrows.

"Friends!" Ercole called to the room, and everyone hushed.

"Many of you have heard of the famous She-Wolves of Siena, but few have been blessed to see one in action. I can attest, after meeting them on the battlefield, that they are indeed formidable. But soon I shall have this one at my side—as my bride." He gestured to me with his good hand but then laid it to rest on Celeste's little shoulder in subtle threat. "She shall be Firenze's to claim as their very own!"

The room erupted in cheers, and I blinked back rising tears of rage. The knight came to me, and everything in me wished to grab my bow and send an arrow into Ercole's neck. But then I would promptly be killed, and Celeste would be left alone. Ercole smiled, seemingly reading my thoughts. I set aside my wine goblet and mask, took the bow, and awaited further instruction.

The doge was accustomed to entertainment. Would this suffice?

"Lady Tiliani, please strike the top of this magnificent cake," Ercole said, gesturing to a towering confection on a side table.

I drew my arrow and let it fly even as he took two steps away. It pierced the center of the top layer and hit the back wall. Women gasped and polite applause arose.

"Well done, m'lady," the doge said approvingly from his seat on the dais.

"Another!" the dogaressa cried, clapping her hands.

"The third candle on this candelabra," Ercole said next, gesturing to it as he passed.

I aimed and released my arrow, neatly snuffing out the third candle. More gasps and more applause arose.

"My goblet!" cried a drunk man, raising it high in the air. Guests around him moved away, both frightened and entranced.

I hesitated as he wavered with each breath he took. But I timed my breathing to his, aimed, assumed, and shot where I believed his goblet would be a second later. It struck the side of the glass, and wine sloshed all over the man. He was outraged, but everyone around him laughed, chiding him for his foolishness.

"Here!" Ercole called on the far side of the room. He turned Celeste toward me, a large apple on her head.

I lowered my bow, aghast. "Nay."

"Do so at once, or I shall hand your bow to the finest Fiorentini archer in the room." A sly smile spread across his face. He knew I would not trust another.

"What do I receive if I am able to do this?" I asked, trying to buy time.

"What is it you wish, my love?"

I bit the inside of my cheek, wanting more than ever to silence him with an arrow. To keep him from any other words of love that felt like diving into mucky, slimy waters. *Direction, Lord. Show me.*

The words emerged before the thought was fully formed in my head. "To return to the borderlands before our nuptials. To gaze upon the hills I love outside Castello Paratore before we wed. For a sennight to receive guests from Siena for the wedding feast, as well as my family."

He squinted, considering me and—likely—my true motives.

"Agreed. We shall return. But we shall wed within *three* days of returning to the castello." He took a step away from the girl. "No one important to the Forellis lives farther away than that. And we shall leave on the morrow."

"So eager to bed a She-Wolf, my lord?" cried a man.

"One has to move fast when in pursuit of *lupe*!" returned Ercole. "See how long the lady has spurned suitors!"

I ignored them. Stifled my rage at how easily he set aside Valentino's claim on my heart. We were returning to the border! And Giulio had heard it—they would have three days to help see us freed. I hoped he was leaving even now. That he and Luci would reach the city gates before they were locked for the night.

"Close your eyes, little sister," I called to Celeste, gratified when the girl immediately did so. But I could see her trembling hands. I needed her as still as possible. "Think of being safe at home." I drew my arrow, and a bead of sweat ran down my temple. "Think of being held in the arms of your dear mama." As I said the last word, I sent my arrow flying, and it neatly split the apple in two.

The room erupted in cheers. Celeste, eyes wide, flung herself into Maria's arms, crying.

"Is she not the finest shot you have ever seen?" Ercole cried, stretching out his good arm. "And now she is all ours." He paused halfway across the floor. "One more, my darling." He made an O-shape with his thumb and index finger and lifted his arm straight above him. "Make it through that, and I shall buy you the finest necklace the goldsmith has to offer."

I gaped at him. "What happens if I strike you instead? You risk losing a finger, m'lord, at the very least." I was stalling. I knew if I even grazed him, there would be repercussions.

"Do not be a fool!" called the doge. "You are already one hand down!"

The room laughed with him.

"Come now," Ercole chided, concentrating only on me. "I know you can do this. And I want all our friends here to see how I now trust you, as they may too." He stared at me. Daring me. It was a matter of pride for him now.

I bit my lip and drew my arrow, my aim hovering over his throat. But if I even maimed him, Celeste and I would likely suffer.

I hated the man. Hated him so much that it sent my hands to trembling. I lowered my bow.

"A bit of wine for the lady!" Ercole called. "She fears harming her handsome husband-to-be! She fears I will not have one good arm with which to hold her!"

Women twittered and fanned themselves. A servant offered me a full goblet, but I declined it.

Grace, said a voice in my head. *Mercy.*

Leave him to me, the Lord was telling me. He was leading us. I had a way out of the palazzo and would soon be back on Siena's border. So close to home, to Valentino. To hope.

I lifted my bow, my hands steady again. Sucking in my breath, I let the arrow fly.

Ercole pulled back his hand so fast I thought I had hit him. But he laughed and sucked at a scratch, then shook it as if to shake away some pain. A lady nearby handed him a handkerchief.

I released my breath. He was not seriously injured. I had only grazed him.

And as reward, we would head south come morn.

32

LUCIANA

Giulio took my jug of wine and set it on a table. "We shall go," he whispered.

I was glad he knew what he was doing. Because after watching all that come down with Tiliani, I was a bit shell-shocked. Had she really just shot an apple off the top of Celeste's head? Another through the hole of Ercole's fingers? I knew how much it must've taken not to shoot him instead. But then all might have been lost.

I followed him down the servants' stairwell and to the kitchens. We ditched our cloaks as we went, revealing our mediocre costumes. Knights stationed there did a double take as we left before any of the other party guests.

"*Mia moglie è malata,*" Giulio said, taking my elbow.

I swallowed a grin as I ducked my head, bringing a hand to my belly. *My wife is ill,* he'd said. I liked the word "wife" on his lips. I mean, I *really*, really liked it.

"Go with God," said one knight, opening the door for us.

And just like that, we were on the streets of Firenze again. A city bell clanged their warning. We had to hurry if we were going to get out the city gates before they were locked for the night. Once out of earshot of any other pedestrians, I said, "I feel terrible leaving them behind again."

"I do too," Giulio said. "But it was a brilliant move on Tiliani's part. She bought us time. Time to convince the Perugians to stand down. Time for the doge to convince the nobles of Arezzo. And time for us to rescue her and Celeste before Ercole forces her to marry him."

"What is to keep him from changing his mind? For not pressing her this very night?"

He shook his head. "'Twas too public. He will not want that many people witnessing him going back on his word. She did not ask for much. And he wants to return to the border anyway. To his mind, he needs to return to see Siena—and the Forellis—vanquished, once and for all. He shall want to revel in our misery. Parade Tiliani about where Valentino can see her."

I shivered, thinking about delivering the news to Val. It had nearly been his undoing, seeing her go. But now? Believing that there was even a chance for Ercole to annul their marriage and claim her for his own? Ercole would need a dozen additional guards to face down Valentino's wrath.

TILIANI

Ercole took my hand, and we joined in the next line dance and then the next, with music and steps that reminded me of far happier occasions in Siena. I was glad for the distraction—the excuse to not have to talk—and the ability to search the room as I turned this way and that. A number of servants wore their deep-hooded cloaks, but none looked in my direction as most of the guests did. I prayed that meant that Giulio was gone, taking Luciana and anyone else with them out of this cursed palazzo. I could breathe again as I imagined my friends making their way through the city gates, on to meet with my uncle and Nico. Could this mad plan work? Could Siena summon enough fighting men to drive Firenze back? Even reclaim Castello Paratore?

Because I never wanted Andrea Ercole Paratore within my sight again. Even now as he took my hand, I fought to not wrench it away. Or not to slap his satisfied, gloating face. He was reveling in this—this illusion that I was vanquished. But I had to feign acquiescence for now. For the good of my people, my family, and Celeste.

Celeste. Maria had ushered the weeping girl out of the salon soon after I had pierced the apple atop her head. Would she ever forgive me? Did she understand why I had to do it? I hated the idea that I might have broken the trust that had been forged between us over the past month. Once we had a moment alone, I hoped I could make amends.

When the doge and dogaressa departed, I tried to make my escape too. But Ercole pinched my arm and hissed, "You shall stay by my side *to the end.*" So dutifully, I remained, telling myself again and again to do nothing to rile him. Celeste had suffered enough this night. I did not want to give him any excuse to traumatize her further.

Finally, the last dance was done, and more guests departed, leaving few but Lord and Lady Garamondi. I stood beside him, gracefully saying farewell to each of them. Most gazed upon me like an exotic animal in the doge's menagerie. Something fascinating but not entirely trustworthy. Did they not know that my heart beat in tandem with theirs? That we all—whether Sienese or Fiorentini—bled red? That I had hopes and dreams and fears, just as they did? Why did it have to be that one city conquered the other? Why could we not simply live in peace and partnership? I recognized anew why Aurelio, my papa, and Zio Marcello had dreamed for the same, and forgave them again for trying to force it into place.

"They shall accept you in time," Andrea said, pulling me closer to his side with a broad hand on my far hip as we finally left the grand salon. "Once they know that you can be trusted. It may take years, but in time . . ."

I nodded. "And what is to transpire in the meantime?" I turned to face him and broke his hold. Trying not to let him see how his touch sickened me. "How do you envision this union making things right?"

He stared down at me. All the servants disappeared, sensing his mood, and he ushered me into an empty room. "How does this make things right?" he asked, closing the door with deceptive calm. "How does this make things right?" he repeated, this time, more strident.

I took a step back and he followed, trying to get ahold of himself. His good hand went to the back of his neck, massaging it. Then he drew himself up and stared down at me. "Do you know how I longed for you while I was in the service of your father?"

I frowned. "What?"

"Never would you even look my direction. Not until you caught me with that maid . . ."

"You were a knight in my father's *service*," I said. "'Twouldn't have been proper." Not that I would have ever wanted—

His hand came at me, lightning fast, and he pinched my chin painfully. "So high and mighty!" He leaned closer. "I knew you looked down upon me. I *knew* it. And then and there, I began to plan. I would become the lord with the authority to claim you. And the magician able to outwit you."

I stared back into his hazel eyes, alight with intensity. He had planned all of this to . . . win *me*? All of what he had put my family through, all of what people we loved had suffered, was all due to a warped desire to win *me*?

I could not help myself. I shook my head and his hand broke free. "This is not the way to win a woman, Lord Paratore. Not win her heart."

He drew himself up. "I need not your heart. Only your body. Your title. And to know that what once was denied me," he bit out, leaning so close I felt his breath on my cheeks, "can no longer be denied." A slow smile spread across his cheeks. "You shall become mine, Tiliani. As soon as we are certain you are not with child. On the morrow, you shall be sent a tonic. And the morrow after. Part of why I agreed to your delay for our nuptials was to be certain you are rid of it. I want no doubt to the paternity of our future child."

"For the future of our republics, m'lord," I said, bowing my head, even as my mind screamed *nay*. For if he thought I fought him on this, he would be watching like a hawk to make certain I drank every drop.

"Very good," he said approvingly as I met his gaze, seemingly somewhat placated by my feigned subservience. He tipped my chin up, studying me, and I willed away any fight. For my baby's sake, I could not fight him now. "Very, *very* good." He bent to kiss me, and I averted my lips, only allowing him to graze my cheek. He laughed lowly. "You may deny me now, but not after I take you to wife, Tiliani. Then—"

"Nay, m'lord," I said earnestly. "When I am your wife, I shall know my place, my duties. I confess I . . . I did not know how you yearned for me when you resided at Castello Forelli." I smiled and ducked my head as if shy. Even as if I was flattered. But inside, I was thinking *it shall be over my dead body that I shall ever be your wife.*

I did not know what would become of Siena if I denied him. But I did know that I had to fight with everything in me to keep it from happening.

He put a knuckle under my chin. "I find the waiting . . . delectable. Come now. Let us return to our home." He ushered me out, and in time, the other Paratore knights fell into line surrounding us as we walked through the streets in relative silence, Maria and Celeste right behind us. Once in the palazzo, Ercole ushered me to my room and, holding my hand, looked down at me. "I know this has been a great deal for you to grasp." He paused. "I admire how you have ceased to fight me."

"Thank you, m'lord."

He lowered his chin. "They *are* marks of agreement, yes? You are not plotting . . ." He paused to dig the toe of one boot into the seam between the fine marble stones at our feet. "Against me?"

I blinked rapidly. "Plotting?"

A tiny smile tickled his lips. "Nay, I thought not. Because," he paused to trace a slow line across my clavicle—a touch I fought not to break—"if you thwart me, if you even attempt to *waylay* me . . ." he leaned closer to whisper in my ear, "it shall not be you, but Celeste, who suffers."

I stepped back and knit my hands before me. "Thank you for your word of caution, m'lord. But I assure you that I want only to restore Lady Celeste back to the loving arms of her parents. And I shall do everything I must to ensure that is done." I hoped it was a sweet smile upon my face. Because inside I was thinking I would do just that. As soon as he was dead.

Leave him to me, the Lord had said. It rang through my head again then.

"*Buonasera,*" I said, bidding him good night.

"Buonasera, my lady," he said with a satisfied nod, allowing me to depart at last.

I entered the room and closed the door quietly, when I longed to slam it shut and lock him out. But the bolt was on the outside, of course. With my back to the door, panting, I felt him slide it into place. Locking me in. Trapping me.

And as he strode away, whistling a tune, I sank to the ground, my skirts mounding about me. And finally, I could let the tears of frustration and fear and fury slide down my face.

33

'Twas Celeste who found me, come morn, still with my back against the door—as if I could keep the monsters out—and the kohl around my eyes streaking down my face.

"M'lady!" she cried, hurrying to my side after she and Maria entered via a hidden door between our rooms. She flung herself into my arms.

"Celeste! How did you get in here?"

"We cannot stay long. Maria knew of the door. Lord Paratore does not."

Maria gaped at me. I had given into slumber right there against the door, still in my terribly tight stays and gown, my "tail" spread out beside me. I was certain I appeared half dead.

"Celeste." I cradled the child's head against my chest. "Might you ever forgive me?"

She drew back. "For saving me? Maria said that any other in that room would surely have shot me at that distance!"

"I am so sorry," I said. "If there had been any other option—"

"You did the best you could," assured the girl. She glanced at our maid. "Maria helped me see that. I-I only regret that I had not your fortitude afterward."

"Oh, dear one," I said, gripping her cheeks, "you have already endured far more than any young woman should. I shall do my best to shield you from what is to come, but I fear we have some trying days ahead." I finished in a whisper, eying Maria. Could I trust her to keep our secrets? Had she not come to my aid in explaining my actions to the girl? Shown her in here this morn, ignoring Lord Paratore's obvious wishes?

"Come to the baths, m'lady." Maria offered her hand, as if in response. "You do not wish the master to find you in such a state."

"Nay, I do not." I groaned as I rolled to one sore hip, objecting to my choice to sleep all night against the door. I rose, noting how my arms were sore too—mayhap the tension of holding my bow taut for so long last night. I closed my eyes, viscerally longing for Castello Forelli. For Valentino. For sparring and patrol and not this nightmare of courtly maneuvers.

"A hot bath will set you to rights," Maria said, offering her arm.

I took it and rose. "If only that was all that was required."

"You may be surprised," she said with a wink. "When the maids arrive with your tray, insist upon a visit to the bathing rooms. You shall not regret it."

I did as she suggested—after the two of them had disappeared back into their own room—and with some relief, discovered them again in the bathing wing—a luxurious series of rooms that included an *apodyterium,* where one undressed, *caldarium* for a steam and dips in a warm pool, then a *frigidarium* to cool. I had elected to sponge-bathe since our arrival, feeling more vulnerable in the bathing chambers, disrobed. But by the time I finished that morn, I wanted to install the same at Castello Forelli. Never had I experienced anything like it. In the caldarium I had been soaped from tip to toe and rinsed, several times, gradually heating in the steam. In the frigidarium, a maid massaged my sore muscles with oils as I cooled, until I was loose and languid, ready to do naught but lounge about.

But there were things to do. Lord Paratore had called for us all to pack and be on our way within hours, intent on reaching Castello Paratore on the morrow. I wondered how my friends and family fared. If they were already en route back home. If they were sending emissaries to all who needed to be contacted. I wondered how the doge had fared with the nobles from Arezzo.

So much was beyond my control.

As the maid left me in the cooling chamber—scents of rosemary and lemon rising about me—I prayed. For our safety. For continued direction. For mercy along the road, every step of the way. *I love Valentino, Lord,* I prayed. *I love him. Please let us honor our marriage vows. Help me find the way! Direction, direction, direction.* Would I forever be praying to be shown the way?

Celeste, fresh from her own bath, joined me, all wrapped up in a towel like we had never seen before. Turkish, the maid mentioned. But when she left, the girl curled up beside me and together we just breathed.

"We shall find our way," I said after a while.

"I know it," she said, cradled under my arm.

"Does it bother you, that I have accepted his request for my hand?" I whispered.

"Nay." She glanced up at me, all pink cheeks and bright eyes. "For I know you did so for Siena, and in doing so, to spare me. Thank you, m'lady."

I squeezed her tightly. "Of course. I would do anything, my friend, to spare your family any more pain. If Lord Paratore is anyone's trial, he is mine alone. We had always planned to help you find your way to freedom. That is why Luciana and I asked to attend you."

"You are as brave as you are beautiful, my lady."

"And I could say the same of you. I think we shall be friends for years to come and tell tales of our last eve together to everyone we meet."

She straightened and grinned. "No one shall believe us!"

I squeezed her hand. "We shall have reenactments, but use dummies, of course."

"That shall be grand!" she grinned. "How my friends will squeal!"

I contemplated her as I returned her smile. Yes, how her friends would *squeal*. Because they were so young they would see only the excitement, not the terror. A terror I was certain she now understood. I took her hand in mine. "Celeste, we shall encounter more strife in the days to come," I whispered. "I shall do everything I can to keep you safe. But I shall need you to respond as a She-Wolf would to my commands, understand? When I tell you to duck, you do so. When I tell you to run, you do so. My goal is to get you safely back to your family. But in order to accomplish that, I cannot doubt you will do as I say. Agreed?"

"Agreed, my lady."

"Every order, the second I command it?"

"Every order."

I took a deep breath. "With God's favor, we are going to survive this." I gave her a squeeze. "Thank you for seeing it through with me. This is far more than a girl of your age should have to endure."

She rose and straightened her shoulders. "I am a lady, am I not? Lady Celeste Romano. Would you have not done the same, at my age?"

I grinned at her. "I would hope, friend. I would sincerely hope."

Maria returned and helped us dress, winding our hair into knots. As we sat side by side, I thought, *this is what it would be like to have a little sister,* and I felt the familiar longing for a sibling—especially a girl. My own little brothers had died young, and my cousins were like siblings in many ways, but the closest I had to a sister was Ilaria Greco. I was thankful for her, but a sister-bond was special. I could see it between my mother and aunt. My hand went to my belly. If I was with child, was it a girl?

I had not been sick for two days, but I had not started my monthly courses either. Was it merely the upheaval in our lives that kept it at bay? I knew such things could interrupt a woman's cycle. Mayhap I could tell Lord Paratore that I had been mistaken—that I had confused a stomach ailment with potential pregnancy.

I was in the midst of hoping that he had forgotten to call upon Sir Cafaro for the tonic that might rid my body of a babe when a knock sounded at the door and we heard the bolt slide backward. In strode Ercole with Sir Cafaro on his heels, carrying a common water vessel. I rose, trying to ignore my shaking knees.

"Please fetch a cup, girl," Sir Cafaro said to Maria. He set the bottle on a small table by the settee.

She bobbed a curtsey. "Yes, right away."

"I-I do not think there is any need for that, Sir Cafaro," I said.

"Nay? Have you begun to bleed then?"

"Y-yes," I said, lying through my teeth.

Andrea narrowed his eyes, and his lips drew back in distaste. "We shall need to see the blood upon your garment or sheets."

I froze, caught.

Andrea closed in on me and Celeste. "I told you," he said, staring down at me, "we cannot wed until we are certain you are not with child."

"Then let us wait until the morrow, or the next. We do not wed for three days."

Maria arrived with the cup and turned her back to us as she set it on the table. Only I saw her depart again, her back to us the whole time. But the men looked only at me.

"'Tis best to take the tonic for three days. And it might cause some cramping," the physician said. "You do not want to be ailing on your wedding day." He turned to pour me a cup. "Now drink this down at once. Then another right after. 'Tis best to get it to your gullet as quickly as possible."

"I-I do not wish to," I said, backing up a step. "My grandmother is the only one I trust to formulate medicinals. I do not want any long-lasting harm to come to my womb." Placing my hands on my belly, I cast a desperate look to Andrea. "Nor do you, my lord."

Sir Cafaro let out an exasperated breath and drew himself up. "Your doubt in my skills is an affront. I assure you that I am the finest barber-surgeon within three days' ride. And you are not the first woman I have assisted in this way."

Ercole moved behind Celeste and stroked her hair. "I am done waiting on a woman's cycle. And I want to be certain you do not carry the traitor's brat."

He pulled Celeste closer to him, his hand sliding beneath her neck. The child's eyes widened, pleading with me to come to her aid. Ercole's eyes held nothing but deadly intent.

"Oh, do drink it down, my lady," Maria said, hands fisting in her skirts. "'Tis for the best for all. I shall see you through it." Her warm brown eyes told me something else. To trust her?

"Yes, yes," Sir Cafaro said, irritated with my delay. "Your maid shall be with you every step of the way. And we are soon to set off for the border. You shall need these few hours to allow your body to . . . process the tonic."

I lifted the cup to my lips, sniffed it, as my eyes darted from one to the next. Mayhap it would not work. Mayhap I was not even with child. And was my responsibility not to see *this* child before me—Celeste—to safety? I could not do that in the heart of Firenze.

"It smells and tastes a bit foul," Cafaro warned. "Another reason to drink it quickly."

Seeing no way out, I prayed for protection and drank the cup down. But it tasted like nothing at all. It tasted like . . . water.

"Allow me, sir." Maria took the bottle from the surgeon and filled it with the remaining liquid. "Make haste, m'lady," she said, those brown eyes again telling me to trust her.

I took the cup from her and dutifully swallowed the remains, pretending to scowl in distaste.

"I shall fetch you some watered wine, m'lady, to rid you of the taste," Maria said, taking the cup from me. She still carried the bottle—a bottle she had managed to switch with water! "And you should lie down."

"Yes, yes, I should," I said, my hand again going to my belly. I grimaced, feigning illness already.

"We shall leave you to it," Cafaro said, rubbing his hands together. "And I shall return to check on you before you depart."

"Thank you, friend," Ercole said, leaving Celeste and

walking him to the door. "You shall send two more treatment tonics with us?"

"Of course, my lord."

Celeste walked with me to the bed chamber, her eyes filled with concern. She wound her small arm about my waist, and I gave her a small, reassuring smile.

"My lady," Ercole called.

I glanced at him over my shoulder, brows furrowed as if I might be sick at any moment.

"I appreciate your obedience in this manner. There shall be more babes for you to carry in the future. Those that shall proudly bear the Paratore name."

I could not even summon a suitable response. He was utterly reprehensible. So instead I bolted for the chamber pot in the next room, pretending to retch. Celeste closed the door, blessedly forming a barrier between us and the vile man, while I continued to gag. Maria arrived from the servant's entrance and rushed over to us, her hand to my back. "My lady!"

I lifted a hand to her, gagged and coughed again, then panted until I heard the bolt slide back into place. Then I rose and enfolded the maid in my arms. "Thank you. Thank you, thank you, thank you!"

"Of course, m'lady," she said with an impish grin.

"What can I do to repay you?" I asked.

Her gaze moved to the door, obviously thinking of Lord Paratore and the repercussions if we were found out. "You mean to escape, yes?"

I gaped at her. How did she know? But then, servants often observed and understood far more than we thought they did, attuned to the small details of their masters and mistresses as they were.

She took my expression as response enough and squeezed my hand. "If you do, please take me with you," she whispered. "I have family in Siena and wish for employment with anyone but *him*. There is not a woman in his household that is truly safe."

34

LUCIANA

We watched as the train of wagons and people on horseback arrived at Castello Paratore. Situated on the cliff a quarter mile away, we had a clear view of the whole, long parade of men. And weapons. Ercole was not arriving ill prepared; he was clearly preparing for potential war. I swallowed hard. Glad to see the women . . . but not the armaments.

They had in their train of goods a trebuchet as well as what looked like a cannon, the first of its kind. "That's a thing now?" I asked my brother in English as he settled down to his belly beside me. "Cannons? I thought they were only in Asia in the fourteenth century."

He grinned sardonically. "Therein is the tragedy of the American public school system. Clearly, the Chinese were trading weapons earlier than we thought. Or Ercole is a more erstwhile tradesman than we gave him credit for."

I sighed and looked back at the cannon snaking its way up the road to Castello Paratore, with her crimson flags waving in the wind. "Let's hope they are as inaccurate as they are primitive," I groaned.

"Let's hope," my brother said. "What's the plan of attack?"

"We have none," I said morosely. "Other than all of Siena assembling at our back in three days' time."

"Nothing like a battle to kick off some wedding festivities. Ercole will be a total Bridezilla when things don't go his way. I can't wait to watch it come down."

I laughed. "Me too. As long as we can get Til and Celeste outta there first."

"He's not likely to let them wander in the glen, looking for herbs. I doubt he'll let them out of the castle before it's done."

I sighed heavily. "Have you heard anything from Cardinal Borgio? Anything on the Arezzians?"

"Not yet. But the dude wants that roof for his cathedral, sis. He *wants* it. And Marcello promised him the funds up front, if he could help us with this, uhh, challenge. And a little persuasion with the Perugians. Maybe we'll get confirmation today."

Challenge. We were watching enemy forces assembling with new weapons. Two of our own disappearing behind enemy lines. One betrothed to the most hateful man I'd ever met.

"There are things to do, bro," I said.

"Oh, yes," he answered. "There are definitely things to do. Beginning with keeping Valentino from tearing on over to Castello Paratore when he finds out his *wife* is there." He looked at me, his expression tender. "I'm so glad you're not in there too."

"Me too," I said. "But I also hate that I had to leave them behind," I said again.

"The lengths one has to go to, to avoid brain surgery in 1372 Firenze . . . You didn't think that would go well?"

I snorted a laugh. "Just pray we get them to safety before all this comes down, will you?"

"Done."

TILIANI

Castello Paratore had more men inside her walls than I had ever seen. My heart had sunk when I glimpsed the cannon and trebuchet they hauled from Firenze. It sank further when I saw how many knights accompanied us. And further still when I saw the massive encampment on the north side of the castello— all Fiorentini, not even the promised forces from Arezzo and Perugia. But the sheer number of men inside Castello Paratore itself threatened to bring me to the edge of despair. Never had I seen so many ready to defend her and Firenze. I did not think that this many knights had come against us since before I was born.

How was I to escape with Celeste and Maria in tow? I could not get them over the edge, as Luciana had. I could not risk Celeste's safety. And while Maria had surprised me with her bravery, I did not know if it would extend to rappelling. Besides, every knight on the allure would be on the lookout for such an attempt again. Those on watch the night Luciana escaped had received floggings.

We were unloading our trunks when someone came to the door. Here, too, a bolt had been installed on the outside. We straightened as it slid open. Maria answered the knock and revealed a manservant with two armed knights behind him.

"Lady Forelli," said the man. "Your elders have come to call. Lord Paratore requests you join them in his receiving room at once. You are to leave Lady Celeste behind."

I glanced back at Maria and Celeste. "I shall return as soon as I am able," I said, giving them both a reassuring nod. It heartened me that the most dangerous man in the castello would be in my presence, not menacing them. I followed the servant, the knights directly behind me. My heart pounded at the thought of seeing my parents, my aunt and uncle. Mayhap they might be able to negotiate with Lord Paratore anew!

"Ahh, there you are, my sweet," he said, as we entered. My elders were clearly perplexed by his endearment, but they said nothing as they came to hug and kiss me.

"Are you well?" Mama asked, holding my hands and taking a step away to examine me.

"Very well," I said. "As is Lady Celeste. Please send word to her parents that Lord Paratore is looking after us both."

"And well I should," he said. "Please. Come and sit and we shall tell you what has transpired."

We stepped closer to the large window that overlooked the castello courtyard, teeming with knights sparring and patrolling and servants carrying goods. Had he asked to see them here so that we would all be reminded of how he had us outnumbered?

"What has transpired?" Zio Marcello said, declining wine when Andrea offered it. He looked from me to my captor and to me again. "Out with it. You arrived carrying weapons that do not suggest the peace we had hoped for across the border."

"Weapons I hope to never have to employ," Ercole said easily, sitting down beside me with a goblet of wine in hand. "Think of them as nothing more than assurances that the vows I exchange with Lady Forelli shall take place as planned."

I stared at my uncle, then my parents. 'Twas best if I kept quiet. If I did not explain it right, Lord Paratore might take out his rage on me later.

"You intend to wed Tiliani?" Papa asked, feigning surprise and confusion. "What of our daughter's marriage to Sir Valeri?"

"Ahh, yes, that. My cardinal in Firenze has annulled Lady Forelli's marriage to the traitor. Imagine my joy when she accepted my bid for her hand." He gazed at me in delight. "We shall wed in three days' time." He leaned forward and put his goblet of wine on the center table, then looked to my father. "Forgive me for the unorthodox manner in which this has transpired. I would have come to formally ask for her hand, of course, but then this came to me as the best solution."

"Annulling my daughter's marriage and *forcing* her to take your hand," Papa said, his lips in a grim line.

"I prefer to think of it as making things right," Andrea said. "I have long admired Lady Tiliani. And now that I am Lord Paratore, I am a suitable husband for her." He gestured to the busy courtyard below. "You see that we have the means to meet you in battle, but we prefer to ensure peace for decades to come. Why lose more lives on the fields and forests between us when we could begin a life as peaceable neighbors?"

"I thought you planned to wed Lady Romano, when she came of age," Mama said.

"Yes, well." He sniffed, picking up his goblet again. "I found I was not willing to wait that long. Not when Lady Tiliani was so readily available. She has come to see the wisdom of it, as she once did with Aurelio. Yes, my love?"

I forced a smile and nodded with him, then turned bright eyes on my elders. "I am willing to do this for the good of our republics," I said.

"But you-you love Valentino," Mama said. Clearly, they were playing the role. For them to dumbly accept this new course would alert Ercole to mischief.

"I do," I said with a sober incline of my head. "But I love Siena more. And as Lord Paratore has said, he has made himself a quite suitable husband. I shall have all I ever need in his care."

Papa stared at me. He knew how I loathed the man beside me. "Very well," he said, taking Mama's hand. "We shall prepare for the wedding festivities in three days' time."

"'Twould be most appropriate for it to take place at Castello Forelli, the bride's home," Zia Gabi said.

"Nay, nay," Andrea said. "I fear that my bride shall remain inside these walls until she bears my heir. At that point, we can resume normal relations."

I tried not to gape at him. He intended to keep me as prisoner until I bore him a babe? That could be years! But then I saw the genius of it. He figured that by then, he would have wooed me, beaten me into submission, or would hold the child back as guarantee that I would return.

"That is preposterous!" Zia Gabi said. "We agreed to this arrangement only on the terms that Tiliani, Luciana, and Celeste would have the freedoms to which they are accustomed. Visitors—"

"Oh, you may all visit any time you wish. But I fear when Luciana chose to . . . depart Castello Paratore, our original agreement became null and void. I must have assurances that neither of the remaining ladies shall attempt to do the same."

"Mayhap"—I reached out to take his hand shyly—"you shall send Celeste home to Castello Romano as a gesture of good will. Would that not soothe these tensions?" I asked, silently begging them to agree to it. If I could get Celeste out and send Maria with her—

"Nay," Andrea said with a laugh. "The girl shall keep you company until you bear that babe. I would not want you to grow lonely, my dear." He squeezed my hand.

Mama did not miss it. "But you shall allow us, her family, to come to call every day?"

Andrea nodded. "Yes, you four. Not Luciana—who I assume is back to tapping her way about Castello Forelli?"

None of them said anything.

"And not Valeri," he went on. "My men would tear him apart. Nor Luciana's brother. You four. Oh, and her grandmother, especially since Tiliani seems to favor her care when she ails. Any day. Every day. Twice a day," he offered magnanimously. "I am all for building family ties and can assure you safe passage, unmolested. In time, you shall see I am not the man I was."

Nay, I thought. *You are hundredfold worse.*

35

The next morn Maria came in and opened the lone shutter that covered the narrow window of my room. She turned to me with a smile as I sat up in bed, rubbing my eyes. I had not been able to sleep much last night. Now my wedding was to be in two days.

But when she handed me a basket and I opened it, I smiled too. "Is this what I think it is?" I asked, looking in at the rags stained red with blood.

"'Proof' for Lord Paratore," she whispered. "I shall go to him now, before he arrives to watch you drink more of that wretched tonic. Tell him you sent me."

"That is a brilliant plan." I sank back with relief to my pillows. I still had not started my courses and again felt a bit queasy this morn. My heart leapt. Could I truly be carrying Valentino's child? I thought of telling him and how he would grin. How it would tip up the sad lines around his eyes. How he would anticipate the baby's arrival, month by month. But we had much to accomplish before that day.

"Please. Hasten to Lord Paratore's chambers," I urged. "Mayhap it shall dissuade him from coming to see me at all this day." Men were so odd when women were having their courses. As if we suffered some malady each month that might be catching. Would he want to delay our wedding when he learned of it? A few more days would allow more to be accomplished by the Sienese.

The woman set off and Celeste stirred beside me. She groaned and put the blanket over her head. "Did you not sleep well?" I asked.

"Nay. 'Tis too noisy with all the men about this castello," she groused.

I agreed. The men had stayed up late, drinking, gaming, and singing. Many had come down our hall, passing us en route to their own quarters. "Come, let us dress so we might break our fast. Mama and Zia Gabi said they would come to visit this morning."

Together we helped each other lace up stays, and then we brushed out our hair. I braided mine and wound it into a knot. I grinned as the child followed suit. "There we are!" I said, admiring the little beauty. She would draw a long line of fine suitors when she came of age—suitors *she* could choose from. I prayed that this place would be a distant memory when it occurred.

Maria came in, the basket still in her hands.

"Were you able to see Lord Paratore?"

"Indeed," she said grimly. "Alas, he still insists on watching you take another dose of the tonic this morning."

"Do you think you might be able to switch the vessel again?" I whispered.

"I can try. But I shall need a distraction."

"I can help!" Celeste offered excitedly.

A knock sounded at our door, and the bolt slid back.

"Are you certain?" I asked, and she gave me the barest of nods as Andrea strode in.

He was in a new, finely embroidered tunic, silk shirt, leather breeches, and polished boots. Even his sling had been made of a new fabric that matched his tunic again. He carried a small pottery pitcher in his other hand. My heart sank. He had transferred the tonic to a new bottle—one like none we had in the room.

"I heard your news." He bent to kiss me on both cheeks. I made myself stay still. "But to be certain, I want you to take one more treatment."

"Yes, m'lord," I said. "Of course. Whatever it takes to set your heart at ease."

"And you should be quick about it," he said. "Your mother and aunt are at the gates."

"Oh, I am so glad they have come to call," I said.

He set out a cup, shook the bottle, then pulled out the cork. He poured my cup to the brim, and I took it from him as if glad to do so.

Celeste cried out in terror. "A mouse! Just there under the cabinet!"

Ercole spun. I quickly poured the contents of my cup into my lap, hiding the stain in the folds of my skirt.

"We shall have to find some new cats to keep you company," Andrea said with a shake of the head, watching as I made my "last" swallowing motion and lowered the cup from my mouth. "The castello is rife with vermin."

He poured the remains of the tonic into my cup. This time, it was Maria's turn, screaming so loudly that the two guards outside the door came bursting in. She pointed to the same corner. Again, I dumped the liquid into my skirt.

"'Tis nothing!" Andrea snapped at the men. "Only a mouse, scaring the women!"

The guards smiled and retreated. Andrea took the cup from me and nodded approvingly. "Very good. I shall leave you to it, now. Shall I send your mother and aunt here?"

"If you please," I said, covering my mouth as if feeling ill already.

"There shall be a guard inside with you. No whispering," he said sternly. "Only ladylike conversation. Mayhap you should plan for the wedding feast?"

"Of course. There is much to be accomplished." I let out a little gag.

"Yes, well, I hope to see you this eve when we sup. Providing you are feeling . . . improved."

"Yes, m'lord," I said, gagging again. Celeste rushed to bring me a pot, and Ercole promptly scurried away as fast as the feigned mouse might have done.

We covered our mouths, trying not to giggle too loudly, but it was hopeless. I rushed to the bed chamber and flung myself on the bed—wet skirts and all—to bury my face in the deep blankets while I laughed. Celeste and Maria did the same, and their merriment made me laugh all the harder.

Maria was the first to sober. "Quickly, we must get you into a new skirt before the guard arrives with your kin." She motioned me up. We were just getting the new black skirt tied about my waist when my aunt and mother arrived, followed by the keen-eyed Captain Sartori. I knew Ercole liked having him present at meetings because he often noticed things that the lord missed. We would have to take care. But Zia Gabi and Mama were clever. They would find a way to tell me what I needed to know.

We kissed and hugged and sat down around a table. Maria brought us watered wine, a round of cheese, grapes and bread, since we had yet to break our fast. I ate hungrily, glad that I was not truly vomiting. Belatedly I saw that the captain had noted my appetite and put a hand to my belly.

"Are you unwell?" Mama asked in concern.

"Only a bit of monthly trouble," I said, grimacing. I reached for a goblet next, setting down my bread.

"We can bring you some fennel and chamomile on the morrow," Mama asked, referring to Nona's favorite remedy for cramping.

"That would be welcome," I said. "Now tell me all of what is new at Castello Forelli."

Her eyes slid to the guard. "Oh, there is a tad more activity with all that is transpiring here, of course. But we are most interested in talking about your nuptials. Which gown shall you wear?"

"Lord Paratore has told me he purchased a new gown for me." I looked her dead in the eye. She would know I would want to choose my own gown.

"How generous of him!" said Zia Gabi. "What of the wedding feast? We have sent invitations to nearly a hundred people. I would expect many to attend. Shall we contribute a few lambs and pigs? Our cooks are eager to assist as well."

"I shall sit down this afternoon with the cook here and find out what he has planned. Then I will send you a note on what would be most helpful."

"Very good." Mama turned to her side and offered me a wrapped bundle. "I purchased this book for you. I thought it would help you pass some time, reading it with Celeste, when she is done with her daily studies."

"Mama, that is so kind!" I said, untying the twine and unwrapping the leather-bound tome. Most books were far too expensive.

"It is a Norman romance," Zia Gabi said meaningfully. "It shall aid you in feeling like you are a hundred miles away when the walls of this castello are closing in."

Captain Sartori moved over to us and put out his hand. I passed it to him, praying there was not a key or some other thing inside for him to discover. But after flipping through the pages for a few moments, he passed it back to me.

"I loved the third and twentieth chapters, especially," Mama said in English. I knew just enough of their native tongue to catch what she was saying. *Third and twentieth,* I repeated silently.

"In Tuscan, please, m'ladies," Captain Sartori said.

"Oh, I only said that I especially loved the romance," Mama said, her face the picture of innocence. "Appropriate for a bride-to-be, yes?"

He only grunted and resumed his place by the door.

"We shall need to come to you early on the day of your nuptials," Zia Gabi said. "We can assist you with your hair and dress. On the precipice of your future, you do not want to be alone."

"Nay," I said. "It would bring me much comfort to have you with me." They were planning something big. *An escape read.* On the day of the wedding. I only hoped we could see it accomplished *before* I was actually wed to a different man than Valentino Valeri.

36

Valentino looked like he hadn't slept in weeks. I suppose he hadn't much, since we'd left almost six weeks ago. And now, with this news? The Forellis did their best to comfort him. Padre Giovanni assured him that his marriage to Tiliani would stand, regardless of what the cardinal had decreed. But it was to me he kept returning, asking the same questions, wanting to hear the same stories of how she fared, how she managed Lord Paratore, how her heart could not have changed.

I was sure that for him, it brought up all the old baggage he'd had with Aurelio. Was he standing in the way of something she really wanted? Was he objecting to a union that could truly establish peace? On the flip side, how could he ever trust her with a man like that?

"No one can," I said to Valentino when he asked me about it again. "He is a snake in the grass, preparing to strike. Til knows that too." We walked with Giulio along the allure at sunset, enjoying the view of the golden light sifting through a dense canopy of trees and across the rolling hills covered in grapevines. I'd always been drawn to the golden hour, but since regaining my sight, it was as if it tore at my soul to miss it. Buzzing bees flew through lavender waving in the breeze, sheep bleating, warm sunlight streaming across the hills, showcasing so many hues of green. At this time of day, it was hard to imagine anyone could be contemplating a battle at all.

"She wants to be nowhere but here, with you," I assured him, looping my arm through his. "It drove her mad to be away from you. And she consistently told Paratore that her heart belongs to you alone. The only thing that could make her pretend to agree was to get closer to home and to protect Celeste. She knew she could not escape that palazzo in the heart of the city. She had to get here to have a chance. 'Tis brilliant, really."

"'Tis dangerous."

"An escape is always dangerous," Giulio put in. "But Tiliani is brave and clever. Trust her, friend."

"Trust her love for you," I added. "Only a few more days, and surely you shall be reunited."

"If God smiles upon us," he said morosely.

"He will," I said with more confidence than I felt. *He has to. Doesn't he?*

"Thank you, my friends." Valentino turned to kiss me on both cheeks, then gripped Giulio's arm.

Giulio put his free hand on his shoulder. "Try and get some sleep, brother. We shall need you in fighting shape in the days to come. *Tiliani* shall need you in fighting shape."

Valentino nodded, blinking weary eyes, and left us. I watched him go, his shoulders slumped, his gait slow.

Giulio wrapped me in his arms from behind and nuzzled my neck. "I know how that feels. Every day away from you felt like an eternity."

I nodded, remembering the pain of it, both external and internal. It was all kinds of wrong to be in love and split apart.

"Shall we marry on the morrow?" he whispered, kissing my ear. "Go into battle as man and wife?"

"Nay," I said with a smile, in response to the idea and the tickle of his scruff against my skin. "I want to marry you on a perfect eve such as this, with only the scent of lavender and sage on the wind, not impending war." I turned in his arms and looked up into those handsome blue eyes. "I want to be with you for the weeks that follow, to travel with you, explore with you, be alone with you or in gatherings, right by your side. And I do not want to carry a sword for any portion of it."

He gave me a sorrowful smile and then a soft kiss to my forehead before placing his head alongside mine. "That is a fair request. So shall it be." We stood there a long moment before parting a bit as two knights strode by on patrol, laughing under their breath.

"Watch yourselves," Giulio growled.

"Yes, Cap'n," said one with a grin.

"Is this truly the best plan? Sending more of our own inside?" I whispered. I looked northward, where Castello Paratore lay.

"Time and again, the Forellis have seen that the only way to conquer that castle is to do so from within. It passed into Forelli hands only when they were on the inside. So we shall use this wedding to get the greatest number possible into her courtyard. And then we shall show the Fiorentini just who they have trifled with."

"It will tear Valentino apart to not be with us inside," I said.

"Which shall make him all the more effective at tearing down her walls," he said with a gruff laugh.

"So we are to enter, dressed for a feast? Surely Lord Paratore shall have every one of us searched. Domenico and I are used to fighting without weapons. But what of the rest of you?"

He gestured to our own small trebuchet below, completed earlier that morn, and understanding dawned. "You plan to lob swords and shields inward?" I frowned. "What if they miss? What if it crashes against the wall instead?"

His dark brows lifted. "Then we all shall have to be very quick about disarming our foes."

Inwardly, I groaned. Nico and I had experienced enough medieval battles to know how it took only one strike to kill a person. Even minor wounds could quickly become infected. He and I would have to be on our game to give our loved ones the edge they would need.

TILIANI

I paged through the book again and again but could not find anything in the third or twentieth chapters. It seemed as if it might be a decent story—read beginning to end—but I could find no clues within those chapters. But then I thought back to our meeting and how the guard had been listening to every word. Mayhap Mama was referring to another third and twentieth reference. I checked the third and twentieth sentences of the first chapter. Nothing.

Then I went to the third page and saw a word so lightly underlined that one had to really search to see it. *Perugia*. The author had mentioned Perugia! What were the chances that a French novel would mention the republic? I eagerly paged forward. On the twentieth, another word was underlined in the middle of a sentence: *absent*.

My heart leapt. They had done it. Perugia would not answer Firenze's call against us, as a favor to Cardinal Borgio. And if the doge had done what he'd promised and called away the Arezzians, then we again faced fair odds. Power and hope surged through my veins. I did not have to agree to this marriage to Paratore. The plan bloomed in my mind. The only reason my elders were agreeing to Andrea's proposal was to get inside Paratore's gates. I huffed a laugh. He was *inviting* them in, eager to rub their noses in this newest victory. *So many of my people, inside the gates!*

I had been raised on the lore of Castello Paratore falling, of how it had come to be Castello Greco. And that had happened only when my elders fought from the inside out. That was what they were planning. That was why they had agreed to this mad plan, regardless of the threat to either Celeste or me.

It was because they knew we could take her back. Drive the

Fiorentini back and reestablish the border. We would all breathe much easier once we reestablished the border we had defended for twenty years.

A tap at my door brought my head up, and I remembered myself. Remembered I ought to be encouraging Celeste with her embroidery, rather than letting the child mindlessly play with a pair of dice, trying to come up with a pair of sixes. Or at least be reading with her, this time of day. I awkwardly set my book aside and stood, smoothing my skirts.

Lord Paratore, dressed in new finery, looked down his nose at me. "You are not dressed to sup," he said.

I glanced down at my gown, one I'd worn through the day. "Are we expecting guests?"

"Nay. But as Lady Paratore, I shall expect you to change into finery each eve as the ladies do in Firenze."

"Forgive me, m'lord," I said. "I did not know that was your preference. Do you wish me to change?"

Celeste scrambled up from the floor and took my hand, tense.

"Not this night. But from here forward. Summon the seamstress, the tailor. Order what you ought." He stepped into the room and picked up my book from the settee. I tensed. "I hear your mother brought you a gift."

"Oh, yes," I said, waving it away as if it were a trifle. "A bit of generous distraction for me as I await our nuptials. She knows what it is to anticipate a wedding."

He turned and gave me a long look of cold perusal. "Is that all she gave you, my love?"

I paused, feeling the chill, the suspicion. "That book alone," I said steadily.

He gave me a cold smile. "May I borrow it this night? I confess that I, too, need a bit of distraction as we await our wedding night."

"Ahh, but I was so looking forward to reading a bit more," I tried.

"Only until morn," he said, tucking it under his arm, decision made. "Now come along. Supper awaits."

37

TILIANI

The night before the wedding, I tried on the gown that Andrea Ercole Paratore had ordered made for me in Firenze. It was a royal-blue silk, with so many blue beads sewn into the bodice it resembled more a chest plate than a normal bodice. And the skirts . . . the train stretched behind me in a yard of silk. The fabric hugged my arms and then dropped in elegant loops at my wrists. The bodice stretched from shoulder to shoulder along my clavicle, but in the back, dropped daringly low—to the center of my back.

I gaped at my image in the bronze mirror, then glanced behind me at all that exquisite fabric. 'Twas the wedding gown of a royal, not a lady. 'Twas the wedding gown of a queen. And it had obviously cost Andrea many a gold florin.

But I would have to find a way to cut off that train on the morrow.

Had he planned it intentionally? Another means to waylay me? Curtail my progress? Did he suspect what was about to unfold? Had he seen the same clues in the book? He had not returned it to me the day before, nor mentioned it. I dared not either.

I cast aside thoughts of the book and concentrated on the problem at hand. There was no way to tuck that much fabric through my legs and into my waistband to be ready to fight. Nay.

If I was to be any use at all, I would need a dagger—and a sharp one at that—to saw through the fabric.

But I had no dagger. Only hairpins. And Andrea had meticulously kept anything sharp from my reach. He watched me at every meal.

Maria appeared and put a hand on my shoulder. I met her gaze in the bronze mirror. "I found this for you, m'lady," she said, placing a large butcher knife on the table before me.

I took it in hand and instantly felt strengthened. "Oh, my friend," I whispered. "You do not know how this shall aid me. But where shall I put it?" I gestured down to my skin-tight bodice and shook my head. The knife was large enough that the outline of it would clearly show.

Hands on hips, Maria gazed about. "Try this." She reached for a hair net. "Tie it to your thigh."

"Excellent idea," I said, immediately hiking up my skirts to do so.

"I have them, on occasion," she quipped. She lowered her voice. "I-I did something else."

"What?" I rose to test out the hold on the knife.

"Last night, I managed to slip a quiver of arrows and a bow into that massive urn to the right of the Great Hall doorway. With luck, no one shall discover it before the feast."

A thrill ran through me, and I embraced her. "Thank you, Maria," I said. "I do not know how to express my gratitude."

She squeezed me tightly. "Live, m'lady. You must live and see me and Celeste to freedom alongside you. That is all the gratitude I can hope for."

I pulled back to look at her. "You shall always have a home with me," I whispered.

She smiled. "Let us see to our future then, m'lady." She left me then, to look after Celeste, and I stared at my own blue-eyed reflection. My mother's eyes. A She-Wolf's. Born of another era, brought to us for a purpose. Just as I was here for a purpose, now.

The thought of it startled me.

I was here for this moment, for this place, for this time. *God has a purpose for me.*

And it was not to wed Andrea Ercole Paratore.

It was to take him down.

LUCIANA

Nico handed me a new tapping stick outside the Great Hall that morning. "You gotta keep up the ruse," he said, stating the obvious. As much as I hated it. "They don't know you're not blind. We've told our men to pretend you're still blind. Even though Lady Adri found that super-fantastic-miraculous plant in the forest that made all things right. Healed you within days and all."

"Okay," I said. "Can you ease up a little on the sarcasm? Isn't it just a little miraculous? I got a head wound in battle that should have taken my sight—and more—but the tunnel healed me. And then did the same for Giulio, en route back! That's gotta be *God*, Nico. No bones about it." I lifted my hands.

He shrugged. "Yeah. Maybe. Whatever. But for now, we can use it. The Fiorentini assume you are blind. That'll give you a momentary edge when the battle begins."

"True," I said, starting to imagine the scenarios.

He gestured to the tapping stick in my hands. "*And*, that one separates in three segments."

It took a moment to see, but there they were. Three different segments. I turned the stick with both hands, unscrewing each part. At the end, impaled in the next, was a long, lethally sharp blade. I huffed a laugh. "Brilliant."

"Dead brilliant," he said. "You can hand them off to others while we take down some Fiorentini and liberate their weapons for the good guys."

"And gals."

"*And* gals."

"What will you try and smuggle in?" I asked.

He shrugged. "Those guys will be looking for daggers and such, so we can't bring much." He flashed me a grin. "But I'm smuggling in some tiny packets of poison and sedatives, courtesy of Adri. The lady herself shall carry her own share. None of us will take a sip of wine, because Adri and I are going to do our best to slip a bit into every pitcher. Also, take some pork but don't eat it. Cook is roasting it with something nasty inside that will hopefully make everyone sick within the hour."

I blinked at him as I took all that in. "Even Adri is going in?"

"Oh yeah. This is it. The Forellis and Grecos are all-in. They believe the more of us that can get inside, the faster Castello Paratore shall fall."

I swallowed with effort, my mouth dry. "Who shall see to Castello Forelli if *we* fail?"

He paused, sobering at the thought. "Her heirs, Fortino and Benedetto. Chiara Greco will remain behind as well. Lady Adri wants a healer available. Everyone else shall be inside—or bringing down that wall."

Even Lady Adri—now in her sixties—intended to enter Castello Paratore's gates. They left nothing behind but the remnants that could hold the line. But the OG—Marcello, Luca, Gabi, and Lia— all intended to be in play. My breath caught. They were not old, at least by modern standards. But if they perished . . .

What would become of those who remained? What would the castello be like without them? Without any one of them? To me, now, they were all family members. And I had to do everything I could to make sure they returned home.

3 8

LUCIANA

At dusk, we proceeded into Castello Paratore in pairs, with the Forellis leading the way. As expected, each guest was asked to give up their weapons, which the men did, leaving a heaping pile of swords beside the guards' barracks by the gate. But in addition, each man was patted down from neck to ankle for additional blades. Given who they were—She-Wolves and their companions—even the women were led into a private chamber for maids to do the same. None of it came as a surprise.

After I was searched, I returned to Giulio's side, still holding my tapping stick. They had barely examined it when I explained what it was for. Only cast me hateful, patronizing glances that I, of course, ignored—for I was pretending not to see. Ilaria made a show of leading me out of the women's room and helping me to take Giulio's arm again. Two by two, we were greeted by Lord Paratore and Captain Sartori and sent on to take our seats on the opposite side of our Fiorentini contemporaries, already seated. I could see over Ilaria and Nico's shoulders that five musicians played lively, joyous music in the corner and wine was already being poured.

My stomach clenched as we neared our turn to greet Ercole. Giulio's hand stretched out on the small of my back, encouraging me onward. Hearing him speak, I guessed it was Captain Sartori beside Ercole, especially after he glanced over at me, curious, and

I saw that his eyes were ringed with laugh lines. How had anyone with a modicum of humanity come to serve one such as Andrea Ercole Paratore? Was it out of duty to the republic?

We stepped forward. "Lord Paratore," Giulio said stiffly, inclining his head. "Thank you for welcoming us."

Paratore sniffed and adjusted his bound arm, still in a sling. "*Welcome* is an errant word when it comes to whom you escort."

I lifted my chin and stared at the center of his chest, as if I did not know where to find his eyes. "My departure did not impede your goal of wedding, so mayhap we can set it aside for the evening."

"After all, Luciana is dear to your intended," Giulio said. "To not have her here would bring sorrow to Tiliani's heart."

"They speak the truth, m'lord," Sartori said, when he hesitated.

"Very well," Paratore sniffed. "Sup, witness our vows, and then be on your way. For I cannot countenance your presence the entire eve."

"As you say, m'lord," I said, with a dip of a curtsey.

Giulio led me to our place at the table—escorted by a servant—and I realized I had been holding my breath near Ercole. Oh, how I loathed the man! How I longed to look him in the eye! Spit in his face! But we had discussed that since he had not permitted me to visit, he might turn me away at the door. At least I was in. Giulio gave my back a tap of congratulations, and I resisted the urge to smile.

The wedding feast preceded the vows, and I was relieved to see that all the tables had been brought out into the courtyard—three long lines of them—probably because there were more guests than could be accommodated in the Great Hall. I guessed about forty per line of tables. This was excellent news for us. We'd be closer to the gatehouse and faster to bring it down. And the men's forfeited weapons were in closer reach too. But our guests were but one-third of the total. I knew that Marcello and Luca, Gabi and Lia, had invited their most capable friends, risking the offense to less capable but more senior friends. In time, those others that might feel snubbed would be glad for it. Because this was going to be a tough night.

I hoped that Giulio's plan to airlift some weapons in would work. While the wedding guests around us were presumably unarmed, I could see—with surreptitious glances—a good thirty men on the walls were armed to the teeth. To say nothing of the hundreds of Fiorentini encamped on the far side of the castello.

Siena had arrived to back us up and had their own encampment at the creek. Five hundred more were a mile distant. A hundred mercenary knights were in Castello Forelli, and Monteriggioni had men only an hour away, due to begin their approach shortly. Our masses would put the Fiorentini on edge but not alarm them. The Forellis assured me that it would be expected, each side standing on alert until this wedding was complete. But they would be expecting this night to be all celebration. Not battle.

Giulio and I would fight together, as would Ilaria and Nico. Our primary goal was to make our way along opposite sides of the walls and to get the gate closed before any—or at least many—of the Fiorentini outside could make their way in. We were already going to be outnumbered inside, four to one, judging from what I could see.

We didn't need the odds to get any worse.

TILIANI

With one glance, I knew my kin—all dressed in their fine blue tunics with the gold embroidered wolf—were prepared for battle. They did not want—nor did they support—this wedding. They already loved Valentino Valeri, as I did. I did not know how they planned to accomplish it, but the knowledge that it was already progressing gave me the confidence I had been lacking. I lifted my chin and pulled back my shoulders—as my mama and aunt had long taught me—and with a wink to Celeste and Maria, strode out to meet Lord Paratore.

To me, he would always be Ercole. *Our nemesis. There had been a good Paratore, dear Aurelio.* But this one was all his evil forefather. The Paratore who had nearly killed my aunt. Who wanted to kill my mother. And who had tried, on numerous occasions, to kill them all.

By the twitch of his lips, I knew Ercole was holding back a smile of victory. I was so close to being his—and this territory secure—that he could barely contain himself. He wanted to gloat. To say things that would shame and chide my loved ones.

His mouth spread in a handsome arc, and for the first time, I could see why some women favored him. He was a charmer, and he knew how to play his part. By the tilt of his shoulders, his outstretched arm in welcoming me, I knew he sought to appear as naught but the innocent, eager suitor. A husband-to-be fully embracing his nuptials. I could hear the women about the tables sucking in their breath, feel them leaning forward.

Charm is deceitful, Nona had often said. And here, embodied, Charm showed his face.

I begrudgingly had to admire him, as much as I hated it. For his prowess in negotiating the people and politics to get to this place. For how he had circumvented true authority and severe repercussions as he climbed up a slippery slope to triumph. I hoped *that* showed in my face as I grinned and took his proffered hand, turning to the crowd sitting at the tables.

"Ladies and gentlemen," Ercole said, lifting my hand, "I present to you my intended wife, Lady Tiliani Forelli." He turned toward me, staring only at me—as if we were a couple deeply in love. "Together we shall change the future of both our republics. Together we shall change the future itself."

People clanged their knives against their goblets, and cheers arose as Ercole drew me closer and lowered his forehead to mine. "This is a good thing, Tiliani. A right thing. Are you with me?" he asked. And for the first time I had ever known him, I faltered. Because in those words were layers of unspoken need like I had never heard expressed. Did he truly believe it? Or was this merely his latest manipulation?

"Of course, my lord," I said, hating the words as they spilled from my mouth. Because even as Ercole deserved nothing but a double cross, it felt wrong in the face of the first truly felt emotion I believed I had ever heard emerge from his lips.

He was right, just as Aurelio had been right.

For the right couple, this union could truly change the course of history for our two republics. And I knew that Siena needed such a course change, to avoid being conquered. But I also knew that *we* were not the right couple. My heart belonged to Valentino Valeri. And Andrea Ercole Paratore was a twisted, troublesome mire that would only take me and mine down with him.

39

It grated at me to watch Paratore lift Tiliani's hand in triumph and kiss it as the crowd applauded. I clapped, of course, but used my "blindness" to be looking askew, to the allure, studying the timing of the watch, distracted as they were by what was coming down in the courtyard.

He escorted her to the end of the first table, where a servant drew back her chair, and she gathered her impressive, cumbersome train to sit. She looked incredible, like some sort of full-on medieval queen in that elaborate blue gown. Valentino would be climbing out of his skin if he were here. But then I noted the Fiorentini woman across the table was watching me. Taking measure of my gaze.

I sat back in my chair and asked Giulio to pour me some wine. He whispered to me that it was at ten o'clock, and I tentatively reached for the goblet. Pretended to almost tip it and then grasp hold. I feigned an eager drink, not knowing if my brother or Adri had yet had opportunity to poison the pitchers.

"Permit me to introduce ourselves," Giulio said to those across the table from us. "I am Sir Giulio Greco, and this is Lady Luciana Betarrini."

I gave a vague smile in an arc, as if I wasn't certain who was before me, even as I took in the three Fiorentini, now introducing themselves—Lord and Lady Gordi and their son. They looked upon me with condescension and sorrow for my infirmity. We exchanged some niceties before Lord Gordi boldly inquired, "Tell us, Lady Betarrini. How did you come to be blinded?"

I paused because he knew full well how it had come down. I doubted he had a single fellow citizen of the republic who didn't. "Well, unfortunately, my lord, my skull was bashed upon a rock by a Fiorentini knight."

Our end of the table grew silent.

"How, my lord, did you come to be sighted?" I asked.

Uneasy laughter erupted.

The Fiorentini said, "I can only bless my mother for that. My father was quite blind come the end."

"Sometimes," I said with a smile, "we must become blind to truly see."

"Indeed." The lord lifted his goblet to me as I steered my eyes left of him. "Indeed," he repeated to himself.

The food came then, huge platters of roast pork and beef and cauldrons of vegetables passed among us. Giulio did his part, serving me and handing off the dishes to the next as people chattered and laughed nervously. This was not the easy conversation experienced at Castello Forelli—this was the talk of nervous folk. Seriously nervous folk.

And that's when I realized that the Fiorentini were as on edge as we, which offered to even the playing field. At least a little.

TILIANI

"You do not eat, beloved," Ercole chided, looking at my plate.

"I confess, I have little appetite," I said, giving him a sorrowful look.

"Ahh, the bride's anticipation has curtailed her appetite for all but one thing," he said for the table at large, who erupted in laughter and clinked their goblets together.

I smiled, even as I noted that the entire table was full of Fiorentini. My parents, my kin, were one table away. Beside us but not one with us. An intentional divide? Or a slight?

I pretended to ignore it and cut into a bit of beef, which my mother had assured in a whisper was safe. Had they accomplished what they intended? I wondered, chewing the meat that seemed too dry to swallow. I longed for a swig of wine to wash it down but remembered Zia Gabi's subtle admonishment to avoid drinking "too much wine" during the festivities. Instead, I chose a goblet of water.

Down the table, at the end, were Celeste and Maria, dolefully watching us. I had no understanding if this was going to unfold over an hour or the entire night, but just as I thought it, a lord halfway down the table covered his mouth and lurched away, narrowly avoiding vomiting over his tablemates.

While some reacted in dismay, others began to cover their own mouths and heave breaths. In my side view, I knew it was happening at other tables too. The poison was taking effect—not a deadly tonic—but rather a very unsettling stomach ailment that would likely trouble those who partook for several days hence.

And at that same time, knights on the allure shouted an alarm and pointed to the sky. Together we looked up and saw a massive, netted bundle of swords and shields, bows and arrows, come over the top of the wall.

With horror, I saw it catch on an outcropping and come to hang above the courtyard in a great cacophony. Too high for us to reach. Every one of us knew what it meant, Fiorentini and Sienese alike.

The battle line had been drawn . . . and it was down the center of Castello Paratore.

I shoved back my chair and ran toward the urn that I hoped still contained my bow.

But Ercole was right behind me, stomping on my train and making me fall to my knees. "What have you *done*?" he seethed, grabbing my arm and looking about. "Take her to the dungeons! With Lady Romano! Make certain she is secure!" He thrust me into Captain Robostelli's arms as I rose.

We were bodily hauled to the dungeon, even as chaos erupted all about us. Two knights held me, two little Celeste. Maria was left behind, screaming her dismay, asking to go with us. The cold slam of the top iron door cut off her cries, and we were hastened down the steep steps to the dark dungeon. I closed my eyes as the knights banged me against the wall and roughly clamped manacles on my wrists. They rammed the cell gate shut, and one sneered, "That'll keep you *safe* until Lord Paratore comes to fetch you."

Is this how it ends, Lord? I cried silently as the knights left us, racing to return to the battle above. They had left but one meager torch on the wall. I wrenched one wrist and then another, tears of frustration racing down my face. I could hear the sounds of all-out battle above as the door at the top briefly opened. Men and women screaming, crying out, swearing. *After all we have endured? Help me! Show me! Allow me to have part in this battle for victory!*

I glanced down at Celeste, huddling beside me, tears running down her face. And I was taken by how young she was. How small. I caught sight of her thin arms. *She* had not been chained to the wall.

I knew we were terribly near where the tunnel extended. Where they might set fire and bring down the wall. How soon would they attempt it? Even now, they might be adding tinder and wood to the fire that would bring this side of the castello down.

Regardless, we had to escape, and fast.

"Listen to me," I said to the sniffling child. "I have a knife tied to my thigh. These chains are too short for me to reach it. Lift my skirts and get it."

She moved tentatively, and I bit back a scream. "Make haste, Celeste! Do not worry about keeping me covered."

Moving faster, she untied the knife and handed it to me. "Good girl," I said. I put the tip of the knife into one manacle lock and twisted. I let out a breath of excitement when it popped open. Then I went after the other one.

LUCIANA

I had unscrewed my stick under the table and handed the makeshift daggers down to Giulio and Ilaria, keeping one for myself. The knives on the table were terribly dull and of little use to us, but as we leaped to our feet and ran toward the gatehouse, I saw one of our knights stab a Fiorentini in the eye with one. Another Fiorentini knight—clearly not ailing as others were—ran toward us, sword drawn. All around the tables, our people fought off the Fiorentini or ran, trying to arm themselves. The only good thing about that was that most of the archers on the wall were kept from firing at us, afraid of hitting their own people. Still, arrows struck two of our knights as they ran for the wall turrets.

The knight before me called me a foul name and struck, intent on eviscerating me. Moving on instinct, Giulio pulled me back. I shook off his hands and leaped toward the knight, slamming my palm up his nose, instantly breaking it. He screamed and dropped his sword, which Giulio picked up. I left the knight to him and pulled my skirt up between my legs, tucking it in the waistband. Now my legs were free.

Another Fiorentini charged toward me but then pulled up, gaping at how I'd fashioned my gown—and how I wore leggings beneath. I pivoted and kicked him in the chest, sending him to his butt. Without pausing I struck his head. He passed out in the dirt.

The first knights from outside streamed in, meeting the first of our knights to reach their discarded weapons. I looked around for Nico, desperate for somebody—anybody—to close the gates. Every single one of the Forellis was engaged. A mighty clang sounded— terribly close to my ear—and I whirled. Giulio had narrowly met the sword strike of another knight who had crept up on me. I stabbed the man with my makeshift knife and ran toward the gates. With relief, I spotted my brother as he broke free and ran with me. Arrows rained down around us, sticking up out of the dirt, and we zigzagged to make it harder to strike us.

He grabbed one giant door and I the other, even as more men charged in. More of our knights—armed now—engaged them. Some tried to drive them back. With but three feet left to close, men on the outside pushed against us, recognizing what we attempted to do. "Help . . . us!" I cried, my feet sliding backward. Giulio slammed into the door beside me, letting out a guttural bellow as he pushed. Others joined, pushing and pushing. Lia had retrieved a bow from the stack of weapons at the gatehouse and began firing back at archers targeting us. Through sweat dripping down into my eyes, I saw an arrow strike the door right beside my head. Giulio did, too, and grimaced, shoving all the harder.

I turned and looked for my brother. "We have to go outside!" I shouted.

His eyes told me he agreed. We weren't getting anywhere.

"Nay!" Giulio grunted. "Stay . . . beside . . . me."

"If we do not . . . get this shut . . . we will all die!" With that I released my press against the door and slipped through the gap, my brother right behind me.

Those outside were taken by surprise. I grabbed the first man's arm and twisted it up and behind him, sending him to his knees. I rammed my fist into the second man's throat, making him fall back against those behind him. I broke the first man's wrist with a wince, hating the sound of it but knowing it would keep him from striking me with his sword. Nico bumped up against me, but I ignored it, going after a third man. The gates finally shut, and with a satisfying clang, we heard the crossbar fall into place.

"Awesome," Nico panted, his back to mine as we both engaged our next adversary. "Now it's just us against a hundred bad guys."

40

The cell door proved even more challenging than my second manacle lock. But when the tip of my blade bent and I pulled it out to examine it, then reinserted it, the lock finally turned. "Thank you, Father!" I cried. We ran up the stairs, and at the top, I pulled Celeste close to me. We could hear men crying out. Someone screamed in terror, another in rage. "When we are outside, I want you behind me at all times. Do you understand? At all times. If I run, you run. If I stop, you stop."

"Yes, m'lady," she said dutifully.

"We are going to run for the Great Hall. With luck, my bow shall still be there. Once I begin shooting, you begin cutting this cursed train off."

"I understand."

I took her small hand in mine.

"M'lady?"

"Yes?"

"Will this make me a She-Wolf too?"

I laughed under my breath. "Friend, if we can get through this, I am going to bring you a Forelli tunic for you to keep forever." With that, I slammed open the door and ran toward the Great Hall. Archers on the wall shot at Forelli knights below. I needed to get to my bow to help defend them. *Please be there, please be there.*

One man aimed toward us but then lowered his bow,

recognizing me. Was he afraid to shoot because I might still become the lady of this castello? He had likely seen me hauled to the dungeon. Regardless, I took his confusion—and hopefully others'—as divine intervention. Anything to help us take our next breath.

We turned the corner, and I cried out in relief when I spied Maria, cowering behind the giant urn. Two men fought right beside her. One was Carlo, a well-loved Forelli knight. His eyes widened as he saw me over the shoulder of his assailant. Their swords were locked above their heads. I rammed the knife into the Paratore knight's kidney and retreated under the short roof of the Great Hall, shooing Celeste behind the urn with Maria.

"My lady!" Maria said in relief, as I spied my bow and lifted it out. "I had intended to fetch it for you," she said, "but then . . ."

"I understand!" I lifted a quiver to my shoulder and strapped it on. "Please, help Celeste free me of this train!" I knelt and began targeting the archers. The first tumbled over the inner wall and fell with a sickening thud to the ground. The second went over the far side.

I saw my mother—over by the gates—take down two more. Men ran along the allure. A few were engaged by Forelli knights who had managed to make their way upward. Wedding guests were still vomiting. Some appeared to be asleep atop their food, still seated at the table. So many of the Fiorentini had ingested the poison!

But then my eyes found Ercole, and he had clearly seen me. He hadn't eaten much at the table, and mayhap our pitcher of wine had not been drugged. Enraged, he strode toward me, a shield before him, Captain Verga at his side. He ignored a charging knight, eyes only on me. Verga turned to answer his attacker.

He lifted the shield when I tried to shoot his head. I drew another arrow and managed to strike his calf. He went down with a cry, staring at me in surprised outrage. Was it just now dawning on him that I was in on this? That I truly never intended to be his bride?

Men on the allure shouted, and archers turned outward. Sienese knights were obviously charging toward the castello. I shot one archer in the back, sending him careening over the wall. My mother shot another. I moved out from under the short roof to better aim at a man lifting rocks to pommel our knights outside the walls, trying to ignore the fact that Ercole was breaking off the shaft of the arrow in his calf.

I knelt, aimed, and shot the rock-bearing knight, drew an arrow and turned to face Ercole again, who hobbled toward me. With only one good hand, he would have to use the shield itself against me. What frightened me more was that Captain Verga was directly behind him, and the big man now carried a mace.

LUCIANA

"Give me a boost for a donkey kick!" I said to my brother, even as I locked arms with him, back-to-back. He bent, and I used every ounce of pressure I could produce to kick the knight in front of me with both legs. He careened backward, taking out several of his fellows.

"Now me!" Nico said, and I immediately bent and lifted him on my back.

I hadn't a moment to take stock of his success because the next guy coming at me swung a huge sword. He missed, but just grinned, as if silently telling me he was only getting warmed up. But hearing a great roar, he paused his advance. Together we looked to the side. A huge group of Sienese knights rounded the corner of the castle and charged toward this group of Fiorentini.

Everyone but the two knights Nico and I currently battled turned to meet their charge.

Nico grinned at me, blood-spattered and panting. "Good timing."

"I'll say." I ducked to miss the first strike of my opponent and tried to stab him, but missed. I pivoted as he brought the sword down again, and this time it was so close, I could feel the wind off it. But I immediately grabbed his sword arm, twisted, and sent him over my shoulder. It knocked the wind out of him so he could only stare at me in alarm as I kicked him into unconsciousness. "I'll take this," I said, grabbing his sword.

I eyed Nico, who was having more trouble dispatching his knight. "Send him over me!" I cried in English, sliding behind the man after he struck at Nico.

Nico immediately went on the offensive with a roundhouse kick and three quick strikes to the man's face, neck, and chest. The man stumbled backward and then fell over my hunched form. His neck broke on impact. "Uh, yuck," Nico winced, giving me a hand up. "I have to say that I wish we were playing by tournament rules here."

"Yeah," I said. "If only all these guys didn't want to kill us."

We considered moving out and into the fray below us but then decided to remain where we were. Being on the ramp by the door was a bit confining, but at least we had a better chance at keeping enemies from circling behind us. And we liked having a slight height advantage with the slope of the ramp.

That was when we smelled the smoke. "Did they do it? Start the fire under the wall?"

"I hope so!" Nico picked up a short sword from a fallen knight and crouched, preparing for the next two knights coming our way.

I picked up a shield. But when I saw who approached me, I took a startled step backward. My mouth dropped open. "No, it can't be . . ."

"Luci," Nico said, glancing my way. "Get that shield up!" I

dimly recognized that he was kicking at his attacker, trying to sweep him off his feet.

But my eyes were on the hulking knight coming my way with a sneer on his face. I took another step back and blinked.

Because he looked like the man who had almost killed me.

The man who had taken my face in his meaty hands and rammed my head against the rock so many times that I'd fallen unconscious . . . and awakened without my sight.

"Luci!" Nico grunted, trying to choke his assailant now, even as the man tried the same on him. "It . . . isn't . . . him!" he gasped.

Distantly, I knew that Giulio had killed that man. Distantly, I knew this man had to just *look* like him. But if it wasn't him, then it had to be his brother. Maybe even a twin himself.

And one thing was clear in his narrow-eyed glare. He was looking for a big ol' serving of payback.

41

TILIANI

"Maria! Celeste! Go inside and lock the door!" I cried, as they cut off the last of my train.

"But m'lady—" Celeste began.

"Go!" I cried, shooting at Captain Verga as he edged ahead of Andrea and lifted his mace. He appeared well used to the heavy weight of the spike-laden weapon. My arrow went wide. I fought to ignore the rising of the hairs along my neck, the shiver of fear that ran down my back.

I bent and picked up a short sword from a fallen Forelli knight and frowned at the two men advancing upon me. Smoke rose from the south side of the castello. They had done it! Set fire below. But Papa said it could take an hour—or days—to bring down the wall. It depended upon how well the mortar held up and how many timbers were embedded under the stone.

"What have they done?" Ercole shouted at me, pointing to the smoke.

"It appears they set your wall afire," I said dolefully, lifting the sword when they were too close to shoot another arrow.

"You dare to try and take down the very castello that could have been your *home*?" he sneered. He rammed his shield against my sword.

"I never wanted this castello," I grunted, striking at him again. Verga had taken a step back, awaiting his master's command.

"But I shall gladly help Siena wrest it away from you!" I added with the next strike.

My sword slid off the broad face of his iron shield. He tried to ram me with it again and caught my shoulder. I backed up a step, wincing.

"Did you ever truly want peace between our republics?" he asked. "Or would you have murdered Aurelio in his sleep?" He swung his shield, but this time I managed to dodge it.

"Aurelio Paratore was the last decent Paratore to live. Together, we might have succeeded with that dream. But as I have told you, my heart has always belonged to another. In the end, Aurelio respected that. *You* never did." Utilizing a move that Luciana had taught me, I swung my sword down toward him. And when he lifted his shield to parry, I crouched and kicked the leg that had been pierced by my arrow.

He screamed and almost dropped his shield. His face grew ashen, and he hobbled backward, calling me foul names. "Kill her!" he screamed at Verga. "Kill her *now*."

The knight lifted his mace and swung it in a slow, terrifying circle above his head. He passed by Andrea and ignored two men parrying to our right, solely looking at me. I could not keep my eyes off his weapon. So great was the circumference that I knew my short sword would be of little aid.

LUCIANA

"You . . . killed . . . my brother!" cried the giant man, uttering a word with each savage strike of his sword.

I barely got my sword up in time to keep the guy from cutting me in half. And with each successive advance, my defense grew perilously narrower. I panted with the effort, but also—I distantly recognized—in panic. My vision was tunneling to black, and it was so much like when I was blind, it set my knees to trembling.

"Luci!" my brother called, rolling on top of the Fiorentini knight and digging his thumbs into his eyes until the man screamed. "Get your head in the game! *Now!*"

I gripped the sword pommel with both hands. I shook my head a little and took several deep breaths, willing oxygen into my brain and the panic away as we circled each other. *I cannot give in to panic. I cannot give in to panic. I cannot give in to panic.*

I focused not on his face, but his chest and arms. I could take this man down. I knew just how to do it. He was massive and strong, but his size made him slower. I would use that to my advantage.

Nico dispatched his adversary and, with a growl, rammed his shoulder into the man attacking me. Surprised, the guy staggered to the side, and his sword dropped a bit. I did not hesitate. I whirled and landed a roundhouse kick along his jaw. But as I followed through, the tip of his sword grazed my leg, slicing into it. I winced but returned to my stance of readiness, trying to ignore the blood seeping into the cloth, refusing to think about how deep the cut was.

Nico leaped in again, trying to grab the man in a wristlock, but didn't get quite the right grip. The man growled and circled, using his momentum to send Nico tumbling away. But as he did so, I moved in, landing strikes to his gut and then his chin and leaping away before his next arc of the sword came down.

He did not stop his advance. Over and over again the sword came in downward strikes toward my shoulders, and I repeatedly took a step back. When my back met the castello gate, I gasped. I had lost track of my perimeter. *Rookie mistake,* I thought, thinking back to my sensei's constant instruction.

But Nico ran at full speed toward us, his arms pumping. I knew what he was about to try, so when he leaped into the air, I dived out of the way. Nico landed on the giant man's back, bringing an arm under his chin. The Fiorentini staggered forward, colliding with the gate, but he kept his feet. I scrambled to mine and grabbed the man's dropped sword and got ready to stab him, but Nico was not letting up. Desperate for air, the man clawed at Nico's arm, leaving bloody streaks, but my brother held on.

Long seconds passed by as the knight staggered, stiffened his knees, and then staggered again. When he at last passed out, Nico broke the man's neck as they fell. He grunted as he took our assailant's weight and slammed to the ground.

I winced when his head hit the stones and hurried over to him, pushing the hulking knight's body off him. "Nico . . ." I said, reaching for his hand in concern.

He gave a grimacing smile. "I'm okay, I'm okay," he said. "Let's just pray that those guys don't have any *more* brothers."

I laughed under my breath and looked up to make sure no other attackers were coming our way. But the Sienese had succeeded in pressing the Fiorentini back. The bulk of the fighting had moved a few hundred paces north. My heart pounded with renewed hope, even as I gazed about in horror at the field of battle.

So many men lay dead or dying. So many cried out in pain. And there was so much blood. There was a man lurching forward, missing a hand. Another with his mouth open, staring down at his own intestines coming out of his abdominal cavity. Fiorentini and Sienese alike helped their brothers move to safety, north and south. How many more would die before this day was through?

Please, Lord, let this lead to peace. Not an all-out war, I prayed.

But then side by side with my brother, I returned to the fray. Because more would die until those in power called a truce. And until that time, I wanted to defend every one of the Sienese I could.

TILIANI

The captain swung his massive mace, and I narrowly ducked the first pass by my head. The second smashed the edge off the huge urn beside me, when I leaped back. But it broke his momentum, and before he could swing it around anew, I jabbed at him with my sword, aiming for his kidney. Anticipating my move, he pivoted, and my sword merely grazed him. He jammed his mace-wielding arm down on my elbow, and my sword skittered to the ground as blinding pain ran up my arm to my shoulder.

"Kill her!" Ercole cried. "Kill her now!" He hobbled closer to us.

The knight grabbed my wrist and pulled me toward him. He dropped the mace and drew the long dagger at his waist. But as he did so, I remembered a move that Luciana had taught us. Since I could not break his grip, I turned my hand upward, which forced his palm up too. I then used my other hand to dig into the meat of his thumb. Instinctively he released his grip, but I held on and used my other hand to push back his knuckles and twist his arm, driving him down to his knees to keep me from breaking his wrist.

Once on the ground, I kneed him under the chin, and he fell to his back. A passing Forelli knight killed him with a single thrust of his sword.

But my eyes were on Ercole, who had picked up the mace and now advanced on me, hate glowing in his eyes. "I have been told," he said, taking a step as I reached for my sword again, "that neither Arezzo nor Perugia are answering our call."

"What bothers you, Ercole? That Firenze shall have to fight a fair fight?"

"How did you manage it?"

I said nothing, knowing that would make him all the more furious and susceptible to making a mistake. And I needed him to make a mistake. He was already swinging that hateful mace. I had the sword, but that mace kept my opponent out of reach.

"How did you manage it?" he screamed, hobbling toward me.

Above him, three Paratore knights fell in quick succession. One shot came from the inside—my mother? Ilaria?—but the other two had been from the outside. Two more fell right after. The men from Siena's encampment had to have arrived! I could hear men's cries as the Fiorentini fell back, the Sienese right after them. And great clouds of gray smoke now billowed upward, the fire truly taking hold.

Ercole glanced that way, too, well aware that the massive wooden beams that stood beneath the wall were burning. As soon as they gave way, the wall would likely collapse.

"Yes," I said with a smile. "Even if you kill me—even if you kill every Forelli knight inside your walls—*your* wall is coming down. And when it does, Siena shall sack this castello again. We are moving the border back to where it stood for decades. When we had peace. And today, or on the morrow, Ercole, you will die."

With a growl he came after me, hobbling faster than before and swinging his mace. But he lurched to a stop when an arrow pierced his throat from behind, the bloody tip emerging beneath his chin.

His eyes widened, and his mouth dropped open in shock. Mine did too.

Ercole released the mace and fell to his knees before collapsing face-first to the stones, dead at last.

I looked up and saw my beautiful mother slowly lowering her bow and closing her eyes in relief. I longed to run into her arms, but did what I had to instead. I went for my bow and arrows.

Together we ran and dodged and downed man after man. In time, only a few Paratore knights remained in battle, and once Captain Sartori paused to take stock, he cried out, "Men of Firenze, hold! I say *hold*!" Slowly they followed his lead. And each took a knee and laid down their weapon.

We had done it—we had truly done it.

We had retaken the castello.

42

LUCIANA

I leaped to the side as a Forelli knight cut a Fiorentini nearly in half, covering me in blood in the gruesome spray.

I grimaced as I wiped red from my eyes and looked down at my already-soaked tunic. My thigh wound bled pretty badly, so I'd stopped to wrap a cloth above it, creating something of a tourniquet. And I knew I should stop and elevate it, but in the heat of battle, that really wasn't an option. The Fiorentini were moving toward retreat—we could feel it—but hadn't given up yet.

My brother finished off his latest opponent and did a double take when he saw me. "Uh, Luci . . ."

"Yeah, yeah," I groused. "I know. I look like I stepped out of a horror movie."

"As a victim."

"Got it. You've taken your own share, bro." Blood soaked half his head, neck, and shoulder. His face was ashen, clearly feeling the strain and the looming exhaustion. Mine was likely the same. My whole body had set to trembling.

I glanced around in terror, for the first time wondering if I *could* face another adversary. Or if my body was just done. But nobody seemed to be looking our way. The bulk of the battle line had again moved northward, leaving only a few people in combat, the rest dead or dying.

A shout rang out from the castello—now to our south—saying

something we couldn't quite make out. But men repeated it, carrying it forward. "Castello Paratore has fallen! *Castello Paratore has fallen!*"

Sienese knights whooped and raised their bloody swords, and some Fiorentini knights frowned and redoubled their efforts. Others, beaten and bone weary, took a knee and set down their weapons. I shouted it with Nico, mouths cupped by our blood-soaked hands. "Castello Paratore has fallen!"

It was like a wave moved through the men ahead of us. Again and again we saw Fiorentini either fight all the more fiercely or give up.

Three riders cantered forward, one carrying Firenze's flag, two carrying white flags. "Fiorentini, surrender and retreat!" they shouted, making the Sienese lift their fists in victory or fall to their knees in praise as their counterparts paused in shock for a moment and then reluctantly did as they were told.

Wearily those able-bodied Fiorentini who remained picked up and carried any wounded comrades that had a chance and, with heads bowed, moved north. Meanwhile, the Sienese did the same, heading south.

We heard the crossbolt of Castello Paratore's gates once again slide open, and the great gates creaked as they widened. Sienese and Forelli knights streamed out and down the entrance ramp. I blinked woozily, suddenly feeling dizzy. But I'd caught sight of Giulio and raised my hand. "Giulio!" I cried, moving toward him with steps that felt like I waded through water.

"Ilaria!" my brother called with a *whoop*, surging forward, finding some hidden last well of energy that I couldn't seem to summon myself.

Giulio and Nico smiled at each other as they passed, each going to his lady. I frowned though, seeing how bloody he was. Surely he was just like me—covered in our adversaries' blood, not his own. My vision tunneled, and I stopped and took deep breaths, refusing to pass out. Not now. Not when we were tasting victory.

Giulio reached me and wrapped me in his arms. "Ah, love. I so feared for you!" He gripped my shoulders and drew back, searching me from head to toe. "Where are you hurt?"

"My leg," I said, eyelids so heavy I could barely keep them open. "Adri needs to see to my leg."

And before I knew it, he'd lifted me in his arms, and we moved back to the castello. "I shall get you to her now."

"I don't think it's too bad," I said. "Surely there are knights that have wounds far more grave."

"We shall get you inside the walls and allow her to determine that." He laid his head against the top of mine as he carried me. "Thank you, God. Thank you for sparing us."

"Yes, thank you," I said, looking up into the pale blue sky of twilight, then to Giulio's strong, determined chin. "Thank you," I said again, and allowed my weary eyelids to close.

TILIANI

Mama and I retrieved Maria and Celeste from the Great Hall, and we were walking across the courtyard when the gates creaked open. Valentino was among the first to enter the castello, and he ran when he saw me, as I did toward him.

We crashed into each other, hugging and kissing and searching each other's bodies for injury. Then kissing again through our tears of joy and relief. We had lived through it! Survived! We would have another day together, and another after that. Gradually, the cries of pain and pleading for help brought me back to the needs at hand. "Val, we ought to—"

"Yes, yes," he said, taking me by the hand. "We shall do so together."

We found a man with a deep laceration at his elbow, rapidly

bleeding out. I bent and ripped a long strip from my undergown and handed it to Valentino. "Tie it above the elbow," I said, having watched my grandmother and Chiara do the same. "As tightly as you can."

He bent to the task, speaking lowly to the wounded man, giving him words of encouragement, asking about his wife, his children, gently reminding him why he ought to fight to survive. I smiled, somehow falling in love with Valentino all over again.

I turned to another man in the throes of death. He thrashed about and only quieted as I came near and took his hand. "My-m'lady," he gasped. "It hurts so! It hurts so very much!"

"I know," I said, tears springing to my eyes. "Thank you for your sacrifice for our cause. Thank you for helping save me and all of Siena. I shall make certain your family knows that you died a hero. They will not be left alone nor penniless."

The fear in his eyes eased, and he grimaced, grit back a cry, and drew in one final breath before he went utterly still. Tears welled and ran down my cheeks as I looked down at him and then about the courtyard. How many men had died this day? How many families would receive the unwelcome word instead of their loved one at their door?

We had to find our way to peace. We simply had to.

After laying the man's hand down on his chest, I looked for the next I could comfort or treat. But then I saw Giulio come through the gates, carrying Luciana and bellowing for Adri. Domenico and Ilaria were right behind them. *Oh, nay,* I groaned inwardly, the scene too close to the last time Luciana was so terribly wounded. How had she been outside? I knew she had run to help close the gates . . .

I searched for my grandmother, too, and Giulio and I saw her at the same time. I rushed toward them as they reached Nona, who was desperately trying to staunch a terrible wound in a young man's belly. She bodily leaned on him, her hands covered in blood. More seeped between her fingers.

"She is unconscious?" Nona asked.

"Just moments ago," Giulio said, face wan.

"Set her down. As gently as you can. Tilly, help him find where her wounds are."

We could clearly see she'd tied a tourniquet on her thigh, and her leggings were soaked, but we could not tell how much of the blood was hers. "Search her, Giulio. See if you see any other wounds. Start at the top of her head and move down." I took a dagger and cut open the legging, exposing the deep laceration that extended from beside her knee to the center of her thigh. "She shall need stitches for this one," I said. "But I do not think it hit the artery."

Thank God. Because if it had . . . I shuddered at the thought.

Giulio finished his search along her body, and then we gently turned her over. He started at the top of her head again, moving down, and I searched the back of her legs, buttocks, and back. Our eyes met and we both shook our heads.

"It has to be this one wound," I said to Nona.

"Very well, tear off more cloth and wrap a big band of it around the wound as tightly as you can, over and around, over and around. We shall decide who gets stitches first, but we need to stop her bleeding. She has likely lost just enough to pass out."

"She shall recover?" Giulio asked.

Nona flashed him a smile. "Did you not see her wade *outside* the gates with none but her brother at her side? If you ever doubted it before, do so no longer. Your lady is a She-Wolf, Giulio. She shall recover."

43

So, yeah, getting stitched up in medieval times was not any more fun the second time around. And it had made me question my decision to stay here, given that our lives seemed to frequently be in danger. I was walking the hills outside Castello Forelli—blessed peace upon us for a good six weeks now—alone, because I'd had a rather confusing argument with Domenico. He was settled here now, thriving, and couldn't believe I was questioning it anymore. But he hadn't been the one that was stabbed and stitched up twice, nor the person who truly knew what living blind was like. And we couldn't rely on the time tunnel any longer to heal us in a crisis. After that near-miss with Manero, I doubted we'd get in and out again.

When I saw Lia at the top of the hill, sketching, I almost turned around. I wanted to be alone, have space to think. But then, had she not likely gone through similar feelings when they'd first gotten here? Maybe God had placed her in my path for a reason. I trudged up the hill, and she gave me a gentle smile when she spotted me but kept on sketching.

"May I?" I asked before circling around to peek over her shoulder at the drawing.

But instead of a picture of the beautiful landscape ahead of us, I discovered she was drawing a woman in repose, hands clasped, chin lifted, the tiniest of smiles on her lips as she looked up to the sky.

"Whoa," I said in English. "I'd heard you were good, but—well, that's amazing."

"Thank you," she said, shading in a bit of the woman's gown.

"Who is she?"

Lia's hand paused, holding the charcoal. "Her name is Peace. When I am in search of peace, I try and imagine myself like this."

"Does that work?" I asked, sitting down on the autumn-dry, crackling grass. I pulled up my knees.

She gave me another gentle smile and I saw the deep wrinkles around her eyes. And I remembered that this was a woman who had seen strife over the years. And glory. Bone-searing pain. And exquisite pleasure. "Sometimes, yes," she said, "sometimes, no. It depends on how open to really welcoming peace—regardless of circumstance—I am."

I nodded, absorbing the wisdom of that. *Regardless of circumstance.*

"You're wondering if you should stay," she said, returning to her sketch. "Here. With us."

"It's not the people," I said quickly. "The people are the best part."

"Especially one person," she said, her lips tipping upward.

"Yes," I admitted, thinking of Giulio. Headstrong, passionate, stubborn, and well, just pretty all-around fab. "I honestly can't imagine leaving him. Or all of you. It's . . ."

"Everything else," she finished for me, still shading. "I had similar questions when we were first here."

"What settled you? Made you sure?"

She smiled and let out a whisper of a laugh. "Oh, hon. I don't think anyone who makes a hard decision is ever a hundred-percent certain it's right. They just make the best call they can with the info they have at the moment and pray it'll turn out okay."

"And that worked out for you?"

"Yes. And no," she added gently. "Would my sons have survived if we had lived in modern times?" She paused and looked to the distance. "Maybe. But would I have ever found the right man in modern times and married? Maybe. Been able to have kids at all? Maybe. All I knew was that *my* family was here. And the man *I* loved was here. And with those two factors in play, I had to make the best of it, regardless of what came my way."

"If you had the choice again? If you could go back in time and choose the future or now, would you make the same decision?"

"I would." She paused. "You are at a crossroads, friend. Clearly wondering if this should be your decision too. Sailors throw out weighted lines to measure how many fathoms deep the bottom is. The question is—how deep are you willing to go? What are you willing to risk? There is heartache and happiness, regardless of when you live. My life has been a good one. I have Luca and Tiliani, the whole clan—friends included. You and Nico now. How we live—all together—cannot be found in the future. And I believe it is how everyone was meant to live. Loneliness is an epidemic in our own time. Here?" She smiled and gestured about. "Sometimes I seek solitude. But I shall never be lonely again."

TILIANI

Valentino wrapped me in his arms from behind as we stood on the wall and looked down at what remained of Castello Paratore, now once more Castello Greco, after the Forellis returned it to Giulio. We were in the process of erasing all the foul memories this place held, beginning by destroying the keep, Great Hall, and gatehouse, and rebuilding it in a new design reminiscent of Castello Forelli. Repairs on the broken wall were complete. Together, Valentino and I, Giulio and Luciana—and eventually

Domenico and Ilaria, I hoped—would make this imposing fortress a home, as my aunt and uncle and parents had in theirs.

"Giulio has asked me to be captain of his guard," Val whispered in my ear.

I smiled and turned to wrap my arms up and around his neck. "He chose wisely."

He took one hand in his and kissed it. "You think so?"

"I know so. He could not find a finer man than you. And together, we shall make this place a fine home in which to raise our child."

He gave me a quizzical look. "Our . . . *child.*"

I smiled, staring into his somber eyes, and watched as they filled with joyful tears. "Tiliani. Are you saying . . ."

I nodded eagerly, tears filling my own eyes even as I grinned. "Yes, yes, beloved. You are going to be a father. And you shall be as fine a father as you shall be a captain."

Then he was kissing me, our teeth clicking together because we could not keep from smiling. We laughed and hugged and kissed again, all while I thought that I had never, ever imagined I would know joy like this. As a She-Wolf of Siena. As a mother-to-be. And as Valentino Valeri's wife . . . forever.

LUCIANA

I thought of Lia's sketch of "Peace" as I climbed the hill again a month later, on a beautiful, crisp late-autumn evening. I was so thankful to feel, at long last, as peaceful as that sketch had depicted. I was making the best decision I could at this moment—taking Giulio as my husband—knowing I could never willingly leave his side again. To say nothing of the Forellis or Grecos. For as I approached them all on Domenico's arm, entering their

U-shaped formation, it was as if they gathered me in and held me as their own. I was one of them now, even as I became one with Giulio.

Golden light swept through the grapevines, still bearing the last of the fruit ready for harvest. The sun was setting with gorgeous hues of gold and coral. A red-tailed hawk turned slow, lazy circles high above. But my eyes couldn't leave Giulio for long, his sapphire eyes glistening.

Giulio lifted his warm hands, seeking mine, and I took them. Father Giovanni began the short ceremony, and I think I managed to repeat the words he gave me to speak. But my heart pounded with joy and with hope and with love as the priest wrapped our hands together in his stole, blessing us. We exchanged our vows, were pronounced husband and wife. And when Father Giovanni began to say that Giulio could kiss his bride, he laughed, and everyone around us did too.

Because Giulio was *already* kissing me in the most thorough, searching, passionate manner to date. And then he picked me up and carried me down the hill, grinning at me like I was his most coveted prize, everyone cheering behind us. But I felt like *I* had won, on so many fronts. Finding life and love, against all the odds. *Thank you, Lord,* I prayed, staring at my new husband and looking over his shoulder at my family. *Thank you.*

ACKNOWLEDGMENTS

This book was one of the hardest of my career to write, because I had many hurdles along the way. I threw out my back so severely, I was in and out of bed for weeks. After that, my puppy got hit by a car and broke her pelvis in three places. Have you ever had to keep a puppy on "bed rest" for twelve weeks? Right?! I laughed, too, when they told me. And then my beloved mom had a stroke and died within days. She had suffered for decades from rheumatoid arthritis, survived many surgeries, but was so doggedly attached to us and this life, we somehow thought she'd be with us for many years to come. I am torn between gratitude to the Lord for sparing her any further pain on this earth and just really missing Mom. I know those of you who have said goodbye to loved ones understand.

Given all of that, I was really stuck on edits. It's hard to think about a fantasy novel when you're dealing with the harder—and very real—aspects of life. You'd think it'd be an escape, right? Nope. Life has been too real of late. I am so thankful that my editor, Nadine Brandes, could come beside me and do yeowoman's work in getting me over the precipice and on to finishing. I'll forever be grateful to her. I'm also thankful for Sarah Grimm's solid copyediting and Megan Gerig's proofing (who caught a few lingering sight issues with Luciana, along with other critical things—writing a blind character is tricky!), as well as Cheryl

Crawford and Melanie Stroud helping me with final reads. All mistakes are ultimately my own, but it's not for a lack of trying to find them!

Nick and Abby Pugh once again assisted me on jiu jitsu advice, since I only wrangle terriers and a grandchild, not people. Nadine Brandes rewrote my rappelling scenes, since she's actually done it and you'd never find me on anything higher than a ladder.

Thanks, dear friends, for making me look like the expert I most definitely am not.

Historical Notes

Much is unknown about medieval Italy and the intricacies of politics, especially in English-translated resources. Even Italian resources of the time can conflict (as do their English counterparts), because medieval historians conflict. So I have taken liberties in describing how cities and republics came against one another in battle, all under the umbrella that this is historical *fantasy*. That said, I did try and represent all that I knew was authentic to the time, the best I could. There were continuous battles between the powers of the era—whether they be smaller kingdoms or republics—and that included those who were "owned" by the Roman Catholic Church, a major player.

Masquerades were not truly in fashion until about a hundred years later, but I took the liberty of inserting one here because surely there had to have been some trial runs, right? Plus they're just so much fun, I couldn't resist. (So don't Google it and take me to task. I knew what I was doing.) That said, masks arrived in Europe in 1268 and were banned from games. (Fascinating, eh? I'd love to know more about that.) And the doge of Venice at the time was given to extravagance, had true menageries (with elephants and exotic bears and monkeys, poor things) and full-on festivals where they sent an "angel" down on a wire from towers to the piazza below. If you want to see that in action, check out my original River of Time Series, specifically *Deluge*. If that was going on, a masquerade isn't hard to imagine too.

Practicing medicine in medieval times was definitely a developing art, as depicted. There were some good things happening (major use of God's bounty of herbal remedies) and bad things (bleeding as a means of healing and rudimentary surgery). As much as I am a daughter of a nurse, and granddaughter of a doctor, I took liberties where I saw fit, all the while trying to be true to the story and the time.

About the Author

Lisa T. Bergren is the author of over seventy books, in a variety of genres, from children's picture books to YA, women's historical fiction to nonfiction, as well as gift books. She is the happy grandmother ("LoLo") of a growing toddler she gets to frequently see/babysit, the mother of three grown, beloved children in town, and wife to Tim, her treasured husband of thirty-some years. Together they manage his business making ducks out of old ranch fenceposts (RMrustic.com) and their two furry-faced babies, Whinnie and Willow, while they dream of their next trip abroad and next recipe from the *New York Times* they want to make for dinner. For more info, see LisaBergren.com and follow her quarterly e-newsletter!

www.LisaBergren.com
Facebook.com/LisaTawnBergren
Instagram.com/LisaTBergren

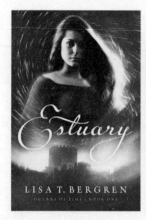